THE SWORD OF GOD

THE SWORD OF GOD

ANN CHAMBERLIN

EPIGRAPH BOOKS
RHINEBECK, NY

Printed in the United States of America.
Book and cover design by Barbara Patterson.

Epigraph Books
22 East Market Street, Suite 304
Rhinebeck, New York 12572
www.epigraphPS.com
USA 845-876-4861

Hardcover: ISBN 978-1-936940-43-1
Softcover: ISBN 978-1-936940-44-8
Library of Congress Control Number: 2012947765

For Jeri

MAIN CHARACTERS
OF THE SWORD OF GOD

In order of appearance; * indicates a real historical character.

*Khalid ibn al-Walīd (or al-Wahid) abu Sulayman—(d. 642 AD)
> Called "the Conqueror," the main male focus of the story. Muhammad the Prophet's most famous general, conqueror of both Iraq and Syria, famous for never having lost a battle, fighting either against Muhammad or for him.

*Abd Allah . . . . The Prophet's father, who died before Muhammad was born. Also, in this book, the name of Khalid's fictitious eunuch scribe.

*Abd ar-Rahman ibn Khalid ibn al-Walīd
> Son of Khalid the Conqueror.

Rayah . . . . Twelve-year-old focus of the story in Tadmor.

*Sitt Sameh . . . . Rayah's mother, a strange woman of the desert who hides on the third floor of the turpentine sellers' home in Tadmor.

Sitt Umm Ali . . . . Rayah's neighbor and instructor in religion.

Adilah. . . . . Rayah's "aunt," the woman who raised her.

Bint Zura . . . . Sitt Sameh's mother, Rayah's grandmother.

*Omar ibn al-Khattab. . . . . Second khalifah (successor) to the Prophet and a distant cousin to Khalid.

Umm Taghlib . . . . A witch, priestess, or kahinah of Taghlibi origin but having sought refuge among the Tamim. She is mother to Bint Zura, grandmother to Sitt Sameh, and great-grandmother to Rayah.

Umm Mutammim . . . . . . Khalid's milk mother, birth mother to his milk brothers Mutammim and Malik of the Tamimi tribe.

*Mutammim ibn Nuwaira . . . The older of Khalid's milk brothers, a famous poet, blind from childhood.

*Malik ibn Nuwaira. . . . . . . The younger of Khalid's milk brothers, sharif of the Banu Tamim.

*Al-Harith ibn Suwaid . . . . . A herdsman working for Mutammim and Malik ibn Nuwaira, childhood companion of Khalid who gets lost in the desert as a boy.

Ghusoon . . . . A young woman, Rayah's friend, driven to madness due to being forced to marry against her will. Rayah healed her in the first volume, allowing her to marry according to her own wishes.

*Muhammad . . . . The Prophet.

*Khadijah bint Khuwaylid . . . Wife of Muhammad the Prophet.

*Musaylimah ibn Habib . . . . . Called "The Liar" in Islamic tradition a native of the oasis of Yamamah, near present-day Riyadh, a wonder-worker, poet, and prophet who opposed Muhammad.

Terms used in Arabic Names

Abd, feminine Amat . . . . . . "Servant, slave," used frequently in pre-Islamic times in front of the name of any divinity to whom a child might be dedicated, used in Islam in front of any of the ninety-nine names of God as popular masculine given names.

Abu . . . . "Father of." This becomes "Abi" in the genitive case, but I usually keep it "Abu" in an attempt at simplification.

Al . . . . "The." In front of certain consonants, the "*l*" changes to that consonant (as in az-Zuharah).

Banu . . . . "Sons of," used to indicate desert tribes by reference to their distant ancestor.

Bint . . . . "Daughter of."

Ibn . . . . "Son of," used to form patronymic last names to this day. Actually pronounced "bin" when in the middle of a name, I've kept this spelling to cut down on confusion.

Umm . . . . "Mother of."

Ummi . . . . "My mother."

AUTHOR'S NOTE

Can I be assured that my faults will not devolve upon the scores of teachers, family members, friends, librarians, and publishing people who have allowed my consuming passion to become theirs, if only for an hour? Hoping this is the case, and that my need to acknowledge them outweighs other considerations, here is a list of the most outstanding: Linda Cook, Jeri Smith, Francesca Koomen; all the women of the Wasatch Mountain Fiction Writers—some of whom had to struggle with this for a thousand pages before it began to grow on them; Teddi Kachi, Solmaz Kamuran, Karen Porcher, Curt Setzer, Ernö Steinmetz, Ralph and Ute Chamberlin, my mother; my sons, the one who laughs at my Arabic and my camels, the other at my computer skills; Drs. Leonard Chiarelli, Laurence Loeb and Peter von Sievers; Marian Florence, Rod Daynes, Giles Florence, John Keahey, Connie Disney and members of Xenobia writers' group. Natalia Aponte, Linn Prentis, Christine Cohen, Vaughne Hansen, Virginia Kidd of blessed memory. Paul Cohen, Maura Shaw, Joe Tantillo. New to this volume is Lauren Manoy, with whom I can talk linguistics and children, and Barbara Patterson. All of the wonderful people I met in Syria. And of course, as always, the woman whose face veiled behind coins and shells in the Sinai desert first set me on this journey.

Those people I may have overlooked know who they are and know that I couldn't have done it without them. Thanks to one and all.

This is a historical novel. I have invented things, lots of things, the biggest one being Khalid's relationship to the woman called Sitt Sameh in this volume. No, I know of no tradition that says he was her father. But he did exist, fighting both for and against Muhammad at the dawn of Islam in the seventh century AD. And so, by God, did she.

On the other hand, I did do my best to accurately research. This novel was the product of a burning desire to answer, for myself, "What were the people in the time of the Prophet, blessed be he, thinking, doing, feeling?" So many things, even most things, are supported by one hadith, tradition, or another. This is not to say that the traditions don't contradict themselves; they do. This is not even to say I actually believe the tradition I have chosen to follow is, in every case, the most accurate one. It was the one that best suited the story.

One final note: The land between the Tigris and Euphrates has always been called "Iraq" in the Arabic language since before Muhammad. It means "the fertile or deep-rooted land." This is not an anachronism.

1

I am the pillar of Islam!
I am the Companion of the Prophet!
I am the noble warrior,
Khalid ibn al-Walīd.
            —Battle cry of Khalid ibn al-Walīd

Dictated in the garden of Khalid the Conqueror in Homs, Syria during the twentieth year of the Hijra, 642 of the Christian era.

The walls of Damascus gleam before the armies of Islam in the heat of the summer sun. The mainstay of Rome in Syria, the ancient city's great ashlar blocks stand the height of six men. Impregnable, they say. Certainly to barbaric men of the desert.

Then I give my war cry.

I give my war cry and ride to the head of my faithful army to meet the Roman commander.

Instead of drawing to duel at once, he speaks in Arabic learned during years in the eastern provinces of his empire. "O Arab brother, come near so that we two may parlay."

He would duel first with words? Against us who have the poets and the Word of the Quran? But for one moment, fear churns in my stomach. Muhammad is dead. And I don't have the greatest living poetess at my side. In fact, I've come surging all this way with Islam as the excuse; truly, however, for her—

But that is pagan idolatry. The Sword of God must lose with such an admission. And the Sword of God must not lose.

I reel my horse just beyond the commander's lance throw. Let no one see through my soul. "O enemy of God," I call back. "Come near me yourself so that

I may take your head."

The sun glints off his heavy armor. It must be like an oven in there. And under the red horsehair bristles of his helmet, sweat must blind him. Far better to be in clothes suited to this place. Far better to be under a red turban within which is wound a lock of the Prophet's hair, blessings on him. Better to have the wind whipping through my loose robes.

Still the fool talks gently, as if coaxing a wild colt to him: "O Arab brother, what makes you come to fight?"

If he only knew. If any of them knew.

"Have you no fear that if I kill you, O Arab brother, your men will be left without a commander?"

"O enemy of God, I have with me men who regard death as a blessing and this life as an illusion. And who are you against such a force?"

That I pretend he is a nobody finally irks him to a loss of patience. He has a battlecry of his own: "I am the champion of Syria. I am the killer of Persians."

"What is your name, infidel?"

"They call me Azrail, named for the Angel of Death. And I say to you, leave our land. Go back to the howling desert God made for you."

I throw back my head and laugh. "You know nothing of God. But we submit to Him and to His Prophet. Your namesake is looking for you, O Azrail. He looks to take you to hell."

Now, at last, he draws. But I am faster. I have my own namesake, Sayf-Allah, the Sword of God. As it comes singing out of its sheath, I hear the men behind me growl like a thousand bull camels in rut as they urge their mounts to charge. Sayf-Allah is a thirsty bit of iron and sky-stone. Once drawn, it never drops back into its sheath until it has drunk like a camel after a fortnight's march. Before I resheathe, even impregnable Damascus shall be mine, and all of Syria shall tumble after her like overripe fruit right into our laps. My fruit this day is the Angel of Death himself. I charge, looking straight at the eyes within that death's head of a helmet. I charge and do not flinch.

Al-hamdulillah, by the grace of God and by His sword, all mine.

All but one thing, hidden in a veil—

And from that veil, the Angel of Death rises up to fight me again, death's head and all. Only this time, the odds are so much more in his favor—

"Master, you have a visitor."

My scribe lays down his pen. It is just as well. He had me dithering on about the wars, the battles, the victories. There are plenty to tell those stories when I am gone. But the other stories, the tales only I can tell. . . Is there time before Azrail finally comes to claim me and I cannot defy him? Or stop him with a sword?

"It is your son come to visit. This should cheer you."

So not Azrail. Not today.

Whom between the two, my son and the Angel of Death, do I dread most to see? To me, the answer is an equal toss of *al-maysir*, those ancient divining arrows of the Arabs. Revelation teaches us they are an abomination.

"*Asalaam alaykum*, Father."

Abd ar-Rahman. A beard covers that face I knew as a baby. He still looks presumptuous with all that facial hair. Can there be grey in it already? Impossible. The old eyes are failing worse than I thought.

Abd ar-Rahman is tall and lanky like his mother. I remember her long arms snaking at shoulder height to the trill of a drum. I don't remember much else. She sealed a trade alliance.

He is not my firstborn, not the boy who gave me the honorific Abu Sulayman. Sulayman, my first-born, died a martyr during the conquest of Egypt.

There is a bronze cast to Abd ar-Rahman's hair—also from his mother—exaggerated by henna. He covers the grey there, too? Like the Prophet did, blessings on him. But the eyes—the eyes are not the seer's blue. Not what I seek for. The eyes are mine. I might as well be looking in a mirror.

"*Wa alaykum asalaam.*"

I don't stand to receive his embrace. I figure that's my prerogative, even now. Fathers deserve some respect. Or has Islam done away with that, as it has everything that went before? Certainly if the father holds to misbelief, a son has the right to set the old man at naught. Abd ar-Rahman must content himself to kiss my hand, this man whose foot receives the kisses of anyone in Homs with a petition. He relishes desperation in his petitioners. Yes, he and I are much alike. Too much.

"They tell me you aren't well, Father."

Who's they? I'll have their heads. I look sharply at the scribe, who doesn't meet my eye.

"*Al-hamdulillah*, I am well enough." Even at my age, a man has some pride.

"I thank the Merciful One to hear it."

I'll lay ten dirhams to a toss of the arrows he lies through his teeth. "And you, dear son?"

I hear about the grandchildren he does not bother to bring to me from his palace adjacent the mosque—the palace that used to be mine. He can step directly into the mosque to lead Friday prayers.

Someone has started a rumor that the Prophet did not think it seemly for the imam to be too much among the people. The Muhammad I knew never would have proposed that even for himself—blessings on him.

I hear about the latest cases Abd ar-Rahman has decided, some gossip out of al-Medinah to prove how favored he is by Omar, my fool of a cousin. I feel myself dropping into an old man's doze.

That is when Abd ar-Rahman comes to his point. "I understand you are having your memories committed to writing."

Now I put an edge on my glance towards the scribe. He shrugs innocently and remains standing in the shadows. But he didn't have a chance to clear away his parchments and ink, of course. There's no denying the fact.

"I should like to have a copy when you're done," Abd ar-Rahman says.

He won't take the time to hear it from my lips. He will have someone glean the useful parts for him. Otherwise, he will keep it in his storeroom, then have his scribes consult with mine and come up with something no petitioner can refute with a tale of his own. An immutable hadith he can preface with: "And I Abd ar-Rahman the son of Khalid the son of al-Walīd heard my father say that he heard the precious words fall from the Prophet's own lips, blessings on him—"

I hem and haw, playing the forgetful old man for all it's worth.

When he grows impatient with that, Abd ar-Rahman says: "And the sword? And the turban? You don't use those now. I am your son. Give them to me, at least on loan. I have a commission coming from al-Medinah in a day or two. Your relics will bolster my case."

Yes, I can see it. My sword unsheathed but drinking no blood, the turban on a little stand, as if my head were on a lance. He already has all of my fortune and my station. He only lacks—and feels the lack of—the moral backbone to go with it.

He gets me to promise, "I'll think about it." That is enough to remind him of a pressing appointment. He kisses my hand again and turns to leave.

After seeing our visitor to the door, my scribe returns to our place in the garden.

"But to whom does a man leave his things, other than to his sons?" So says my eunuch-scribe, one whose father's legacy to him was that he will never know flesh of his flesh. He'll be spared that thorn in his side, *al-hamdulillah.*

"Unlike God, praises to him, men also have daughters," I remind him.

"To whom the Holy Quran grants only half a son's share of inheritance."

"Or two-thirds if there are three or more daughters. Requiring of the judges great exercise of mind to figure out so many parts of a whole," I mutter. "So, you with the head for figures, what part of the fortune I won at sword point during my life—the fortune taken from me by khalifah's decree, now that I can no longer defend myself swinging a blade as once I did—what part does this sword, this turban—oh, yes, and this, the most important—?"

"This" my scribe counts as little more than firewood when I produce it. But I rub my hands over it as if I could rekindle the fire of youth from it, the ruined acacia frame of a woman's camel litter.

"Although in a world where women carefully gather their animals' dung to dry and burn, that is some worth, I suppose," he finally concedes. Does he mock me?

"Do these three possessions make two thirds of a whole?" I insist. "For a daughter? In the eyes of a judge?"

He figures, the creases furrowing his eunuch-naked face. Yes, he decides, that would be fair. For a daughter. "But surely the sword should go to a son. That seems only just."

Just, yes. But what of mercy? The Rahman part of my son's name he seems to have forgotten. That part of God's name. The womb part? For the word mercy comes from the same root as that part of a woman. I think of women. And of God . . .

"Master, are you asleep?"

I start from my dream and lie. "No, no. Come, boy. In the name of God, take up your usual cushion there. Take up your reeds again as when my son so rudely interrupted us."

He does so, this eunuch-scribe with the emerald in his ear.

"What were you dreaming—er, thinking of, Master?"

"Of the time I met the Angel of Death on the battlefield before Damascus."

He hurries to unfurl a fresh sheet of parchment. In all our time together, I haven't spoken enough of battles to suit his taste. "And you bested him, by the grace of God?"

I laugh and reach for the blade I never had far from me since it first came to my hand. I ignore the twinge in the side such exertion gives me. "I chased him down, that Azrail. He parried, but I hamstrung his horse, so— Then led him away in chains, gaining a vast ransom for the coffers of Islam." I do not add, "Booty they begrudge me."

"Tell me more."

But then I remember another hamstringing, spurting blood and splaying grey tendons: the white camel at the Day of Dhu Qar before I ever heard of Islam. Another victory, Dhu Qar, but there the defeated was a woman, the woman I loved. And she went as spoil to another man.

In the cool of my garden, the sword grows too heavy in my hand and sinks, still in its sheath and silken wrap, to the carpet between me and the scribe's scratching pen.

As if jinn crawled under the skin of my arm. Come to claim their own.

I shake my head to rid it of the unwanted vision. Coughing with the effort, I say, by way of weak apology, trying to laugh, "He is the wiliest of enemies, age. Age refuses to meet you head-on in honorable combat. He creeps up on you from behind and disarms you before you know he's there, before you can turn to defend yourself.

"So," I order. "Write."

2

**They saw the sorceress; the corners of her eyes
were like swords with blood-stained blades.
—Mutanabbi**

*Though he fought it with courage and defiance, age was getting the better
of my father. The death he would die, he realized, would not be that of
a man—in battle—but the death of a slave or a caterpillar. He would
bundle himself up in a fat cocoon and simply drift off to sleep one hot, Meccan
afternoon . . .*

"Master?"

I wake with a start and realize my scribe has had to prod me awake once more,
from just such a sleep as I used to find my father in. I want to excuse myself, but what
could I say? Azrail is with me again, breathing cold on my neck. I haven't much time.
God grant me—

My scribe is gentle with me, as with an infant or a wounded animal. "Sometimes it
takes more of a man to sit down and accept that painfully slow death," he says.

"You mean than it does to charge madly upon the enemies' swords when one is
young and foolish?"

"Exactly."

"Well, I have not yet accepted my own old, cocoonlike death, at least, not with
grace. Pass the anise seeds."

I always get a gurgle of anger in my stomach when I think of the injustice of it all.
That I, who once laded the Angel of Death with chains, am now forced to wrestle him
in the quiet of my own garden. And I thought I had some precious hope of paradise
which my father did not have.

Anise helps. Cracked between my teeth and warming all down to my belly.

*The day came when Father accepted the fact that he would not lead another
caravan. He called me in to him and told me so, charged me with the family busi-*

ness, his creditors, his clients, his alliances. Some of these were so long-standing that they had been included in his inheritance, too.

That was when he gave me the sword.

I had not spent the first twenty-five years of my life unarmed, of course. But compared with this blade, I might have been defending myself with a fibula.

Now, in my own old age, I sit bundled in my own garden in Homs. The cocoon I have strength to unswaddle today is that of my sword, Sayf-Allah, the Sword of God. The silk shimmers to the ground, sending a shimmer down my spine. I pull off the sheath—although it takes two yanks rather than only one—

And I let it fall.

I have to have a eunuch place it in my right hand, that hand whose strength I once gambled the jinn for. With difficulty, I keep my hand from trembling under the weight, under my anger at my own weakness.

There. I let the heaven-cast steel catch the sun. I present it to the admiring eye of the eunuch. How will he describe this in his parchments? Are there words enough in a sea of ink?

The scabbard and hilt bore signs of time: the enamel worn through all the colors to its base in just the outline of a man's grip. Gems had fallen from their settings in hours when the clean simple blade was worth more than a fistful of pearls. Its age was that of twenty men; something immortal clung as well in its power to send a soul to eternity. Never in all its years of frequent and even use had rust come to damage its perfect balance.

I bowed my head as my father strapped the sword belt across my chest; I would draw over my left shoulder.

My scribe bows his head now in my garden in Homs, he who will never draw.

Homs, in Syria, is but one among the scores of cities I conquered with this sword across two empires. The whole city is mine—and yet it is the narrow place of my exile. My cousin Omar reigns as khalifah of all the Muslims, a force this sword and I helped to create. He forbids me ever to return to Mecca. By God, I was born in Mecca as well as he, as well as the Prophet, blessings on him. Mecca was where my father bequeathed me the world he had created, where he died.

My eldest son Sulayman died during the conquest of Egypt, God grant him a martyr's reward. My son Muhajir has spread, in his turn, to the winds as he spreads the Faith, at the point of his own sword. And there were those who died when the plague swept through their cradles. I had thought to make up for the loss of my daughter in other wombs, the more fool I.

Islam calls my forty sons martyrs, martyrs to an affliction an all-merciful God sent in the first place. Wonderful are the ways of God. Islam hasn't done away with mysteries; if anything, it's made the dissonance greater. My point is, those little graves cannot inherit my sword.

Only my son Abd ar-Rahman remains in Homs, serving as governor here under the newly appointed Muawiya, son of the first khalifah Abu Bakr. But Abd ar-Rahman is faithful only to Omar, not to his own father.

To which of them should I pass the sword in my turn? Only this one is left to me, this "son" I hired in the marketplace last month because he understands the mysteries, not of the sword, but of pen and ink. He will never have sons of his own, this eunuch, corrupt product of the corrupt past I overthrew.

And yet, I begin to see he may, after all, be my path to progeny. Not to sons, but to a daughter. A daughter I never claimed, fearing she would prove my weakness. Yet she has overcome me in the end. Not on the battlefield, as I thought, riding bare-breasted in a litter borne on a white camel, a feast for every eye.

Hidden instead in her harem from the eyes of all men. Even mine, old, dry, and sun-blinded as they grow.

If only God grants me time and holds Azrail at bay.

This scribe must write.

That first time on my own, after my father's retirement, I reached the distant markets of al-Khatt in Bahrain. Here, at the head of the waters of the Gulf lying like polished steel, gathered the dhows. Their sails themselves folded like the wings of nesting rocs, those great birds brought in sailors' reports from afar. Along with the tales, from India and beyond, the ships carried goods to make an Arab dream of conquering lands to gain more.

Here, I decided to have one of the local craftsmen refurbish and enrich the hilt and scabbard of the weapon my father had bequeathed me. It was little enough that I could do, I felt, to add to the honorable name of all my fathers. I left the sword with the man throughout my three-month stay in his land, but every week or so I returned to him. From Bahrain's markets, I'd gleaned another square of cloth filled with fresh-caught pearls. Or he would offer me a new piece of amber or coral or tiger's eye stone. For a price, he was only too happy to work them into the design for me.

He was also proud to display the sword before his shop. It became famous. I heard myself pointed out here and there in town as "the owner of the sword in Abu Rabi'a's shop." Everyone knew what sword that was, and gazes—somewhat envious, somewhat afraid—followed me. Some good contracts for my desert-raised horses fell my way in this manner.

But I had another reason for putting off the final payment and claiming my property. Two days before I planned, if God were willing, to leave Bahrain, I finally had the courage to approach the worthy silversmith with the idea.

From my robe I removed the soft gazelle-skin bag I wore secured about my neck. Without a word, I loosened the drawstrings and carefully poured the contents out upon his felt-covered counter.

He did not ask, "By the God of my fathers, what have you brought this time?" He knew what they were when he saw them, glossy black as if they'd already been through his furnace. He did ask, in an awe-filled whisper, "By God, where did you get them?"

"In the desert," was my sparse and evasive reply.

"But what shall I do with such heaven stones?" the smith said weakly, encircling his fingers in the shape of an eye as a sign against the evil.

A sign such as my scribe makes now. "Heaven stones? Stones fired by God to send jinn falling from the sky? *Mashallah*, I heard rumors that such made the metal of the Sword of God, but I didn't believe it. Where did you get them?"

I do not tell him the tale of my night of possession by the sacred well of Nakhlah. Not yet. I have never told anyone that. Nor did I speak of the wonders flying like burning arrows through the night sky.

Soon. But not yet.

"I want a new blade for this sword," I told the smith. "Your cousin is a swordsmith, I am told."

"Yes, yes. One of the finest, thanks be to Manat. But . . ."

"Will you introduce us?"

"Not heaven stones. He will not touch heaven stones."

"Why not?" I asked, hurt as if I were a child getting his hand slapped.

"Too dangerous."

"Too dangerous?"

"He does not know the skill." The smith shook his head and clicked his tongue. "No, skill is not quite the word for what such work requires. Magic. One needs to know the secrets of the beings who appear in a puff of smoke. Men have died. Men have been killed and a curse laid upon whole families for unwisely attempting such a thing."

"Still it can be done. It must be done."

"There is one swordsmith in al-Khatt . . . "

"Take me to him."

"To her. It is a woman. A kahinah."

The craftsman stared hard at me with his small lashless and bloodshot eyes. The import of his words sank in to me. Then he relieved me of that stare and went, as it were, into hiding for the process of bargaining.

"I will take you to her for fifty dinar."

"Fifty dinar!" I exclaimed. "I shall find her out myself."

"That would be impossible. Forty-five."

"I am charged less for escort across the wildest stretch of desert. Do you think she might kill you?"

"She might," and he made a sign against evil again. "One cannot tell with Rudainah. Forty."

"I will give you fifteen, not a dinar more."

"Very well, thirty. Because you are my friend."

I paid him twenty-five and have always felt I got a bargain.

❧

Abu Rubi'a indicated the outcrop to me. Then he backed off and left me to climb up to it on my own. A spring bubbled forth from this stone on the very brink of the waters of the Gulf. In this land, mineral reigned. All that was not mineral to begin with sweated to join it in a moment. In this land, the bubbling, moving, vibrant life of a spring was a miracle indeed.

Part of this pure water channeled off to fill a great basin. Here Indian bamboos stood stacked. They soaked and waited to be straightened into perfect lance shafts, the death of tribesmen and the burden of poems throughout Arabia.

This task occupied a crew of strong and well-built men. They were all the sons of a single blessed mother. Yet she was called by none of their names; her own name was greater than any of them. Her name was Rudainah, and a spear or a sword made on this outcrop would be called Rudaini throughout the land. Such a weapon could make a man famous, but it would always bear her name and not his.

Still, I saw no woman as I approached. A small hut made of unbaked mud-brick sprouted by the spring. Indeed, it stood so close to the spring that the waters had worn away a corner of the edifice. To come and see who had arrived, a small child used that as an exit rather than the roundabout doorway her elders were obliged to use. The ruins of a second such mud hut also stood on the outcrop. The crumbled and worn walls looked like a meal had been made of the solid form of the mud. Swallowed and half-digested before disagreeing with the belly, it had then been spat up and left there to rot.

Dry channels told me the history of the spot: The spring had bubbled up under the earlier house's corners, too. In fact, it was probably the blessing and the curse of this household that wherever the mother set her hearthstones, there pure water shot forth.

Presently, a flock of women complementary to the crew of men followed their children out. They stood and stared. They did indeed seem to be a flock of birds, blackbirds, come to settle and preen themselves upon that rock. They all wore the burqa, the curious beaklike mask that veils the women in that part of the world.

I guessed that none of these fowl was the sword maker. I was right. "Mother!"

the eldest of the brothers called when I handed him my sword and my pouch of stones. "He wants a sword."

An old, frail woman stepped out of the hut. Her eyes were shot with blood— from years of working over a forge is the mundane explanation if I could convince myself it was not from staring face-to-face at jinn.

Her eyes were blue.

As much as I could tell beneath the sleeves of her gown, old flesh slipped over the muscles of her arms like the fabric of a second garment. How she would manage the great hammer blows needed for the task ahead, I couldn't imagine. But perhaps that was what she had those big, burly sons for.

Her hair of equal parts deep black and pale white stood out on end in a perfect circle all about her head like the rays of the sun. Yes, unlike her daughters-in-law, she was unveiled. She did not even wear a hair veil, but her eyes immediately met my stare with ferocity, as if she had snapped out loud, "Who are you? You would dare to even think in your mind to tell Rudainah what she should wear?"

The son approached his mother to hand her my sword and my stones. Never had I seen such deference, such honor, and yet such warm love in a son. Most mothers must wait until they are on their deathbeds for such a sight. This woman lived with it all day, every day.

Rudainah took my things from her son and gave me another long, hard stare. "Fool," her eyes chastised me sharply. "How did such a fool as you come to own such treasures, eh?"

I hung my head, astounded that anyone could make me feel shame, let alone a woman. Her look seared through the top of my head and demanded without mercy, "And how many old mothers will you bereave of their sons with this? How many daughters will you abuse?"

Her son heard what her eyes said, too. But just as he reached out a hand to relieve her of what was so distasteful to her, she pulled the stones to her and seemed to say, "Very well, I'll make this for you. Perhaps you may fall on it and rid the world of your own fool self."

Then, without an audible word, she turned and entered the hut.

"No, my friend," I tell my scribe. "Do not ask me how she did it, bound heaven stone to the old, earthly steel to make new. I do not know. It was magic. The secret of the jinn whispering through the bellows to her."

The eunuch-scribe forgets his conversion. He begins to cross himself, then simply says "*Mashallah*" for protection.

It is better not to think too long of such things. They have power to possess over space and time if you linger on them.

From the full of the moon to the dark, ignoring the date I had made to leave,

I waited. I waited as only the sounds of hammering and hissing water came from the hut. What magic did she employ, of all the rumors I have ever heard? Did she slake the white-hot blade in chicory water? Did she braid hard steel ingots brought with her bamboo from India around a softer core of iron, "male cutting edge surrounding the softer, flexible female" as the poets like to phrase it? Did dark spells weave the pattern of serpent skin to a surface like water, water and sword both indispensable to life in the desert? Did she even proof the final product in the body of a condemned criminal manacled live to the roof of her crumbling forge?

All I needed to know is that one day, at dusk, she finished. She brought it out like the pure, clean blade of a new moon rising. At least, that is how I saw it. She herself handed the weapon to her son as if throwing rubbish to the dogs. But the man took it with a full share of the reverence that was its due.

"Hey, Arab." She did not just stare her words this time but actually spoke with all the harshness I had imagined in her stares. "I'm keeping this," she said, and held up one lump of heaven stone she had not incorporated. "Count it as part payment."

I nodded without a second thought and took the wondrous blade to myself. The blade was still warm to the touch, like the stones had been when they'd fallen. The polish was so clear, I could look in the blade to adjust the angle of my red turban. I felt more emotion than I had felt on being handed my first-born son.

I strapped it to me, the Sword of God, that has given me my name more than any son.

And see? As with everything else, it seems to me now, I owe it to a woman.

3

In the Name of God, the Merciful, the Compassionate.
Praise belongs to God, the Lord of all Being,
the All-Merciful, the All-Compassionate,
the Lord of the Day of Doom.
—First Surah of the Quran

Tadmor (Palmyra), Syria, twenty-fourth year of the Hijra,
643 of the Christian era

"Rudaini."

In the little room on the third floor, Sitt Sameh—recluse from the world, healer, converser with jinn—breathed the name of the legendary spear maker's creations. She spoke it, conjuring, into the hollow formed by their three pairs of bent knees, the circle the eunuch-scribe's voice had just vacated as he came to the end of a chapter in the Conqueror's record. As Sitt Sameh said the word, she lifted the sword off the rug between them in the same gesture the Conqueror must have used when he first took possession of his treasure, although here a sheath still swaddled it from the world.

"Rudaini." Again.

Rayah—her daughter, her listener, her mere eavesdropper, perhaps—had no doubt that in tents in the desert, spears bearing this name still swung. Kept in places of honor against the center pole by sons of famous fathers. The weapons dated to the Days of the Arabs, the times Muslims were beginning to call Jahiliyyah: the Times of Ignorance.

This, however, was *the* sword. The sword the kahinah Rudainah had forged of elements of heaven and earth because no male smith dared, as the parchments of Khalid the Conqueror related. The sword that had grown beyond her, its maker, taken the name of one God above all others, and conquered empires in His name—not hers.

Still, now she had the blade in her little room, Sitt Sameh named it for a woman, as if she had just welcomed a friend to come and help her while away the hot, sleepy hours.

It was hot. And dry, for this time of year. The rains should have started a month ago—more—but they had not. Rayah's nose itched with the dryness; sometimes it bled. Islam blowing out of the desert might have brought the desert with it, even here to the oasis. In which case, prayer and words of the Quran offered up by the local folk should have blown in a storm. They had not.

"It is God's will" was all people could say about the drought as they had said about the plague five years before. Certainly there was nothing for a twelve-year-old girl to do but sit and listen.

At some point, having been built by oasis dwellers, the room must have had a regular roof: a palm trunk across the center, perhaps, laid with sturdy fronds and pounded earth. At some point, before Rayah could remember, this construction must have needed repairs. And, instead of more palm and dust, Sitt Sameh—for who else would it have been? —had made her own roof: heavy black worsted like the goat hair tents of the desert, tied down with twisted hair cord but still able to lift and breathe with every passing breeze. Unprotected by a better roof, the walls of the small room had also crumbled.

Rayah had never gone into the room much before. She had avoided it as the women who raised her—the turpentine sellers' women—taught her, resorting there only for the most serious injuries and illnesses. They had also taught her, or let her believe, that her mother was dead. She had watched the walls disintegrate as she had grown. They stood now only to her chest in some places, lower in others. Smooth plaster outside crumbled to reveal the rough straw- and hair-crammed center of the brickwork like gobbets of spat-out gristle.

To the roof fabric, then, with rough, finger-long stitches, new lengths had been added. Sitt Sameh rolled them up to catch the air, down for shade as the sun moved, battened them in the cold just as a tent in the desert functioned. Her calloused hands kept working, spinning the threads to replace those panels that wore out or crumbled to dust in the fierce sun. Always it seemed the intensity of her spinning held a determination to swirl away from clay walls altogether. Indeed, the wind breathing through the wool, blowing away the clay walls grain by sandy grain, rewarded her diligence.

From where she sat on the rug, hugging her knees, twelve-year-old Rayah watched Sitt Sameh. She scrutinized the woman's thin features, dark as if she'd only just left the sun of her desert. The desert tattoos, protective dots and lines on forehead and chin. The steel blue eyes. This stranger Rayah had, for the last months only, been forced to recognize as her mother. But her father? The rest of her kin? There were only the sword and the other relics the eunuch had brought with him from Homs: the Conqueror's red turban and the broken wicker of an old camel litter.

Until that moment when she gave it a woman's name, Sitt Sameh had ignored the sword. The red silk and the acacia frame she had welcomed with caresses, but the sword she ignored. She ignored it as if she did not want the taint in her room, all the space that was left to her, she who had once strode the vast desert with brave, bare feet. Now Rayah watched Sitt Sameh, in one move, snatch the weapon up and unsheathe it, holding it like a bolt of lightning frozen between sky and earth.

The eunuch sat cross-legged, watching too, the emerald winking in his ear. "You have handled that blade before, Lady."

"How do you know that?" Sitt Sameh turned the blade so it caught the sunlight where it squeezed in through gaps in the tenting. Rayah stifled her breath at the flash like falling stars.

"My master, blessings on him, told me that tale as well," the eunuch said.

"Then the old man is more honest than I gave him credit for . . . for a Conqueror." Sitt Sameh trusted her father no more than Rayah trusted Sitt Sameh as her mother.

"He had no reason not to be. He was old, sick. His command had been taken from him. He already knew, I think, that you must inherit these things."

Sitt Sameh watched the sword as if something other than the twist of her own wrist made it dance with light. "Does it still cut draped silk?"

"I know no reason why not."

Sitt Sameh waved her hand in the direction of the red turban the eunuch had wrapped around the sword to travel.

"You would test the blade on the silk headdress, Lady?" His hesitation did not stop him from handing it to her.

"I suppose not, stiff with sweat and dirt as it is. *His* sweat." Sitt Sameh found the thought distasteful.

Instead, after a moment's thought, she unknotted a corner and removed what looked like a lock of hair.

This shocked the eunuch even more. "The Prophet's hair, Lady, may God reward him?"

"Just one."

She plucked one of the hairs, grey, from among the orange-hennaed lock and handed the rest back. Abd Allah took the lock, kissed it, and reverently knotted it in a corner of the turban once more. His reverence did not stop her from dropping that grey hair, watching it float, watching it split over the upturned, magical blade.

A shiver ran down Rayah's spine. "Will you not put the sword up now, Mother? Resheathe it?" the girl almost begged.

"Do you not know?" A subtle threat wove its way through Sitt Sameh's voice with its desert accents. "This Rudaini sword has a deep-forged trait. It cannot be resheathed until it has drunk its fill of blood."

"Oh, then why did you not keep it—?"

The look in Sitt Sameh's eyes was as sharp as the blade. Rayah's heart raced, and she bit her tongue over her words. Before, when she'd imagined the mother she'd thought dead, she'd always imagined of someone she didn't fear quite so much. Someone softer. Someone for her tears.

With ceremony, Sitt Sameh laid them side by side, sheath and naked sword. The three people sat looking at the display, the unspoken threat suspended in their midst.

"How did the Conqueror come by such heaven stones?" Rayah finally found the courage to ask.

"Does he say how?" Sitt Sameh demanded of the eunuch. "Does it tell that tale in the tangled vines of your parchment?"

"It does, Lady." The eunuch's hand, soft and unnaturally long-fingered for a man, gently stroked his trove of ink and parchment. "It's here, all of it."

"His version." Sitt Sameh nodded skeptically.

"Then tell me yours, please—Mother." The word still seemed a strained fit on Rayah's tongue, sometimes more than at others.

Sitt Sameh ignored her. "But first he has to glorify himself at the fall of Damascus."

"True," the eunuch agreed. "He did speak out of order. More and more towards the end. The end of our project."

"Damascus, which he claims as his own with all the rest. He forgets Khaulah bint al-Azwar who faced the forces of Caesar Heraclitus alone with nothing but her spear to rescue her brother taken captive."

The eunuch shuffled his leaves of yellowed goat skin. "I do not remember that."

"Or the story of Aban ibn Sa'id's widow who picked up his fallen bow and had the defenders on the walls afraid for their lives with the accuracy of her shots. Does he mention her?"

"No—"

"And then, of course, the city would not have fallen, even to this day, if it had not been for the marriage of Jonah, the son of Marcus, Jonah the Lover and his love. Does the great Conqueror say anything of her?"

"Not that tale, either."

"No, he would not tell the tales told in the harem, not even the tales Muhammad's women told, those women who knew him best. The traditions, the hadiths, of Ayesha bint Abi Bakr, the Prophet's favorite child-wife, the memories of his own daughter Fatimah."

"Blessings on all the Prophet's household," Rayah said. "Let me get pen and parchments, Lady, and I will write it all down before they are forgotten—"

"Where will you find parchment here in Tadmor?"

"The sharif will have some," Rayah suggested.

Sharif Diya'l-Din was on Rayah's mind much these days. She had saved her friend Ghusoon from marriage to him with his bad teeth and paunchy belly. The name still gave her a bad feeling in her stomach, however. She mentioned it now just to prove she wasn't afraid.

"No," Sitt Sameh snapped.

"I only thought—he will have parchment for the trading accounts that have made him so rich."

"You think of that one so much, you will conjure him into your life," Sitt Sameh warned. "More than he already is, the Gods forbid."

"I don't have that power," Rayah protested. "Only the—" No. Not the Gods, as her heathen mother persisted in believing. "Only the Most Merciful does."

"You don't? My daughter does not?"

Rayah shifted nervously. She was only twelve. How should she know what her power was? Until the coming of the eunuch bearing this inheritance—on parchment as well as in sheaths and saddlebags—from the Conqueror, she had assumed she had no power at all. Like any other twelve-year-old girl.

Since the eunuch's coming, however, she had healed her little cousin. She had helped to heal others. She had healed her friend Ghusoon who had gone mad in the desert over her forced marriage to the sharif. But was that a true healing? Just finding a way for the other girl to become betrothed to someone else? Someone other than the old sharif with the bad breath who, to judge from the disruption he had since brought to Tadmor, must have been possessed by a demon instead. The sharif only got away with it because he was who he was, and everyone called the girl "irrational."

Rayah doubted very much that she could have such an effect, any effect that was not God's will in the first place. Much more, she did not think this could affect her, in any case.

But many things she had doubted, thought impossible in fact, had come true over the last month.

4

You only do we serve; to You alone do we pray for succor.
Guide us in the straight path,
the path of those whom You have blessed,
not those against whom You are wrathful,
nor of those who are astray.
—First Surah of the Quran

"**N**o."

Sitt Sameh was talking to the eunuch again. That showed how much power a twelve-year-old had, Rayah thought.

"Do not try to trap my words in ink on parchment, *ustadh*," Sitt Sameh said to Abd Allah's preparations, "where men can adjust them to suit their ambition. Keep such tales as they were when women first told them, painting each other's hands with henna, weaving, spinning in private as they did so."

"Then did you, Lady, actually sit with these famous women?"

"Many women. Over the years."

"I mean, the Prophet's women, may God shield them. With Sitt Fatimah and Sitt Ayesha?"

"I did. Which is more than the Conqueror ever did, no? If he has the piety he claims."

"Tell the tale. I am not a man, Lady," the eunuch said, "as you must know."

So Sitt Sameh picked up her spinning to begin.

"But, Mother, we must soon go to the wedding," Rayah had to interrupt. "Ghusoon is marrying her new betrothed. The festivities begin this evening. Please don't tell these tales when I'm not here. I hope you will come to the wedding, too."

"And I wish you would not go," Sitt Sameh said. "This marriage would not have happened without you. This is when the old sharif's anger will reach its peak against you, my daughter, may Allat shield you."

"But Ghusoon is my friend, and all my family—I mean, the family of the turpentine sellers—is going. I can come to no harm with them." They had, after all, raised her with more care than her own mother.

"If the Gods will. Do not speak with such assurance of that which is yet to occur. Unless you yourself prophesy."

"Of course not, Mother." Rayah shuddered with horror at the very blasphemy.

"I'll go with the girl, too, my lady, if it will set your heart more at ease," Abd Allah the eunuch promised.

"I don't know that I can fight it," Sitt Sameh said, "if she wants to go. But you must let me tell you one more thing." The spindle dropped, the yarn twisted on its base.

"Let me remind you of Bint Zura, my mother, your grandmother," Sitt Sameh said with a nod to her daughter. "How she saved her mother the kahinah from death by stoning. How Bint Zura then rode bare chested in the sacred litter, the *qubbah*, on the back of her sacred white camel into battle on the Day of Dhu Qar."

Rayah could hear the wedding preparations below her in the house of the turpentine sellers, those she called her "aunts" and "cousins" laughing with one another, sharing jewelry and veils. That present made her impatient with the tales of the past told in this room. "But we've heard all that."

Sitt Sameh ignored her. "How out of the battle dust came the man she had seen by al-Hira's well, a man who pursued her to her convent sanctuary, who still wore her red underdress as a triumphant turban on his head, Khalid ibn al-Walid. This was long before he got his famous sword, long before Islam. Nonetheless, he came, drawn like a thirsty camel to the well. And where before she had encouraged him, even protected him, now she cursed herself for a fool.

"The men of her tribe clustered around the white camel, defending these sacred emblems of their honor. But such was Khalid's right arm that they could not stand against him. And then, her beloved camel screamed. It lurched back onto its hind legs, and she slipped that way toward the ground. She saw the blood spurting from her mount's rear legs. A man carapaced in Persian armor had cut the white tendons, and the camel, for years her best friend, would never rise again.

"In her grief, Bint Zura hardly noticed when she was given as booty, not to the man whose eye she had caught, but to the one who had cut the tendons, al-Harith, a lowly herdsman's son. Months passed before she came to appreciate this gentle man's kindness. Then she thought al-Harith just didn't force her because of his good heart. She began to care for his flocks. After an even longer time, she realized why he didn't have a wife to head his tent already. She realized, when he came to slip under the rugs beside her at night, that a childhood accident had made him a little less than a man. He was incapable not only of making her his concubine but of giving her the child, the daughter she needed to pass on her magic, her blue eyes."

Sitt Sameh's own blue gaze pinned Rayah to the carpet where she sat. "The accident had left him, by heaven's will, like our friend Abd Allah here, made so by men's greedy hands. So, no matter how al-Harith's flocks grew and bore twins under her care, Bint Zura herself would never become a mother."

For a minute, Rayah ignored the bustle downstairs. She knew her mother was telling her how similar she thought their lives must be, so different from everyone else who knew their parents and what their well-trodden paths would be. Had betrothal, even to the right man, brought her friend Ghusoon perfect happiness? And could Rayah herself be happy with the same fate?

Sitt Sameh was also telling Rayah what her duty was—to likewise pass on her gifts and with them, the wrenched and difficult life. Rayah didn't want anything to do with it.

"But you were conceived, after all, Mother. For here you are."

Sitt Sameh nodded.

"What happened?"

"Bint Zura was content with al-Harith as a husband as he, who could never marry another, was with her. She was content with the animals that bred so richly under her hands. But she wasn't content with her own infertility. And so, she began to work a great magic to overcome the impossible situation. When her captor, her husband, al-Harith, was away with the flocks, she went alone behind the striped center curtain of her tent. She removed her veils and undid the braids of her hair so it lay in ripples over her shoulders. She unknotted her belt. Over a low fire, she waved the rags of her blood and the fox's skull, things she usually hung from the center pole to frighten away Those of the Place. She stoked the fire with arugula seed—sometimes called 'Ayesha's plant' for the prophet's wife who knew its properties to make herself the favorite. Bint Zura stoked the fire with the peeled white insides of green poplar and almond and plane-tree wands from the settled lands. The tent filled to choking, and the smoke leaked out at the seams.

"She performed this rite once, twice, and the third time found her by the sacred palms and the well at Nakhlah. Here she drank the water and sacrificed a young he-goat to smear its blood on the trunks of the trees along with her own. Blood on her face as well, she began to sway in the smoke. She swayed until first a humming rhythm and then the words came to her, words of power, of poetry."

Rayah found herself reciting the opening verse of the Quran: "*Bismillah ar-Rahman, ar-Rahim.*" The world's first poem—and the last. The words revealed to the Seal of the Prophets, blessings on him, must protect against the evil lingering in any poetry revealed by jinn, by shayatan, during the Times of Ignorance.

As Rayah recited, and as her mother went on with the tale, Sitt Sameh carefully picked up the two halves of the Prophet's grey hair from where they'd wafted to the carpet. She held them up to the light between thumb and forefinger.

"And because Khalid ibn al-Walīd's was the hand under which her misfortune had come, his was the name she began to conjure. Only she conjured him by his birth mother's name, which she had taken care to discover was Lubabah, the Little One."

"His foster, milk family was more important to him," Abd Allah the eunuch pointed out. "He himself said so in his account."

"Mark well, child," Sitt Sameh insisted to her daughter, "it's always best, when working magic, to know the birth mother's name of him you wish to conjure. It gives you more power over him than against a single-layered wall of men."

Rayah found her pious words stifled in the presence of her own mother's. She wanted to swear by God she would never work magic. Healing was one thing, useful, helpful. The dark arts, however, God cursed. With a breath, she managed to continue her recitation. Still, it made her uneasy. The names of God in this verse, "ar-Rahman, ar-Rahim," the Merciful, the Compassionate, came from the same root as the word for a woman's womb. And what else must Bint Zura have conjured by to fill the emptiness inside her? And did it work, this magic? Not yet, her mother seemed to imply. But how and when?

The tension gnawing within Rayah burst suddenly in a pop of flame that made her jump. The flame vanished as quickly as it had come, leaving only a ghost of black before her eyes. Lingering smoke did not fill the little room as it had Bint Zura's tent, but a wisp of it did certainly rise from Sitt Sameh's hand. Ash blackened her fingers, and the acrid smell of burnt hair came to Rayah's nostrils strong enough to make her eyes water. With her thumb, Sitt Sameh reached across the rug between them and smeared her daughter's forehead with the ash, in a pattern like her own tattoos.

Rayah couldn't see the smear, but thought she could feel it, tight and hot. She knew it was there, a smear of the Prophet's hair. She reached up in horror to wipe it away.

"Don't." Her mother's voice stopped her like the thrust of a knife. "It will protect you when you go to this wedding tonight. If you must go. For jealous spirits lurk there."

Rayah jumped to her feet and ran downstairs. She soon found herself safe among the "cousins" and "aunties" in their happy, carefree preparations.

"Oh, Auntie Adilah. Would you? Would you lend me your fine blue veil? Thank you." A kiss on the hands. "It doesn't call too much attention to my eyes? Well, yes, then the red is better."

Even as she said these things, however, Rayah's spine prickled with a sense of their hollowness, of the double world behind them of jinn and magic she had tripped into when she had entered the tent room.

Auntie Adilah considered. "Yes, the red suits you best. But go and wash your face. Get that smudge of ash off your forehead."

Rayah disobeyed, something she'd rarely done before.

And as long as the smear stayed between her brows, she couldn't escape the throbbing doubt: Muhammad the son of Abd Allah, born in Mecca in the Year of the Elephant, more than seventy years before, was the Seal, the last of God's Prophets, blessings on them all. His general, Khalid the Conqueror, claimed her mother as daughter, herself as granddaughter. Both of these things seemed easier to accept than the maternal half of her origins.

What was this woman perched under the very roof of the house of the turpentine sellers like some sort of carrion bird? What was this running in Rayah's own veins and flashing from her own blue eyes?

5

As for the unbelievers, for them garments of fire shall be cut and there shall be poured over their heads boiling water whereby whatever is in their bowels and skins shall be dissolved, and they will be punished with hooked iron-rods.
—The Holy Quran 22:9

I look at my scribe, dappled in the shade of the pomegranate tree, laying out his ink and parchment to begin the day. "It's been a while since you've nagged me like some old woman."

"I nag you, my lord? God forbid."

"Yes, you nag that you want to hear about the Prophet, precious blessings on him. Do you no longer care to hear?"

The sharpening of the quill halts midstroke. "God forbid, of course not."

"You are not more interested in my women?"

He does not know which way to jump. I am gratified. What I once did with my sword—tease a man near to death without ever running the blade home—I can still do with my words. Of course he wants to hear of Muhammad. Such tales—he thinks—will make his fortune.

"Very well, today I will tell you a tale—the first—where the lives of my women and the Prophet intersect."

"God give you the strength, Master."

"Here we come, O ye Gods, here we come."

This was years before I inherited the sword. My father, hale and strong, and I, my wound still tender from the battle of Dhu Qar, were returning to our home in Mecca. We stopped at the border of the precinct to pray and, with those words, we entered the Navel of the Earth.

Mecca. The spot first created in the world. Within its sanctuary, the truce of God reigns. We had to unstrap our arms and pack them; all feuds and thoughts of blood revenge must be left behind. To receive their punishment, adulterers and thieves are dragged beyond the circle of stones; the manslayer seeks asylum at Mecca's altar. Even the beasts, save those meant for holy sacrifice, and plants, save the one shrub necessary for the work of smiths, are protected by the divine laws.

The present-day pilgrim will not be aware of the changes wrought in Mecca by the Prophet's revelation, blessed be he. Changes to the Ka'ba, the Holy House, however, are remarkably few. The Gods, of course, are gone. There is only One. Banners and curtains aplenty covered the walls then, as now. But then they were not limited to the current plain black (one God, one color); they were as colorful as a desert rainbow. Some embroidered with words of poetry (that very few could read but all had memorized), some patterned, some shimmering silk, and some of fine gold—they all enfolded the shrine.

Above the statue of Hubal himself stretched one ancient red-stained camel hide, but otherwise the whole interior of the House with its treasures, its Gods, its sacred pit communicating to the netherworld, they were all open to the heavens by day and by night. The walls surrounding the Gods' courtyard were only the walls of the neighboring houses, although of course the wealthiest men with the largest houses claimed space closest to the sanctuary. We entered through alleys between the private homes.

Father and I went first to salute each of the three hundred and sixty Gods that stood about the clearing before the Ka'ba. They marked the points of heaven with their wood and rock figures. The circumambulation, so we believed then, was a reflection of the planets circling overhead. I kissed the black stone and made thank-offering to Hubal of the Red Hand.

But even as I did, I had my doubts—

"So you, Master, were a *hanif*, a hater of idols and believer in one God, before Muhammad?"

I do not disabuse my scribe of his faith in me. But as my lips met the cold, lifeless graven image all those years and miles ago, my heart was really asking: "Thank-offering? For what? For this wound I got battling before the white camel at Dhu Qar? My love Bint Zura was defeated at my hand and given to another there. My life is worth nothing now."

Divine duty accomplished, I returned to my father's courtyard where my mother and brothers, sisters and wives awaited my homecoming. Not until then was I told that I had become a father again and presented with little—Well, I cannot remember which son it was. He could already sit alone and smile—but not for me. He was afraid of me. By the full moon, he was off in the desert with a foster family. They had only waited for me to see and accept him before sending him to this best sort of education, the same as I had had among the Tamim.

My returning rite that year was to be the last time I would ever see Mecca's great Holy House in that ancient and venerable guise. God decreed that just two nights after my arrival, the House suffered an even greater calamity than the seasonal bouts with jealous dust and flash flood.

The night was reserved for women at the Ka'ba. What their private rites were, I do not know, for even male infants at the breast were never allowed in with their mothers at such times. I had heard the ritual invocations women chanted as they circumambulated the holy shrine, their cymbals, their drums. And they lit the place, for on such nights, the darks of the moon, the whole town could see a golden glow dancing beneath the stars, over the Ka'ba walls.

On this night, however, I awoke to see the dance of firelight on my bedroom wall brighter than ever before. And the air choked with smoke. Quickly wrapping a cloak about myself, I went down and joined the rest of the Quraysh in horror to see the entire sacred precinct a vision of the flames of hell.

During a devotional frenzy, perhaps, coals had caught the bright, blowing hangings. In a moment, flames had engulfed the entire sanctuary. Ignoring the half-healed wound in my side, I joined the pitiful effort to carry goatskins of water from the closest well. What gurgled out of the narrow necks was little better than spitting. Then the screams began, and the horrible smell of burning flesh—

The Day of Dhu Qar danced before my eyes, the screams of my beloved as her camel fell. The effort to make the flashbacks stop split my wound open again. Blood seeped through my cloak, and I didn't care.

Heaps of women's clothes and veils must have been among the first things to ignite. Women began running out. Their long, unbound hair singed, red burns crosshatched their naked skin. That was how I learned in what state women performed their secret rites.

Men threw their cloaks over their kinswomen and led or carried them weeping away. As long as the precinct was sanctified to women, however, no man dared to profane the space. No one carried a goat skin in to pour out closer to the flames. No one went in to assist those who might be wounded or trapped, or even to rescue the generations of pious gifts that formed the Ka'ba's treasure: gold goblets and bowls carried across the desert, gem-encrusted statues, precious silks.

And some women refused to expose to profane eyes what is sacred and should be veiled to all but other women and the Gods.

"Umm Sulayman. Here comes Umm Sulayman," men close to the door announced, averting their eyes.

My wife Umm Sulayman burst out into my arms. I slapped smoldering sparks out of her hair and threw my blood-stiff cloak over her. More bodily comfort I could not give in public eyes, but I could relieve her of a priceless casket, still hot to the touch, she'd had the presence of mind to salvage.

She hardly cared about that. "Umm Khalid. Alas for Umm Khalid," she gasped.

At first, I couldn't understand what she meant. I was still so much in the recent past of the Battle of Dhu Qar. "You mean Bint Zura, alas for her," I wanted to say.

But this was how I learned that my mother clung to modesty until the end of her life and stayed within. She was among the fourteen who died.

We went in to retrieve the bodies, after the ban had been lifted and the ashes cooled. We could not tell one woman from the next, all burnt and black and flexed into tight, infantlike positions. I helped to scoop out fourteen graves in the desert with my hands, shallow trenches, but not so shallow as a man's final resting place: If she is to rise again, a woman wants earth to cover her breasts. As modesty in life had cost her that life.

Fourteen shrouds we couldn't keep from being charcoal smudged—I helped gently to lay them down. Fourteen sheep sacrifices I attended, fourteen stones I set on fourteen memorials. And all the while I didn't know whether it was an old woman or a virgin to whom I did these rites, an ugly face or a fair, my closest blood kinswoman or a stranger. At the time, I thought, such are the Goddesses, unknowable and all phases of womanhood at once.

Now I recite:

> "If she was a doer of good, please increase the reward of her deeds.
> If she misbehaved, please forgive her misdeeds.
> O Lord, deprive me not of her reward,
> And let me not be misguided after her."

The entire sanctuary burned to the ground. The sour, sickening smell of burnt wool and flesh hung over Mecca, strung between the surrounding mountains, for a week.

I sat in mourning, receiving condolence calls in my father's quiet and dignified majlis. Not even here, however, could I escape the wild screams of tearing hair and breaking bangles and clawing faces. The sounds tore in from every woman's apartment in town. They reminded me of what I had lost the day I won at Dhu Qar. I have to confess to a pang of jealousy: a man's grief is permitted no such outlets.

I didn't miss Umm Khalid, my birth mother, so much. My first memories of her were of a stranger I shrank from, crying into Umm Mutammim's skirts. I missed the idea of Mother more. Because I had not seen her face in death, it might have been Umm Mutammim, my milk mother, who had gone in the flames of the Ka'ba. The thought that I wouldn't see her when next I went to the desert—I could sink my nails into my own flesh and draw blood at that thought.

And at the thought that Bint Zura was dead to me.

The entire town of Mecca fasted for three days to avert the Gods' anger. Light headed and open to the jinn and things beyond, we got up a procession with banners and drums and incense to take the House's rescued treasure back to its place. This included the casket Umm Sulayman had rescued, a pathetic few other items polished of soot, not taken by the Gods to themselves in the holocaust. After we had performed our seven circumambulations in this manner, the elders of the tribe moved cautiously to set the bier holding the treasure in its proper place.

It never got there.

The men stepped back in horror, spitting against evil and tumbling the treasure from its bier. A monster of a serpent had engendered itself out of the ash. No soul dared approach. I saw the thing with my own eyes, as black as soot and as big around as a man's arm. I had to spit against evil myself.

Well, by this time the superstitions of the populace had reached a fever pitch. Signs and portents appeared everywhere: monsters were born; women wept that the curds would not come; comets flared in the night sky. When men met for qat during the day, no speculation invoked laughter as being too far-fetched. When women turn to prayers, charms, and weeping, men ask rather, "Who is to blame, that we may drag them outside the city and have wild horses pull them to pieces?"

Some blamed the Abyssinians, some blamed the Jews. They were the same groups who blamed the sons of Judah or of Africa for smallpox or for poisoning the wells, although such things affected Jew, African, and Arab equally. Some blamed the envious magic of the Christian slaves. The poor man was blamed by everyone he owed. The rich blamed each other.

I do remember, too, a novel idea presented: the One God was angry at the many imports, false Gods and demons, with which He was asked to share His House.

Someone actually said: "It's the Gods themselves who ought to be dragged out and buried."

A silence fell upon the group, but whether it was horror or concurrence, I couldn't tell.

My scribe leaps on this, as well as a man sitting cross-legged on cushions can leap. "A new saying of the Prophet, precious blessings on him." My man will trap the thing like some rare beast and show it for dinars in the market.

"No," I tell him. "I cannot say for certain whether it was Muhammad ibn Abd Allah who spoke such pious and high-minded words or not. I rather doubt it. This was before his calling, you see, and he was not the sort of man to speak up in public council before the angel drove him to it. Indeed, I don't think I knew who Muhammad was at that time, beyond perhaps being able to pick him out as one of the clan of Abd al-Muttalib by the resemblance of mouth and nose."

"But he must have made some impression. The Seal of the Prophets could not pass through the world without something—some glow, some difference—from other men."

"Couldn't he?" I wonder. Can the same be said of all the anonymous men crowded together in a city like Homs? "Very well." I give the eunuch this. "Everyone knew that the only son of Abd Allah was the one who had married the widow Khadijah for love. That was notoriety of a kind, perhaps, which a true man would rather not gain."

"So such ideas of the One God truly were in the air?"

"But of course. The *hunafa*. Did not the Prophet teach us that Submission is the natural religion of all people, from the day of creation on? Some men never forget the purity with which they are born. In any case, four or five men of note in Mecca especially favored the idea. They would meet of an evening, or take retreats into the mountains during holy months, or converse at length with the Jews of Yathrib or Christians they met on caravan to Syria. No, my good scribe, it was not necessarily Muhammad who made the suggestion to bury the Gods. The suggestion did not meet with much success, in any case. One God was powerful. Why shouldn't three hundred and sixty Gods be three hundred and sixty times more powerful? It is only parents who corrupt the natural religion of children, as Muhammad, blessed be he, did say.

"But let me get back to our confusion, poor mortal men, with no voice of the Gods to tell us what should be Their will."

"The women are to blame," someone said next, and that suspicion proved infinitely more popular than that it was the Gods.

"There is reason in that," someone else agreed.

"Indeed. It was during women's rites that the fire began."

"And the serpent, like the beast that threatens us now. It is a well-known symbol of the powers women invoke."

"Their bringer of wisdom and grantor of new life, not evil."

"But what may be good for women may be bad for men. Such things weaken us."

"Make us unable to approach our Gods, surely."

"They are only foolish women, careless with a brazier."

"But to condemn women? That would be as good as condemning the Meccan race to oblivion."

"No," most finally decided, "women must be protected in their weakness and their folly as well as in their virtue."

So discussions continued, often throughout the night, with little result. I didn't say much. I was as yet too young to be much of a voice in the majlis.

The greatest matter was that when they spoke of women and of things of the spirit, I couldn't help but think of Bint Zura. I couldn't help but think of her much of the time, anyway, being young and in love. I was, you may well say, enchanted, and the tumble of the white camel in the dust of Dhu Qar had not broken the spell. If anything, it had tied the magic tighter, penetrating to my every fiber like smoke through the seams of a tent.

In these difficulties with the Sacred House, the words of the Christian hermit came back to me so strongly. "The coming salvation of the Arabs." The thought would not escape me. If I had Bint Zura here—her mother, the kahinah, too, perhaps—the evil jinn could be lured away from this profaned shrine. What had been done by a woman could be undone by one. But how could I bring that woman I had so destroyed to this spot? How could I even mention her name among the great ones of my tribe? The thought was like the itch of my slowly healing wound.

Then heaven grew impatient with us and took matters into its own hands.

6

Muhammad is not the father of any man among you, but he
is the Apostle of God, and the Seal of the Prophets: and God
knows all things.
—The Holy Quran, Surah XXXIII

The men of Mecca had erected a portico of palm fronds just inside the sacred precinct. They had meant it merely to be a temporary shelter for the treasure until we decided how to proceed, but the structure seemed more and more permanent as time passed. Men gathered in that shade on hot afternoons. They sat and debated. They stared in mute silence across the ashes, cringing in horror from the unnatural reptilian coils that slithered through the ruins from time to time.

I was there with many others, including my friend Amr, one afternoon when a shadow slipped across the sacred compound. Looking up into a sky of faultless blue, we saw an eagle of wingspan greater than any man had ever seen before.

"It's a sign from the Gods," Amr just had time to mutter as the creature wheeled once slowly overhead.

Then, suddenly, the bird dropped like a stone into the serpent's very nest. A fanged, black head reared up and struck.

Men were calling the rest of the town now to come and see. I was on my feet. We all watched with awe.

With a back sweep of its wings, the eagle leapt away and hissed. Fangs struck ash into clouds; the serpent hissed back in dry fury. Red talon gashes streaked its scales.

The serpent struck again. The bird danced out of the way.

Again the serpent struck. This time the bird lunged even closer to the head and stuck. The great wings flapped to keep balance as the serpent writhed to escape. The head, the worst hazard, stayed pinned to the ground.

Then the heavenly creature stabbed the creature of the earth through the neck. The spine broke with a crack. A screech of triumph, of benediction. A heavy beat of wings labored under the burden, and the bird carried the snake off, limp and lifeless, to feed its eaglets, touching me with its shadow.

"What does this omen mean?"

This prattle had only half begun when a new issue arrived. A rider on a lean camel rode into Mecca from the coast.

"The winds of heaven blew a Greek ship against the rocks of Jeddah last night," was his message.

The words were hardly out of him before half the men in town were saddling their swiftest mounts and stringing a line of pack camels behind them. Jeddah is but a night's ride from Mecca. I went too and saw the miracle: great beams of wood strewing a barren, treeless land. Also washed ashore from the wreck were bundles of precious fabrics, gems, incense, and tools. We scooped them up and loaded all the camels could carry.

We consecrated every bit to the rebuilding of the Great House, including the sole human survivor of the wreck, the captain. Because he admitted to having worked in Egyptian shipyards, this man was immediately made head builder. This Greek's name was Bakum, and he was a Christian.

A cast of lots chose my father of all Mecca's great patriarchs to pray over the rubble. On a morning, already warm, in late summer, in the midst of the gathered guardians of the Holy Place, he assured God, who had convinced us of His petulance: "O God, do not be afraid. We mean what is best for You."

It was my father who first put forth a hand to clear the half-standing old wall and its ruins. He lifted a blackened stone and tossed it to one side. When all saw that he did so with impunity, the rest of the town joined in the pious work.

Father had to leave shortly after that on his yearly trade caravan. The wound in my side still had not completely healed, so I remained behind. Not that it distressed me so very much, not as much as it had when I was ten years old and I had thought I should die if I could not tempt someone into letting me stowaway. I did not feel capable yet of returning to the sons of Tamim (at the time I thought I never should be able) to see my daughter of Zura made al-Harith's wife. She might be carrying his child, perhaps. At least his firewood.

Instead, I went to the center of town to watch the building of the House nearly every day. Towards the end of the work I was well enough to lend a hand myself.

When all the rubble was cleared, we discovered the foundation to be of fine, firm marble.

"These are the remains," some said, "of the foundation laid by Adam at the beginning of time."

Others were convinced otherwise: "These marble slabs are nothing less than the very foundations upon which the whole world rests."

This theory received support when Bakum the Christian set his crow to pry them up. Suddenly the earth shook beneath our feet as if it were a live thing with whose aching tooth he had tampered. The lurch threw me to the ground in clouds of dust and chaos like the end of time. I landed hard on my wound and cried like a child.

When the dust had cleared, an inscription appeared on one of the cracked marble slabs. A learned Jew was called in to read it.

"I am God," he read, "Lord of Mecca. I created it on the day that I created Heaven and Earth and formed the sun and moon, and I surrounded it with seven pious angels. It will stand while its two mountains stand, a blessing to its people, with milk and water."

So Bakum put away his crowbar. He didn't touch the foundations, and the new House grew upon that base.

In layers of shipwrecked Greek wood and grey stone cut from Mecca's hills, the Great House rose. As many of the original stones as possible were reincorporated. When the House was finished, it rose two-and-a-half times the height of a man, by far the tallest edifice in Mecca, as suited its greater worth. Obviously, many other stones had had to be cut and smoothed for the work. Instead of being level with the surrounding courtyard, the opening of the new door in the Ka'ba was placed over a man's head. It could only be reached by a ladder. This way, neither floods nor dust storms nor unworthy men could make their way in to desecrate the inner sanctuary. A true roof of Syrian construction, with beams and slabs, protected the top.

Our women busied themselves weaving and embroidering new, colorful hangings. The many different idols, those who had not burned, were cleaned, rubbed with oils and scents, and set in their places once again.

"But the Prophet?" my scribe protests, for the light is almost gone from my garden, our work almost done for the day, and the Muhammad I promised him has yet to appear.

"Patience, patience, by God, he's coming. That short, solid figure of the orphan son of Abd Allah ibn Abd al-Muttalib surfaced as separate from all his kinsmen. Muhammad the Messenger is coming, and nothing can stop him. It happened on this wise."

My scribe gives a great sigh and reaches for a sheet of fresh, new parchment.

The Ka'ba was complete. There only remained the task of replacing the most sacred object of all—the Black Stone —into the eastern corner of the shrine. Some say that this Stone is an angel fallen from heaven, once white, now stained to obsidian by our many sins over the ages. I never remember it being anything but a deep, shiny black in which one could see one's reflection if the light were right. And many years of the wicked Time of Ignorance had yet to pass.

"But who should have the honor of finally lifting the Stone back into place?" became the question.

Bakum the Egyptian, for all that the project would have been impossible without him, was a Christian. He could not be given the task. He'd even been known to scoff at our ancient ways. The clan of Kusay, guardians of the Ka'ba? They had glory enough already and, because of the fire, old rivalries that deemed them unworthy had flared up again. Al-Walid my father might have won the honor, as he had been the one to start the enterprise with prayer. But he was out of town, and I was not considered my father's worthy substitute, not yet. The honored Abu Talib, the honored Abu Sufyan—many were the names presented and supported by their various factions. But as with blame, honor too could find no unanimous voice.

Finally, it was decided: "Let the will of heaven manifest itself, in this as it has in so many other things connected with the House. Let the final word go to the first person who should walk into the courtyard of the Ka'ba this afternoon."

Even as the elders spoke the agreement, I turned with the rest to look at the gate to the sacred enclosure. Framed within its arch stood a figure in brown, leaning heavily on a staff. He walked as one dazzled, having just come from a fast of days, maybe weeks, in the desert. A certain glow lit up the patch of face above his beard, more than sunburn. And as he walked towards the shrine to perform his rites upon returning to town, he muttered to himself the invocation: "Here I am in answer to Your call. Here I am, O God, here I am. You have no partner . . . Here I am."

Heaven sent us the son of Abd Allah, blessings on him, who in those days was called Muhammad the Trustworthy. As everyone said, he would rather die than mislead a donkey.

The men of Mecca crowded around the new arrival. Muhammad seemed neither flattered nor amazed that heaven should have given him this responsibility by leading him through the courtyard at just that moment. Nor did he immediately turn the honor over to his uncle and one-time guardian, Abu Talib, as some protested he might, Abu Talib being the greater man.

I studied Muhammad as he stroked his beard and considered the Great Black Stone. Under the glow, his complexion was pale, his hair and beard dark and meticulously tended. His dark brows formed a straight, unbroken line above his eyes; where the brows met sprang a mole. Such a mole, people said, was the mark of an extraordinary man. Fastidious, clean, neat to distraction—his appearance, we now know, hid more disruptive things brewing.

It must have been the eyes—the blue eyes.

"What? The Prophet, blessed be he, had blue eyes?" my scribe asks.

"But of course," I reply. "The true sign of a seer. Don't they tell you that in market gossip?"

My scribe shakes his head, his emerald earring dull, and scribbles fiercely.

So there we were, standing around the ruined Ka'ba, seeing, really seeing the son of Abd Allah for the first time, blue eyes and all. Now here is a fellow— *I thought. But what sort of fellow, I could not say.*

At once the answer to the problem of the Black Stone came to him; you could see it pass like a torch through the night across his face, in those pale eyes. Quickly, he took off his cloak and spread it on the ground. Then he hefted the Stone and gently laid it in the center of the cloak.

"Now," he said. "Every leader of a clan may take a corner and lift together."

His idea brightened face to face around the ring, torch lighting torch. His wisdom was cheered, God was praised, and the Stone was lifted into place.

In the harem that night I heard Muhammad called "blessed" and "inspired." None of us could foresee to what extent God the All-Seeing meant these things to be true.

7

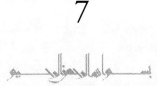

What is religion? A maid kept close so no eye may view her;
The price of her wedding-gifts and dowry baffles the wooer.
—Al-Ma'arri, the blind Syrian philosopher

Aunt to the groom, Sitt Umm Ali spat at the bride. All the older guests did, those women past childbearing whose jealousy of a young life on the brink of rich fertility might cast the evil eye. Best to admit to such destructive feelings, Rayah knew, than to pretend they didn't exist.

Younger women danced. Hips and shoulders waved and jerked like troubled water in a well, breasts shimmied in blatant womanhood. No jealousy here. Wedding drums and trilled ululations sent their pulse as high as the stars, and the stars throbbed in response over the congregated women.

The bride, Rayah's friend Ghusoon, sat cross-legged in the place of honor, elevated so everyone could see her.

Ghusoon kept her eyes down, but no tears of terror made the thick kohl run down her cheeks as they did with most other brides Rayah had seen in the short years of her life. Ghusoon ate no more than any other bride of the roast lamb, the strengthening soup of lamb intestines, lemon, mint and chickpeas, or heap after pyramidal heap of pastries stuffed with the new crop of dates. But every now and then, a little smile twitched at the corners of the painted lips. For Ghusoon was marrying the man of her choice.

Such joy, Rayah knew, was dangerous. She wanted to warn her friend: "Don't tempt the jinn." But it wasn't her place to say. And plenty of other things could give the warning to her—if only joy had not stuffed her ears.

The headdress and necklaces Ghusoon wore had been passed around the town of Tadmor from mother to daughter since ancient Roman days of prosperity. The ornaments taught a bride's head and shoulders the weight of her new responsibilities along with her glory. The pearls glinting in a hundred well-trimmed oil lamps were dredged up from the days when pearls from the Gulf had been easier to come by in this desert oasis. A reminder of the days of Queen Zaynab, in fact—whom the Romans called Zenobia—and a reminder that the vigor and joy of youth would not live forever.

Most importantly, the pearls winked back at well-wishers like eyes themselves. They turned away any evil that might dare to settle on the bride and her future life. Tendrils of henna decorated the bride's hands and feet with signs of ruddy fertility—to ward off other jinn who might seek to enter and curse her young body through these vulnerable, exposed limbs.

And Sitt Umm Ali spat, over and over, under her breath and without real spittle.

Sitt—Lady—Umm Ali taught Islam to Tadmor's young women. That new, powerful weapon against unbelieving fire spirits in the world could not squeeze every last drop of jealousy from a heart. In fact, Rayah was beginning to see, the Faith might make a person even more conscious of shadows that lurked in the world, more anxious to thrust them out.

The other Sitt in Rayah's life was Sitt Sameh, the woman she had only just come to accept as her own mother. The close connection hadn't yet let Rayah drop the honorific—yes, the edge of fear she felt in that woman's presence. Still, what should she fear when Sitt Sameh herself seemed much more fearful of something that had no name? Sitt Sameh had not even dared to leave her room on the third floor of the turpentine sellers' harem to come to the wedding. Perhaps there wasn't spit enough in the world to drown Sitt Sameh's jealousy?

The night air braided the celebratory smells together: hot oil from the lamps, the press of sweated perfumes, fat cooked crisp, honey and mint all dried like henna over the incense braziers. Amid these smells, through their twists of smoke, the bride drew Rayah's attention, like everyone's. And yet, Rayah found herself trying to resist. She knew everyone must accuse her of jealousy, since the groom had asked for her hand before, when Ghusoon had been promised to the old sharif with the bad breath.

Should Rayah spit, at only twelve years old?

No. Rayah wasn't jealous. She was young, not even come to a hip-twitching, breast-pulsing womanhood yet. She had had no desire to marry young and handsome Jaffar herself and wished the couple well.

Nonetheless, she knew she was responsible for her friend being happy and not a heap of abandoned bones. A month ago, Ghusoon the bride had been wandering mad in the desert, and Rayah had cast those demons out of her. Would she or no, Rayah was a descendant of Queen Zaynab and of other women of power in the desert. Such women were familiars, makers of treaties, with the tribe of Those of the Land and Waste Places, those whose names one dared not speak—the jinn. Such women did not seek to crush the Others as Islam did, rather to make treaty, however uneasy, with them.

Except that faithful Muslimah Sitt Umm Ali still thought she had to spit.

Rayah's blue eyes announced to the world that she had been born with this power, although she herself, through a long struggle, was only just coming to accept it. Along with accepting the mother who had given her both eyes and power. And if Ghusoon the lamp-lit bride dazzled the night more than the stars, Rayah knew herself to be that light's shadow. In truth, she couldn't say whether the gazes turned on the bride were more of joy for Ghusoon—or simply avoidance, fear, of having to look in Rayah's own dark corner of the assembly.

All of Rayah's household, the extended family of the turpentine sellers, had come to the wedding, and she had come with them. Everyone, with the exception of the only one whose blood she actually shared. Of course, Rayah had wanted to come, to rejoice, to celebrate Ghusoon's triumph—and, yes, her own. Now she saw that perhaps it would have been better to do as her mother always did. Her mother never left her small room. So it had been all the thirteen years since the turpentine sellers had taken her in, a woman, an anomaly, without friends and protection, pregnant, hunted, alone.

Where and what her mother's more distant past was, what had brought her to that moment, Rayah did not understand. In fact, she was afraid to learn, and blessedly, no one had told her, in all her twelve years. But that summer, the eunuch Abd Allah, scribe to Khalid ibn al-Walid abu Sulayman the Conqueror, general of the great armies of Islam, had come to the house of the turpentine sellers. He had worn down Sitt Sameh's protective walls, so that she had broken the silence. She had told Abd Allah and Rayah of her mother and her mother's mother, the power they had wielded in the desert before the rise of the Prophet Muhammad, blessings on him. Sitt Sameh was trying to teach Rayah to embrace the heritage neither of them could escape, in any case. But of herself—Sitt Sameh still said nothing.

As Rayah had healed the bride, Sitt Sameh had healed the groom. The circumcision that made him a man and prepared him to marry had gone awry and threatened to kill him. Sitt Sameh had healed the fever. Still, the healer never came out, least of all to weddings. Not even to weddings she made possible.

Should Rayah, her daughter—now also a healer, would she or not—should she do likewise?

Or should she spit?

Avoiding the bride, she looked down through the railing upon the men celebrating the groom on the floor below like the mirror image of the women. The warlike steps of masculine line dances stomped the courtyard dust, their unsheathed swords flashed like lightning. Rayah thought of the other, superior, heavenly sword, lying at home, unsheathed on Sitt Sameh's rug, and shivered in spite of the heat.

Away from the dance, at the edge of that assembly in the place she occupied above, Rayah caught a glimpse of the eunuch, the wink of the emerald in his ear. The men tolerated him among them, but barely. Men didn't spit, never admitting to any jealousy festering their hearts. So one whose virility had been sliced from him, what did it portend to have him cheering on the groom who must perform in just a little while?

Rayah wanted to give the eunuch an encouraging smile but knew he wouldn't see her. Worse, the men would resent any invasion of womankind upon their sword-wagging world and make things even more uncomfortable for him. Perhaps they both should have stayed at home.

Suddenly, the spitting became a frenzy. Every woman reached for a muffling veil and pulled back from the bride. The girl must go forward on her own.

Down below, the groom, cushioned on a shield on men's shoulders, made his final proud circuit around the company. Four kinsmen of the bride came up the stairs two at a time to bring Ghusoon down with the same ceremony, except that her conveyance was a serving tray. It wouldn't be long now. After parading together, the couple would be carried to the tent pitched in the courtyard. There they would finally, completely unite while the party lingered encouragingly without, awaiting the stained sheets that would prove the bride's virginity.

"I can't wait to see this," rumored someone close by. "That might convince me a jinni did not have her first."

Rayah couldn't tell who this was, the face veiled. But from beneath that veil came spitting, a clink of amulets and a sideways look in Rayah's direction.

To avoid more sights like this, Rayah took advantage of what had been her place of lowest honor near the railing. She did not stand, but only had to shift around on the carpet and press her face through the wooden slats. Standing women crushed above her, clapping, singing shrill, trilling triumph, spitting. Rayah had the best view when the bride, completely veiled in gauze like a birth caul, pearls winking, emerged from the womb of the staircase. The men's shouts of triumph and greeting shook the very plaster Rayah sat on.

Then suddenly something crashed louder than all singing and shouting together. Rayah tried to lean even farther: the sound came from somewhere downstairs and to her right. She could just barely see yet another great brass tray and the sweets its toppling must have spilled. Not a good omen, such an accident caused as men's exuberance released. Still, not the end of the world. The dancing and union might just continue, and all would be well.

"Inshallah." Rayah joined a dozen voices around her in saying against evil.

But no. It was no accident. Or the man who had done the deed decided now to expand his disruption. He strode to the center of the yard, parting the couple and their bearers. From the angle of turbans, Rayah might not have recognized him. But belly and backside rounded him fully beneath the turban. A little monkey perched on his silken left shoulder, gnawing on one of the stolen sweets and chattering. And the man himself must have indulged heavily in the garlicky soup, for she could smell his breath from one floor above.

Sharif Diya'l-Din, the old man Ghusoon's parents had wanted her to marry. The thought had sent the girl reeling, mad, to the desert.

Now, it seemed, the thwarted groom had gone mad instead. And at the mere sight of the glittering bride, even completely veiled as she was. Only you couldn't call it madness, could you? Not in a merchant as rich and powerful as Diya'l-Din. Not in a man, who never spat against his own recognized weakness. Curses were his response, insults and threats.

"By God, Abu Isma'il," he roared at the bride's father. The poor man still had a smile frozen on his face, his hands still high in midclap. "You have saved me a bride-price, *al-hamdulillah*, the price of a madwoman. But I shall use the amount to destroy you in the marketplace for this insult. With God's will, I shall do it. The jinn, my ass." The great hulk lurched then towards the door.

The collective intake of breath among the women was enough to make the lamps dance. The man had called undue attention from the bride to himself—then back again. A terrible omen. Worse, to actually speak the name of the fire spirits, to tempt them to come to him—or to her—

Men from the bride's family and the groom's were at the irate man's side in a moment, turning him back so as not to compound evil words with a breach of community. Immediately, Diya'l-Din understood his mistake and took control of himself. He could not attack other men's women, even now, as Ghusoon made the dangerous pass from father to husband, where they might drop her.

One creature, however, was free game.

The sharif turned so violently, the monkey had to cling for dear life. Consoling kinsmen dropped away. "You."

For one dreadful moment, Rayah thought he meant her. His gaze was lower, however. No, he couldn't attack Rayah. Nor could he attack her mother, safe in the harem. But he could attack the next closest thing: Abd Allah.

"Yes, you. Eunuch."

Abd Allah bowed low, his earring winking. Perhaps he tried to make his voice deeper, but he lost that battle. An adolescent gurgle was all he managed. "At your service, most gracious lord. But, please, sir, later. Let us not disrupt the honor due the young couple."

Diya'l Din would not be deterred. "You say you come from Homs."

"That is so. But can't it wait?"

"Do you not also come from Abu Sulayman, Khalid the Conqueror of Syria and Iraq?"

This news sent a murmur through the crowd. There was a name to conjure by, half fear, half honor.

Abd Allah made another attempt to lower his voice. "Sir, in consideration of matrimonial harmony, let me come to you tomorrow for whatever concerns you—"

"No. We will discuss this here, in front of all. You come from the Conqueror?"

"By the grace of God, it is so."

"An emissary from such a great man, such a servant of God, his very sword has that name, Sayf-Allah."

"May God favor him and all Muslims."

"*Amīn*," echoed any number of the assembly. The men carrying the happy couple rocked in place under their burdens, not knowing what to do.

The sharif went on, the monkey chattering in chorus. "And yet you do not come to me or to any of the great ones in our community."

"That is so," agreed some of the crowd, mostly downstairs, among the men. "A slight, an insult."

"Why is that so?"

"My commission was not to the great, but more humbly, as suits myself. I was sent to those—" Abd Allah worked to be circumspect in mentioning the harem. "To those behind."

"Why, in God's name?"

"As he approached—approaches the end of his life, God have mercy on him, the Sword of God realizes he has—he has left some things undone. In his glory, some of the lesser things—"

"Eunuch, you slipped." Diya'l-Din crowed in triumph. His monkey chattered. "Let me call the assembly's attention to that slip, something that I learned on my most recent trip west to Homs, Damascus and beyond. This half-man cannot have come at the Conqueror's bidding. Do you know why he cannot have done so?"

"Why?" urged some of the hearers. "Tell us your news, O sharif."

"The Conqueror cannot have ordered him because he is dead."

Rayah herself joined the gasp, even as she felt the legs pressing around her move back to avoid touching her. Maybe the eunuch had told her mother, but she herself had not known. Perhaps she should have guessed. Slips like Abd Allah had just made now. He had made them before. But she had willed herself not to hear them. So she could delude herself longer that it was good to stay and listen to the stories the eunuch brought? Because they came from a powerful, a *living* man?

"God grant him peace." Abd Allah bowed his head over his folded arms.

"Because he never knew peace while he was alive." Rayah almost heard the eunuch say that out loud. But maybe it was the whisper of a jinni instead. The air felt like that around her, heavy, twisting, a gathering storm.

Some among the hearers added their own wishes to this prayer. But not everyone did. They didn't want to miss what other news the sharif might divulge.

The large, angry man was not slow to satisfy them. "God will not, however, grant him peace, but consign Khalid ibn al-Walid to hellfire. The man died in disgrace, cast off by his cousin Omar, khalifah of the faithful, may God preserve him and the Muslim cause. The man succumbed in his final hours to the very heresy God willed him to fight all the rest of his years. That is the word in Homs, where he may rot in his grave."

The party erupted in horrified comment.

The moment he could claim attention again, Diya'l-Din drove on: "This death occurred long before this eunuch can have left that western city to arrive here. The unsexed one lies when he says he comes under orders."

"You do not understand, then, how orders can come after death, through writing," Abd Allah said quietly. "How orders can be part of a man's last testament. I find it remarkable that a merchant should not understand this."

"All the worse for you, eunuch." Diya'l-Din sprang to his conclusion. "And for those you come to visit. They are tainted by this falsehood, this backsliding. Worse, who knows but that this servant even raised his hand against his master?"

"If you accuse my master of backsliding, perhaps his death was a good thing, nothing of which to accuse me." Rayah's heart sank. Abd Allah was clutching at straws. And such straws might stab him.

"You confess it then?"

Abd Allah realized his mistake. "I am not guilty of Abu Sulayman's death. Nor of his heresy, if indeed there was heresy here."

"You would doubt the judgment of Omar ibn al-Khattab?"

"Blessings on him," was all the commitment Abd Allah would make.

Triumph grew in Diya'l-Din's voice. "Those this prevaricator came to visit—this possibility must taint them as well. Poison, possession, communing with jinn, the weapons of women and the weak. They are all among us, even in this union of families. Yes, I suspect them all."

And so did the whole wedding party. Diya'l Din cried over their jabber: "Arrest him. Arrest the eunuch. Pull the truth out of him, with hot pincers, if necessary." Ten men moved to obey.

"I go with you willingly," Rayah heard the high, reedy voice say before the eunuch—and yes, her friend—disappeared from the courtyard below. "So as to leave no more blot on the happy couple."

Putting the couple to bed in the pitched tent was an afterthought. The party broke up quickly, as if someone had rumored plague in the house. Were the sheets stained, proving no jinn had had the bride before? No one stayed to see. There would be much more blood in Tadmor—soon.

Sitt Sameh had said, when she worked the cure, that the young man might never be able to perform his husbandly duties. Rayah remembered this with dread as she, too, left the party along with the rest of the turpentine sellers' household.

On the dark threshold, where no one saw, she spat. But was it too little too late? Not just for the bride, but for everyone she held dear?

8

O Prophet, say to your wives
If your desire is for the present life and its finery,
Then come, I will make provision for you
And release you with kindness.
But if you desire God, His Messenger
And the Home of the Hereafter
Then remember that God has prepared great rewards
For those of you who do good.
——The Holy Quran 33:28–29

I make a minaret of my fingers and, over them, ask slyly: "Suppose we start today with Khadijah, daughter of Khuwaylid?"

"The Mother of the Believers?" My scribe's eyes light up and wink like the emerald in his ear. "May God favor her."

"Still—a woman."

Ah, but close enough. Who in the world does not bless Khadijah bint Khuwaylid these days? The first wife of the Prophet, blessings on him, she believed in him first of all and gave him the freedom to pursue his mission. But there were many times, I'm sure, when her father cursed the day she first blackened his face with shame. Such is the willful way of daughters, some of them . . .

"So write," I order.

I did not see my milk brothers again for several years. When I did, it was not because I had returned to the desert of the Tamim, where I'd been put to the wet nurse as an infant and raised with them as closer than brothers. Nor had I returned to the town of al-Hira which must always remind me of where I'd first laid eyes on Bint Zura and fallen in love. Instead, my milk brothers came to Mecca, to participate in the annual pilgrimage, to our newly repaired shrine, the Ka'ba. They also meant to take profit from the joint fair, of course. Their herdsman had been unusually successful at breeding in the last years.

"And Muhammad, blessings on him?" my scribe asks. "And Khadijah, may God favor her soul?"

Very well. I can no quicker return to Bint Zura now than I could then, with all the world's other concerns whirling around me.

Muhammad, blessed be he, was preaching by then. But how many pilgrimages had it been since the Angel Jabra'il first visited him on the mountain? I cannot say with certainty. Two or three, perhaps. I counted my years by other events in those days.

Actually, my milk brothers, Malik and Mutammim ibn Nuwaira, had closer connections with Muhammad than I did at that season. They accepted the hospitality of a blood kinsman of theirs, Abu Hala al-Oseyyad the Tamimi, for the holy month. Abu Hala had been a long-time resident among us in Mecca, furthering his mercantile ambitions as a client of a clan of the Quraysh. In his early years here, Abu Hala had taken himself a wife of the daughters of the clan of Asad, to help his position and prove his stability in the community.

"You said we would begin with Khadijah bint Khuwaylid, blessings on her."

Is the fellow going to sulk? Just like women, these sexless ones.

This woman he took to wife was none other than Khadijah bint Khuwaylid herself, blessings on her. Her first marriage. She had borne Abu Hala a pair of sons, but—

But Abu Hala found her too willful to be endured. A harem could not contain her nor keep her from meddling in his affairs. He divorced her.

Abu Hala saved his life by doing so, or so the rumors said. Khadijah's next husband had not the courage to divorce. The only way to end the contention in the home over who should run the business was for him to die quietly. He left it all, without further argument, to the controlling hand of his widow, Bint Khuwaylid.

Khuwaylid despaired for his daughter. She was now a proverb in the town for a woman who will accept no bridle. How was a man to endure watching how well she ran her business interests, turned her profits, and refused the new matches her father devised for her?

Still, it is as the proverb says, "To every out there is an in." For Khadijah's hard and outward soul, the Omnipotent One created the soft and inward soul of Muhammad ibn Abd Allah. As soon as death had taken Khuwaylid in the Wars of Wickedness, and even though she was fifteen years Muhammad's senior, the match was made. Khadijah did the proposing, hired the Messenger of God to husband as she had first hired him to drive her camels when he was the orphan son of a nobody, a dead nobody at that. Khadijah prepared the feast and provided her own bride-price. Khadijah continued to run the business and the household, raise the children, discipline the slaves and the neighbors as well. She was a formidable source of energy, indeed, this daughter of Khuwaylid of the sons of Asad.

Muhammad was lucky. Blessed by God, perhaps, it were better to say. Praises to Him. Who else would have had the son of Abd Allah, poor as he was? Who else but Khadijah would have left him free to think, to dream, to fast, to pray? It was a perfect match and had endured, up to the time I am remembering, for fifteen years or so.

Perhaps the only blight was that, among all her other skills, in this third marriage, Khadijah bint Khuwaylid had given birth to only daughters.

So this is how Malik and Mutammim, my milk brothers, first came to hear of the Well-Trusted One of Mecca, that orphan son of a nobody, Muhammad ibn Abd Allah, blessings on him. Their kinsman Abu Hala had two sons by this divorced wife Khadijah bint Khuwaylid. These young men had true, male names, and these had been pronounced aloud at their circumcisions for the whole community to hear and remember them as men. Still, everyone called them by the names Khadijah had given them as infants, Hala and Hind, women's names, one, indeed, named for her own sister. The Prophet's wife, may she rest in peace, had lost a number of sons at birth and thought this would be the best way to fool the jinn into leaving her boys alone. Femininity in infancy may be the death of daughters at their fathers' hands. In this case, it saved Khadijah's sons. But then, Khadijah always bargained well, even with the jinn.

I think, but do not speak, of my own cheating of the jinn, of Mutammim's blindness. Of his brother—

"Master?"

The scribe recalls me to the task.

Hala and Hind, fair-skinned, slender youths, lived with their father, of course, after the divorce, and kept his tribal allegiance. But they went often to pay their respects to their mother Khadijah, fearing her wrath if they did not. During these visits, the boys learned respect for the gentle and loving ways of their stepfather.

"Let me get this straight," my scribe interrupts. "Your milk brothers were kinsmen to the Prophet's stepsons, blessings on him?"

"I would have said Khadijah's sons in those days. She made a better connection. Relations multiplied. We worked at them as a woman works at her loom. Kinship was the net by which we did business and became rich. Relations were better than money invested in Indian spices."

So. At this particular pilgrimage, my milk brothers gave their young kinsmen, Hala and Hind, the honor of leading them through the rites. I felt a twinge of jealousy, but Mutammim and Malik were staying with Abu Hala, after all, and blood is thicker than milk. And they did come to invite me to join them in the rite.

Here were my milk brothers, hardening into manhood. Mutammim was totally blind now, having given his sight to the jinn as a child to save the herdsman's son, al-Harith. Or rather, I should say, having given his sight for the strength of my right arm. I could never look into the milkiness glazing his eyes without that twinge of guilt. Probably I should have felt more.

In place of physical vision, however, he had gained wisdom, and Malik, though the younger of the pair, had the brawn for the two. Malik's features had grown strong and sinewy under a thick, full beard.

We embraced. Unashamed of the tears in our eyes, we thanked the Gods for our reunion. But the moment I laid eyes on them, more than their own health, I wanted to know about those behind them, their women. What had been a dull ache of longing for all the intervening years became a sharp pain upon actual sight. Their mother, my milk mother. I wanted to know I had not buried her after the fire that destroyed the Ka'ba, as I had imagined. Layla bint al-Minhal, Malik's wife who had once been betrothed to me. Their herdsman, al-Harith. My milk brothers spoke of great success with the herds. Was that slight, shy, almost beardless al-Harith's doing? I would have to see it to believe it.

Only slowly would I work up to my true concern, Bint Zura, so as not to draw undue attention. I tried to tell myself she was no longer a daughter, the girl I had fallen in love with at the hand of a jinn-possessed monk in al-Hira. More guilt, twisting like a knife in a camel's hamstrings. She must be a mother, stinking of sour milk and dirty swaddling . . .

No, I would not believe it. I would have to see that, too.

My milk brother Malik only answered my first, politely vague questions with, "Fine, fine, thank the Gods. Our women have come with us and are camped out in the desert eastward."

"There's no water there," Mutammim reminded his brother. "We must send them waterskins from Zamzam. Don't forget." That was all.

I knew I would have to put off any further details until after the pilgrimage. We mustn't keep the Gods waiting. We went together to get our heads shaved.

My scribe stops to sharpen his pen. "So there was much of the true pilgrimage we know today, upon which I will go if God favors me, that was the same in the Days of Ignorance?"

"Much was the same. Much was different. The shaved heads were the same, no doubt given us from Ibrahim, the Friend of God." I feel a chill he cannot feel, not yet, as I go on to say, "As was the ban on weapons. Of course a man needs a knife to complete the pilgrimage with the blood of a sheep, but always, always these were left outside the Ka'ba. The only sacrifices within the precinct were those of birds, who had their necks wrung. Blood running down rocks was for the *baytels* outside as well."

Usually, no Meccan came to the compound during the pilgrimage if he did not have guests. But as we entered, there was Muhammad ibn Abd Allah, alone at his prayers beneath the portico. Hala and Hind, breaking from our staid procession, went to pay their respects. Their stepfather sat on his mat, dusty to his turban from praying, his beard grizzled, his eyes—his blue eyes, God favor him—keen and alive like no others.

Hala and Hind introduced my milk brothers to Muhammad. Hala and Hind found it easier to be warm to this dreaming stepfather of theirs than to their own father. I hung back a little awkwardly, uneasy around so strange a personage. I didn't know Muhammad well, only by sight.

"And for the replacement of the Black Stone," my scribe says.

"Yes, and for that."

Except for his wife Khadijah—and she encouraged distance by being a woman—Muhammad ibn Abd Allah wasn't a relationship for an ambitious man to foster. I stared instead at the sacred compound as if I were a first-time pilgrim, as if I hadn't been familiar with its three hundred and sixty Gods since childhood.

A thousand thousand feet had pounded the ground to a dry ocher that rose to meet the white-shrouded knees of the pilgrim's izar. Dust met the bare knees of those who believed the Gods preferred us to come before them naked. A slight breeze blessed the blistering air and stirred the banners overhead, the incense braziers whose fires the heat made invisible. The heavy thud of drummers, the squeal of flutes, the cacophony of a score of different chants burdened the air. Every tribe chanted at once, trying to prove whose God was strongest by how He had blessed His followers' lungs. Before them, some carried their tribe's standards: tassels, tinkling bells, or decorated camel skulls. Incense poured from the House itself between the maw of brightly colored hangings.

I saw it all without really looking, without really hearing, without really smelling. But because I held back, I did hear one thing: I overheard someone mimicking the sons of Abu Hala's greeting to their stepfather.

"Peace to you, O Muhammad. Madman. Jinn-possessed."

9

In the Name of God, the Merciful, the Compassionate.
Say: O ye unbelievers! I shall never worship that which ye
worship,
Neither will ye worship that which I worship . . .
To you your religion and to me mine.
—The Holy Quran 109

"**M**adman. Majnun."

I knew the voice even before I turned around. Other tellers of this tale that I have heard are reticent to name the names of those who participated in this incident. I am not. They say that since that time, all have submitted to God, so all is forgotten. But I haven't forgotten. It was my cousin Omar and other young men of his clan.

"The same Omar ibn al-Khattab who now commands the faithful, may God lead him and all Muslims aright?" my scribe asks, unable to conceal his shock.

"The same," I assure him, "who now accuses me of heresy. Blame shifts like a mirage, does it not? At the whim of whomever is in charge."

The eunuch straightens his parchment with the discomfort of it all.

"*Have you no manners, O son of al-Khattab?*" *I hissed at him then. "Even here, in the Ka'ba?*"

"*Have you no sense, O son of al-Walid?*" *Omar flung back.*

I took a step closer. His face had not firmed up much in manhood and was covered by a thin, patchy beard. His naked, sweat-oiled scalp only accentuated his pastiness. I could see in his eyes: he had not forgiven me for breaking his leg when we were children. Perhaps he felt it, every time he knelt before the Great House, every time he climbed up the stairway to see the idols within, and I was glad. I hope he feels it to this day, every time the rains come. But his fury went deeper, even, than that old score.

"That man Muhammad is mad," Omar continued. "And dangerous. Haven't you heard him preaching? Here, in the middle of pilgrimage? He wants to rid this holy house of every God, every God but his. Such an insult he would offer to our many guests. He's the one who needs to learn manners."

"He's not preaching now," I retorted, "so leave him in peace. This is the pilgrimage."

The fact of the matter was, though I had heard him preaching—no one in Mecca could avoid it—I always went the other way when I saw Muhammad gathering a crowd. I remembered the mad preacher in al-Hira—"the coming salvation of the Arabs"—another holy place, another pilgrimage. No, Muhammad did not make me comfortable. But then, neither did Omar, and Omar seemed the more volatile in that hot morning sun.

Hala and Hind had done with their greetings now and began to lead Mutammim and Malik to join the rest of the worshippers.

"The mother's darlings with the sissy girl names." This Hala and Hind did hear. Omar meant them to. "Can't live without hiding behind women's skirts. They've caught madness from their stepfather, see?"

Khadijah's two sons ignored the comment. They seemed all too used to such things. They edged their way past Omar and his companions, led Malik and Mutammim to face the Black Stone at the eastern side of the Great House. I hurried to join them, and we began the rite: "Here I am, O God . . ."

Because of the pilgrimage, the Ka'ba compound was crowded. Each man of Mecca jostled to give his guests the best places, giving an arm to the elderly, carrying the very young on his shoulders. Each taught the proper dialect and form of the prayers to those from other tribes—but only if his guests weren't content with their traditional forms and Gods. Then he might introduce them to Hubal of the Red Hand or to the feminine trio of Allat, Manat, and al-Uzza, as a tribesman might introduce guests to his great sharif.

Fine young men such as Malik, Hala, Hind, and I were well able to fend for ourselves in the press. Even blind Mutammim had no difficulty keeping up, his hand on Malik's shoulder. Away from Mecca, my milk brothers sometimes ran across the desert together that way, Malik keeping a flow of cautions going through his brother's ear.

Believing that the Gods loved exertion as much as devotion, we made our first three circuits in half the time other parties did. We moved on the outside—like more distant planets in their spheres, perhaps—then dashed in to touch and kiss the Black Stone for the removal of our sins before dashing back out again.

No doubt Hala and Hind felt a particular proprietary reverence towards this phase of the rite, remembering their stepfather's deed in replacing the Stone during the recent restoration. In any case, they didn't use as much caution as they might *have bringing us back out into the outer circle on the third circuit. They let Mu-tammim jostle into a man from another party, then Hala actually trod on another man's trailing* izar, *almost pulling it from his waist.*

I am convinced this wasn't mere inattention on the part of Muhammad's step-sons. The man whose thick waist almost lost its covering was Omar ibn al-Khattab.

"Watch where you're going" and "Clumsy madmen" interrupted the flow of prayers.

We got clear with as much dignity as we could and continued our rite. We had four more circuits to go, and these could be taken at a more leisurely, more careful pace.

On the second of these four, one voice rose above all the cacophony of chant and invocation. "In the Name of God, the Compassionate, the Merciful. There is no God but God."

I drag my hands over my face and wonder aloud, "What, for the love of God, was Muhammad the son of Abd Allah thinking, to say such a thing that day of pilgrimage?"

My scribe, shocked, says what he must. "Of course, the angel Jabra'il guided the Prophet's actions, blessings on him, in the face of unbelieving pagans."

My scribe, I remember, is another Abd Allah, one who must have chosen that name upon his conversion. What name did he choose earlier, when they cut his sex from him? That seems a greater life change than to profess one God above all others.

"Of course."

What else can I say? Although I have to wonder, what kind of merciful God is that who'd rather hear His name pronounced than prevent rancor? And was Muhammad mad? Jinn—or angel, rather—possessed? Or merely mad like a fox?

And my Bint Zura?

"Write," I order.

I stole a glance at my two young companions. Neither Hala nor Hind betrayed the least flush of embarrassment to hear their stepfather raising his voice in such words again, even at the pilgrimage. Instead, I saw that they had given up the more general invocation they had been reciting while my milk brothers and I used the verses peculiar to the Tamim. They were reciting along with Muhammad: "O ye unbelievers, I worship not that which ye worship."

Muhammad passed beyond my view, but when we came around the Great House again, I spotted him at once. I was at the threatening end of his raised staff.

The true object of his aggression was an idol particularly favored by women. I do confess, it was a bizarre thing, heavily inspired from the Egyptians: a God with a huge male member carved of wood. Unveiled paraders raised and lowered the pulleyed phallus as they prayed for many strong sons.

"Ah, the evil of the Time of Ignorance," my scribe exclaims.

But it was no more bizarre than, say, the camel skull perched on a pole and hung with amulets that rolled red eyes in its empty sockets and clapped its naked jaws together to increase herds. The virile God had been part of that tribe's tradition, and part of the pilgrimage at Mecca, as far as anyone knew, since the beginning of time.

Muhammad's staff arched. It crashed down upon the most remarkable part of the idol in a way that made me flinch, even for wood.

"Blessings on God's Messenger," says the one whose own fleshy parts received worse.

I dropped my arms from their prayerful attitude, protectively to my front, and stopped circling. Neither bit of wood broke, in spite of a sound that cracked against the walls of the compound. Muhammad's staff arched again for another blow.

"I shall never worship that which ye worship," I heard him say.

Another crack never came. Omar and two of his party had flung themselves between staff and staff. My cousin wrenched Muhammad's weapon out of his hand. The staff arched again, and this time it landed hard upon the older man's back.

Hala and Hind had vanished from my side. I saw them there, in the center of the rising dust, come to their stepfather's aid, taking the blows for him.

"Take Mutammim to safety," I told Malik, but he didn't need to be told.

I rushed myself to the fray.

"Upon whose side?" my scribe asks.

"I didn't know then and I don't know now. I just wanted them all to cease."

"For shame. For shame. In the Ka'ba. At the time of pilgrimage." I shouted in choppy phrases as I reached in and pulled one of the clan of al-Khattab off the growing heap, then another.

"Blasphemer," this one shouted back at me, then another. "Kill that blasphemer. He would deny most of the Gods of the universe."

A fist came for my head. I sparred it with my upper arm, caught it and yanked it behind the man until he yelped for pain and sank to his knees. I kicked him aside and reached into the knot of struggling bodies for someone else. My hands slipped on the sweat of a naked back. I caught this one by the tail of izar *tossed over one shoulder and ripped the length of cloth from him. He came up fighting, but I got my own fist in hard to his jaw before he could reach me. Something cracked, and I tossed him aside, too.*

The jinn had my right arm.

The next back I met owned more aging flesh. It sat on his ribs like a smear of pottage. Muhammad the son of Abd Allah. He wasn't actually landing blows, I saw, but he was shouting encouragement: "God is great, God is great."

I yanked him away, too, none to gently. "Go on, get out of the way, old man. You've caused enough trouble for one day."

Finally I came upon Hala, near the bottom of the heap. Blood from his nose stained his whole face, dyed his pilgrimage garment. A good-sized wound stood out on his bare scalp as well. He looked a bit dazed. I had no trouble picking him up, like an idol himself, and pulling him out of harm's way.

"Come on, you son of a madman's whore." I heard my cousin's voice behind me as I daubed at Hala's face with the corner of my izar, *looking for any worse wound.*

"You've drawn the boy's blood," I told Omar. "You'll have blood money to pay. Let that suffice."

"I won't. I won't let blasphemers live."

A rough hand fell on my shoulder, but I shook it off. "Don't you dare, Omar. Remember last time we crossed?"

That was the wrong thing to say. Of course he remembered; it made him angrier. All I heard was a bestial growl, but I had his shadow in my view. As soon as he took one step closer, I would whirl around. I would go in low and get him right where old Muhammad had gone for on the idol.

Hala gasped. I thought he must be choking on his own blood, and I yanked on his shoulders to help him cough it up. But a look of staring horror in his eyes made me turn even though Omar's shadow held steady.

"Go on, Omar," I said as I turned, "let it—"

I met my cousin full in the eye—and couldn't conceal a gasp of my own when I saw the unsheathed dagger in his hand.

"A weapon in the Ka'ba? Omar, now there is blasphemy." No matter how much of this brawl Muhammad had provoked, my cousin had come to the ritual armed. He had expected something like this to happen.

Women screamed. The rest of the worshippers stopped any attempt to complete their circuits now. I felt them stepping away from us like inhaled breath.

Omar's wasn't the only blade. Metal glinted in the hand of each of the others in his party.

"Put up your weapons, men," I said. "For shame. I won't have kinsmen of mine sullying the name of Hubal with such things."

Others joined my chorus, low, calm.

Then behind me, I heard Muhammad's brazen sing-song: "O ye unbelievers! I shall never worship that which ye worship. Neither will ye worship that which I worship."

"Shut up, fool," I shouted.

"With no knowledge you were hearing the angel's voice." My scribe shakes his head over what he has written.

The man on Omar's left lunged. I kicked up swiftly. The contact broke my bare toes, but I caught the attacker just on the wrist, sending the knife flying into the hot Meccan air.

The man on Omar's right thrust, nicking me on the shoulder as I managed to trip him to the ground.

Omar, still armed, lunged to his left, past me, in the direction of Muhammad's unstoppable voice. I whirled around, hoping to catch Hala up out of harm's way. Somehow I held him fast instead, even as he tried to move to shield his stepfather. The blade meant for Muhammad struck him instead, low, in the belly.

With a shriek of "God is great," he buckled over the wound, even as I continued to try to hold him upright. Another man stabbed Hala. I dropped the body that was already a corpse. Another man stabbed. Omar yanked out his blade and stabbed again. Then he turned from his deed and fled the sacred precinct.

Stumbling backwards, I ran into Hind, into Mutammim and Malik. I wanted to throw myself in my milk brothers' arms, to find comfort there from the horror I'd witnessed. But a veil seemed to have fallen before Malik's face, as impenetrable as Mutammim's blindness. A kinsman of mine had killed a kinsman of theirs. If this were not the Ka'ba, if my milk brothers had been armed, they would have been honor bound to take Hala's life from Omar on the spot. And if, because Omar and his companions had already fled, they could not shed the blood actually responsible for the deed, they had every right to shed mine. I had to stand alone, so alone, and stare in wordless horror. I stood and stared until the flies gathered, drinking up the blood that had spilled upon the sanctuary dust.

Then Muhammad came and knelt in Hala's blood. Gathering his stepson up in his arms, he rose on unsteady legs. He left the Ka'ba and carried the body home to Khadijah. No woman's name had saved the boy from this. Without a word, Mutammim and Malik, whose mother's breasts I had shared, turned their backs on me and followed after.

And all I could think as I hobbled away on my broken toes was, I wish I'd learned news of Bint Zura before this happened. I wished to all the Gods I had.

10

Who can describe the nature of God,
The Living, the Eternal? His throne
Extends over worlds and worlds
That no imagination can compass.
      —The Holy Quran, Surah II

"**O**h, God, keep us from evil."

Auntie Adilah had pushed ahead of the party of women returning with subdued spirits from the wedding. Her sandals slapping on ancient flagstones and softer dirt alike, she had outrun the torches. Now, to dispel the gloom, she greeted each member of the harem as she came in under the silver hand with its blue eye by blowing in her face and murmuring over and over, "Oh, God, keep us from evil."

Rayah allowed her elders to enter and receive the blessing before her.

"Oh, God—"

As Rayah stepped over the threshold, the invocation stopped. No breath of grace dried the sweat on her cheeks.

"Oh, God," Adilah sighed at last, holding her hands before her in a protective gesture. "Save us from such a child."

Tears of hurt stung Rayah's eyes. The wedding had exhausted her, feeling the community's collective though unexpressed doubts about what she had done to Ghusoon and how she had done it. Then had come the open hatred which had culminated, when Sharif Diya'l-Din couldn't reach her among the women, in his taking the eunuch Abd Allah away—where? To do what? Rayah knew she would need all the help she could get to fight the battle to save the scribe come morning.

"Auntie, please, why don't you bless me?"

"I cared for this child as my brother Yaqub of blessed memory charged me to do. Sisters, did I not? Witness that I did."

"As God is my witness, Adilah, you did." A few yawns stretched among the answering mouths. It was late. What was Adilah on about that kept them standing here when their beds beckoned?

"I cared for her as for my own. More than for my own, for I never married, gave up all hope of a house and home and children to call mine for that one."

Rayah wanted to run to arms that once had comforted her, but suddenly she didn't dare. They would not welcome her. Demiella and others took Adilah's shoulders, her arms, and tried to calm her, to bring her in. Their actions were in vain; there was no doing so. But they had ceased to reach out to Rayah at all.

"I gave up my belief in Isa ibn Maryam and His blessed Mother for that one."

Adilah's sharp pointing finger accused Rayah. But the longing with which she spoke the name of the Christians' devotion indicted herself as well. Maryam, the mother of Isa the Nazarene, had a whole chapter of the Quran which Rayah had memorized as particularly appropriate to young women, but such devotion as Adilah had just expressed—

Demiella took Adilah's shoulders again, but a little more carefully this time. "Surely, Sister, you do not regret that you submitted to Islam when the rest of us did."

Adilah's voice caught in her throat, but she made no out-and-out denial. "Isa and His mother know what is in my heart."

Demiella withdrew the comfort of her touch as if Adilah's shoulders scalded her. She stepped back. "You could die for this."

Adilah's path to justifying herself consisted of quoting another. "'It will be safer for the child and its mother,' he told me."

Who had told her? Surely not Isa himself. But "the dead" did come as a jinn-whispered reply in Rayah's head.

Adilah shook off the whisperings in her own head, whatever they might be, and plunged ahead with her accusation of Rayah. "And so what happens as soon as she is old enough? Does she sit down and listen to my story, ask me how to behave? No, a strange eunuch comes from far away. She listens to *his* story."

"I'm sorry, Auntie. I didn't ask him to leave Homs and come here."

Remembering how abruptly and violently the wedding had ended for Abd Allah less than half an hour ago, and how they were returning without him, Rayah had to continue, "But how could we have let Sharif Diya'l-Din and his ruffians—?"

"A blister on your tongue, child, for speaking thus of a respectable man," said Demiella.

They had forgotten Adilah's confession for the moment. All of the women of the harem were glaring, forming a half-circle of solidarity against Rayah's lone self.

Rayah paused only long enough to discover that no blister had grown on her tongue before finishing her thought, something she never would have done even three months ago. "How could we have let the sharif and his ruffians say and do such things to a guest of this house?"

"Children should be seen and not heard," hissed Falak.

"Then I must cease being a child," Rayah heard herself say as if some other being had power over her tongue. She managed to keep it to a mutter, but the power was still strong enough that most of the women heard and took another step back under the protective hand of Fatimah.

"That eunuch a guest of this house?" Demiella was the first to find a retort. "Yes, for our sins."

"What sort of guest is he?" Adilah entered on her sister-in-law's side. "He makes us interfere in other families' marriages."

"What I did for my friend Ghusoon—only I didn't do it. It was—it was—"

"Demons."

Adilah's anger knew no doubt about what dangers the harem faced here. After her brief, subduing outburst of Christian faith, she was retaking the charge here, but even Falak nodded knowingly.

"No, Auntie," Rayah heard herself say. "I will not confess that what I did for Ghusoon was bad."

"When this is the result? A child who talks back?"

Rayah pulled her veil across her face. She was not a child who talked back. She never had been. And yet—what else had she just done?

"Shame for the house of the turpentine sellers before all our neighbors for this stranger we have taken in and yet cannot protect." Falak threw up her hands

"And you were always such a good child." Demiella had to add her part, shaking her head in its party-worn ornaments. "Until this eunuch came."

Rayah did feel shame for how the pompous old sharif had pulled attention and happiness from Ghusoon and Jaffar. But that wasn't her fault. She found herself incapable of feeling the full measure of guilt the aunties wanted her to.

She tried to justify herself again. "What I did for Ghusoon had nothing to do with Abd Allah. Why should he suffer? Why should they take him captive?"

"Good riddance," snorted Demiella.

"Yes." Adilah's venom cut even deeper. "When they might have done better to take you and that mother of yours."

"Come, sisters." Falak tried this much reconciliation. "Let us at least enter the harem so the whole house doesn't have to hear our discord. Women's bickering shames men as well—but only if they have to hear it."

Rayah suspected the men were having their own arguments over this matter. She wanted to be there, speaking for her friend among the half of humanity with the power to actually do something. In any case, here in the between-world, Adilah wouldn't budge. She stood still blocking Rayah from reaching the protection of the harem where she had lived all her life.

"After all I've done for her." Adilah threw her case on the attending court, be it ever so wide. "When she comes of age, does she sit down to hear *my* story? No. She listens to that witch we have harbored, Sitt Sameh, who did nothing but push the baby out into the world, an orphan, a bastard no man would claim."

"But Khalid ibn al-Walīd claims her," Falak suggested.

"A man who is dead," said Demiella. "A man who died in the khalifah's bad graces."

"If we believe the old sharif."

"The child sits and listens to a eunuch, a stranger. When do I get to tell my story?"

Rayah stared at the woman who had raised her. Is that all anybody ever wanted? To have their side of the story heard? "Tell it to me, Auntie. When we wake in the morning and are refreshed, tell me your story."

As that only seemed to make Adilah angrier, Rayah tried again. "Or let the others go to sleep now. I will stay and listen—but inside."

Rayah realized she had not kept the pity from her eyes as she said this. As Sitt Sameh and Abd Allah's stories were teaching her to see, she was a young woman with her life before her. Adilah had made all the choices she would be allowed long ago. That was sad, and it was hard to see that such sorrow was merely the way God had created the world. Rayah did realize that pity was the last thing Adilah wanted. The very sight of it now heightened her anger.

But Rayah was angry, too. A demon seemed to possess her, demanding its right to at least examine lives lived before hers for what was good or bad in them before she made her own choices. "What is there to say of your life?" she demanded of Adilah rudely.

The whole harem caught its collective breath at the audacity of Rayah's question. In truth, how dare she judge choices made under pressures she did not understand, pressures long buried and forgotten?

With her harem sisters' support, Adilah pulled herself up unapologetically. "I changed your swaddling. I sat up when you, child, were feverish. I kissed the skinned knees and sang the lullabies."

Rayah tried to swallow her anger, for Adilah spoke truth when she listed all the things she had done for her. Sitt Sameh had done none of these maternal things, and when Rayah turned her back on Adilah, she was ungrateful.

But the demon inside Rayah would not be still. "That makes a story? A poem?"

"Not in the world's eyes."

Adilah truly seemed afraid. Was that her problem? What had she to fear in such a retiring life as she had chosen? Did her beliefs make her afraid when they ought to give her courage?

Before Rayah could form this thought into words, Adilah went on. "Not in your blue eyes that always seemed so blinded to me." She sighed, pleading now. "Why must you take this dangerous path when I only ever tried to make the world safe for you?"

"Why can't I be more like you, do you mean?"

Auntie Adilah's reaction rang with hurt. In a moment, she recovered enough to lash back. "Yes, exactly. After all I have given of myself, why can't I have had more effect?"

"I'm trying to be like *me*, Auntie. I need to learn what sort of woman I am."

"Why can't you be the sort of woman I am, when I put so much love and care into you?"

"You're not happy, Auntie, and I'm sorry for that. Your talents have been hidden."

"What do you know of it?"

"I don't know much, I confess. But I'm trying to learn. I'm trying to learn God's will for me."

"'God's will' for you? A different will for you than for any other woman in all the world? One thing is certain, He cannot want you to be like the mother who bore you, hunted from any home and family. A jinn-haunted madwoman."

"God made the jinn, beings of fire and smoke, as well as each of us."

The wedding torches had been extinguished so that but a single oil lamp still burned in its niche, fire and smoke, causing the familiar figures of the family to dance like otherworldly creatures on the walls. When she had spoken their name, Rayah had felt the jinn's presence, a curl of cold smoke rising along her spine. She knew they fueled this confrontation. To what purpose? Should she just be the plaything, first of a childless woman and then of malicious beings who, without flesh of their own, sought to possess the flesh of careless mortals?

Rayah groped for words to express herself as a stranger might grope along this hallway, a little fearfully. Nonetheless, she pressed on. "And I have come to feel something of their presence in me—"

Again the family women caught their breath. Most of them took this chance to hurry their children off to bed. There went little cousin Bushra whose broken skull Rayah had healed less than two months ago with a single touch and a few pious words. The girl's mother had no interest in learning by what power the cure had happened. One or two women stifled dizzy laughter at such a conversation, and all touched their amulets as they left. Rayah found herself alone with Adilah now, her way into the harem still blocked.

"I won't have a child grown too big for my arms laughing at me," Adilah said.

"God forbid. I'm not laughing, Auntie."

"Nor do I want your pity."

"I do not pity." Rayah knew that was a lie, at least in part.

So did Adilah. "Oh, a pox on it. You won't know until you have a child of your own. You should just marry. Then this house would be rid of you, and maybe the woman upstairs would leave, too. Go back to the desert whence she came."

More tears spilled down Rayah's cheeks. "For all your care, Auntie, I do thank you." But to be so unloved by the woman who'd raised her. And the others—their eyes weren't even wet. To know that this was the extent of the embrace of the only home Rayah had ever known—

Then again, any girl knew her days at home were numbered, as any woman raising children knew the days with her daughters, at least, were likewise numbered.

Any girl but Adilah, who had never married. Had she wanted to? Had she been in love but thwarted? There was that woman's story. But would she ever tell it?

"My marriage is not in my hands, Auntie." No more than yours, Rayah wanted to add but resisted. "It will be as God wills." As it was with you.

"Not so." Adilah rejected this consolation, spoken and unspoken. "For didn't Diya'l-Din's sister-in-law speak to me at the wedding just now? 'We should join our households at a similar event in the near future,' she said. 'Since my brother was thwarted with this marriage to Ghusoon, his attention has been drawn to your Rayah.'"

The words punched Rayah in the stomach, threatening to bring all the wedding dainties back up again. She never should have saved Ghusoon. It drew too much notice to herself, and that was never a good thing for a girl. She saw now just how bad attention was.

"Yes, the sister-in-law will visit us within the week to begin arrangements. Marry the old man. That's all my care is worth on a thankless child like you."

"But Auntie—" Rayah stopped herself.

Adilah had lost the gist of her own thought. As if in a trance, she turned slowly this way, then that, taking in the space around them, the windowless hallway where male majlis converged with harem door.

Another smoky shiver ran up Rayah's spine, for in the light of the single lamp, more shadows danced than their two solid figures could have cast.

The voice Rayah then heard belonged to a man she didn't know. "For the safety of this woman I love but can never have, for the child that is not mine but I love unborn."

His tall shadow stood where only men of the family came. His hands rested on the shadow that was Auntie Adilah, bidding her a farewell full of care and grief and at the same time constraining her, holding her back.

"Should it come to this, give up your Isa and your Maryam and convert to the new religion to protect them. Promise me you will do this, for life's continuing is more important than any religion."

Adilah's brother, Yaqub, about whom nobody spoke much and whose place was marked with but a hollow stone in the family tomb tower. A jinni had taken his shape, his voice. Rayah's eyes, her accursed blue eyes, stung with the sight. She understood, but she almost wished she did not have such powers.

Adilah's next words confirmed Rayah's ghostly vision. "He said it standing in this very hall as he bade us farewell. Going to join the forces of collapsing Rome against the fresh and vigorous Muslims."

Rayah could see the man was going to fight dressed only in his workman's tunic and cloak for the cold desert nights, armed with no more than a terebinth scraper.

"Why do you do this, brother?" The voice of shadowy Adilah spoke. The flesh-and-blood Adilah moved her lips over the remembered words, but she dared not speak them aloud, even after all these years.

"I must if I am a man," came the jinni-brother's reply.

"But why? Everyone is hoping this storm will quickly blow over."

"It will not do so."

"How do you know? How can you have so little faith?"

"Or so much faith in a poem of prophecy I have heard."

"You are no longer a man if you die. To what end? Not one other man of Tadmor has answered the emperor Heraclius's desperate call."

"And who can blame them? The emperor is not of their faith."

"He is a Christian." Adilah of old expressed her shock at a contrary notion.

"But a heretic," her brother insisted. "For centuries now, hasn't the Roman Empire—this so-called Christian empire of Constantine sucking power towards Constantine's city—hasn't it oppressed you of the Syrian faith?"

Rayah could see by the lamplight how even just remembering the words of Adilah's dead brother made the older woman nearly double over with pain. "You of the Monophysite faith," he had said, no longer "we." Adilah's brother Yaqub had changed so much on this last trip to sell turpentine in Damascus. Too much. And if he insisted on dying for this change, he could never change back, to rejoin her. Still, she loved him more than anything. More than Isa and his beloved mother Maryam? Why did heaven demand that she make this choice?

"Which Christians have been fed to the lions to seal our faith?" Adilah pleaded history with him, hoping that might win her case. "We have. Which have had their churches and monasteries burned, their voices drowned out at so-called 'councils'? Which have had to flee to the safety of God in the desert? Or even beyond the desert, to Persia? Do not fight for this godless emperor."

"I do not go to fight for him, only on the side that I wish might win, the lesser of two evils. In truth, what I fight for is older than your Christianity, older and closer to the desert we inhabit than this new gloss. A deep, sweet well. I have found it, and I must fight for it on the Roman Christian side, even though the prophetess has told me the Muslims must win."

"If she believes they are fated to win, yet she opposes them, what sort of prophecy is that? Demons, not God. If this is so, then why, oh why, brother, don't you fight, if fight you must, for the Muslims under Khalid ibn al-Walīd? You say most men of our faith will do so, seeing the new religion as liberators."

"Because—" And the shadowy man looked up, up to rest his gaze for a moment on the hand and lapis lazuli eye that protected the women behind him. His gaze rose further then, as if he could see through that ceiling. He looked up to that place where that stranger woman with the demon blue eyes and heavy with child was pitching her tent on the turpentine sellers' roof.

"Because while I was trading in Damascus, a pregnant figure all in veils came and begged that I should conceal her from the Muslims. She spoke—she spoke her poetry, told me her tale, and I believed."

The Adilahs, both of flesh and shadow, bent over a stomach sick at the thought of the danger, both to her brother's body from heretic hunters and for his immortal soul. But he would not let her dissuade him.

"Yes, Sister," said the shadow with the terebinth scraper, "I believe in that woman's verses more than even what your priest preaches and what your martyrs have shed their blood for in the face of the oppressors from Constantinople."

"'My' priest, 'my' martyrs, not 'ours.'" The real Adilah choked on her sobs, on the choices she had made when that had been her power. "My brother, who had always been so close to me that I never wanted to marry. He could say this to me, ask these things of me? He could, this and more."

"I believe in one grain of sand as opposed to the great sandstorm of belief sweeping over us." The jinni shadow had its last say, then swirled away to smoke as the lamp wick sputtered and popped.

"Then—then he was gone, never to return," Adilah whispered hoarsely.

Silence echoed off the white-washed tile of the corridor, off the courtyard beyond. Although darkness still draped the world, the linnet had begun to sing in the jasmine vine, the brokenhearted sweetness of its lost love. Every splash of the fountain rang in the hollow space. Rayah didn't know what to say.

Finally, Adilah did. "As part of your mother's story that so consumes you, child, ask her. Ask her to tell you her real name."

"Her real name? Not Sitt Sameh?"

"Just ask her. Then marry that old sharif. Leave this house finally, finally in peace."

11

بسم الله الرحمن الرحيم

These are the tribe's commanders,
its nights, its protectors of law;
they are like the bounteous spring to their neighbors.
— The qasidah of Labid ibn Rabi'a

Tension hung in my father's majlis as thick as smoke. And there was no more room to sit. Younger men had climbed on the roof and pulled aside palm thatching to hear. Such a crowd should have convened in the assembly hall, the Dar al-Nadwa, with its round windows of alabaster cut so thin light came through and spread the rich carpets with the color of butter. But the tribe of the Quraysh, the people of Mecca, were rent down the middle by the murder in the sacred precincts. No emblem of community could stand any longer; this is what Muhammad had done.

I provided armfuls of the best qat, but nobody was chewing. The heap remained green and untouched in the center of the room, crowded by all the men of our clan who claimed a place. Qat would have calmed them, and no one was calm. No one had any desire to be.

For several moments, I longed for my father's presence, acting as host in my place. I desperately wanted his guidance. If not that, then I wanted the comfort of my milk mother's arms.

Hala the son of al-Oseyyad the Tamimi had died; blood flowed in the Ka'ba sanctuary. My tribe must answer for that blood—against the blood of my milk tribe. In such circumstances, my seeking the comfort and wisdom of Umm Mutammim was out of the question.

Then I comforted myself. I had the backing of all the rest of the Quraysh. Abu Sufyan was there, Muhammad's uncle Abu Talib, Abu Bakr, al-Khattab Omar's father—although not the murderer himself. They would be very careful not to let him out of the sanctuary of his mother's harem, not with sons of Tamim in the *streets, thirsty for his blood. I was glad to see Muhammad had stayed away as well. I only had to provide the cushions, the pomegranate juice, melon seeds, the qat— and now I saw I didn't even need to provide that. I would just sit quietly and let them speak. Among such men, an answer would come. The best possible answer.*

I let Abu Sufyan take the place of honor. He was a large, fleshy man, loud of voice and broad of hands. His face was florid with fury above a beard just streaked with grey, but like the leader he was, he too was letting others do most of the talking.

"It's not as if my son were without provocation," al-Khattab said. "Muhammad, this son of Abd Allah, has been preaching his message publicly—in the midst of the Ka'ba—throughout the pilgrimage, offending everyone."

The company nodded. They had all seen him, heard him.

"I find it odd that someone as innocuous as Muhammad should take up such a task," Abu Sufyan mused.

"He should let his wife Bint Khuwaylid do his peddling," said one of the younger Meccans present. "She'd meet with more success."

Everyone laughed, grateful for a moment's relief from the tension.

"Otherwise, there seemed no need for particular alarm in this preaching, did there?" Abu Talib agreed. He was Muhammad's uncle and head of his clan. The deep furrows where his eyebrows met, the family trait, showed how his soul was torn. He'd never liked the orphan with whom he'd been saddled. Now the fact that he hadn't been able to control the man reflected poorly on him as a leader.

"Mecca is much like al-Hira, my brothers." Abu Bakr spoke in a voice striving for calm. He would marry his son Ali to Muhammad's daughter. How close the ties went then the rest of us could only guess. "We have always prided ourselves that it is so. Any man can claim an audience to promote anything, from Isa ibn Maryam to cheap amulets or untanned hides. He can take up a stand next to any pillar in the holy compound he cares to."

"Waraka, Khadijah's uncle, used to stand in just such a place while stirring a lively interest in Christianity," remembered one of the greybeards present.

"You don't have to listen to my nephew's blather," Abu Talib suggested.

"He's not simply preaching for something," Abu Sufyan said.

"No," another agreed. He opened his mouth to say more but was stopped by a confusion of commenting voices.

"The Ka'ba has already absorbed three hundred and sixty various deities, including Isa and his lady mother," were the first words I picked out of the rest.

Someone with slurred speech said: "Room can always be made for others."

"But there are no others," I heard Abu Bakr say, and it made me nervous. "There is but one God, as Muhammad says." Fortunately, not too many also heard him.

Someone else said, with more edge: "That's just the point. Muhammad preaches against 'all other Gods but God' in such fierce terms of hellfire and earthquake that the very basis of the pilgrimage is threatened."

"I have not seen this," Abu Talib admitted. "But then, I have been avoiding the pilgrimage crowds."

Trying for lightness, I said, "Yes. No one comes interested in horse flesh."

"I was there," someone insisted, "paying my respects along with the rest—"

The tale had already been told so many times that those who had not been there knew it as well as those who were. Or perhaps better, for their mind's eye saw the scene from many angles. But we had to tell it again, the snippet of one voice after another, to remind ourselves the true horror of all that had happened.

"A young man—of a guest tribe, not even one of our own—has died."

"Murdered in the Ka'ba."

"The shrine will have to be purified before the pilgrimage can continue."

"And so shortly after we had to totally rebuild the place. A bad omen."

"Rebuilt it with Muhammad's help—remember that."

"Purification can't come cheaply."

"But we must do it."

"The priestesses of al-Uzza will want a say in this."

"And Manat. Do you think any of our wives will let us in to them if we don't see Manat satisfied?"

"And what of the God Muhammad attacked?"

"That Egyptian prick." Nobody laughed at this attempt at humor. We couldn't afford to offend any Gods in such circumstances.

"What sorts of gifts will be needed to appease Him?"

"Do you think, even if we do purify the place, that any who were there today will come again, bringing their much-needed trade?"

"Yes, what tales will they take back to their home pastures? No one in their tribe will come again after this."

"We must hand Omar the son of al-Khattab over to the Tamim for justice."

Al-Khattab gave a groan of protest against the obvious conclusion that all discussion boiled down to.

"Not just Omar, but the others who were with him as well."

"Otherwise we'll have war with the Tamim."

"And their tribal territory sits across our trade routes."

"Omar is a good boy," al-Khattab insisted. "He doesn't do things unless others lead him astray."

"Well, then maybe he should learn more backbone."

"You can't say Abu Omar's son wasn't provoked," Abu Sufyan said. "The son of

Abd Allah had actually lifted up his staff and made to topple one of the gods from his incense-wreathed pedestal."

"Lifted his staff against a God? Muhammad dared so much?"

This brought a number of the men to their feet, their hands at their dagger hilts. "Where is he? Where is the dog's son? Muhammad is the man we should throw to the Tamim."

A cacophony of voices gave their opinions, none waiting for the other to stop.

"Too much for any proper Meccan to endure."

"We have clients to consider."

"Wives, children, slaves."

"Egypt is such a market for the gold from our hills."

"Who knows but what that particular God might not be responsible for three-quarters of all the income we might make in a single year?"

"Or that God's particular tribe."

"Which amounts to the same thing."

"And you see?" Omar's father spoke again. "My son only moved to stop this blasphemy. He cannot be blamed if his piety was too strong. The Gods moved him to their defense."

"But he did go armed to the shrine. That doesn't speak of piety."

"Hala saw his mother's husband so unfairly outnumbered. He made a move to defend him."

"Hala doesn't—may the rain fall softly on his grave —he didn't actually believe what Muhammad preaches, did he?"

"By God, I've heard him confess with my own ears."

This was Abu Bakr again, speaking quietly, and perhaps no one else heard him but me. I immediately wished I hadn't heard him. It sent a cold shiver down my spine. Muhammad was mad. And the madness was catching. It started with the immediate family, then went to the clan. Was the tribe next? If Abu Bakr could succumb—by Hubal, no Syrian plague could be worse, and the pure desert was usually free of such things.

"I'd always found Hind and Hala to be such promising young men. Tamimi though they are, they are—they were—an asset to Mecca. More so, I must say, than I ever found that dreamer Muhammad."

Abu Sufyan commanded enough respect that he turned the tide of the conversation when he said: "This fine boy—I say it even though he is not a Qurayshi—this fine boy is dead, while Muhammad, whose madness is truly to blame, walked away without a scratch."

Both Abu Bakr, Muhammad's kinsman by marriage, and Abu Talib, his kinsman by blood, grew pale.

"As if protected by a charm," someone said in the hollow tones that evoke the jinn.

"What is it exactly that Muhammad was preaching?" someone else asked.

"Oh, the usual madness," replied a skeptic. "'Give up false Gods and prepare for the world to come.' He says he is the Apostle of God."

"Was not Khalid ibn Sinan sent from God to the tribe of Abs in just such a fashion?" one asked. "Such is the tradition of their poets."

"One Hanzala ibn Safwan preached to other tribes," said the next.

"Not only preached, but worked miracles as well," agreed the third.

"Have you not heard of Isa the Nazarene who healed the blind and lame in Syria? And then rose from the dead on the third day. Or so the tale goes. I don't say that I believe it."

"One Samayfa of the Himyari tribe is said to have hidden himself for longer than three days."

"Several hundred years, I heard tell when I was in the Yemen recently. And then he reappeared, to the wonderment of all."

"I myself saw a great worker of wonders," said yet another. "When I visited my kin among the Banu Hanifa in Yamamah. One called Musaylimah lives there who preaches against many Gods. I heard him with these very ears, by al-Uzza, and he was not struck down. And then, I saw him work a miracle. No, this is not hearsay. I saw it with my own eyes."

Here, to the momentary entertainment if not belief of all, this man called for a narrow-necked flask from the harem and a wild partridge's egg. He tried to explain just what miracle this prophet of Yamamah called Musaylimah had performed. The man tried to tell us that he had actually seen just such an egg be drawn by magic through the narrow neck and down into the body of just such a flask without break-ing the shell. But none of us could see how such a thing could be. After a few broken eggs, no one answered the teller's earnest voice with belief.

I grew impatient with what seemed to have turned into idle sport when mat-ters of life and death were at hand. And yet, this banter around the circle was not without its meaning in my heart. What did this rash of heavenly dealings mean for the Arabs? I puzzled over the future. The talk certainly made me remember "the coming salvation of the Arabs." And that made me impatient.

I shifted nervously upon my cushions as if they were a stranger's. And then, at the first lull, I said, "Kinsmen, let me go to the Banu Tamim."

Abu Sufyan said, "You, Ibn al-Walīd? You are far too ready for action, as hot-headed youth is. The Banu Tamim will kill you as soon as look at you, for your cousin Omar's sake. And then what should I tell your father when he comes home?"

"They will not kill me, if the Gods will," I assured the circle of kinsmen. Their gazes had all reverted to me, and they sat stroking their beards in thought, as one man.

"*The Banu Tamim are my milk brothers. For what purpose was I sent to the desert as a child but for this? For what purpose have I sent my own son to another tribe, but in hopes the connection may serve in a similar way in time to come, if the Gods will? I know the sons of Nuwaira. I may convince my milk brothers to take herds or money as blood price instead. Yes, I will even offer my sister in marriage to blind Mutammim to show my good faith. Let the bloodshed cease. Let no more come to pollute the Sacred House.*"

An hour or two more of discussion followed, but I hardly listened to it. I had made up my own mind.

Yes, I had seen the veil of hatred that had fallen over Malik's eyes, a flush for vengeance deeper than ever I had seen him drunk on wine. I knew full well what I risked. I even thought over what weapons I would take with me, imagining I might have to fight my way out of my own milk mother's tent. Imagining in the foolishness of youth that I could do such a thing. It didn't matter. I still would have gone, even without my elders' blessing. In the Tamimi tents were things, too many things, too precious to me to be denied them for the rest of my life even over bloodshed in the Ka'ba.

12

I was sleepless because of a thick cloud, wherein
were lightning flashes,
which rose above the summit of Shi'b.
The Mashrafi sword flashed above its summit,
and the sides of its new, well-guarded mantle gleamed.
—A poem of Adi ibn Zaid

"Welcome home, Daughter."

Sitt Sameh was not asleep. Did she ever close her eyes? She sat in the light of a single lamp, at her eternal spinning.

Home? Although she had never slept any place else, Rayah had to wonder. Could this place possibly feel safe again?

"Was the wedding nice?" Sitt Sameh pursued when Rayah found herself at a loss for words. The accents of the deep desert sifted like sand over her mother's speech, the desert tattoos shadowed her angular face blue, the desert ring swung in her nose. "I heard the music over the rooftops all the way here. That was pleasant, in the dark."

Sitt Sameh shut her mouth tight then and fixed her blue eyes on her daughter. She was hearing something beneath speech, Rayah's very thoughts. As Rayah had just heard Adilah's. Rayah wanted to run back to the normal world, but she didn't know where it was.

"Abd Allah did not come home with you?"

Then the words spilled from Rayah's mouth. She told it all, just not about what had happened once they came home, what Adilah had said. She concluded, "They have taken Abd Allah prisoner. He's in what was once the pagan temple in the ruins of the Camp of Diocletian."

No more solid place remained standing in all Tadmor. The town's mudbrick houses had begun to engulf the tumbled stone ruins left after the fall first of Queen Zaynab and then, in its turn, of her conqueror, Rome.

Sitt Sameh had let her spinning drop in her horror at the tale. "This is my fault," she said.

"No, Lady, not so—"

"It is," she snapped, her words like a leather lash.

Rayah stood up to the lash, less painful than her own sense of guilt. "It's my fault. I cured my friend and gave her to a different groom. You warned me not to, and you were right."

"You do not know who I am, or you would not say such palliatives."

Palliatives? Were these confessions, which Rayah felt were very grown-up of herself, mere palliatives?

"You are my mother—" She stopped, conscious of how short a time even she had believed it.

"Would you had never come to know it. Sameh is not my real name."

"Not—?" Then what Auntie Adilah had been fuming about in the passage below had some point.

"No, I cannot tell you what it is. It is too dangerous, too dangerous. See what it has done to the eunuch. Poor Abd Allah who, after the death of Khalid is the only other living soul besides myself, once poor Yaqub who rescued me found his own grave—no, I say. I cannot put my only child at such risk. Do not ask me."

Sitt Sameh—who said now Sitt Sameh wasn't even her name—got to her feet. She shoved past Rayah, out onto the flat dark roof beneath a canopy of stars twisted to their autumn positions. Canopus, the star announcing rain, was there, hanging low in the southern sky. And az-Zuharah, the evening star, the demon Goddess from the Time of Ignorance.

"I shall have to leave here," she said.

Rayah, following after, felt her heart skip a beat. "Where—where would you go?"

"The desert."

Worse and worse. The place of the jinn, of savage forces men could not control. All Rayah could manage was a strangled, "No."

"The desert is not so fearsome." Starlight caught the curve of a smile in the older woman's face. "Not to me. You forget. I was born there, in the embrace of a loving tribe. I lived there happily—until—until Khalid and his Muslims made the place burst like a stone in the fire."

Sitt Sameh had begun to pace along the low, rounded plaster wall edging the roof. Then Rayah saw she had brought something from the little room after all. She fingered it now as busily as usually she fingered her tow. It was one of the three things the eunuch had brought with him from Homs. Rather than the fine sword or the red turban that held a lock of the Prophet's hair, blessings on him, it was the most broken of the three: the snapped arc of acacia wood and the scraps of gauze that once had formed a woman's camel litter.

"I will live, if I must, as once my grandmother did," Sitt Sameh went on. "An outcast kahinah under a tent of a single, ragged cloth. I stayed here when I thought of your safety, child. No other reason. I see now I only brought you greater danger. You and all this household who have been so good to me."

Then Rayah saw what she could never have expected, the sacrifice that staying within walls must have been to one born under a hair tent. Stifling, crushing. How many times had Rayah come up to find her mother as she was now, pacing at the boundary of her world that once had spread from horizon to dust-colored horizon? How many times had her mother scurried back to the walls of her little room and picked up her spinning when she found herself watched? How often did she spin, her fingers doing what her feet could not, repeating the movements a woman made in her litter as the camel swung away the vast distances beneath her? How many times had she looked up to the sky, as blue as her eyes, and prayed?

"Will you take me?" Rayah asked, dreading the answer.

"No, of course not. You will stay here, where you're safe."

Rayah felt new guilt for the relief that washed over her. Seeing what had happened to the eunuch that night, knowing her own eyes to be the same color as her mother's, perhaps relief deceived her.

"When will you leave?"

"Tonight. I must leave at once."

"No." The word startled even Rayah, whose mouth formed it. "You cannot go and leave Abd Allah imprisoned like this. He came here for you. It is your fault he languishes in Diocletian's Camp—Lady." She added that last quickly, aware of how rash her demand had been.

"He came here for his master, Khalid the Conqueror."

"The Conqueror who is dead. As maybe you learned weeks ago, but which I have only just learned. And all the town. Dead in disgrace and under suspicion of heresy from the khalifah in Mecca. A connection to him is no protection for me."

"How can I free one whom the Muslims have seen fit to imprison? Surely the eunuch is as good as dead."

"God forbid," Rayah cried. Remembering the anger of Sharif Diya'l Din and how it blew so quickly to the rest of the men, she knew it was probably true. Then she regathered her courage and said: "At least until we learn for certain they have killed him. Please. You must stay until then."

After a moment's silence, Sitt Sameh gave a nod that made the ring in her nose sway. She pushed away from the edge of the roof and made her way back to her little room. "Very well. Until he's dead. I owe him that."

Astonished at her own rashness, Rayah found herself pushing on. "And the story."

"What about the story?"

"You cannot leave without telling me the end of the story. Your part." And maybe even your name, she thought. Auntie Adilah is right. I should know my own mother's name.

Sitt Sameh reached and picked up her spinning again. Her fingers ran over the dun-colored wool like bare feet over desert sand. "It is too late tonight. You have been to the wedding. It is nearing dawn."

"But tell me some. A little tonight." A deep-seated fear had struck Rayah that the moment she let her mother out of her sight, she would vanish, like water on hot stones. Sitt Sameh had, after all, lied before. Her whole life, so it seemed, was spun of lies.

"The eunuch, remember, told half the tale, reading it from his master's parchments. I cannot read."

"Tell your part, anyway. Sitt, please."

A smile twitched at the corners of the thin, hard mouth. Sitt Sameh quickly suppressed it. "Very well. Remind me where we were."

"Your mother, the young woman, had ridden at the head of her tribe in the sacred litter, the *qubbah*, upon her white camel. Her virginity called on her tribesmen to protect their honor to the very last breath."

Sitt Sameh stole a glance at the abandoned scraps of broken acacia, gauze and tufts of black ostrich feathers. "In spite of such magic, however, the Banu Taghlib lost at the Day of Dhu Qar. It was the Gods' will. The camel hamstrung beneath her, herself made a slave of the Banu Tamim." She mourned as if the events had happened only yesterday, to herself more than merely her mother, before she was born.

"She was given to al-Harith," Rayah prodded, "the young herdsman who cut the rear tendons of the beautiful white camel az-Zuharah."

"And not to Khalid ibn al-Walīd, a conqueror even then, but one who had tried, at the last moment, when he saw who was within the litter, to save her. He loved her, you see, a deep love spell of the desert, fed of the fire spirits, of the girl's own mother, my grandmother, the kahinah."

Did Sitt Sameh believe all love to be so, of the jinn? Her tone sounded that way.

"But there remains something important you haven't said about al-Harith who won her," Sitt Sameh went on.

Rayah sorted through her memory. What was the most important fact about the young herdsman suddenly made good by the whim of war, better than birth would have ever granted him. "He ran away as a child."

"That is so."

"Fell down a ravine. Was wounded so they feared for his life."

"How wounded?"

Rayah thought—then suddenly remembered. How it had come up while her mother healed Jaffar, that very night's groom. Things might be the same with him. "Al-Harith was wounded in the groin."

"Remember how he went to the women—?"

"The harlots."

"The women who served the Goddess, yes. What happened there?"

"Even such women couldn't make him perform as a man." Rayah knew she spoke of things of which she, a virgin, had no knowledge, and she fell into confusion.

"Although he had managed to win my mother as the spoils of war, and although he was the kindest of men, al-Harith could never give her a child. A woman of our line must pass on her power."

Rayah knew that last pointed statement was meant for her. She must pass on her power, this power she was still trying to shrug from her own shoulders like a too-heavy cloak.

Sitt Sameh went on as if there were no such burden. "And yet—remember?—her mother the kahinah had blown on knots, worked her spells, conjured the jinn against her own daughter's camel that this should be so."

The fervor of this speech helped Rayah realize that perhaps her mother hoped the story itself would make the cloak less stifling. At least in this knowledge of the past, Sitt Sameh had found the ability to go through all she had to see herself and her daughter alive.

"So then what happened?" Rayah asked.

"My mother, Bint Zura, brought great fertility to the herds of al-Harith," Sitt Sameh continued her tale. "Every womb dropped twins, most of them shes, until the milk flowed like wadis in spate. But for her own womb, she could do nothing. Not until—"

Sitt Sameh had let the spindle fall again. She reached for her few treasures, stacked against her wall. This time, she didn't touch the broken litter, but instead, the sword unsheathed from its scabbard, what the world would consider the prize. The men of the wedding, in their anger, might kill for it—if any of them learned she had it here. Sayf-Allah, the Sword of the Conqueror and of his one God.

13

بسم والم الرحمن الرحيم

**O man, time shall unveil to you things
you did not know, and he whom you never
asked shall yet bring you back tidings.**
                    —Qasidah of Tarafa 'bnu'l-Abd

My milk mother had pitched her tent west of Mecca, towards the pass that leads to the sea. I came on foot, since it wasn't far, just beyond the sacred precinct, and an unmounted man suggests more peaceful intentions. On foot, the familiar smells of my childhood, of an encampment in the desert, came more readily to my nostrils—dung fire, dust, and the shaggy sides of camels. Why do the poets never sing of the smells of the dislodged lover's encampment, evocative even in the dark?

The shadows were long, away from me, those of the kneeling camels' like full mountains. No tent here seemed to belong to al-Harith. I looked for such at once. Of course, a sharif might well leave his herdsman in his home pastures with most of the animals when he came on pilgrimage.

All seemed quiet, deserted. Smoke rose only from the women's section, a fragrance of warm, fresh bread, and I made my way towards that side. I tried not to feel the need to do so, but I found myself trying to walk with stealth. And every pebble I knocked against another rang too, too loudly in my ears.

I can always run, I told myself. I can always fight my way out of this. I always did when we were boys together.

But my palm was sweaty on the hilt of my sword. If I had to use it, it would probably slip in my hand.

I was about fifty paces from the goat-hair house when a figure came around it from the far side. I recognized him at once, of course, and felt my heart surge into my throat. That made it very difficult for me to speak.

But I attempted a "Brother Malik—?"

A whisper of steel was my answer. He was after me shouting, "Vengeance! Blood for Tamimi blood!"

I ran. The wisest thing might have been to run for Mecca where I'd come from. I could still outrun my milk brother, I thought, although I did have a town softness weighing me down. I could even take one of those camels on my way to lengthen my stride.

I ran for Umm Mutammim instead, leaping over goats and shoving camels' broad sides out of my way as I went. I could hear Malik's heavy breathing over my own before I reached the tent sides. He had a much better angle to begin with, of course.

The moment my feet felt the rugs beneath them, I flung myself towards the center pole. Women's screams filled the air along with the wild jangle of the spells my milk mother hung from the prop pole. The force of my hitting it and the clinging afterwards nearly yanked the thing up out of the ground. This threatened to bring the whole tent down on all of our heads. More female screams rent the close air.

Malik grabbed a handful of my hair and pulled it back, exposing my throat to his raised sword.

More female screams—and then everything went black.

Two shuddered breaths convinced me I wasn't dead. Another one helped me identify the smell that filled my nostrils, the warm, blood, milk, wool smell of Umm Mutammim.

Her voice came muffled to my ears. "Khalid is under my cloak, my son."

That's what I'd begun to expect—to hope—this blackness was. I could see nothing, but the idea occurred to me, this is a woman's view of the world. Of course, they took care to have the eye holes where they could see. But that same protection her veil had always offered her, Umm Mutammim had now thrown over me. Few men on earth were so lacking in honor that they would dare to breach that shelter.

"Remove your cloak from him, Mother," Malik demanded. "Let me kill him and slake Hala's thirsty spirit with Qurayshi blood."

"I will not let one boy I suckled kill another," Umm Mutammim insisted. "Not here before my eyes. Not here in my own tent."

My gasps were taking a very long time to return to normal breathing. I closed my eyes to embrace the dark that kept me living and took those deep lungfuls of her fragrance.

"Layla," she called to a woman with her—Bint al-Minhal, I had no doubt.

Layla who had been given to me first by her horse-breeding father and then as booty after Dhu Qar. Layla whose love I had refused. I'd given her—tossed her, in truth, like some old rag—to Malik instead.

"A bowl of milk. Layla, quickly."

The cloak was thrown back. A bowl of fresh camels' milk, still warm, was shoved at my lips.

"Drink," Umm Mutammim ordered me.

I sputtered, then drank, meeting Malik's eyes full of fury over the bowl's rim. The veil of blood lust fell from my milk brother's eyes and, with a sigh, he let his sword drop lifeless to his side. He knew when he was defeated. I had drunk his mother's milk, once in childhood, again now. She had covered me with her cloak. No, there was no way under heaven he could kill me now.

My milk brother resigned. My eyes adjusted to the dimness, I allowed my gaze to slip around the tent. Layla bint al-Minhal sat cross-legged there indeed, the forms of a few other women besides my mother. None of them, I knew in a moment, was the daughter of the Taghlib, Bint Zura, whom I longed to see. Who was, in fact, the purpose I had risked my life just now to try to breach this gulf of honor.

In spite of her lack, the tent was as I'd always remembered it, a haven in the desert's harshness. A butter skin hung in its usual place from the tent pole, just awaiting first light to wake up the world with its sloshing swing.

Malik would have to stay and listen to what I had to say. And I would have to say it. Then after that, perhaps, I could find out what I'd really come to this tent to learn.

❧

In the dark of the night, my milk brothers and I joined the men of both our tribes—Tamim and Quraysh—at Mina, at the bottom of that steep, narrow gorge of bare granite east of Mecca. The bitter cold of the dark desert sank into every bone; sleep came with difficulty, even close to a fire. The devout among my kinsmen prepared to greet the rising sun as God. Something of the same gratitude penetrated my own marrow.

And dawn came suddenly with a sweep of wind down the pass that snapped the flames of our fire like pilgrimage banners. I joined the simple but beautiful prostrations. This in spite of the fact that, to my taste, they were full of fear and pleading. Who would not pray to be spared the wrath of that great ball of fire that would soon turn the world from a bleak and blasted icy waste to an inferno? The sun is a jealous and a baleful deity, the exact opposite of what Muhammad said the Most Merciful is. But the sun is like Him in other ways, even as the prostrations are: born, bred, and come to His power in the desert.

Within the pass of Mina stood three ancient pillars of unhewn stone called baytels. They had been raised, some said, by Father Ibrahim when he was tempted to murder Isma'il his son and thrice resisted the evil being many call Satan. Others turned the tale another way; they thought no inspired man, poet or prophet, should resist his shaytan *or pretend he didn't exist. His shaytan was the only source of his inspiration.*

Be that as it may, the baytels *of Mina ran in height from the tallest in the west, nearest Mecca, to the shortest before the rising sun. Their shadows stretched Mecca-ward—like Muslims in prayer—through the brilliant colors of early day. The oranges and pinks and golds and purples would soon bleach out to an almost uniform white gold.*

The baytels' *shadows stretched likewise through the silence that weighed on the ear. The sheep brought for sacrifice bleated only occasionally. Now and then a man scuffled nervously or hawked with the night chill still in his lungs. The high, lonesome screech of an eagle in her aerie on the cliff. These sounds only intensified the silence in between.*

I found plenty to worship, in any case.

After the rites, we all returned to squat in a circle around the fire. Or rather, in two distinct halves of a circle. For the space and distance left between Qurayshi and Tamimi, the averted eyes, the open glares, stood as physical emblems of the bad blood between the tribes.

In my heart sat the same division. I wanted to be with my milk brothers, but form said I must sit with the Quraysh. Young Hala's murder was the reason we had all come to see justice done, and yet few felt the connection to Muhammad's belief for which the young man had died. Of those who did follow his persuasion, more sat on the Qurayshi side, the side that must pay for Hala's death. And in the face of blood, they must keep quiet about these tenets which many of them held dearer than blood, dearer than life itself.

These rifts, as deep yet as narrow as the very gorge of Mina itself, we had come to try to heal.

Of all the men present, only one belonged to neither side, either by blood or persuasion, and that was as it should be. We called this man the sharif of the Bisha, a tribe of his own above all disagreements, holding neither lands nor followers. By ancient right, his was the privilege and the duty to oversee with impartiality the rites to follow. His family alone was heir to this power and accepted as such throughout all the Hijaz, the barrier of the desert.

The sharif of the Bisha sat in judgment. When a body was found in the desert and the murderer unknown, he was called to find out the truth of testimonies. He was called when objects or herds were stolen and nobody knew by whom—or in a case of oath taking such as the present one.

"Oath taking?" My scribe asks for a clarification.

Of course, they do not use this trial by ordeal in Syria where judges and courts make men effeminate.

"A member of my tribe the Quraysh would step forward in the next few minutes," I explain.

"Would simply speaking an oath be enough to satisfy the wounded Tamim?"

"My clansman would swear, at the risk of severe burns to his tongue, that the whole clan would apologize and keep the peace between us. And the sharif of Bisha knew the Gods he invoked would demonstrate the validity of the oath with the hot iron blade of a sword, to blister the oath-taking tongue or leave it whole."

The sharif was a small, swarthy man with slits for eyes and a thin mouth surrounded by a grizzled beard. He held aloof from either tribe's half circle, squatting close to the fire. He alone was allowed to stoke it with the charcoal and wood—no dung—the parties had brought in equal portion for fuel. He alone could touch the wooden hilt of an ancient sword which rested on a stone before the fire. The naked tip of the sword—about the top third of the blade—the sharif held into the heart of the fire itself. With a magic known only to his blood, he adjusted its position from time to time. This God and then that one he invoked in a distracted undertone as he did so.

The tip of the sword was fire-blackened in parts, glowing with heat in others. It dried my mouth to look at the weapon, the implement of the oath. I stole a glance at Omar. In the midst of his sparse beard, his mouth was working to raise spittle over what must be an even greater dryness.

Under the direction of the sharif of the Bisha, the men began to bargain. What was the life of Hala worth? The life of one young man for the life of another, that was an easy equation. But what when that young life stood against peace and the good name of the pilgrimage? What was it worth then?

The Quraysh came quickly up to the level the Tamim first proposed: the usual forty camels plus a mare and a full outfit for a warrior to sit upon that mare. They would let these stand in the place of a man.

"Now swear to it," the sharif ordered.

Mutammim swore for his tribe, and in such poetical tones that tears winked in eyes on both sides of the fire by the time he was done. Nothing could buy back the life of such a fine young man, defender of the defenseless. But a Qurayshi dagger intended for his Qurayshi stepfather had cut short the life of this brave Tamimi. "Young Hala's example inspires us to offer you this brotherhood."

Then it was our turn. The Qurayshi reply needed to be no more than formula, but Omar, who had done the deed, ought to speak it. That was not the reason for his hesitation. The hesitation came when he saw the sharif of the Bisha reach once again for the hilt of the sword, pull it out of the fire, and study the tip with interest.

The sharif must have noticed my cousin wavering, although he never looked at him directly. Instead, the man began an explanation, as if everyone didn't already understand what should happen next. He spoke as if it had nothing whatever to do with the sudden and uncomfortable lull in the proceedings: "The Bisha must go to the tongue of he who speaks for the offending party. To determine the truth of what he says, of his remorse for the deed, his oath to provide the blood price as agreed and to keep the peace ever after. Should he fail in either of these matters, either he or his clansmen after, though his tongue came away clean on this occasion, the wound will appear for all judgment at the time of failure."

Al-Khattab tried to urge his son to his feet with a nudge. Still Omar didn't respond. He allowed himself to be jostled off his squat rather than respond. He met no one's gaze, least of all mine, but steadily studied the dirt in front of his feet.

The sharif did not intervene, only called again on the Gods. "Witness."

Clearly Omar had no remorse, had no intention of keeping the peace. That glowing end of the sword had him very, very afraid. Who could blame him?

Nervous murmurs had begun. The oath taker should not be urged aloud, for that would go against a favorable outcome. But some Qurayshi must take the trial, swear to the peace. And soon. If the sharif of the Bisha commented on the hesitation, his doubt would work its way into the swearing sword, from hilt to truth-finding tip.

I had sworn to the jinn once before, and then withdrawn my offer of a strip of cloth representing my right arm. My right arm continued strong in battle. But I had been a mere child, frightened, then. I wanted a chance to prove that I was no longer the child. I could keep oaths now, publicly. I was worthy of the deepest trust of my tribesmen—on both sides of the circle.

"I speak for the Qurayshi," *I said suddenly, getting to my feet.* "I'll speak for my cousin," *I added, unable to resist that extra jab at Omar.* "I am not afraid."

14

> So I swear, by the Holy House about which circumambulate
> men of Quraysh and Jurhum, whose hands have constructed it,
> A solemn oath I swear—you have proved yourselves fine masters
> in all matters, be the thread single or twisted double.
> You alone mended the rift between Abs and Dhubyan
> after long slaughter, and much grinding of the perfume of Manshim,
> and you declared, "If we achieve peace broad and sure
> by ample giving and fair speaking, we shall live secure."
> —Muallaqa of Zuhairy

*M*urmurs of surprise, then gratitude and encouragement rose from my kins-men at my sudden announcement. The life of one young man of Quraysh could easily stand in for another, more easily than one Qurayshi could stand in for a dead Tamimi. The look from Malik, the nod of Mutammim's blind head were more encouragement still, the only encouragement I truly cared about then.

I'm not swearing peace to Muhammad after all, I told myself. I'm swearing peace to the Tamim, who are already my milk brothers. Muhammad is the one who should be here swearing. But again he has avoided the responsibility of what he preaches, claiming too much holiness to join us in the real world, in a place where multiple Gods might be invoked. And the truth is, I would rather be conjoined with Mutammim and Malik than with the shifting sands of Mecca's sensibilities.

That is what I said, something along those lines, though what exactly is perhaps better lost, as I am no poet.

What mattered was that my words pleased the sharif of the Bisha. I impressed him with my earnestness, and he stood content. Whatever stumbling language I used, I covered all the important aspects of the oath. I expressed our sorrow—at least mine—over what had happened at the Ka'ba. I recited the number of beasts *and goods to be given to heal the breach, my full intent never to break it again with violence between our blood. I concluded with the names of a God or two and an invocation upon my life and my tongue, which I set to risk to prove the truth of what I said:*

"By Hubal and by the God of the Tamim. By my life and by my tongue." I was not risking my right arm, after all, as once I had done with a witch and jinn in the desert. Only my tongue.

"Good," the sharif nodded. Then with a toss of his head, he gestured me to come and kneel just behind his left shoulder.

With a glare at Omar to cover the weakness in my knees, I did so.

I who dared to break your leg now dare this for you as well, you coward, I thought.

I hoped he got the message.

Taking up the sharif of the Bisha's view of things sobered me quickly. I felt every eye on me. Worse, I saw exactly where the sharif thrust the tip of the sword. No, he did not keep it to the cooler ashes scraped to one side. He thrust it into the part burning white beyond even the usual golden red. The fire, instead of being his friend and kinsman in the operation of the ordeal for others, might have been the object of an hereditary blood feud instead: He thrust to the beating heart.

I suddenly found my mouth very dry indeed.

The sharif handed me a small jug full of water and bade me drink. I longed for it to be cool. It was no cooler than the air in which it stood, about blood heat now as the sun grew higher.

Cooler than the flame, anyway, I tried to tell myself. I took the prescribed three mouthfuls, one after the other, wishing with each my mouth could hold more. Wishing then I could swallow. Instead, I had to spit the water back onto the sand at my feet, where it quickly vanished into the air—the same way it did from my sand-grainy tongue.

After my second spit, the sharif took hold of the hilt and drew the blade out of the fire one last time. "In the Name of God, the Merciful, the Compassionate," he recited over the weapon as he waved it first to the Tamim and then to the Quraysh for their approval. Yes, it was, indeed, glowing hot.

I kept the third mouthful of water between my teeth until the sharif of Bisha had at least passed the invocations to the God Muhammad said we should worship alone. I didn't want this to be a testimony to that man's faith, of his guiltlessness in all of this. That man who wouldn't even put in an appearance when the violence he set in motion was put to rest. "But I am never one of the great ones of Mecca," he might say, in straining humility. Too busy talking to his angels. Unwilling, perhaps, to set the violence to rest at all.

"In the name of al-Uzza, the morning star, and Manat the rising sun. In the name of . . . "

I spat out the last mouthful of water. It was either that or choke and give in to the temptation to swallow it.

The sharif crossed his right arm, the one holding the sword, over his chest so the blade thrust out towards me over his left shoulder.

"Taste the flavor of your oath upon the sword of God," he commanded. "Taste the Bisha."

See how it was. The sharif of the Bisha did not look at me, for I was behind him. He did not hold the sword to my tongue so he could keep it there longer or shorter than necessary according to some corrupt ambition of his own. Of course, the ashraf of the Bisha are not supposed to have any ambitions of their own save justice. Still, this rite guaranteed it. All he did was to continue to invoke Gods to the sword—and watch the faces of the men before him. They would tell him when satisfaction was reached, no action of his. Or of mine.

But my actions had to bring satisfaction to those faces. I felt myself wash with pallor at the thought. Then I saw my cousin Omar's eyes and mouth wide. Determined, I stuck out my tongue—not at him, to the hot, dry, desert air—and brought it toward the sword's point.

I intend to keep this oath, I reminded myself, whatever anyone else's intentions. Whatever Omar's intentions.

These are my milk kin.

What man would say, "For a woman among them"?

But don't let your tongue dry too long in the air, I told myself.

I felt the heat of the sword while still a hand's breadth away from it. No trick was involved. This was like licking a branding iron. The heat radiated like a solid wall around the sword tip. It threw me back again. I hesitated.

Then I reached up and adjusted the red silk of my headdress. As if I wanted to assure myself it hadn't caught fire, which seemed entirely possible. I did this for my milk mother and her sons. Because if I didn't, and the oath didn't hold, I would never see them again without danger of death, theirs or mine.

Because if I didn't, I would never find out what had become of Bint Zura.

I did it for her.

I leaned forward into the heat, through it, closing my eyes against it. I had touched the tip of the sword. I was certain my tongue had touched the thing, yet I felt nothing. I pulled back.

"Again," Abu Hala called out.

The murmur of voices from the Qurayshi side had told me they were satisfied. More than satisfied, they were proud. Almost jubilant.

But *"Again,"* Abu Hala insisted. *"For the life of my son, touch it again."*

"Touch it again," the sharif told me quietly. *I was certain he'd felt the first touch, but he said it anyway.*

So, for the memory of the blood spilled under my arm in the Ka'ba, I did it. And without benefit of another mouthful of water. But I didn't hesitate. For Bint Zura, I licked it again, with my eyes wide open this time, so the heat seemed to blast them like a gust of sand-laden wind.

"Very well," Abu Hala said.

"We are satisfied," Mutammim declared.

The sharif passed me the jug of water. This time he met my eyes and gave a little thin-lipped smile. I tried to return wordless gratitude. I didn't know what his magic was, but at least I didn't feel any pain. At the moment, that was good enough for me. Once more I took a mouthful, spat.

"Show them," the sharif instructed me next.

I got up off my knees and went around to every assembled witness, the Tamim first and then my own kin.

"What's that?" Abu Hala asked, squinting keenly into my mouth like a man about to pull another's tooth.

"Just a bit of ash," Malik said at his side. *His voice and glance said he was as proud of me as my blood kinsmen.*

"Have him rinse again," Abu Hala said. *"It might be burned black."*

The sharif did so, though I was certain if my tongue had burned black in any spot, I would know about it.

"Gone," the dead boy's father admitted.

"Clean," Malik declared, triumphant.

"Clean," all my kinsmen readily agreed.

Even Omar did so, although grudgingly, more grudgingly, it seemed than the father of the boy he'd killed. There was no sign of red burn, white blister or white char. My clean tongue proved the clean intentions of my heart. And so it would remain, as long as the oath held.

The sharif nodded with contentment. The strength of his family's power had proven itself yet again.

"Thus the sword of God," he said, and the way he said it made me wonder if he referred to the weapon—or to myself.*

Of course I meant to keep the oath. My solid purpose kept me from harm on that day.

But now as I sit in the peace of my own garden in Homs, my parched throat craves a drink of the pomegranate juice I can have for a wave of my hand. The tartness stings on my blistered, forsworn tongue like fire. I cannot swallow fast enough, and then it sits in my belly like hot coals.

My scribe leaps up to tend my feeble sputtering.

"Water," I gasp to quench the flames, but even that stings.

The Sword of God. I certainly took on that appellation, by the flames of Jehannam—hell.

But perhaps it would have been better—in this case, at least—to let revenge slake its thirst with blood. Because if you don't have a revenge killing, the unavenged blood creates a martyr. And that's what I handed Muhammad that day, on the tip of a sword.

And only God knew then how, against my best intentions, I would break my oath.

"Now," said the sharif of the Bisha, "to seal the oath with the blood of sacrifice."

And so a sheep was brought, one to each of the stone pillars in Mina. Each throat was cut in the name of the Gods and the blood used to anoint the stones. Some of the party pelted the baytels *with pebbles in imitation of Father Ibrahim's denial of temptation in this spot.*

For me, of course, the important part of the rite had ended when my tongue had been declared "clean." The hard edges between our tribes were smoothed. I went and sat companionably with my milk brothers.

That was when I could finally, finally ask the question I'd carried with me even at Hala and Hind's heels to the Ka'ba: "And what has become of your herdsman since last I saw you? Al-Harith and I were in captivity those months with the sons of Bakr. He and I fought on the Day of Dhu Qar. But he didn't join you on the pilgrimage?" I took a breath, rolled my untouched tongue gratefully through my mouth and added: "And what of the ones behind him?"

Then I received the answer.

"Al-Harith and his family no longer pitch their tents with the sons of Nu waira," Mutammim told me.

"Gone to greener pastures," Malik said. "Three or four years ago he had a re-markable calving and carried all of them over the summer. They had to move off, there wasn't grazing enough for our combined herds. Al-Harith ibn Suwaid is his own man now."

"A remarkable calving?" I asked, astounded. "With what?"

"With those same flea-bitten, swaybacked wrecks he's always herded, mixed in with ours." To hear us talk of these old, familiar things as the day crawled towards its zenith, no stranger would have guessed bad blood had stood between us when the sun rose.

"I've never seen anything like it," Mutammim added. He made the sign that mimics Hubal's raised red hand, protecting the company from all the things in this world that are not to be understood. "Every single one of them bore twins, mostly shes. Even so, there was so much milk he had to buy a couple of slaves to help his

poor old mother and his wife out with the churning and the cheese making."

*His wife. Someone had mentioned her. Bint Zura, I had no doubt they meant.
But how to ask more?*

*"They did come as far west as at-Ta'if with us this year," Malik managed to
interject, before Mutammim was on about the herdsman's marvelous success again.*

*"By the looks of things, there's another good year coming up for him. Suwaid's
second son married way over his head and his daughters, grown smooth and plump
on the cream, are spoken for in twenty directions. I've never seen anything like it."*

*"What the Gods allow!" I exclaimed, the traditional phrase one says to put the
power of the Gods between you and the ill effects of amazement, not to say jealousy.
"What is it?" I went on to ask, as if he described some sort of plague instead of a
remarkable good.*

*Malik reiterated his magic sign with a grunt and a shrug. "Al-Uzza knows,"
he said.*

"After al-Harith finally got a wife—" Mutammim spoke of her again.

*"And didn't we all think he'd never manage it?" Malik interrupted with a good
humor that was going to drive me to distraction in a moment.*

*"After that," Mutammim continued, "Suwaid let age take hold of him, and
he put our old playmate in charge of the herd. That seems to have had something
to do with it."*

*"But al-Harith is no magician, by God. Well, you remember him, Khalid. He
married while you were with us last, as I recall. That Taghlibi girl he took in battle.
But of course you were playing* al-maysir—*winner take all—with Death at the
time and perhaps do not remember."*

*"I remember," I said, and made the same sign against amazement Malik had
made. I understood, or thought I understood, more of the source of Suwaid's fortune
than my milk brother did, but I was no less filled with wonder.*

*How could she abide such a mundane existence? How could she go from nun
to* qubbah *rider to captive wife, and yet bring great fertility to each occupation? I
wondered . . . I wondered so many things.*

*"And al-Harith's tent itself?" It made me sick to ask this, but I had to do it. "Is
that as fertile as his flocks?"*

"Now that is doubly strange," Malik said.

"Has he many sons?"

"No. He has none."

*No. None. Al-Harith, whom even the women under the red kerchiefs could not
make perform.*

*My wonder, more complicated, was also longer lived than Malik's. My milk
brothers were on to other things. And the name of the town of at-Ta'if had begun*

to drum in my head.

"How has your wound from Dhu Qar healed?" asked Mutammim, "Manat preserve you."

"Yes, and when will you thrill us all by seeking another?" asked his brother.

"Very shortly, by al-Uzza," I replied, "if this business over Hala and Muhammad his stepfather hadn't been cleared up so nicely."

"Thanks to your iron tongue," Malik said. Every vestige of his attempt to kill me less than one turn of the sun ago had vanished into our old comfortable companionship.

"Yes, and you'd be obliged to give that wound to me."

"Thank all the Gods it never came to that."

His brother echoed the feeling and then said, "You'll come and stay with us in our tent for a while. Our mother would love to see you, you know."

"More than just when she's throwing her cloak over you to save your miserable skin," Mutammim teased.

"No," I told them. At-Ta'if. They'd said al-Harith was in at-Ta'if. "No," I said again. "Something presses."

"Oh, the ways of these townsfolk," Malik said. "Always in a hurry."

"Something more pressing than us?" Mutammim asked. "By Hubal, what can such a matter be?"

"I cannot tell you."

"If you cannot tell us, your own kin, it cannot be that important."

"Nevertheless, it is so."

After that, and after the sacrifices were just a pile of bones, I left my kin, both milk and blood, to decide without me just how the forty camels would be delivered. For my part, I set my horse's head towards the spot where the morning star rises out of the gorge of Mina. By the time it did rise, I had reached the Valley of Nakhlah, halfway between Mecca and at-Ta'if.

15

They invoke in His stead only females; they pray to none else than shaytan, a rebel.
—The Holy Quran 4:117

With a sudden movement and a hiss like an adder in the sun, Sitt Sameh plucked the sword from its almost-forgotten bed upon the carpet. She waved it once above her head, a gesture from the battle-leading *qubbah* that took Rayah's breath away.

Then her mother replaced it, again like a snake, and continued Bint Zura's tale as if she'd done nothing. She told the details lovingly as if she, Sitt Sameh, had been there, in the long past. But it transpired before she was even born.

❧

Swift, brute violence is in the land. That cannot be denied. It's in the way of the land. That must be learned before the finer, softer touch. Violence is in the air one takes into her lungs. It's in the sun, that old woman who, being barren herself, resents the life in anything else and destroys it with the evil eye of her vindictive glare. It's in the rains—when they come, if they come—that tease the flocks into the bottom of the wadis with sweet green grass. Then, with no more warning than a low rumble like a ravenous stomach, it sweeps them away in a flash of flood, herdsman and all.

But these things are merely on the land, about the land, and not the land itself. The land itself is the most violent of all. It is not within the knowledge of man how the Gods made this land—if They made it at all, for it has a deep, thoughtful mind of its own. But even the most ignorant of men—perhaps because he is ignorant—cannot spend much time among the valleys and the crevices, the plains, the dunes and the high places, without getting a feeling for the sternness of the land. Its unforgiving nature and the holocaust that must have been its birthing.

A woman can stand on certain high mountains and as far as the eye can see are only other high mountains, equal in barrenness. Cores of lava stand, thrown up the color of coagulated blood. Sheer cliffs hundreds of times the height of a man rip and heave from once-level plains, one portion above another under incredible pressure. Sand dunes creep over the land like something alive. And everywhere water, wind, and sun have been at work, whittling away, making smooth places rough, then fickly changing their minds and smoothing them again.

Erosion is no less violent for all the time it takes. Erosion is part of the land. The patience required of a woman in the desert is like the patience of the elements working at a limestone mountain. Most men would be driven mad.

And with such patience, Bint Zura bided her time, a prisoner and a wife in the tent of al-Harith, the man who had cut down her treasure, her white camel az-Zuharah. She looked over her flocks in the violent, jealous land where she made them flourish.

Sometimes it seemed as if life consisted of nothing but the watering of flocks and herds. One well was not out of sight before her thoughts and aspirations turned to the next. Would there be enough water there? Would the walls have collapsed and have to be redug? Would other herds under careless herdsmen have befouled it, leaving the excrement floating a hand's depth on top of the water and the flies swarming? Would the water level be high or low, so low that the work of drawing it would take all day?

Until one day, Bint Zura left them all untended. She entered the violent desert alone and went to find her mother.

She hadn't gone but just out of sight of the dust raised by her animals when a gust of wind raised other dust. The dust began to twist around emptiness, dancing before her. With a little cry of fear, Bint Zura clutched her amulets against evil. She twisted herself and began to run back the way her bare footprints led. After three steps, her footprints vanished, a scree of sand sifted across the outcrop of rock. She turned again. The dust devil twisted still, hissing as it went. She would return to the life she knew, to the flocks that were fertile enough, even if she couldn't be. She could follow the sun well enough—

Then—the dust demon spoke. At first she could make out no meaning, only she knew the hissing had turned to words. Then she heard her name. Not Bint Zura, daughter of her father. The name her mother had given her, her, born in the holy *qubbah* between the sacred shrine at Nakhlah and Mecca of the Quraysh. The name her mother had never been allowed to use. "Amat al-Uzza, handmaid of the Goddess."

The demon was asking her to follow it.

The young woman did.

And when her shadow grew long behind her, the wind suddenly stilled. She found herself at the base of a tumble of rock. There, under a single scrap of tenting, sat a white-haired woman—her mother, Umm Taghlib. The dust demon flew to the yarn she was twisting, shrank, took its shape.

"Peace, my daughter."

"Blessings on you, my mother." Bint Zura sat in the day's last shade opposite the old woman. "You called me?" For she understood now that she had not been following her own will when she left the flocks that afternoon.

"Your womb stays empty, child."

"And is that my fault?" The dryness in Bint Zura's throat would not let her slide over the anger she felt. "You were the one who made al-Harith cut my camel's tendons in the heat of Dhu Qar, who made us lose that battle. Here I am, a captive in a strange tribe, captive of a man who will never sire a child. All thanks to your magic."

"Yes." The old woman nodded. "Did I not conjure valor into a man who never knew it before or since? Did I not, years before that, conjure him in the fall that made him less than a man, conjure the Fire Ones to save him in the desert where otherwise he was condemned to die?"

"Yes, Mother, you did. It would have been better had he died."

"Ah, hush, child." The kahinah glanced toward the charms dangling from her tent pole: tufts of ostrich feathers broken from a woman's litter—Bint Zura's own litter—among bones that appeared human. "You do not understand the power of your own tongue."

"What power?"

"You make every beast you touch grow fertile."

"What of that, if I cannot help my own womb?"

"Isn't your man kind to you? Doesn't he fairly worship the ground you walk upon? This from a man who won you in battle. When else have you heard the like?"

Bint Zura considered. "This, too, is your magic?"

"What mother wants her daughter's day-to-day life to be a torture?"

"I would not know, for I will never have a daughter of my own."

Umm Taghlib looked to her amulets again. The glance alone—for no wind blew—set them gently swinging. "No. Do not curse yourself with your own tongue. Form your mind around the desire of your heart. For now is the time. Now you will truly know your own power. Now—now is the time to work your own magic—for yourself."

Bint Zura sat. Her mother span. Nothing happened.

"What am I to do?" The young woman finally lost patience.

Twilight had come and, between them, the tiny fire winked on the verge of going out.

"Build up the fire against the chill of night," her mother replied. "But think, think well what should go into the burn."

Bint Zura thought, but there wasn't much time. The next heartbeat—or the next—the fire would go out. How would they start it again? No tent nearby from which to borrow coals, growing too dark to see to easily strike a flint. She couldn't imagine that her mother, poor as she was, would ever burn anything but dried dung.

Nonetheless, Bint Zura spoke the instant the idea entered her mind: "Holy acacia. Wood of fertility."

"Very good. And, as the Goddess is merciful, I just happen to have some here."

How a back existed to a tent that barely owned a top, Bint Zura didn't know. But from that back, her mother did indeed draw forth bundled, broken sticks of acacia.

The moment she felt the curve they'd been arced into, Bint Zura knew: "This is the litter—*my* litter."

"I found it broken beyond repair on the battlefield of Dhu Qar, yes. Never fear, I saved the tufts of feather." Another glance toward the charms at the tent pole. "That will be enough to renew the *qubbah*. When you need it."

"I am a captive wife. I will never need a sacred litter again."

"No. But your daughter will."

"I will never have a daughter—"

"It will be as the Gods will."

It had grown too dark inside the tent for Bint Zura to read her mother's face. Even in the dark, however, she felt the bore of her stare.

Quickly, Bint Zura set to feeding the fire, first with threads torn from her own hem with their heavy wool smell. Puffing, puffing, not too hard, just enough—

While she worked, her mother spoke. "Do you hear the news in the desert?"

Puff. "What news?" Puff.

"The news from Mecca."

Puff. "What know I of Mecca? My father—" Puff. "—Always made the pilgrimage to al-Hira—" Puff. "Among the Christians." Puff.

"So think on al-Hira."

Bint Zura didn't like to. There her father had tried to sell her to a convent of nuns. There her mother had almost been stoned to death before the sacred *baytels* of pilgrimage. Had the old woman forgotten?

"There you met—" her mother said.

The very last thing Bint Zura wanted to think about. That son of the Quraysh. That young man who had been everywhere on the battlefield of Dhu Qar. Al-Harith might have been the one to actually cut az-Zuharah's hamstrings from under her. But her loss was really due to that son of Quraysh named Khalid. That strong, jinni-charged right arm of his, impossible to fight against.

She had seen him through the curtains of the *qubbah*, and it had made her heart pound. With fear? Yes, but also—also with something else. For the moment he had laid his gaze on her within those curtains, he had turned the thrust of his efforts, trying to spare her, trying to fight on *her* side.

For, of course, she had seen him before that hot day of battle. In al-Hira. At the hand of her jinn-possessed father. "The coming salvation of the Arabs." Khalid was his name. Khalid ibn al-Walīd abu Sulayman. Of the Quraysh, of Mecca. Abu Sulayman. So he already had a son. Which meant he already had a wife. At least one.

And he had seen her and followed her—or so it seemed—from convent to tent, all over al-Hira.

Such a man, a fearsome, fiery man. Something to avoid.

Yet even as the thought of him burst in her mind, and she tried to push the thought aside, the acacia wood caught fire.

Her mother had begun something about that Qurayshi in al-Hira, but she did not finish her thought. She returned to Mecca instead: "They say a prophet has arisen in Mecca."

"In Mecca?"

"I am not so ignorant of Mecca and its holy Ka'ba as you. I gave birth to you, there between Nakhlah and Mecca. Just as we reached the point where pilgrims shout: 'Here I am, O Lord.' There, indeed, you were."

Such talk made Bint Zura uncomfortable. "Yet another prophet to the Arabs? In Mecca?"

"He is not a prophet just for the Arabs, but for all the world." Her mother shifted in the darkness. "So they say."

"Not for me." Bint Zura surprised herself at the force of her reply.

"I only report what they say."

"Not for me—or mine." Bint Zura said again.

"His name is Muhammad ibn Abd Allah."

"I said, I am not interested."

"Muhammad has, they say, no son but only daughters. Interesting, don't you think, for a man who is supposed to have power?"

The fire was burning well now. A single curl of smoke twisted over it like a jinni. "Please, mother, I am not—"

"He is Qurayshi. Cousin—to another of that tribe."

Bint Zura would not think of that Khalid. "How am I to work this spell?" she demanded.

The firelight caught her mother's smile. "Take the spindle," her mother said.

Bint Zura did.

"Spin."

Bint Zura did, trying not to think of Khalid ibn al-Walīd all the while. She thought instead of the smoke, twisting the smoke into the twist of her wool.

"Cut off a good length."

Bint Zura set the wool between her teeth and bit.

"Now—begin to tie the knots, blowing on each one. Call on the Goddess, our Lady of Nakhlah, as you do. And when you come to the sacred Valley where first I felt the pangs of your entering the world—"

16

Liken my weeping eye to a waterbag
dragged down the well slope . . .
Spilling water into channels
as grain husks part
from the ripening fruit . . .
—The Hanging Poem of Alqama

"**W**hat?" Rayah prodded Sitt Sameh. Had the older woman fallen into a trance with the rhythm of her recitation?

The story of one mother speaking to her daughter had stopped in the middle. The cessation jarred another daughter into her own speech, into a later time and place where Sitt Sameh felt less comfortable, where the way ahead was more difficult to see. The sense of seeing one mirage reflected within another made Rayah dizzy; the layers of womanhood like layers peeling from an onion made her cry.

"What happened next to my grandmother?" she insisted nonetheless. "She was blowing on knots over a fire, working a spell which the Holy Quran expressly forbids—"

"Blood feud broke the pilgrimage peace. Young Hala died, as the eunuch just read to us from the Conqueror's account."

Rayah couldn't see the connection yet.

Heedless, her mother went on, "Omar ibn al-Khattab killed the stepson of Muhammad ibn Abd Allah, the son of Abu Hala the Tamimi of my mother's husband's tribe."

"Omar ibn al-Khattab, the present khalifah. Did he we follow truly commit this blasphemous murder? Was it really as the scribe read to us?" Rayah had her doubts about magic, but this she found even harder to believe.

"Even so, although no one now will mention it in public. At this time, as we have also heard from the Conqueror, my mother and her husband's people traveled with the poet Mutammim and his brother the sharif Malik of the Tamim as far as at-Ta'if. They had meant to sell many of their surplus herds here, perhaps for the pilgrimage at

Mecca. Instead al-Harith found himself and his overabundant herds stuck out in the desert, away from water."

"Didn't his milk brothers just tell the Conqueror that the herdsman had had unusual success with his herds since he'd taken your mother to wife?"

"And so he had. But she had gone out into the desert alone to visit her mother concerning her own fertility, as I have just related."

"They had no water?" Rayah asked.

"They had driven the animals across the desert, expecting to draw water in at-Ta'if for the usual consideration when they got there. You should know that your grandmother did not care to raise camels since the loss of her sacred white camel az-Zuharah, and probably her magic would not have worked on them in any case. Of course, people cannot live in the desert without camels, particularly in that part of the desert, so it was a strain on the sheep and goats. Many could not stand at the end of the trek and had to be carried. The children in the company whimpered weakly for thirst. The sight of at-Ta'if's wells cheered everyone. They hurried forward, pulling the collapsed leather water troughs out of the baggage even as they ran. Sometimes not even bothering to unravel the ropes in their haste.

"When, however, the local Banu Thaqif saw al-Harith setting peeled wands of hazel, acacia, and almond beside his water troughs even before he let the herds drink, as my mother had taught him to do—"

"Wands? What was the purpose of these wands?"

"Ah, well you ask." Was that pride in Sitt Sameh's blue eyes? "Magic. To bring the ewes to heat, to fill their udders."

"Of course."

"The Banu Thaqif cried, 'Witchcraft. He will steal the milk from our herds' udders to his own. Our rams will spend their best seed on his ewes.' And they stoned sheep and shepherd from their water."

"The Banu Thaqif?" Rayah remembered the name now. "They did the same thing to the Prophet, blessings on him, when he went to preach submission in at-Ta'if. Sitt Umm Ali told us the story."

"Ah. And what is that tale?"

Was Rayah really able to add her own part to the story rather than just listening to grown-ups expound? Did that mean she led the story, a little? Did changing the story then change the past, as each of the adults tried to do?

Should that be the case, she spoke carefully. Especially since it concerned the Messenger of God. Future generations would model their behavior after his history. "His face bleeding, Muhammad, precious blessings on him, stopped at their well to wash himself—"

"That would be the same well from which they drove al-Harith."

"But I heard nothing about them prohibiting Muhammad water. No, they left him pretty much alone because the angel Jabra'il came to him there—"

"Ah, his jinni. His shaytan."

Rayah's blood chilled. "Not 'jinni.' God forbid. That—that other word. Angel." The choice of word was very important.

Sitt Sameh smiled as if indulging a child, but bowed her head.

"The angel Jabra'il came and asked if the Messenger, blessings on him, would like the whole stiff-necked town to be dashed to pieces between the two mountains that flank either side of at-Ta'if."

"And what did your prophet reply to his 'angel'?"

"He begged Jabra'il to spare them. He prophesied that the day would come when the Banu Thaqif would produce sons who believed to a man."

"And so it has come to pass," Sitt Sameh admitted. "See what a prophet you follow."

Rayah's mother then continued with her version of earlier events.

"'We cannot go to Mecca for our water.' Bint Zura had suddenly, inexplicably returned from the desert to the suffering group of husband and herds. She retook charge. Slung low around her hips and woman's swinging cradle of flesh, she now wore a knotted cord.

"'Our men are not safe to leave the camp for fear of the blood feud with the Quraysh in one direction, at-Ta'if in the other,' she continued. 'But a woman—I will take a caravan of empty waterskins myself with one servant and bring back what will save us all.'

"And then, even though camels were sacred to her, she knew some had to be sacrificed because she had not been in at-Ta'if to turn the charge of witchcraft. She allowed the last resort of the desert for the sake of the whimpering children. Not looking in the camel herd's direction, she said, 'Cut open the belly of a camel for the water pouch inside. One a day until I return.'

"'Where will you go?' al-Harith almost feared to ask.

"Bint Zura realized now the Gods of necessity had brought her at last to the place her mother wanted her to visit long before. 'Nakhlah,' she said. Not too many camels, then, would have to die. 'I will put myself under that shrine's protection and the Goddess, since the Gods of at-Ta'if turn a dark eye to us.'

"So she set out alone with the caravan of thirsty camels, two flaccid waterskins slung on each animal's sides. And as she approached Nakhlah, to the south she saw a tiny dark cloud along the horizon. The wind died; the sun was enveloped in veils. A peculiar depressing feeling overcame her. The knotted cord about her waist tightened. The camels grew restless. Only with difficulty did she keep them in line, and she longed for another hand to help."

"So what happened at Nakhlah?" Rayah asked.

"That—" said Sitt Sameh, twisting the blade of the sword so it caught the lamp light and bounced it against the far wall. "That you would do best to learn from Khalid the Sword of God himself."

Sitt Sameh looked toward Abd Allah's abandoned parchments. Was that a tear in her blue eye? "And our door to that knowledge is shut within the prison at the Camp of Diocletian."

"I will do what I can for Abd Allah tomorrow," Rayah offered.

Sitt Sameh nodded.

"You must try, too."

Sitt Sameh dropped her spindle and rubbed her hands together as if to rid them of the cramp.

"Mother, you must. His life is at stake."

Sitt Sameh nodded once.

Rayah breathed easier. "And if all else fails, I can take the parchments to him in prison and have him read them to me."

"Child, that would be dangerous."

"I'll do it anyway. I must know the whole history."

Sitt Sameh nodded again. "He remembers how it was, the Conqueror does, how his sword and my life were forged together on the same night."

❧

And God willed that Rayah succeed in what she proposed.

And the eunuch read.

17

And remember the brother of Ad, when he
warned his people beside the winding sand tracts—
and already other augurs had passed away
alike before him and behind him . . .
And when Our signs are recited to them,
clear signs, the unbelievers say to the
truth when it has come to them, "this is manifest sorcery."
—The Holy Quran XLVI:20, 7, the Surah of
the Winding Sand Tracts

A *boy learns the swift, straightforward violence of the raid first. It is in every-thing he will ever meet. He cannot survive if he fears the violent or resents it. He can survive very well without patience.*

And yet, this afternoon, I look from my scribe who sits with his pen poised, ready for my next words. I look at the splashing fountain under the pomegranate instead.

"You've been after me about where I got the heavenly stones to make my sword," I say to him.

Eagerly, he reaches for more parchment.

"They came as a result of something even more important. To do with a woman."

A bit of his eagerness fades.

"But now is the time to tell it. It must be told. Back before Rudainah. Back . . ."

And the words come to me:

A man will simply never be great without the power of slow erosion behind him.

Drawing water requires great patience, and sometimes it seems as if life holds nothing but the watering of flocks and herds. Boys and youths with their whoops and hollers have the strength, but they have much to learn before that strength can match the skill and dogged patience of a woman. From the cradle, a son has known that violence will make or break him in the desert, swallow him whole or refine him to gold. Will he have to draw the sword and fight for those wells?

It takes years before he understands the other side, the side that will make him most honored in the tents of the Arabs. Only with patient coaxing, with wooing— yes, call it the recitation of poetry, for it is that, too—can he do those things that really make the difference in the end.

That is it: the slow, watchful circling of a hawk like the one that has hung in midair all morning, flitting through the pomegranate leaves. At last, it sees its time. It strikes at whatever has not been able to endure the desert.

So with the drawing of water. One who has not patience and a light, jiggling touch on the rope should not draw.

Like counseling in the tents, like drawing water, so must one deal with women, when one is man enough to handle them. Some men never are.

To others, this wisdom comes only in old age.

That morning in the Valley of Nakhlah, I made a great mistake. I let time press upon me until I thought I would burst with anxiety and haste.

She is near, just in at-Ta'if. Near, near, kept beating like the sun on my head. Bint Zura—

My slaves were taking slow and lazy turns with the bucket at the Valley's only and sacred well with its low stone coping. My men leaned far out over the deep, wet space because there was no wheel or pulley.

Finally, I lost patience with them. I waved them to one side with a short temper. The rope, I saw, had knots. Like the spell thread of a kahinah.

"Fool!"

Did I speak to my men—or of myself? For I yanked—and ripped the leathern bucket, our only bucket. I lurched forward to grab it as it tumbled, spurting against the wet-darkened rocks.

I saved it. I came up wet but rejoicing. I had kept the bucket in its hooped wooden frame from tumbling, knotted rope and all, to the bottom of the well.

"She just reached right up and tore it," one of my men said, awe forcing his voice to a whisper.

For when I held the dripping bucket up, the sodden, raining leather showed a gap it would take the patience of a woman to sew back up.

Nakhlah's spring was sacred to the Goddess al-Uzza (the Prophet, blessed be he, would call her a demon) in those days of ignorance. It was "She" my man meant. The place was as favorable to the tribes of jinn as it was to men; it was haunted. The one man convinced the other with his tales. They both stood staring and stupid with fright.

The keeper of Nakhlah's shrine came out from his shade under the three sacred trees. He looked with no lighter eye than my men upon this sign of his divine mistress's displeasure. He was a scabby old fellow; his hair grew in sparse tufts here and there upon his head and also from his chin. He closed like a wound beneath a scab when he saw what I had done.

"Yes," he replied when I asked if he could provide us with a bucket. "Is it not a pious duty towards pilgrims?"

Then he named his price.

"Pious duty!" I cried. "To fleece the destitute pilgrim?" I could buy the whole Valley. And yet, in my foolish haste to leave Mecca, I had not brought the price of a date stone with me.

The man narrowed his eyes. I think now perhaps the Goddess gave him warning that I was not to be trusted, that we would meet again in fatal circumstances. Whatever grudge he bore, he bore it deeply and was not to be entreated.

We had some food with us, stolen from Umm Tamim's harem, but this old man turned his nose up at it as defiled and refused to take it as payment.

I cursed the fellow, the various demon Gods, the jinn I assured my men were not there to hear me, and the forty generations of the lousy goat whose skin had torn. None of this had any effect. I had only myself to blame for this predicament, myself and my nervous anxiety to witness the miracle of al-Harith's herds.

"The coming salvation of the Arabs," indeed. Well, at that moment, my only hope of salvation from the plague of thirst was to get another bucket as soon as possible. I sent one of my men back on a trusty camel all the long way we had just come to get one and a little spending money, too, just in case. Until he returned, there was nothing to do but sit down under one of al-Uzza's sacred acacia trees and wait, trying to raise spit. And so I did, contemplating the stubborn, patient hills around Nakhlah, cursing their ancient wisdom.

❧

The heat of the afternoon had passed and wound slowly down to the end of the day. I had dozed, I know it. What brought me awake was the sudden twitch of the sand at my feet like the skin of a horse tormented by flies. The unnatural silence of bustards gone to cover hung in the air.

The greatness, the hollowness of the desert had always been like a mother's arms to me. But then, before I'd quite fathomed what this subtle, silent shifting of sand meant, the desert suddenly exploded in all directions about me with a sandstorm.

"Thank God," my heart said. "An excuse at last to do something."

I jumped to my feet, stumbling against the wind, to the spot, not ten paces away, where my mare was hobbled. I hoped to lead her to shelter.

Sand saturated the sky. When I'd stood up I could still see my horse. By the time I'd gone three steps, only the setting sun, a greasy smear in parchment, gave me a hint as to which way was up and which down. My robes tangled with uprooted, *flying thorn about my ankles.*

I staggered far beyond where I knew the mare ought to be. I could not see so much as her wind-whipped tail. I shouted out orders to my man. He had also mysteriously disappeared. My voice swirled around and was lost two steps from where I stood.

And then it took more strength than I had to stay upright against the earth-become-air. It was heavy enough to be like daggers hitting my face and hands, fine enough to enter like choking incense with the air into my lungs. I swaddled my mouth and nose with red silk bands from the end of my turban. Particles forced their way through its weave. I smelled sand, I tasted sand, sand deafened me. On an already-dry throat, the grit was brutal.

So again I was forced into inactivity. An insidious something is doing this to me, I thought. Something that does not use conventional weapons, something which could not be faced in battle like an honorable man.

I sat down where I was, like a coward, with my back to the enemy. I took what cover I could beneath my red headdress and heavy, rough-weave cloak. I waited, near childish tears in my frustration and my anxiety.

The thought blew into my mind: the jinn. Once it entered, I could no more spit it out than the sand gritting between my teeth. Who else could make a horse and my slave simply disappear? To open my mind, like my mouth, was to let more in. The jinn. What else could explain this ability of grains of sand to break their common rules of behavior and fly like winged locusts?

Again, I fiercely squashed the idea. I had been in many sandstorms before and should know better than to think them unnatural. If I could do nothing physically, at least I could control my mind.

And yet shadows moved in the storm. Shadows that looked not so much like wolves or afrits as they looked like nothing. Great yawning pits of nothing, no rock, no sand, no light, nothing. With no one around to verify my existence maybe my horse and my man had not vanished after all. Maybe I had. Maybe I had collided with one of these holes and blinked out of being.

I struggled against these fears. They threatened to overcome me like some giants of ancient times, risen from the mythical, mountain-like graves.

And then, just as quickly as it had roused, the air dropped into stillness again. Shaking myself from the layer of grit like a dog from water, I wiped more grit from my eyes. I spat, I coughed. I looked around at a world unchanged, unmystical as it had ever been. I laughed at my fears as at a nightmare by daylight. Indeed, the thought that entered my head with the first clean breath of air was the Christian monk's words in his rolling voice: "You shall behold the coming salvation of the Arabs." I dismissed the prophecy. If anything is the Arab's salvation, it is the won-

derful calm that comes directly after a blustering show of the almighty power of the voice in a sandstorm.

Did I say the storm left the world completely unchanged? No, not so. There was my horse, just four paces on; there was my man, emerging like a moth, complete with moth-grey dust on his face and hair, from his cocoon bundle of cloaks. But there also, across the well from us, was pitched a tent. It stood as natural and as unremarkable as if it had been there all the time.

It was not our tent. Men alone do not need tents. A tent bespeaks women, and women always bespeak a tent not too far distant.

How did the tent (and the women) come to be there? No one but the stingy caretaker had been in the Valley when the storm began—was that not so? And he had hidden behind his mudbricks. Tents are not pitched in a storm. Women have not the strength and slaves not the lust for punishment that such a task would entail. Even pitched tents usually blow away. Best to leave the bundles of black felt tied to the camels' sides and huddle there oneself until the whole thing passes.

Or had the wind full of tiny blades pushed me and horse and slave to a spot within a mirage where it wanted us to go?

The storm, thank Hubal, had passed; I would not entertain fantasies of spirits. I could think that, as has been known to happen, the storm had passed by one side of the Valley while only a bow's shot away the land had remained completely unaffected. These tent builders had swiftly gone to work while we had been suffering blindness and confusion.

God knew best the meaning of this. Whatever it was, I was so bewildered from my battle with the wind and the sand, and busy seeing to our animals, that the party in the tent made the first overtures. A slave strode his way around the well to bid me welcome as if I had not been in the Valley first. He informed me that his master was not at home, but that his mistress, in the master's name, bade me come and be her guest.

The world had not quite settled from its tantrum as I answered the invitation. Stirrings lingered in the sand as if in warning. The sun had set during the storm, dropped beneath the hills of distant Mecca. A void rose in its wake, drawing wind after it like spilled water drawn into the insatiable ground. Not the violent wind of the storm, but a breathing wind skidding sand across the bare stone in whispers. It rustled in the dried acacia. For some reason, I remembered the dying breaths of my old grandmother, those last desperate attempts to cling to life.

A single whirlwind danced about the corners of the tent as we approached. My man made signs against evil.

As we drew closer to the tent, the pattern of stripes woven into the side curtains told me: Taghlibi. My heart began to pound as I thought of what that might mean. I had killed enough of the prime of that tribe surrounding their sacred white camel to blood-feud away my sons and all my brothers.

I hesitated only a moment. She had sent her servant without knowing who I was in an honorable display of her tribe's hospitality. Her one word of welcome was a sure and strong immunity against her husband's wrath. I had the three days of a guest's sanctity.

But plotting my future was interrupted by a glaring inconsistency in the present. The trappings on the riding and pack camels crouched about this Taghlibi tent were of the sons of Tamim. Indeed, some of the animals I knew from long association. Had there been a raid? Mutammim and Malik had said nothing about any raid. Or— Such a confusion of emblems was also the natural inconsistency that comes of a woman weaving her own tent in the pattern she had learned as a child, whatever her husband's affiliation. If she were powerful enough to do so.

Only one son of Tamim I knew had taken himself a wife of their great enemies, the Taghlib. A wife won in battle.

And before my heart could throb again, she herself passed from the shadow of the tent into the fading light. She held a great bowl of her camels' milk, frothing and warm, towards us.

Her best dress hung from the center pole of the tent as a sign of especial welcome. My brow heated with recognition beneath the ruins of a previous garment, red silk and now sand-blasted.

"Strength to you, O cousin of my master," she greeted me with more brightness than even form required. She didn't seem at all surprised to see me. A frisson of jinn breath skittered like sand down my back

"God give you strength, O wife of my cousin," I replied, grateful for the reflex of ceremony.

My woman from the well.

18

I recalled my youth and was filled with
longing as her camels set out at evening,
while the doves rose, hovering in the air
above us like swords unsheathed.
— The qasidah of Amr ibn Kulthum

In spite of her married wife's veils, I recognized her. Her eyes were the same: hazed and yet all-seeing, twin wells reflecting the glory of heaven without compromise. A yank of fear assaulted my stomach; I was falling to the bottom of those wells with an eternal fall. I could not stop the result of my own cumbersome weight intruding itself upon her airiness.

By my life, with what calm she ushered us in and bade us be seated! Was not my heart beating enough to shake both of us? By God, what control she had over her voice (and her voice over me) as she spoke the niceties of welcome!

"Your husband is at at-Ta'if, my cousin?" I asked.

"Yes. He trades his surplus flocks for their good wheat and fruit, al-Uzza bless his prospects."

"You are not with him?"

"He sent me away, here to take refuge in Nakhlah."

"Sent you away? Why?" How could any man bear to do such a thing, I wondered?

"The people of at-Ta'if—suspect his flock's success."

Reason dawned clear to me. "Suspect it's your doing rather than his own superior herdsmanship. They suspect witchcraft."

"Please." Her veils hid all but her deep eyes, and even these she averted at my words. "You are thirsty, my guest. Please, drink."

And I did, still trying to meet her eyes over the rim of the skin bowl. In some passion very close to jealousy, he had sent her away. I would have done the same to her. To have such a woman walking through the streets of at-Ta'if, pulling every *gaze after her, if not for lust then for desire of her power. Such a woman I would sink so deep in a walled harem—if she were mine. But she was not mine, I had to remind myself. Very difficult, as the salty drink, at blood heat, cleansed my throat of sand and warmed my insides.*

I understood no more of the matter. Even this she did not tell me in so many words, did she? That would have been a criticism of her husband and her master. Few women would express such things to another man.

And she has a master, another, not me, I reminded myself.

Still, the phrases she used were chosen like the colored threads worked on the border of her best dress. The garment moved on the tent pole as if alive in the early evening air above our heads. The skill of the born poet larded her speech. I saw a landscape with every word.

I realized I had never heard her speak before. Not with this ease and naturalness. All women gain confidence when they become mistresses of their own tents, I thought. When their menfolk are away. And when people suddenly find themselves related by marriage, they are no longer strangers. Perhaps her husband had spoken of me to her. What had he told her? I was anxious to know. Good or bad?

And yet I had the sense that her ease was more . . .

I found myself thinking of the small, hollow, stone mounds men build to trap hyenas and foxes: The predator creeps in to eat the meat set on the cozy inside, only to have the roof tumble down and crush the life from him. Was this a trap? I looked sharply at her, trying to pierce the veils for a clue. I had killed many sons of Taghlib at Dhu Qar, her kinsmen. She beguiled me into her revenge . . .

She has other cases against me, too. This marriage was only a glorified slavery. Al-Harith lacked so much of what makes a man—see how no cradle hung from the poles of this tent. Reason enough for a woman's vengeance.

Let her murder me, I thought. Most men die for less just causes.

Al-Harith's wife smiled until her cheeks pushed up her eyes into a double smile, as if she knew my mind and said to me, "There. Rest on that thought, that thought alone of all your fears: the inadequacy of my man."

But my emotions had carried me away with them. What she actually said next had nothing to do with her husband or with any of the fanciful alleyways my mind wandered in.

"And how do you come to be at Nakhlah yourself, my cousin?" she asked simply.

I heard you were in at-Ta'if. I was travelling, like the she-camel with painful dugs home to her calf, to see you, your miracles here in the desert.

No, I couldn't say such words. I'd rather cut out my own tongue.

The predicament with the bucket? I'd die of shame. But my mind was so full of her presence, I hadn't come up with any alibi to spare me that shame.

While I stumbled for words, my man spoke up beside me: "The prankish jinn of the well have torn our bucket."

"My own fault," I confessed. "Childish impatience."

"By the prankish jinn of this well," our hostess said, her eyes crinkling with a smile again. "Now, before the light goes, I shall mend your bucket."

Already color had washed from the landscape leaving only grey and black. But Bint Zura did not hesitate. She quickly patched the rent with rawhide and a bit of thong. Then she called up her slaves. Al-Harith had slaves! She set them to drawing from Nakhlah's holy well, first for us and afterwards for their own animals, to fill the many skins she had. With both our mended bucket and hers, the task took only half as long. When I protested that we should wait for light, she had torches of dry acacia brought. When I protested that the men were tired, she set her own hand to it. Her steady patience required more of the self than the brute strength needed to topple a great and ancient standing stone.

By God, the sight of her by torchlight! She burned brighter. When I close my eyes, the image she cast in the night still burns upon my eyelids, leaping black upon the red blood vessels. Her hips, banded by a tight, wide girdle, caught the light away from the darkness of her slender waist. They were like the curves of a vessel, just pulled from the coppersmith's fire, glowing like forged metal, firm and hard. But if I could touch them without my fingers turning to cinders, I would find that firmness but an illusion. In the heat, her hips would be pliable, nearly liquid. And hollow, a rich, open vessel.

As the last of the animals drank by torch- and moonlight, Bint Zura took a small handful of grain from her girdle. She sprinkled it around the well. "For the prankish jinn," she whispered and smiled when she found me watching her.

This devotion drew the sulky keeper of the shrine out of his four walls. He was Dubayya, a son of the ancient family of shrine guardians, the Sulaym. When she gave proof of an honest pilgrimage, with no mockery or rudeness such as I had shown earlier, he turned cordial enough. Opposed to my first impression, I now found him wise in the ancient and reverend lore of his tribe. He did not even seem to be as ugly and scabby as I had thought him at first. Bint Zura radiated; anything she shone upon waxed attractive.

Al-Harith's wife pressed a real Persian gold piece into old Dubayya's hand for his trouble. "Thanks be to al-Uzza," she told him, "great prosperity has come to my master's flocks. But, alas, my own womb has been unable to meet that fruitfulness these four full years. For this reason we have made the pilgrimage to at-Ta'if to pray for a—well, my husband wants a son, of course."

"Of course," Dubayya grinned and nodded. This was his business.

"At-Ta'if is such a fruitful land," she continued, "where wheat or palm or pomegranates leap from the ground. Shrines to the Great Three, the givers of increase, stand there. But even so far away as our native pastures, I had heard of this spot in Nakhlah, sacred to al-Uzza, the Strong, the Powerful, the Quickener of Seed. She of the black Ka'ba stone into which sin sinks and returns to life. And so I came."

The old man nodded and smiled again. He promised, come morning, to show her all the ancient rites by which women coming to Nakhlah had made heaven work its magic in their favor since time began.

"Is there not something to be done by night?" Bint Zura's tone was so subtle, the man did not realize she was second-guessing the sacred knowledge women usually paid extra for. "A certain spot where one should sleep beneath the open sky to work the true efficaciousness."

"Yes, indeed," Dubayya said, and pointed in the direction where I had last seen my horse and camel before night obliterated them. "Fifty paces over there is a small hill and, just beyond, a low, cradle-like valley. That is the spot."

Bint Zura seemed to mark it well in her mind, though who can ever tell what a woman behind a veil might be noticing?

"But I do not advise you to sleep under the open sky tonight," Dubayya warned.

Bint Zura nodded solemnly at his caution. Earrings whispered against her neck beneath her veil as she did so.

"Why do you say that, O son of Sulaym?" I asked. My man and I had intended, in all good faith, to spend the night in the open.

"Where do you come from, man, that you do not know? That you haven't seen?" was the reply I received. "From at-Ta'if in all directions, from north and south, from sundown to sunrise, they have seen it. Wonders, ominous portents in the sky. Stars falling from their spheres and great blazes of light, like streaks of fire, with tails like the thoroughbred mares of the jinn."

No, we had seen nothing like this in Mecca. Granted, we live between four walls and a roof in Mecca. During the month of pilgrimage, the blaze of torches and bonfires all but obliterates the sky's night lights from dusk to dawn. Still, messengers from the desert would have brought the word—yet I had heard nothing.

"Muhammad makes them godless in Mecca," was Dubayya's verdict.

I protested that I certainly never listened to such a madman, but my protest was half-hearted. I was busy looking out of the tent to try to verify the wild tale. I saw only the sky as I had always known it, with stars so placid and calm, they seemed to be half-shut, like eyes heavy and drowsing with sleep.

"No, no sign of the wonder yet tonight," Dubayya assured me. "You would know it if you saw it. Perhaps the sacrifices have satisfied heaven's anger indeed.

"The people of at-Ta'if have been so frightened by these signs," the guardian continued. "They slaughtered one third of all their flocks, both male and female, to appease the lowering sky. 'All day they lobbed about hacked meat and fat like fringes of twisted silk.'" I knew he quoted the poet. "Milk and cheese are now such rare commodities in town."

"From a distance, it smelled to heaven of death, unburied offal, uneaten meat become inedible with maggots," Bint Zura concurred.

I saw easily how in such a place, a man like al-Harith, with prodigiously fecund flocks, might be the object of dread. I got the impression, however, that al-Harith's wife, when she returned, would manage to be received in the community as something of a deliverer.

Was this the "coming salvation of the Arabs"?

"And yet," Bint Zura said thoughtfully, "perhaps these signs are not signs of evil at all, but of great good. My mother just told me it is so."

The kahinah, then, was not dead. I flexed my right arm, feeling it still jeopardized as it had been since my earliest childhood when I had offered its strength in exchange for al-Harith's life—and then cheated. What else had her mother told her?

"If something is awe-full," Bint Zura continued, "it is not necessarily disastrous. The Gods are to be feared by lowly mortals such as ourselves. Such fear, rather than being harmful, can be our salvation. Like the jinn, the Gods may be a power for good if they are rightly approached."

"Can you tell us the meaning of these signs, then?" I asked her. "Your mother . . ." I hesitated. At this point, I wanted the old man back in his hut. I didn't like him eavesdropping on such a conversation.

"No. My mother taught me that if I could fathom all the things of the spirits, then they would cease to be of help to me. We should rejoice to be witnesses and servants of such wonderful powers. Just so the herdsman may rejoice to be in the service of a great and just sharif, a woman may rejoice to serve her husband and master, when he is kind and generous."

Bint Zura's next words were a leap away from the somber, painful subject she had been pursuing. She ordered her slaves to hurry up with the roasting, for she had had a young ram sacrificed. So we feasted that night. Then, satisfied in belly but nothing else, I rose and stood in the tent doorway, studying the stars, dull as they burned through the lingering sand from the storm. I had wagered my arm to the jinn but withdrawn it. Did that mean I would never see wonders?

19

O night, you deny me greatly
The love I loved early in the day.
Those black-white eyes, if they gazed at you,
Would cast upon you a sorcerer's spell.
Is she jinniyyah? Is she human?
Or between the two, a thing more majestic still?
    —A poem of Bashshar ibn Burd
    (died c. 784 AD)

Animals slept. Men feasted on roasted lamb flavored with wild onion and other herbs, delicious but strange. They sopped up the juices with fingertips full of boiled burghul and gossiped until the night and full bellies made them sleep as well.

A camel saddle cradled my head. My mind murmured, drowsed, started awake, then drowsed again. It was comfortable now, my mind, lulled, satiated. I assured it that it need work no longer that night. After all the sandstorm emotions I had set it through since I'd first spoken to my milk brother Malik back home in Mecca, my mind seemed grateful for the leave.

Al-Harith's wife sat still where she had been all night, spinning. She had eaten nothing; even a male host eats but little with his guests. I expected soon to see her set down her distaff, pick up the tray of leftovers and retire with it to the harem. Indeed, sometimes as I drowsed, I dreamed that she had done just that. I dreamed she slept alone and faithful to her husband and master on the other side of the curtain. She had fulfilled her duties so as to bring him shame neither for niggardliness nor for immodest behavior in his absence. In the morning, she would leave at first light to return to her people with life-giving water.

That was how things should be, how my mind, craving sleep and dreams, had decided it must be. Life is so much easier when its rules are obeyed. Safer, more restful to think that her effect on me was a youthful infatuation. Good food and a night's rest could make me outgrow it. Come morning, we could take a friendly, yet politely cool, leave of one another. At some future time, some future watering well, we could meet by chance with the ease of any folk related by marriage and fosterage: "Strength to you, O my cousin."

Yet when I opened my eyes, I found she still had not gone behind the curtain. She sat immovable as ever by my side, so close I could have reached out and touched her knee if I'd dared. And she was not yet relaxing with sleep, but sat very straight, taking so little space that only by standing could she have covered less. She seemed to be listening intently for something. I listened for a while, too, but heard nothing save the usual night sounds of a camp in the desert: the cough of a herdsman breathing camel dung smoke; the frenzied but brief yap of a dog thrilling to new territory; the grunts and snores of the camels, crouched like a range of rolling hills outside; the screech of a hunting owl.

She must be hungry. I dismissed Bint Zura's curious rigidness. I was too tired, too contented to wish to engage any spirit, even her highly tantalizing one, in battle.

But the unwatched direction is always the source of the most devastating raid, as they say; it comes when one refuses to expect it.

❧

Later, when Rayah was telling Sitt Sameh what the imprisoned eunuch had read to her as best she could remember, her mother stopped her at this point with a touch on her knee.

"He won't get this part right."

They spoke in the dark, because recitation needed no lamp. The whish of spinning, the drop of the weight still accompanied the tale.

"And my Rayah should know how such spells work: peeled wands, knots on the threads."

Rayah could tell the spinning had stopped for a moment. Probably Sitt Sameh circled her head once with the thread, the traditional way to measure work; thirty-five rounds enough for one tent warp. Even that didn't need a light. Only the fact that Rayah never heard a puff of breath from her mother assured her that Sitt Sameh wasn't working spells that very moment.

"Herbs in the lamb broth," Sitt Sameh went on, her voice becoming a chant as she listed love herbs. "Arugula—Ayesha's plant. Hair of a fox's tail—for that beast's cunning. Sparrow's brains, the bones of a toad eaten by ants, her own menstrual blood, her urine, the lamb's testicles, musk—for the odor of that small deer in rut. Those were for him.

"For herself, she had already eaten licorice, *samh* seeds, honey, and sesame cooked into a halwah. She knew another chance at this might never come her way.

"And her chant, which the Conqueror, half-asleep, cannot have heard, or certainly remembered, was a recitation of her own story turned to poetry, on this order:

"Riding like rain upon the white cloud
of the sacred camel of the sons of Taghlib,
I never should have been defeated,
for the power was with me.
But Allat willed that I had come only lately
to exercise it.
I had not the confidence I must have for such work.

Four full years away from my father
and his dead and deadening God,
hearing my mother,
watching the young rams leap
upon the fruitful young ewes to my touch—
Have these things brought full strength upon me?
I fear, stunted by my own mistrust,
I have grown as much as I ever shall.

The son of Suwaid is kind and good.
Yet I curse him for his keeping me captive.
He will never flow with the water
Water I need to quench my thirst.
I shall never fill the true measure
of my creation with him.
Stir up one, O my Mistress,
O my Masters of the depths,
One who for wanton spilling of Taghlibi blood
owes seed of his own to me.
One who will find greater hardship in this life
than he ever would in death."

When she heard the spindle whirl again, Rayah picked up the Conqueror's tale from the parchments once more.

❧

I woke again. The stars between the slash of tent curtain had shifted a little closer to midnight. Bint Zura was speaking now, but to whom I could not say. The priest Dubayya had returned to his little hut. My man was asleep and could not answer her. As for me, I could not understand what she meant to say, so I took it as part of a dream, something to be passively observed, forgotten come daylight.

By my life! I wish I had paid more attention to what she said. It was a sort of enchantment, you see. Indeed, much of it rhymed and had a singsong meter, but all of that I have forgotten by now. And then, instead of the spindle, I saw that the wool she worked was her own hair. She undid it as she chanted, taking off the veils. She reached up and undid the single braid on her forehead, working loose the strands that many days and much grease had hardened and knotted. She rubbed it, fluffed it, and combed it with her fingers until the stiffness was broken. She continued to sit, combing it down across breast and knees in the coppering firelight. Black magic indeed.

By the time I had fetched enough sense up from sleep to realize this, a most unearthly sound bolted me upright. It began as a thin, high-pitched whistle which grew until I thought my head would split. It ended in a frightful explosion, as if half a mountain had fallen from its perch into the valley below.

"God of my fathers," I gasped in the thin air of first waking. I had been unaware of how deeply I had been asleep. "What was that?"

"I do not know," Bint Zura, by my side, replied. The quaver of fear in her voice seemed natural and, if I had any suspicions brought on by her curious monologue, this was enough to dispel them. Other things can cause a quaver in a woman's voice: excitement, exertion, anticipation. Desire. But I took no time to consider these alternatives.

The unearthly sound came again.

"One of the men must have fallen in the well in the dark," I told myself aloud as I scrambled to my feet. "Someone is drowning."

"Perhaps." Bint Zura responded with enough conviction to encourage me to go out.

I didn't stop to take a brand from the dying fire to see by. I never stopped to wonder that the sound did not rouse any of the other men sleeping about me. I thought I was the defending hero.

I found the well silent and undisturbed. The unearthly sound came again, from beyond. Wolves, was my next suspicion. I hurried out to see to my horse. The animals were awake, snorting with fear, but what frightened them I could not see. I walked to the top of a hill beyond and surveyed all Nakhlah, but without result. I began to feel foolish and out of place, alone and awake in this peaceful night. Perhaps the whistle and explosion had been nothing but the echo of a fading dream.

Then Bint Zura stepped out from behind the horse. She had been there all along. As if she were the moon come out from behind a cloud, her presence seemed to brighten the landscape. At the same time, it turned that brightness ashen as the burned-out remains of a great holocaust.

I suppose I started at her appearance, for her words of greeting were: "You are afraid, O cousin of my master."

"The night plays tricks on us, O wife of my cousin."

"On such a night, they say, the jinn tribe comes to their well for water. Women dare not sew on such a night lest their needles inadvertently pierce the waterskins of the Air-Borne Ones."

I laughed, hoping it would ease her and consequently myself. "Virtuous women should be safe in their tents on such a night—sleeping beneath the protection of the tent-pole charms."

Bint Zura responded by quoting a verse of ancient poetry: "'The promise of night is spread with butter that melts come daybreak.'"

Again I tried the tactic of a light-hearted countenance. "Those are the words of a poet so ancient, man has forgotten his name."

Bint Zura's only veil now was her hair. She answered my laughter with a smile of her own, but it carried little lightness with it. "He never had a name," she said. "Those words fell unmade from the sky like a meteor."

Even as she said the word, one meteor streaked across the southern sky.

"Whoever wills, whoever dares, may gather and use them," she continued.

"Must one understand them to use them?" I asked. "For I swear by Lord Hubal I understand but little . . ."

She did not speak at once, but seemed to be thinking.

And this thought was enough to silence me.

At last she shook her head. "I do not understand it."

"No?"

"I do not understand by what burning force and by what ingredients those words were ignited, united, and fused. It is enough to have a sense of them on my lips, as in my fingertips. I pick them out, feel in the darkness their smooth surface and the solid comfort of their heart."

I shivered. "Aren't you afraid to be out in this night?" I asked her. "What about the strange lights they have seen in the sky in at-Ta'if? And have you never heard stories of women alone in the desert ravished by the jinn, forced to bear their black-souled offspring as was our mother Eve? Such women, the poet says, 'have no spouse but the wind.'"

"Aren't you afraid," she replied, "to think of men such as our father Adam? The demon's womenfolk came to him with breasts so pendulous they could throw them *over their shoulders. They commanded him to beget. When he would not, they beat him with whips of fire until he would."*

"Ah!" I cried.

For suddenly the whole southern sky was a sheet of falling sparks. No wonder the people of at-Ta'if had slaughtered their flocks, if they had seen nights like this.

Every falling star, taught the Messenger of God, eternal blessings on him, is a jinni cast out of heaven.

I stopped trying to fathom what she said. Her words echoed, as if they came from the depths of a narrow-sided well. By my life, and indeed, my life hung in the balance there, I had come out seeking some waylaid fellow, only to find that it was I, myself, who had been ensnared.

The whole sky whirled overhead like a chariot wheel. The stars, pegs of molten iron studding the wheel, blurred with their racing. The whistles came again, two, three pitches together, one whistle starting before the last one was finished. Such a sound one hears racing against the wind on a very fast horse. Sparks continued to shoot through the sky over my back. Impacts thudded all around, like giant hailstones imbedding themselves in the soft sand of the Valley. Imbedding in my flesh.

If only I had been able to catch a glimpse of some firm reality about me, I might have saved myself. But I was no longer my own master. To a constraint-hating man, that is as much as saying "I give in" to death. I could not will myself to look else-where than at her hair, which she shook until the light caught in it whirled like the night sky overhead. So had she ridden, possessed, possessing, upon the white camel in the sacred litter on the Day of Dhu Qar. The tresses so thick, they took two hands to encircle. I swept them back and up into my palms, just to see, and the moment I touched them, I was entranced. Hanzala ibn Thalaba's leather thongs never gripped me so tightly.

The rope of her hair let me down into a bottomless well. And in the well, lumps of fire fell upon my back.

Her hair, her power over me, the memory of the qubbah, *these things must have pleased her. She stretched out upon the soft sand, her head pillowed by what nature had so lavishly given her. She shut her eyes with delight.*

The spell on me did not break when her great all-seeing eyes closed under their long lashes and heavy kohl. I watched, transfixed, as she bared first her arms to the soft armpits, and then her breasts, downy-soft and raised as twin white camel calves.

With one finger, like a planet moving through the constellations, Bint Zura traced the tattoo marks on wrist and arm, then shoulders, belly, breast. I followed that touch, first with my own fingers then with my lips as she recited the various figures' names and meanings in a deep, dark woman's spell: wild rue here, asphodel blossom, cross of the sun, dark, protective eye of a Goddess.

I was a slave, her thrall. So must women feel when they are stolen from their tents and made the prisoners and concubines of war. Indeed, Bint Zura must have been made to feel this way by my hand, ravished by my doing and yet not of my do-ing at Dhu Qar. Here was truly an eye for an eye, revenge taken according to strict desert law. I grasped the thin leather body belt about her hips as a coward with a sword at his throat pleads for mercy on his life.

I remembered a more original sensation: that of waking in the predawn dark of my milk mother's tent. I would wake to hear her churning the day's butter. I felt my body, no longer a burden to me, no longer mine to command or to be responsible for. I was in her hands—my milk mother's then, Bint Zura's now—having my body and mind swung, swung with gentle rhythm like the butter skin from the tent poles. Suspended in the air, I lay half-asleep, stupid with sleep, drawn out of myself like the soul in a dream.

I think there was pain as her famine grabbed me in my tenderest part, branded me. Or the falling stars. I do not remember. My helplessness shamed me, but I do not remember that, either. Women, I suppose, must do the same thing: forget a lot, until we men tend to blame it as stupidity. But if it were not so, they could not waken and look the world in the face the next morning. Memory, like a well-armed soldier, wields a shield as well as a sword.

The sun was already letting its blood upon the eastern horizon when memory withdrew its shield, and I awoke. Exposed on a stretch of churned sand, I heard the ghru-grug, ghru-grug of a butter churn being swung, full of the morning milk. Somehow I rallied the strength to rediscover my clothes, to cross the camp, past the camels struggling to their feet, the yapping dogs. I confronted the sound that had taken the best of me in the night.

"A morning of good things," greeted my bursting into the harem half of the tent. "O my cousin, a morning of light."

Bint Zura didn't speak these words. She continued, quiet and veiled, to swing the skin. Her husband, al-Harith ibn Suwaid, had returned triumphant from at-Ta'if some time during the night. The taint of witchcraft lifted by the Banu Thaqif, his herds sold at great profit, those left to him watered and hale.

The moment I managed to catch my breath, I saw that the young fool suspected nothing. Indeed, he was flamboyant and expansive as if he had gotten the better of his wife in a welcome-home tumble. Perhaps he had. I opened my mouth to say something, to accuse, to protest. But who would believe my tale? Death is the fruit reaped by both adulteress and lover when their crimes are known. The life and death of my own little first-born daughter had surely taught me this.

"Strength to this house of hair and its shadow this day," I murmured in formal reply.

Al-Harith led me around to the men's portion of the tent, then accepted a matfuof dates and a bowl of fresh butter reached over the curtain by anonymous hands.

"My humble hospitality, cousin," he said as he presented it.

I knew full well the imprint of that thumb that had served as a ladle to press the butter into the bowl. By God, was it not even then imprinted upon my own flesh, pressed about my loins, affecting the very carriage of my shoulders for all the world to see?

Al-Harith scooped into the soft yellow cream with the point of a date and handed it to me. I could not insult his budding abilities as host. Another and another he offered as he frothed with news of the town and of his lately gained wealth. No mark of that beloved thumb remained. Frustrated, close to tears, I remembered the words of that night: "Night is spread with butter that melts come daybreak."

"Cousin, there are singed patches on your fine robe. Did you lie too near the fire?" Al-Harith brushed at the ashy circles, loosing the smell of burnt wool within the tent.

"I guess I did," was the only reply I could find. I clenched my teeth as his action jarred the blistered flesh of my back beneath.

Later that day, before I rode back to Mecca with a heavy and confused heart, I returned to the little valley Dubayya ibn Sulaym had said was a source of deep fertility. All over the place, I found small bits of black stone, burnt as if having been thrown from a crucible, bits of star fallen and sunk into the yielding earth. I picked up a handful of them, as many as I could find, and took them with me. I had to prove to myself I had not dreamed when heaven fell and planted itself in a womb on earth while the jinn smoked and whistled through the air.

"And that is the origin of your sword?" My scribe looks as if the meat of his kebab were tainted. "The blade known as the Sword of God? The sword forged by Rudainah of Bahrain?"

"Forged of heaven stones. In very deed," I reply, and help myself to a bunch of grapes. "And the origins of my scars."

Then I have to put the grapes down and lift up my shirt to show him the only wounds I ever got on my back: pits imprinted in the pattern of a woman's fingertips gripping in passion. Every other wound I took head on.

20

بسـ̣ـوام الرحمْلايهِ

Nothing benefits more from a long term of imprisonment than the tongue.
—Ibn al-Qayyim

Something scuffed in the sand around the corner of the Camp of Diocletian. Rayah scrambled down off a block of ruined stone.

"Hist. Guards," she warned.

Inside, Abd Allah the eunuch snuffed the lamp he'd been reading by. Rayah had no time to get the pages of his manuscript back. She sank to the ground and froze at the base of the ruins that served as the eunuch's prison.

The guards came in a pair. They stood, watching, listening, a stone's throw from where she crouched. The sharif had chosen big men for the night watch of his prisoner. Their dual bulk seemed to block out half the spangled sky. The spearheads held trembling at the ready caught starlight and were poised to catch her first, before even eyes could.

Rayah worked to still her ragged breathing. She'd first set out to come to the remote spot where the scribe was kept by daylight. But she'd felt the disapproving glance of everyone when she did: everyone from the women at the well to the ploughman and his oxen pursued by dust demons as they prepared the weary earth for winter wheat. So she had pulled her veil close about her and returned home, helping in the kitchen until night fell.

Then, armed with a lamp, the manuscript—although only the next handful of pages, easier to carry and to conceal—and a few fresh loaves under her arm, she had felt no real threat in the empty streets. The veil of the night granted safety.

"Ah, Little Blue Eyes." The eunuch's warm greeting and then his sonorous voice as he read his master's account made her forget even the prison and the danger he was in. As for her own danger—only now did it strike her.

The thump of blood in her ears must surely make the guards find her. It almost made her deaf to their words, hushed and low to each other.

"You heard it too, didn't you?" asked one.

"Yes, a whispering. Coming from over here," replied his companion.

"We could split up and have a look."

Rayah shrank lower. If they looked, they would surely find her.

The second man thought about this, twisting his spear so that the light on the head winked. "I think it's gone," he finally decided.

"It isn't gone." The first man shook his head; he was certain. "It lives here. Why can't the sharif keep his prisoners someplace else? A strong room in his own house, maybe. Where he keeps his boxes of spice and his fine carpets. I would guard the sexless one there. Everyone knows ruins are the haunts of—" The swallow he had to make to get even the respectful, skirting words out was audible. "Fire Folk."

"Maybe the sharif means that our prisoner should die of fright. That would save us a lot of trouble."

"The fellow has no balls. He might well die of fright in this place." The first man shivered then pretended he was merely cold. "Let's go back to the fire."

His companion agreed. "Save us all the trouble of dragging his secrets from him before we take his head off as well."

The guards were gone. Rayah tried again to bring her breathing back to normal. She realized now what her eagerness to hear the next part of the Conqueror's tale had blinded her to. She wasn't as safe here in the dark with Abd Allah as she'd told herself she was. Abd Allah himself stood in danger of death. The guards had said as much. By coming to him, she had joined him in that danger. Worse, she found herself on the edge of the pit filled with the jinn, those spirits of smoke and darkness.

"Rayah?" The wind seemed to blow her name.

Or was it the jinn? The thought that the Fire Ones knew her name made her gasp with fear.

"Rayah." Again.

The guards were gone. "Yes?" The word trembled in her throat.

"Little Blue Eyes?" Abd Allah whispered through the chink in the wall.

"Yes, *ustadh*."

"Are you still there? Have they gone?"

Rayah realized she'd been sitting stunned. Now, at Abd Allah's voice, she roused herself. He was the captive here; she'd heard the guards threaten his life, but she knew nothing to help. Her presence, if discovered, could only make things worse for him.

"I'm here," she assured him. "They're gone. But I should be going, too."

"Of course. It's late. And without an ember to relight the lamp, I can't read any more."

He must be cold at night, sleeping on the ground in the ruin. "Next time, I'll bring a blanket," she told him.

In reply, the roll of manuscript pages appeared in the starlight over the edge of the chink.

"Won't you keep the manuscript here?" she asked.

"No, child. It would never do for our friend the sharif to find words of the disgraced Conqueror here with me."

"It isn't true, what the sharif said."

"What's that?"

"Khalid ibn al-Walid—wasn't he, I mean, blessings on him—wasn't he a champion of Islam?"

"He was. But you should know, child, there are mirages in the desert. The Folk of the Land like to play with human beings and, *al-hamdulillah*, God allows it. People see things that aren't really there. Here. The manuscript. Keep it safe."

Rayah promised she would, but she remembered to add, "If it be God's will." She'd begun to doubt she could. More, she wanted to keep Abd Allah safe. Now that she'd seen how he was restrained, however, she feared that would be impossible.

Abd Allah, too, seemed to have resigned himself to his fate. "And you, Little One. I think you can read the rest yourself, without me." As if he would not be around to read another word.

"Oh, no. I couldn't . . ."

"You found the place where we left off very well," the eunuch reminded her.

So she had. She had forgotten, or rather, not noticed how easily it had come. Because she didn't want to have charmed words without the man who'd tamed them to parchment.

"Your Quranic teacher has taught you well. This is the same language."

The eunuch did not seem to begrudge Sitt Umm Ali this skill, even though her nephew's marriage was responsible for his present dangerous situation.

"And though she can't read, desert Arabic is your mother's native tongue, too," Abd Allah went on. "She can help you."

Rayah felt this as a loss of innocence, responsibility she hadn't seen coming, forced upon her. Never again could she look at a line of writing in Arabic and not know what it meant.

With that ability came the inkling that the stiff parchment Abd Allah handed her was what the sharif really would want, if he knew of its existence. He would want it more than Abd Allah's body in a prison to torture, more than the eunuch's life. For the pages contained the soul of a dead man, a man who had been most powerful in the world, the Conqueror. That was a life worth capturing and racking into the shape of one's own liking. Or suppressing it to flatter those who had the power now. She didn't know yet what was on the sharif's mind. She didn't even know all that the Conqueror had told his scribe yet. But she knew she needed to know. It was part of herself, and who she must be in the new world.

"So go, my child," the eunuch said, as if they would never see each other again. "And God go with you."

Two steps away from the chink in the stone, Rayah knew the terror of her burden. She missed the lamp most of all as she carried it unlit with the last of its oil so Aunt Adilah wouldn't miss it on her sconce. The night desert was cold. She wrapped her veil close about her, grateful for its warmth. Still her teeth chattered on the sandy grit between them. An owl, hunting, gave its mournful cry, and something squeaked as it died within the talons. She could see nothing but stars.

A glow to her right drew her to it, a counter to these terrors. It turned out, however, to be the guards' fire, around which they huddled at the front of the old fortress. Trying to step away from that, her footing left the solid path. She stumbled and felt herself slide, then fall. The lamp dropped from her hands and cracked on stone. Rather than save herself, however, she clung to the leather-wrapped pages under her arms. She landed hard. The pain in her knee made her open her mouth to cry out.

The guards started at the crack of pottery. Their large shadows rose against the firelight. If she screamed—

A sudden presence beside her squeezed the scream to dryness in her throat. Yet, comfort wrapped in the presence, too, so much so, she imagined at first that Abd Allah must have managed to escape and come to help her.

But it was not the eunuch. It was a boy. About her age, his skin was the color of smoke and his dark hair curled like burning greenwood. His eyes were coals and his presence hot and cold by turns. She saw all this because a smoky blue glow haloed him. He carried no lamp. The light exuded from his own pores. He laid a finger to her lips. Its touch was like flame, so the chattering stopped along with the desire to cry. She breathed.

"Hush," the smoky lips mouthed, blowing a sweet incense upon her.

The guards drew nearer, their spears ready. Though her knee and the tears in the corners of her eyes stung, Rayah kept quiet.

"Maryam, mother of Isa, bless me."

One guard asked the old blessing, the other the newer one: "In the Name of God the Merciful . . ."

One sprinkled the contents of his waterskin on the ground, an offering. The boy left her side and flew thirstily to catch the drops. They seemed to hiss as they fell—right through him—to the parched, dark ground. The guards retreated to their fire.

The boy was back at her side in a moment. "Let's go," he said without moving his lips that she could see. "Before the offering dries."

His glow led her wordlessly back to the path and all the way to where the alley to the turpentine sellers' house bent away from the straight, high road. No more words passed between them, only the quiet, comforting, leading presence.

She turned to enter the old ladies' house next to hers. She would climb to their roof as the women slept and so come to her own roof and Sitt Sameh in her little room. First, however, the boy spoke to her.

"Rayah." He said her name. His voice was like the passing of a Christian procession, bells and swinging censors. Something other—and very, very old. They were of another language, the ancient language of the desert. The jinn did know her name.

Then: "We should marry, you and I."

She couldn't possibly have heard him right. "Good night," she told him, and slipped through the door she'd left unlatched coming out.

Rayah found Sitt Sameh waiting for her, spinning by feel alone in the dark as she watched and waited to worship the moon as it rose.

"Did you see him, child?"

It took Rayah a moment to understand that her mother meant the eunuch, not the boy.

"How is he?"

"Well enough, Lady. Wait until I tell you what he read. And he says I could try to read it myself now—" And the boy? Should she tell her mother about the boy?

"I do not like how he seems to have given up on this life already." Sitt Sameh, who never seemed to have cared for anything in her life, not even her own child, cared for this eunuch scribe.

"Shall I start the tale now?"

"No. I have some news you should hear first, daughter."

Rayah felt the chatter return to her teeth at the tone in her mother's words. Exhaustion hit her suddenly, too. She sank down on the rug to sit knee to knee with the older woman.

Sitt Sameh set aside her spindle and folded her hands in her lap as if to still them. "Tonight was not a good night to go to our friend Abd Allah—if ever any time is good."

"Yes, Mother?"

"Who do you think came calling tonight? You cannot guess, so I will tell you. Sharif Diya'l Din's sister."

Rayah's heart rose to her throat. She remembered what Auntie Adilah had said and guessed what was coming.

She pretended she did not. "I do not even know the great lady. How should this affect me?"

"You do not know her? But it was you she came asking for. I had to lie very hard—and, yes, work a spell—to make her believe you were indisposed tonight."

Rayah did not ask her mother to go on. It would come soon enough, the doom she felt just around the corner of the roof, blowing off the desert on a drying wind.

"She came to ask for a bride for her brother. And, since you thwarted him with your friend Ghusoon, he's asking after you."

21

God's revelation is not an occasion
For man's distress: It is a message
To show that God All-Knowing sits
On the throne of mercy and guides all affairs.
There is no god but He: To Him
Belong all the most beautiful Names.
> —The Holy Quran, Surah XX, said to be the
> verses Omar's sister was reading when he was
> converted

Yesterday I sent my scribe home muttering spells against evil, against jinn and burning rocks that fall from the sky. Today he returns in much the same state, only further agitated by the investigations with which he fretted away his evening.

"You don't know how God-blessed you are," he tells me, then proceeds to rattle off a catalogue of men lusted after by the jinn who did not fare half so well as I did. He shivers, cold, though it is the heat of the day. He knows a holy man, he says, an honorable mufti who will come and recite the Holy Quran over me as many times as need be until all effects of that long-ago night are gone. He begins to sound like my third wife.

"Mufti, mufti!" I rage. "What need have Muslims for such upstart entrepreneurs, making profit from the Holy Quran? What need have I for such, I, the Sword of God and one of the Companions?"

And now this fellow would assure me that there are no such things as jinn. "They are mere figments of your imagination, Master, of the dangerous desert. With proper prayers and counsel, you may reach the true oasis and avoid those misleading mirages."

Who is he, this city dweller, this blasphemer? Who pretends to know the Quran and yet does not know what is revealed there concerning the jinn? Is it not said that falling stars at night are God's weapons, bolts of fire, and each brings down an evil, unbelieving jinni?

"I have still the scars on my back from where my beloved's whip of fire touched me," I tell him. "I showed you them yesterday—there, there they are again. There and there, on my buttocks and shoulders."

He flinches from the sight. And I revel in it.

"Shall I forget that night when I have such proof?" I demand. "And what makes that grand 'mufti' of yours think I want to forget? Does a man want to forget the battles that give him honor? Even those battles he lost, does he not keep them close in his memory, to remind him who his enemies are and what his grudges must be?"

My scribe considers, his emerald earring winking. "Many are the jinn, I've heard it said, who became Muslims when the Prophet, blessed be he, preached to them in their haunts in that same Valley of Nakhlah. They warned one another saying, 'O our people! Obey the Summoner of God and believe in him.'"

"There. You see? There is nothing my sword could do to put faith into such beings. They come to Submission of their own, with words, with gentle coaxing."

"They are therefore a sight more pious than stone-hearted men."

"You prejudge them, the jinn, and think them all bad," I tell my scribe, taking another vein. "Their ways are not our way, that is all. We do not understand them, but that, as my beautiful *jinniyyah* said, is good. It gives us a chance to learn from them. You are more a man than looks give you credit for, my friend. Who but a man thinks anyone more powerful than he must, by his very nature, be bad? I have lived my life allowing no one to defeat me in arms. Would you deny me this one sweet taste of humility? I do not resent it. I do not resent that night nor my possession at all.

"True, that night did make me something like you, my friend. For a full year from that night, I could not come near a woman, not even my wives, without feeling fire in my loins and extreme exhaustion. Your mufti friend will tell me this was my imagination, too. Well, it is no fancy that I got no offspring all that year. On three or four wives, that is something of a wonder. I made up for it since then, of course. You may know that I lost forty sons in this recent plague. Forty sons, and I still have others fighting for the Faith in distant lands. Yes, quite a herd of martyrs I created. The gates of paradise must be groaning with them. That fertility, too, after my year of rest, I blame on the night of Nakhlah.

"There are other things to life than offspring, my friend. If you have never found it so, the more pity for you in your condition. But I pity myself for not having discovered that sooner, though I had the best instructress in the world, that daughter of Zura. Maybe it is not the popular, new form of Islam to think so, but I am the Sword of God drawn into the sheath, and that is what I think."

"Is this woman alive? Can action be taken against her? She could be stoned for witchcraft. What is her personal name?"

"She is long dead."

"She's in God's hands, then."

"So she is, but you don't even know her name to conjure by, to curse. I don't know the name to tell you, and even if I did, I wouldn't say it."

"You fear her so, Master? You?"

"Lest I blaspheme."

My scribe looks a little green at this. But the abundance of growing things here will do that to a man. That and the green gem in his ear.

"Before you and your mufti come and disturb the peace of my garden with your jihad against this woman," I tell him, to give him stomach, "let me continue with my tale."

I returned to Mecca where my cousin Omar ibn al-Khattab had never forgiven me for—well, for many things. But the fact that I had sworn the Bisha oath in his stead grated him most at that period. Our kinsmen wouldn't let him forget it. At any majlis, any counsel, someone would bring it up. Not openly, perhaps, but someone would say to me, "What a brave thing you did, Khalid Abu Sulayman, praise the Gods," setting me among the honored men. And Omar they would slight or admonish with more severity than was necessary, for some recent failing, just by way of comparison.

One day it happened that the majlis spoke of Muhammad instead. They did so with growing frequency as, slowly but definitely, he made converts.

"It's just the women, the slaves, the poor," al-Khattab said, trying to console.

"Such fables of the ancients always appeal to those who have nothing else to hope in," Abu Sufyan said with scorn.

"Nevertheless," others said, more carefully, "there is not a clan in all Mecca, from the high to the low, that is not affected."

Still others spoke in turn.

"And it's very disruptive, I must say."

"This kinsman takes my hard-earned money to give as alms."

"I order my clansman to a task, and he refuses to do it because it interferes with hearing the madman recite."

"Or with prayer."

"Or he is fasting."

"Or he refuses because he says it would exploit the widows and orphans."

"How can we have an ordered society when our dependents—women, even— obey some nobody over their own men and guardians?"

"By Hubal, I wish that Hala hadn't come in my way," Omar blurted at last. "I should have killed that Muhammad there in the Ka'ba. Then we could have paid

his blood price—which would have been less than we paid the Tamim—and we'd be done with this nonsense."

All the men either scowled at this or shifted nervously. Omar wanted someone, finally, to say, "Yes, what you attempted on that day was good, son of al-Khattab. We wouldn't have come to this pass if you'd not been thwarted by that son of al-Walid and his vile milk brothers."

But nobody did. They changed the subject completely, to the price of fleeces in the Damascus market.

I saw Omar's face grow florid, his plump fingers working on the hilt of his dagger. I sat smug and listened to the market report with exaggerated dignity.

Then suddenly, Omar leapt to his feet. "Look at you all," he said. "You are content to sit around grumbling in your grey beards while this man who styles himself a prophet pulls society completely from under your backsides. Well, I am not so content."

He unsheathed his sword and waved it dangerously.

"Put up your sword," his father chided him, but the son wouldn't hear.

"By this bright sword of mine," Omar said, "I'll hear no more of that Muhammad! You all talk of oaths, pride yourselves on your tongue-licking oaths. Well, Khalid, you may lick my ass. I call on you all, my kinsmen, to witness that I will not put this blade up again until it wears the son of Abd Allah's blood. The Gods hear that oath of mine."

The few attempts to dissuade him were only half-hearted. Certainly none of them was able to stop him before he gave up swinging the blade at our heads and bolted for the door.

"Son, you'd better go see what you can do to make him cease," my father told me.

"Now just a moment," said al-Khattab, Omar's father. "If our sons come to blows—" He knew I was the better fighter. That had been proved as long ago as our childhood wrestling match.

"But remember whose tongue touched the blade of Bishra, O cousin." My father spoke quietly. "I have a son who knows the price of blood."

Al-Khattab Abu Omar had no choice but to settle back on his cushions. The whole majlis agreed on the point.

My hand on my own hilt, I rose to obey. But I noticed that no other young man was ordered to join me.

"Blood price or no," someone behind me commented, "I hope that lad's rashness rids us of Mecca's troublesome firebrand."

If not of both of them, I thought to myself, Omar and that madman Muhammad. Let them kill each other.

Omar flamed his way through Mecca's dusty streets. I followed at a safe distance.

In the end, I wasn't the one who turned his single-minded purpose. That was left to the intrusion of—of course—a woman.

As I turned right out of the majlis, the sun of the street momentarily blinded me. But that was the way I knew Omar would go, for that led to Khadijah's house. When I could see, I discovered my quarry hadn't even turned the corner at the end of the lane yet. Someone had stopped him there for me.

"Where do you go, O son of al-Khattab, in such a flurry, sword drawn?" I recognized the voice of my friend Amr, on his own way to join the majlis with his slick, oiled beard and fine Persian robes.

Two of us are matched against him now, I thought. Amr will help me end this in an honorable, even amusing manner.

I drew my blade upon Omar's back with less trepidation. The two of them stood, carefully choosing the shade of a broad-bean sellers' awning rather than the sun, no matter the heat of their talk. By the time I came to stand behind my cousin, a wide grin had risen to my face.

Omar explained his red-faced purpose. He'd made some improvements in the plan since leaving the majlis.

Amr laughed out loud, careless of the naked blade waving near his vitals. This only increased Omar's fury. But even I was surprised at what Amr said.

"Before you go to set other people's houses to rights, you should see about your own, O son of al-Khattab," were his words. "Your married sister Fatimah and your brother-in-law have submitted themselves to one God."

The sword flashed and threatened. "You lie. You cannot drag the name of my sister into the streets and live."

Amr avoided a thrust to the belly by ducking behind a basket of broad beans. From this safety he still taunted: "They're even at this moment reading Quran to one another in their house. Go there now and see for yourself if you don't believe me."

So Omar's straight path veered. Off to Fatimah's house he charged.

Amr caught my arm when I made to follow. "Leave them now," he said. "It may be your business to stop him when he goes against Muhammad. But it's not your business to come between a man, even Omar, and his sister."

Since he was right, I gave up the chase and went along with Amr instead. Because I didn't think it proper to return to my father's presence with Omar's tale still playing itself out, I went with Amr to his house instead. There we wiled the afternoon away at more pleasant pursuits . . .

"Master?"

The slave of a scribe has recalled me from such a pleasant memory. Instead of this garden, I imagined myself in Amr's, in hot youth—

"How did Omar, may God lead him and all Muslims aright, rise from the dust of that ignoble scene to sit where he now sits?" my eunuch asks.

"As ruler of all the world's believers, do you mean?"

The emerald winks in a nod.

And so I must tell the story of what happened at his sister's house. Even though I wasn't there, all the gossip of the town filled my ears with before the day was out. And it is a tale that every schoolboy will someday recite, much improved with the retelling.

Omar barged in on his sister and brother-in-law even as Amr had told him they would be. How Amr knew, I never did discover. But Amr, being Amr, son of a house of women that floated the red scarf before their door, had means of his own denied to the rest of us.

Fatimah had barely a moment to stuff the parchment into her bodice. Her husband hid himself quivering behind her defenselessness, and Omar thrust the cold iron of his sword against both of their throats.

"What is this I heard in here?" he bellowed as only Omar could bellow.

"Nothing," Fatimah said lamely.

"Tell me!" Omar insisted, giving his sister such a blow across the face that blood burst from her cheek.

Trembling like dried grass in the wind, Fatimah professed her belief in God and His Messenger. "Kill me, brother, if you will. I will not recant."

Then she reached into her bosom, brought out the Surah, and began to recite: "When our wondrous verses were recited to him, a man of riches and blessed with sons has naught to say but 'fables of the ancients.'" Just the term of abuse Abu Sufyan was so fond of saying in the majlis.

They say the divine power of the words convinced my cousin. God knows best. I know, however, Omar's is not a soul to be convinced by a few puffs of air. Nonetheless, the poetry of what he saw rather than what he heard touched him to the quick: His sister stood there, unafraid in the face of death, brushing her cheek with the back of her hand to keep the tears mixed with blood from dripping onto the sacred text as she read.

Her goodness and purity burst his soul into submission in an instant. How monstrous and wicked he was in contrast. He remembered having sheltered his sister from every harm when they had been children. He imagined how one slip of his sword could have cut her like a thin silken thread, and she would have been lost to him forever.

"What are these wondrous words?" Omar cried.

And the end of this story is that he did not sheath his sword again until he had gone with Fatimah to Khadijah's house—and submitted his blade wholly to the Messenger's service.

Back in our majlis, we muttered to ourselves. My failure to stop Omar's conversion did not receive the censure I thought it deserved at the time. How can you stop what happens in a man's heart? I think older men knew this, my father knew this. The crowd of men gave all the censure to another place.

"Omar is always getting himself in trouble for his rashness."

"Rash fights and now rash conversions and treaties of peace."

"No good will come of it, you may be sure."

Those were our mutterings.

On the other hand, the Prophet, blessed be he, was heard to say that Satan ran the other direction when he saw Omar coming.

❧

And now he sits there, my cousin, down in al-Madinah, and gloats that he felt the finger of God before any of the rest of us. At the time, I had other distractions. We had the spring caravan to prepare. My father had just given me his sword, and I had had the kahinah Rudainah forge a new blade for it, a blade mixed with heaven stones.

I had strapped the Sword of God to my side for the first time. The world must see it to be mine, that it gave me of its glory. For I was riding north to trade in Bahrain, and my next halt, even before the pilgrimage of al-Hira, would be the pastures of the Banu Tamim and my beloved.

22

Don't conceal from God what you cherish in your breast.
What God conceals from you is known to Him . . .
—Zuhayr ibn Abu Salma

"**O**mar ibn al-Khattab felt the finger of God before any of the rest . . ."

By lamplight in the early morning while the rest of the house slept, Rayah attempted what the eunuch had suggested. On her own, she made out that much of the next pages of the Conqueror's dictation. It didn't make her comfortable, however. Something—something was not right, leaving Abd Allah out in his prison alone, suffering for having brought the Conqueror's tale to her. She felt it, a stinging behind her eyes, blue like the Prophet's, blessings on him.

Blue eyes, like her mother's.

The eunuch's imprisonment wasn't the biggest thing preying on Rayah's mind, of course. She'd only been trying to read the parchments as a distraction. Sitt Sameh was not going to help her out of this marriage to the old sharif Diya'l-Din; she wouldn't leave her room to do so. What sort of mother was that?

And the rest of the turpentine sellers' family over supper that night?. They were thrilled at the honor, at the prospect of new markets this alliance with the sharif would open up for them.

Even Auntie Adilah, once her most sympathetic friend in the harem, had brushed the hair out of Rayah's blue eyes and said, "I know, my dear, but this time I think you have no choice. You came out of the harem, made your name infamous in Tadmor, controlling the Ones of Fire, sparing Ghusoon but not yourself. Think. It is better than many a girl may hope for, married to an old man. At least he is a merchant and will be away much of the time."

Rayah brushed the hair out of her own eyes to keep them from filling with tears at the memory. Then she had to blow out the lamp and run. The early morning call to prayer had begun, and she would be late.

"We must pray for rain," Sitt Umm Ali told her class of girls.

"Yes, my father says the grain has dried in the ground for want of rain," said one student.

"Mine will do no more plowing until the heavens bless us," said another.

Rayah remembered the dust demon following the lone plow she'd seen in the field the day before. On her way to the Camp of Diocletian. "Is the lack of rain caused by jinn—Fire Spirits, God shield us from them?" she asked.

The other girls stared at her. What did that have to do with the crisis at hand? their looks demanded. Then one whispered to another, and the explanation came: Rayah was going to marry Sharif Diya'l-Din. She's bound to speak nonsense. Their looks tried for envy, but mostly melted to pity.

They prayed for rain. In her own mind, Rayah switched her prayer in the middle. "Do not make me marry the old sharif," she pleaded. She even remembered the boy of the previous night. "We should marry," he had said. But she didn't add him to a prayer.

Anyway, how could heaven hear her over all the other voices speaking as one? And, she scolded herself, what was her own small discomfort in a world without rain?

The class ended after midday prayers. Rather than return through the alleys and over rooftops to their jumble of homes to help with chores like the rest of the girls, Rayah told them she had to take the right-hand way instead. "I must carry a message to my uncle in the shop where he is rendering turpentine," she said.

The looks of pity were all set in stone now, and the other girls seemed glad to escape from the curse of her presence.

When she got to the shop, however, Rayah waited until her uncle—whom she now knew was no true blood relative of hers—had his back turned in the heavy steam. Then she ran by the shop and quickly around the corner. Beyond the bazaar, she noticed that, indeed, the farmers had given up on their fields for lack of rain. She couldn't help that now, however, but hurried on, out among the ruins once more to the Camp of Diocletian.

"*Ustadh*. Ya, Abd Allah," she whispered at the open window.

No answer came.

Where had the prisoner, her friend, gone? Had the sharif moved him? Where? Surely Abd Allah couldn't escape on his own.

She tried again, as loud as she dared with the guards around the other side of the building. "Ya, Abd Allah."

She heard a sound. The guards? No, from within. And more like the scurrying of rats. In horror, she stepped back.

A gust of dry wind skittered dust, tickling around her ankles, playing with the little bells she wore there, lifting her skirt. A voice murmured behind her: "It's not rats. It's your friend. He's hurt."

Rayah didn't have to turn to see. She recognized the voice as that belonging to the
boy who'd saved her from the guards, who'd walked her home. Who'd asked to marry
her. No, no boy. A jinni. She knew better than to try to catch a glimpse of him; she
knew there'd be nothing but dust. But she also knew that the jinni spoke truth: Her
friend was hurt and needed her.

"Abd Allah, *ustadh*, can you hear me? You're hurt. How are you hurt?"

This time a groan answered her from within the old Roman wall.

She studied the stone of the wall, found a chink where mortar was missing that just
fit her foot. She set her toes in the place, tried to stand. Her foot slipped—then, with
a jangle of her anklets, stayed, as if she'd received a shove from behind. That jinni—

Still, it allowed her to stretch up and catch the sill. Bracing her other foot in a
smaller chink, she hoisted herself until she could peer into the dim dungeon.

A dark shadow in the far corner shifted but made no attempt to rise and come to
her.

"Abd Allah, you're hurt."

"I think—I think he broke my leg." The eunuch spoke faintly, a little grunt of pain
every other word.

"Who? Who did this to you?"

Rayah received no answer but another groan.

"Never mind. I think I can squeeze through this window."

"Don't, child," she heard with the next groan, but ignored it.

"You need help—water certainly. Let me run for water and, inshallah, I'll be back."

No water pooled in its usual places in the old aqueduct, nearby but fallen into
ruin. Rayah had to run all the way to the spring. Here, because of the lack of rain, the
water lay so far down that a line of women was waiting, chatting together, even at this
time of day. They fell silent when she appeared, and looked at her with the same faces
their daughters had done in class earlier. She even heard one of them whisper it to her
neighbor: "That's Rayah. Although she has no proper parentage, and blue eyes besides,
she is to marry the wealthy sharif."

Rayah ignored them. She helped herself to a jug, abandoned because it had a crack
down most of one side. She couldn't go home for a better jug—and face the questions
and demands that she stay and get ready for a visit from the sharif's sister-in-law?

When, finally, she took her turn at the ropes, Rayah found if she held the jug
carefully, no water leaked. It was, however, more awkward to carry it that way than
balanced on her head.

She arrived back at Diocletian's Camp, arms aching and quite damp down one side
of her skirt where dust collected in mud. She ignored these discomforts and managed
to squeeze through the high, narrow window.

"A girl small enough to do that," commented the unseen jinni as he gave her the final shove to the rubble inside, "is far too young to take a human husband. She'd better stick to one of us, like smoke."

"Who has done this?" Rayah turned her attention to the human, the ravaged eunuch, instead.

When Abd Allah didn't immediately reply, she answered herself. "It was your captor, Sharif Diya'l-Din." And she was expected to marry this man? She would die rather than do such a thing.

Only maybe—God forbid. Maybe she would have to marry him in order to save her friend.

"Not him." A pain-filled grunt. "His guest."

Not the sharif? "Who?"

"Someone from Homs," Abd Allah said as she washed the terrible cuts and bruises on his face with the corner of her veil.

Homs. Where the Conqueror lived, where Abd Allah the scribe had taken down his story in the garden.

"You do not know him, Little One." That lip was really bad, making it difficult for the eunuch to speak even so much. A tooth must have gone through the flesh, leaving it swollen. Another pair of teeth was missing altogether. "So do not think of revenge."

Do not think of revenge? This beating had happened, she knew, because of her. The sharif had been unable to get to her—to her mother, rather. But he knew the Conqueror's messenger had come to them, not to him. And now more powerful men were coming from Homs, torturing Abd Allah to learn what he knew. His craving for this power was behind the old man's offer of marriage, of course, more than his thwarted designs on Ghusoon.

Only not the sharif, but his guest. His guest from Homs— Who is he?

The eunuch's nose was probably broken. This monstrous guest would be welcome in her home if she were the sharif's wife? Rayah touched the nose as much as Abd Allah could bear. She felt some of the healing power leave her. The feature might never be handsome again, might always mock the gem in his ear, but at least it wouldn't pain him.

She had to save some strength for the leg.

She moved to the leg now. She pushed the hateful sharif from her mind as she pushed up the eunuch's robe for a better view. She laid a hand on either side of the shin. She felt the softness that should have been hard. Energy began to congeal behind her eyes, in her wrists, like the strengthening broth of boiled bones. She remembered how the pieces of her little cousin's skull, like bits of broken pottery, had shifted and come together under her hands. She knew she could do this, if God were willing. The prayer. She began to recite the Name of God in a prayer: "Ya Latif, ya Latif."

One splinter snapped into place. Abd Allah gasped. She must not let his reaction make her lose her concentration.

"Ya Latif."

"Hush," Abd Allah insisted, clearer now, cutting the prayer and the healing short.

It took Rayah longer to hear what the matter was. The effort of healing put her nearly in a trance. Only when the invisible jinni boy added a hiss of caution did she drop the narrow core of her attention.

Then she stopped too, horror raising her heart and choking her. Beneath her hands, two splinters yearning towards each other strained, then relaxed apart again.

Outside the cell, she heard voices. Very close. Had they heard her? They must have heard her, although she'd been too intense to judge how loudly she prayed.

Chains clanked on the thick wooden door and a bolt slammed open.

"Shall I work on him again?"

A voice Rayah didn't recognize came through the gaping door. From the place she'd managed to hide, directly behind the wood panel swinging in its stone pivot, she could see it wasn't just the guards. Sharif Diya'l-Din and two others, his guests. One was tall, well dressed; a handsome, wealthy man who spoke with the divine, elegant Arabic of the desert. The other, smaller, dark, quick man, the one who spoke this threat, was the elegant one's servant, by the slit nose probably even his slave. Something of Persia accented his speech, the way he seemed to be standing on the brink—of who knew what?

"Please, my guests." This was the sharif. She recognized his speech. It made her sick, as if she'd swallowed a cup of pure oil. "Help yourselves."

Rayah hardly dared to breathe. They were going to beat Abd Allah again? Now, while she watched? She could not keep hidden if they did that. She could not—

The little Persian strode to her friend's side and caught him up by the hair. "So? Are you ready to tell us now, capon?"

Abd Allah groaned in pain, but the Arab said, "What's this?" He picked up the cracked water jug Rayah hadn't had time to take with her. "I thought I said, 'Give him no water.'"

The betrayal allowed the Persian to increase his violence threefold. "Gelding, where is the demon poetess hiding? You gave her the sword? Lead us to her."

Abd Allah shook his head, though even that must have pained him, knotted by the hair in his tormentor's grip as it was.

Faster than she could react, faster, certainly, than Rayah would ever be able to repair the damage, the Persian's hand moved to the side of the eunuch's face. He ripped the emerald from Abd Allah's ear.

Her friend might have screamed, but she didn't hear. Her own scream was too loud in her ears. "Stop!"

Silence strangled as three pairs of eyes found her behind the door.

"By God," Rayah heard herself whisper. "I will not let you hurt my friend."

The cool, elegant Arab laughed out loud, showing teeth pared to points—like a shark's. Quraysh, the Prophet's clan, blessings on him.

Blessings—help me, ya Latif. I could run—help me not to run and abandon Abd Allah. Rayah closed her eyes against the next blow she expected.

"Well, well, well," the Arab said when laughter allowed. "Who have we here?"

"That, I'm sorry to say, O gracious lord, is the girl I told you about." Sharif Diya'l-Din gave the reply.

"The one you plan to marry?"

"Yes, my lord."

The Arab gave a hum of consideration as he stroked his beard.

"Shall I grab and hold her, Master?" interjected the Persian with such relish that Rayah, for horror, thought she would have to make a run for it after all.

"Not necessary, Firuz, I think," the Arab said. "She does not run, you see?"

"Yes, Master." Firuz the Persian muttered in deep disappointment and looked like he'd only be satisfied if he was allowed to turn back to Abd Allah again.

"Trust me, as God is my witness," stammered the sharif, "once she comes to my bed, I will see that she stops running all over creation as she is allowed to do now."

"The thing is," said the Arab, "I don't know if you will gain permission to marry her."

"My lord, I take the privilege of reminding you that the turpentine sellers have overwhelmingly said yes."

"God is all-powerful, mighty," the Arab said.

"*Amīn*," echoed the sharif piously. Then he chuckled a little. "But they have said yes. How could they say otherwise, such poor people, when it is I who come courting?"

"And yet, if she is who you led me to believe she is, with all your jumbled tale told in my majlis in Homs— God's ways are unfathomable."

"*Amīn*. As I told you, she drove the demons out of—" the sharif said, then stopped in bewilderment.

"And now that I see her—yes, yes, I believe it's true. She is brave, she doesn't run. She has the very look of my father, God rest him, about her. You'd find it hard to credit, but I do believe she looks more like him than I, his son, do. And those eyes."

The Persian's nerves in the face of his master's calm graciousness finally got the better of him. He couldn't resist giving Abd Allah a kick. Rayah screamed in protest and left the wall behind the door in order to fall to her knees at her friend's side. If necessary, she'd take the next kick for him.

"Firuz." The Arab didn't have to raise his voice at all. Something when he said his slave's name brought even the malicious violence in those small dark eyes to heel. "If you do that again, I think our sexless friend will not tell us what we want to hear him confirm. Even so, I think now I do not need to have his confirmation. I am not certain you will marry this young lady," the wealthy Arab went on, "because, by the grace of God, if I am right, you need to get no turpentine seller's permission, but my own. If I am right, and I think I am, I am her closest male kin."

The elegant Arab turned the sharpened-tooth grin on Rayah. She felt her blood turn to ice as he said, "I am this young lady's mother's brother, her long-lost uncle, Abd ar-Rahman ibn Khalid."

23

God and the years have taught me
The error and pride of my ways.
O daughter
Pretty, joyous child in the light of our family hearth.
Now I would rather die myself than ever lose you.
—Traditional Arabic poem

Like shifting dunes of the great Nefud sands, a group of fifteen tents spread out long and low across the barley field on the outskirts of al-Hira. A swarm of children came out of these tents to greet me as if a guest were a pot of honey and they, wild bees. I recognized none of them, for even the eldest, who might have been born the last time I was among the Tamim, had had four years in which to grow and change.

Four years to let the matter of Hala die between us, the blood-money camels to grow used to their new herds as if they'd never been strangers. Time to renew the old milk-brother relationship.

After the children came the dogs, the mangy guard dogs trained to circle the encampment by night and lounge on a high lookout point by day, the sleek hunting seluqis. They came to sniff at me in one muttish, yelping pack. Among them I failed to see old Edja, the dog of my boyhood.

"Left him in the spring pastures," a cheery Malik told me as he came to the door of the largest tent. "Edja was too old and sick to migrate further, so we left him."

Trying not to let the death of a dog sadden me, I moved on at once to demand other news. "And how are those behind you?" I asked, meaning his harem, Layla in particular. I knew she had borne her master at least one son.

"My wife? Which one?" Malik asked, opening his small, narrow mouth its full extent in laughter. He had ten children now, he said, and plenty of mothers for them all. Here was a man, my milk brother, who grew in possessions and depen-

dents now that his physical growth had stopped. Layla was rather lost in the crowd. Only I, it seems, remembered how Bint al-Minhal and Bint Zura had clung to one another by the fireside at night to gain courage to face their joint captivity, in the aftermath of Dhu Qar.

My arrival brought every man in camp to the great tent. They came to hear what was new in the world and to dip their thin fingers in the great bowls and platters my milk brother would order up for his guest. Al-Harith was among them, and my heart stopped its easy, homecoming rhythm. This man bent his head and came in under the corner of the tent. He sat quietly not far from his entrance as if trying not to intrude. When form and a deep breath for self-control allowed me to do so, I managed to pose the question to him, "And how are you, O son of Suwaid? And how are those behind your tent curtain?"

Al-Harith was flattered that I should ask and replied: "Fine, fine, thanks be to Our Lady al-Uzza."

The answer was much too innocuous to satisfy me, but then, so had my question been. I could not very well ask, in the presence of all that company, "Tell me, O son of Suwaid, how fares your wife, the Taghlibi Bint Zura, in whom I have a deep interest?" Men have been killed for showing greater tact in speaking of another's woman.

I was pestered with the most questions. The answers, however brief I had the heart to make them, always demanded elaboration. Had I seen good pasture, rain clouds, swollen wells upon my journey? And how were things in the world, in Damascus, in Mecca, in Homs, in Yathrib, in Bosra?

With evening and the return of the herds from pasture, al-Harith and a good number of others slipped out from the company. They went to form a guard at this vulnerable time of day and then see to the division and milking of their own. Only then did I begin my cautious drive to satisfaction.

"Al-Harith is under your protection again I see."

"Oh, yes," Malik replied. "Such is the way of heaven: little bursts of fertility come and go. Now, that is a clan that tries the limits of a sharif's charity."

"I noticed you still call al-Harith only Ibn Suwaid after his father. Has he no sons to give him the name of a man?"

"By my life, no. Now no wife will have him, for it is rumored the women are not to blame in this case."

I found myself blushing furiously and changed the subject until I cooled off my face for a moment. As soon as I felt I could do it with ease, I asked, trying to make it sound like throwing bones to the dogs, "What of his first wife? What of the Taghlibi he won at Dhu Qar?"

Malik paused for a moment to think. Such information was not the sort of thing he usually bothered to stock in his mind, especially not after four years. But soon he said, "Oh, yes—her. I suppose she was still alive when we were in Mecca to see you last."

My stomach lurched over grilled lamb.

"She is dead then?" It took me two false starts to get that out. I had no fear of blushing now. I had gone white as a carcass the townsmen hang up to bleed for cleaning. When Malik grunted in the affirmative, I still could not accept it and asked the cause and the season to add to the evidence.

"Childbirth," Malik said.

"Impossible."

My milk brother raised his brow at me, and I realized I'd spoken my thought aloud with a possessed sort of laugh. I managed to keep the swarm of other things I wanted to say swirling only in my own brain: How could that happen to a woman who urged life everywhere she went? Something about salvation was supposed to inhabit her life. There must be some mistake. You might as well call the sun to rise in the west. Prove it, O my brother. Did you actually see her dead, feel for the pulse in that lovely neck to confirm?

But of course not. The wonder was that he knew so much of his herdsman's wife. Usually a sharif would not even know another man's wife was with child. Women would have washed and wound the body without any man being the wiser, hardly even the husband. If women wailed, the sharif might not ask why before he demanded silence in the face of what Islam now terms a martyr's demise: laboring to bring forth new warriors for jihad.

I couldn't help myself, however. I pressed for one more details. "When?"

The time period he gave me, though he could not be exact, I quickly worked out to be nine months from that sky-swirling night in Nakhlah.

What images flooded into my mind! I relived that night with a clarity of the pain, the sweat, the fears, and the dark exhilaration that only the reality had surpassed. At my side, my newly forged sword seemed to burn as if hot from the anvil, as if the heavenly stones still fell. I got up and hung it from the center pole of the tent, as I should have done from the first.

Malik stopped in the middle of the gossip he was spouting to look at me. "A new sword, milk brother?"

"My father's."

"Let's have a look at it."

Giggling like a girl in a sort of clumsy apology, I changed the subject, as if a man's sword were something private. "I thought . . . I thought you said al-Harith was not man enough to do his own begetting."

Now what had I said? I panicked. I might as well have blurted straight out about that dark and haunted night. But a creeping grief harried the edges of my control.

Malik suspected nothing. "It was only a girl," he said "which hardly counts."

A lot of women's concerns for a sharif to divulge. As if to apologize, he went on: "We both know there was something peculiar about that Taghlibi woman. Those eyes, for one thing. She was the source, or so they say, of al-Harith's brief burst of fortune. It is true, the magic came and went with her. She could get the very stones to mount her she-goats and bring forth twins, that is what they are saying now, those who remember the tale. Surely it was no great feat to get a girl-child for herself from that stump of a man."

A girl, I said to myself, trying to find consolation, trying to keep from tears. A girl. So she is not dead after all. The spirit is still alive, for it passes from mother to daughter, however disparate the father.

Then a new thought entered my head that caused my heart to shudder first, then freeze. Proud and possessive as we men tend to be of our offspring, we realize only too well that a child in no way can survive the first two or three years upon the hard and arid body of a man. And this, I recalled, was not the pampered city of Mecca that looked elsewhere for wet nurses. In the harsh desert, a child without a mother, especially a girl-child, must be given up for the survival of more important persons.

"A girl," I said aloud. "And is she still alive? She wasn't buried with the mother, was she?"

Malik responded with a click of his tongue which I first took to be a sound of exasperation. "By al-Uzza," I expected him to say, "you certainly are interested in petty things these days."

Instead, the click seemed to be one of curious wonder. "Odd that you should ask," he said. "She was meant to be buried, of course. Al-Harith, such a soft-hearted soul, put it off as long as he could. But his fortune began to fail—right from the death of that Taghlibi woman. It was as if his flocks knew she was no longer there to stroke them and whisper their names when they came home at night. An inflammation of the bowels carried off more than half the flock in the first three months. Under such circumstances, one could hardly be burdened with an extra mouth that provided no helping hands. The child was sitting on her own by then, and laughing and smiling, but there was no choice in the matter."

Malik warmed to his subject with no apology or self-consciousness. The details of the story had so impressed him that he remembered every one and elaborated them with flair, as if he had actually been there. And this was the story he told:

It was morning. The herdsmen and young boys had already gone out with their much-depleted charges, the girls to gather dung and water. Only one slave woman was left behind to churn the butter, air the bedding, and mind the one girl-child still too young to be given a task.

Al-Harith gave the word to the old woman. "I must bury it today. Get it ready."

The woman sobbed in reply as if the child had been her own. But she knew there was no escape from this hard thing. She had listened to the infant's hungry whimperings too many long nights. She hung the little girl's neck with every charm and chain and bead she could. The child was delighted with such rattling brilliance, hardly knowing which to play with first. Then, just as quickly, the old woman removed them all again. What use was it to make little sparks against so consuming a fire of Fate?

And so the old woman removed all the jewelry but a single, simple bronze cross. The child's mother had taken the amulet from her own neck when she had learned she'd had a girl, just before she had died. Then the old woman handed the child to its father. The little thing laughed with delight to be in those big, strong hands. Al-Harith had to wipe away womanlike tears from his own cheeks with those hands. The old woman buried her face in her veil in the corner of the tent and wept unashamedly as only old women are allowed to.

Somewhere near that abandoned campsite, if I cared to hunt for it, I might still see the hole that al-Harith had dug, there upon the lonely, barren hillside. The rains of four springs will have corroded the sides so that a casual passerby might think it only a natural sinking in the sand, or a spot where dogs or jackals have dug for bones. But al-Harith put that wound in the earth's side. He was much like an animal at the time, one might say, denying any thought but the under-thought of survival. He had dug it with good straight sides, wide and deep enough to accommodate the body of a little girl not yet a year old who could no longer be provided for.

A wind blew ripples through the walls of the tents. It came across the open spaces and sent those same ripples up al-Harith's spine. So far, his resolve had allowed him to toss in only two handfuls of sand, and the little girl laughed and looked up at him. She thought he meant to tickle her with this game. Her round little knees were kicked up to her waist and her perfect, never-walked-upon bare toes wriggled in the air.

The wind seemed to be trying to speak with him, plead with him to hold back the next handful of sand. But he would not heed it. He could not heed it. A plague if it sounded like his dead wife's voice! A death-dealing drought if it were filled with troubled flocks of birds that all seemed to have her spirited eyes! Something had to give. His people were weak with hunger. He was a man, and a man did not need to listen to his wife when she was alive. He would certainly do what must be done when she was dead.

And then, the earth moved. It twitched beneath al-Harith's feet as if it were some great war horse caught in the shoulder with a lance. For one moment, all of nature paused, holding its breath to see what the great broad back might do. Would the wound prove too much for it? Would the knotted tension in its muscles turn to liquid and sink away, bringing the rider down with it in death?

No, the wound turned all creation mad with pain. It lurched this way and that as if trying to snap the shaft out of its shoulder with its teeth. It threw and trampled everything in the blindness of its rage.

The earth, the desert, that seemed so bleached and dead—one could not even trust it to lie peacefully. Beneath that stark, deceiving calm, hatred brooded. From far away and near at hand echoed the roar as whole mountainsides slipped into valleys. The decimated herds stampeded over cliffs in fright. Tent stakes, as if they'd been hammered into quicksand, quivered loose and the fragile security of home came tumbling down on the heads of the occupants.

Al-Harith ibn Suwaid lost his footing and fell. The level ground he'd been standing on suddenly turned into a narrow ledge of rock; he made the mistake of looking down in fear. He tumbled into the hole by the side of his small daughter. Her he had meant to bury by his own hand he snatched up and hid in the fold of his cloak lest any of the dust the earth threw in its anger should soil her cheeks.

"It was," Malik said, "as if the earth were a blanket having the dust flipped out of it in the morning. I know," he said, "because we felt it in our camp, too, a full night's ride away. And we thought the world had come to an end. Next day, the entire clan of Suwaid, with what was left of their herds, came straggling into our camp. And the little girl, smiling and thrilled with her own small life, was still snuggled in the protection of her father's cloak, riding with him on his boney camel at the head of the march.

"My herdsman's wife had milk for two, and she nursed the child until she was weaned. But from that day to this, no matter how poor they've become, al-Harith would hear no more of burying infants. The earth had too plainly shown him its displeasure."

Such was the tale my milk brother told me.

That night, on some pretext, I left his tent, left the lights of al-Hira behind me, and went out into the desert alone. I tore my sword from my side and flung it at a scarp of rock. I withdrew it from its protecting scabbard and whacked the blade again and again across the stone, shrieking, howling in my grief as I did. Arrowhead-like fragments flew from the stone, but so fine was the craftsmanship of the sword, so divine its substance, that the blade was not even dulled.

In unendurable pain, I turned that blade upon myself, pressed its perfect point up beneath my ribs. The swordsmith Rubainah might well have set her curse upon it, that whoever should claim such an instrument could kill no one but himself.

The sudden appearance of a voice out of the darkness was all that stopped me. From the direction of the woman's end of a distant tent, I heard a voice raised in what might be the singsong to lull a child to sleep. Only the child herself was chanting, nonsense. Or rather, a long string of rhymes, what poets call feminine rhymes, the most difficult. The rhythm loped along like a sturdy camel. And the rhymes—

I picked myself up from the edge of destruction and moved toward the sound, only to have the rear curtain of that tent stop me.

Then, by most merciful God, I lifted up my eyes and beheld the fall of a single silver star. This one burned out long before she reached the earth, but she seemed to speak to me as she fell and these were her words, "My child. Our little daughter. Look to her, O cousin of my master. Look to her, care for her, for she is greater than I. Look to her for my sake, and I shall live."

24

بسم الله الرحمن الرحيم

**Muhammed is al-Amīn, the Truthful, and he can no more hide
the truth than the sun can rise in the west.
—Said by Khadijah, Mother of the Faithful,
blessings on her, about her husband**

"Yes, I remember the day that strange man from Mecca came to our encampment at the pilgrimage of al-Hira."

In the dark, Sitt Sameh turned from reciting some verses—set to a camel's lope, each line ending with a difficult feminine ending—at the rooftop's edge. The disembodied voice belonged once again to a four-year-old child, motherless but touched by the jinn in the desert.

Rayah had stayed under the little room's tent roofing, watching her mother from what she hoped was a safe distance. She set aside the parchments she'd been reading the moment her mother began to speak. Rayah did not shake off the spell of the chanted words until her mother had rejoined her and Abd Allah back under the shelter and taken up her spinning once more.

Earlier that day, in the prison cell in the Camp of Diocletian, Rayah had found the courage to instruct the governor of Homs, his Persian slave, and Sharif Diya'l-Din how best to take up the wounded eunuch. To her amazement—and it seemed the governor's own amusement—they carried him all the way to the turpentine sellers' house. At the door protected by the silver and lapis lazuli charm, the women of the household took over and brought the eunuch up to the third floor.

The strange men could only follow with their eyes. From her mind, Rayah pushed the thought that these torturers now knew what Abd Allah had been willing to keep from them. He'd been willing to keep it from them at the cost of his life. She had led them here, to her mother, to the Conqueror's sword and his parchments, to herself. The eunuch might be willing to die, but she was not willing to let him.

Here, at last, Rayah set Abd Allah's leg. Her mother recommended a salve of black seed pounded with dates when they wrapped the leg between two sticks, and red cress seed to eat. They tended his other hurts, even the torn ear, with staining turmeric and salt and the rare, ground brown beans called "coffee." The ear would never hold another gem, but when the bandages came off in a week or so, if he wore his turban low, the scar would not be too disfiguring.

Sitt Sameh also gave the patient poppy juice to help him rest and to take away the pain. He was in no shape to be reading, but when awake, he listened to Rayah read with interest, helping her when her Arabic failed. Sometimes he didn't even have to strain his black eye to look at the words he'd written. He'd heard them, after all, just as they spilled from the Conqueror's mouth.

"I remember," Sitt Sameh went on, "that some of the other children dared me to go and rifle the stranger's saddle bags while he sat in the great tent, talking. Already at four years old, they gave me a name for bravery. They also didn't sound a warning, but ran away and hid when they saw him coming up behind me.

"Laughing, the big man caught my little thieving hand, picked me up—then nearly dropped me. I saw recognition in his eyes—a sort of fear and awe mixed, which helped my own bravery to return. The stranger touched the bronze cross on the child-flatness of my breast, then touched his turban. To my surprise, he wore the twin of the amulet I'd cut my teeth on among the folds of red silk."

"What did he say, Lady?" Rayah asked. She still didn't dare call the woman "Mother" with any regularity.

Sitt Sameh laughed at the memory. "I accused him before he accused me, although he had caught me with my very hands in his saddle bag. 'Thief! You've stolen my mother's amulet, may the Mother of Rain pour gentle showers on her grave.'"

The eunuch attempted a convivial chuckle from his sickbed. "The Conqueror, Abu Sulayman—may he find favor with God—he told me he could not look at you without remembering the words of the old Christian holy man, 'You shall behold the salvation of the Arabs.'"

"He set me down, but he would not let go of my hand. I pulled arm's length away, but he would not let go.

"'Come, Little Blue Eyes,' he said. I thought it very strange to see a grown man's tears. 'Tell your uncle—'"

"He almost slipped and said 'your father,'" Abd Allah interjected.

"'—What your name might be.'"

Suddenly, the two adults, the eunuch and the woman telling the story, fell silent. To Rayah, it was as if a waterskin had been dumped over the both of them. She couldn't understand.

"So you told him your name," Rayah urged.

"Yes," Sitt Sameh repeated, as if far away in al-Hira and not there in Tadmor, a place she hadn't left since Rayah's birth. "I told him my name."

More silence.

"Please go on," Rayah urged them.

Neither adult would look at her. Sitt Sameh stopped her spinning and moved as if to set it down.

Rayah couldn't believe that was going to be the end of the storytelling for that day. "'My name is Sameh bint al-Harith,'" she prompted. "Then what?"

"I didn't say 'Sameh bint al-Harith.'" Sitt Sameh set down her spinning with finality.

"Why not?"

"At that time, that wasn't—" Sitt Sameh began.

"No." Abd Allah stopped her. The eunuch was in on this, too. "Not here. Not yet."

"She should be told. The men downstairs—sooner rather than later."

Rayah noticed her mother was in no haste to claim the governor of Homs as her half-brother, unlike the governor himself.

"It's still too dangerous," Abd Allah said.

"What?" Rayah insisted. "What's too dangerous?" Although something in the back of her mind had begun to whir like a waterwheel with the first donkey plod. Something about the cadence of "Sameh bint al-Harith" when it shaped her tongue. The sounds were very close to something familiar, something she'd heard in Sitt Umm Ali's Quranic class. Rayah tossed the thought from her mind, but it had stayed long enough to leave some residue. The name pronounced with spits and cursing.

"Run along downstairs now, Rayah," Sitt Sameh said, "and help your aunties in the kitchen."

"I won't until you tell me," Rayah started to say, a rudeness she'd never dared in front of this mother of hers before.

With a shift of cushions, Abd Allah came gallantly to the rescue. "Why don't you tell us, Lady, about how the Conqueror invited your father, then, to bring his household south to Mecca, working as his own herdsmen?"

"I don't want to hear about Mecca," Rayah said. "I want to know your name."

Sitt Sameh ignored her. Instead, she picked up her spindle once more, although she didn't yet take up the thread. "Mecca, yes. I remember Abu Sulayman's sisters and wives, into whose care I was given, taking me to visit in Khadijah's house."

"You mean, to the very house where the Prophet lived, blessings on him?" Rayah knew she was being lured away, but this event, this sop they'd thrown her, was too juicy to be ignored.

"Yes, although he was never there that I recall. Muhammad went out during the day and left it all to his women."

"So please, tell me, what do you remember of that sanctified place?" Rayah asked, the riddle of the name forgotten.

"I remember a room full of women, Muhammad's stepdaughters mostly, and Khadijah his wife. I remember one called Zaynab."

"Muhammad's daughter, blessings on him?"

"Khadijah's oldest daughter by her previous husband, full sister to the boys Hind and the murdered Hala about whom Khalid told us earlier. The girl had been married to a man before Muhammad received his calling and, unlike her sisters, stayed married afterwards, pagan though her husband remained. I remember that Zaynab commented on my blue eyes.

"'Like our stepfather's,' said her sister.

"'And like the great queen Zaynab, whom the Romans call Zenobia, for whom our mother named me,' said Zaynab. "Perhaps, Little One, God willing, you will lead the Arabs to victory, as she did.'" Sitt Sameh laughed dismissively at this recollection.

"But what else do you remember?" Rayah pressed. "You were in the Prophet's home, blessed be he. You must remember more."

"Apart from that, I remember everyone being sad."

"*Mashallah*, how could anyone be sad who lived in the presence of the Seal of the Prophets, blessings on him?"

"One of Khadijah's daughters by her previous husband, Ruqayyah, had just stolen away from Mecca by night with her husband Uthman ibn Affan and a handful of others. They hoped to find a haven in Abyssinia from the persecution Muslims were enduring in their native town among their own kinsmen. Another of Khadijah's daughters, Umm Kulthum, was also married to Uthman. Both young women had had prior, nonbelieving husbands who had divorced them when they discovered their father-in-law was a madman. Uthman, an early and faithful convert, had taken both sisters on out of the goodness of his heart. He had taken only Ruqayyah with him to Abyssinia, however, for Umm Kulthum was with child.

"Umm Kulthum had returned to her mother's house and, even though everyone told her it wasn't good for the baby, she wept most of every day. One moment, she felt abandoned to Mecca's cruelties by her husband and a greedy sister. The next moment, she considered that her infant must be born fatherless. She feared she would see neither her husband nor her dear sister Ruqayyah ever again.

"'They will drown on the voyage across the sea,' Umm Kulthum mourned. 'Or the Abyssinians will give them no sanctuary. You know, those men of Africa tried to conquer our town the year the Prophet was born, may God further his work.'

"'God willing, the Abyssinians will welcome them. The people there are Christians, after all, monotheists, *hunafa*, as are we. People who also have a book of revelation,' Khadijah tried to cheer her youngest daughter."

"Her youngest daughter?" Rayah asked. "But they always told us—"

"When I met Khadijah bint Khuwaylid, when she took me up into her cramped lap, I thought she was just a large, comfortable, motherly woman. Having never known my own mother, I appreciated that. I realize now that she, too, must have been expecting at the time, same as her daughter Umm Kulthum. After the death of Muhammad's son Qasim at two years old, one or two other sons in infancy, she was carrying the only actual offspring of Muhammad's flesh and blood that would live—his daughter, Fatimah Zahra."

"May God favor him and her," Rayah said in liturgical echo.

"That was the last child she would bear, for she was already forty-five when she and Muhammad ibn Abd Allah married."

"Just a moment," Rayah stopped her mother's tale. "How did you come to be in Khadijah's house?"

"Khadijah's daughter had just fled the town under cover of night, as I said. I suppose there might have been a bit of gloating among the townswomen, come to wallow in another's misfortune. They brought a cloth of goat cheese or a pot of beans, to see what might be done in tragedy. To hold hands, distract children, sweep the floor, wash the pots. Not to make plans for the sufferers or to tell them to accept God's will with fortitude or anything else that might make grief worse. Just to listen—"

"Khalid ibn al-Walid was not a convert at the time, but one of the persecutors. How would his wives and sisters be Khadijah's guests, blessings on her?"

"I think women's lives stay intertwined." Sitt Sameh studied the thread she spun as if it expressed her thought as well as any physical thing could. "There are always births and deaths and marriages. These things are somehow greater than the religious differences that were tearing Mecca apart. Khalid's women did what his pride would never allow him to do."

Rayah didn't know if she believed what Sitt Sameh said or not, but she decided to keep silent.

Her mother continued her tale by recounting words said in the house of Khadijah, first wife of the Prophet, blessings on him, long ago. "I remember Umm Khulthum wailing, 'Oh, Mother, why did you have to marry such a hard man to make him my stepfather? You had a choice of husbands, which none of the rest of us have had.'

"'Muhammad ibn Abd Allah hard?' Khadijah's laughter filled the courtyard. 'Daughter, I'd had two husbands before. You're right, I got to choose. I knew my own mind, and believe me, I know hard men. Muhammad ibn Abd Allah, God bless him and his mission, is the gentlest man I know.'

"That was when I piped up. I remember sitting on Khadijah's lap, hearing this talk and then saying, 'Maybe he is not so hard, but his God is.'

"The buzz this statement caused among a group of women, half Muslim, half not, gratified me. I had said what no one else dared. I had to say more. 'He does not have a son, and this one, too shall be a daughter. He should not give us a hard God. He wants a nice, soft God like Umm Qasim here." And I patted Khadijah's great belly and breasts.

In the little room on the third floor of the turpentine sellers' house, Rayah clapped her hands over her ears, then her mouth, then her ears again. "I cannot hear such blasphemy," she said with a tiny squeal.

Sitt Sameh, who had always been a hard parent, ignored her. "I suppose this is how my name came to Muhammad's attention, his women talking about me after I'd gone. For he sought me out."

Rayah forgot all about blasphemy then. "So you did actually meet the Prophet, blessings on him?"

"I did, and I will tell you how it happened. But first, I need a rest. Why don't you read more of the Conqueror's dictation, child?"

25

Does firebrand Muhammad promise us that we shall live again?
How can there be life for the death-bird and the skull?
Do you omit to keep me from death in this life
And will you then revive me when my bones are rotten?
—A poetical satire by Amr ibn al-Asi

"*The wild desert is not the right place for a child,*" *I tried to explain to my friend Amr ibn al-Asi as we sat together drinking wine in his mother's brothel garden.*

"*Such an upbringing doesn't seem to have hurt you any,*" *my friend said with a teasing fist to my shoulder. "And aren't you always urging the same thing to toughen your sons into men?*"

"*The right sort of upbringing for a son is not the right place for a daughter.*" *Not this daughter that could never be replaced. Not even in the same camp with Umm Mutammim, my own dear milk mother.*

"*A daughter?*" *Amr repeated, quizzically raising a brow at me.*

"*Anybody's daughter,*" *I hastily added.*

Amr shook his head with incomprehension. I hadn't told even him about that night, where the little girl came from. I couldn't tell him, not without sullying the child's name with that of bastard and that of her dead mother with harlotry.

Amr had to ask what everybody else asked, "Of all the girl children to darken their father's faces in a year, why this one?"

The truth was, I wanted Bint Zura's daughter with me. The desert dirah was too far away; I had already missed the first four years of her life, not to mention time with her mother that could never be recovered. Sometimes I had the feeling that, had I overcome my fear of death enough to be publicly with another man's wife, I might have saved Bint Zura from her death. The death that was, in fact, in good part my fault. Perhaps if only I had dared to raid my own milk family—? Impossible.

Whisking Bint Zura's daughter to Mecca with me had been easy. And al-Harith, too; he had to be part of the bargain, of course. I'd given him some small duties with the horses to justify his presence in Mecca. His prospects as Malik's herdsman were limited enough, and al-Harith, too, had ambition for his supposed daughter. The daughter to whom he must always lend his name in my stead.

But no man can have a girl-child always at his heels, taking her to the public places he must visit, and remain a man or protect her sequestered as his honor demands. Bringing her to Amr's mother's place as she was now, for example.

Wives, other daughters—I had all of these still living. Surely there were enough females behind me in town to care for one girl-child with four years of desert crammed into her already. However, one wife—hoping to win favors over another—had tattled to me between bed cushions what had happened with my daughter at Khadijah's. Prophesying to a prophet's harem.

"That the child, my—ward—" I barely kept the word "daughter" off my wine-loosened tongue. "—should have been taken among the Muslim madwomen at all!"

This is what diverted me from settling into my usual manly tasks. I began this panicked hunt for exactly the right woman to buy or marry and set with no other task than to raise this one—whom I couldn't really claim as my own at all.

Of course, no such woman existed. There had been one once, under the white heat of the desert sky. She lay now, however, under desert sands. Or flitting over camel thorn, a night bird after prey. A falling star.

Sooner rather than later, my search brought me to Amr's garden.

"You could do worse than Khadijah Umm Qasim, ya Khalid."

My friend Amr, having refilled both our goblets with wine, leaned back amongst his cushions and studied me. I knew he knew I wasn't telling everything and wouldn't meet his eye. But what? What tight chill of premonition held me back before him? We had been through Omar's submission to the Prophet together, after Amr had told my cousin that his sister was a convert. Listening to Amr recite satirical poems had been the best way to get past that treachery. Having been born in this house where we sat, he more than any could understand and forgive when love makes a man wander. But the world around us did not remain static, and of that I was afraid. Afraid, in it, even of my best friend.

My friend had a tongue like honey on thorns; and my daughter, that warm afternoon, stopped her attention to the Goddess's maids to hear him. Later on she recalled all his poems, word for word, and added her own . . .

As I sit in Homs now, Amr sits comfortably in a hero's villa in Beersheba, revered as Egypt's conqueror. I don't suppose he would appreciate my recounting all the satirical verses his quick wit came up with in those long-ago days. Muhammad, blessed be he, was often a subject of our idle, pagan conversations. Amr might even send a couple of his famous assassins to visit me if he got wind of this. I am close to death and don't really care if it's a knife or this confounded heart that takes me. Still, for old time's sake, I will spare my friend the trouble and expense.

But, by God, we had pleasant times, idling in Umm Amr's gardens. After a morning with the horses, the hawks, and the hounds, to enter that lavishly cool place with the sparkling waters—ah! We would fan incense from the braziers across our faces until they forgot the dust they wore. We would dip our hands in the rosewater and sip her too-sweet-to-get-drunk-on date wine. Her girls would come and curl up like cats at our feet to sing and dance as a background. Even if we were beyond lust, it was nice to sit in this one place in all Mecca a man could go where every companion was not male, a place that was not his own harem riddled with intrigue, jealousy, and children. Here round bosoms and pink and crimson silks softened angular faces and desert-scruffy cloaks. Here Amr and I sat with others of our acquaintance—Omar before his conversion, my brothers, our friends. Older men didn't come here. Here we could speak freely about what we should do with the world when—heaven forbid!—our fathers should die and we would move into power.

Umm Amr, as I've said, flew a red kerchief over her door, announcing the holy services of her girls. The cult of the old love temples in Ephesus and Alexandria, which the spread of Christianity had decimated, still maintained a busy shrine in Mecca. A statue of the Goddess—in marble, so her perfect curves and white, upturned breasts in the old Greek style had not aged a day—stood on an altar wreathed in jasmine. Two or three golden lumps of frankincense smoldered languidly at Her naked white feet. At rare times when worship was slow, Her priestesses, dressed in wisps of light silk to emulate their Lady, carried Her in procession around the Ka'ba. Were they thumbing Her nose at an idol-hating God whose female creations too often sag or are boney with bad teeth? Muhammad had already attacked these holy women when they paraded their God with the large, movable phallus—on the day Hala had died.

That afternoon, in long, loose gowns, the priestesses had all come out of their rooms to play with that rarity among them: a child, my daughter. Mostly they had the Goddess's control of such things in ways of which we male worshippers had no inkling. Childbirth, certainly with its possibility of death, rarely shadowed their court, and then only when it might benefit their coffers.

Oh, don't get me wrong. My heart thuds in guilt and panic enough now. To think that I was more concerned that my little girl had visited with Khadijah than with servants of love! Women whose marriage contracts said such things as "until the lamp burns out" or "until moonrise" were braiding her hair with flowers, painting her lips and eyes. Did they teach her to become one of them?

These giggling girls, however, upheld a pious tradition in the Days of Ignorance. Khadijah and her husband wanted to do away with that tradition, with all tradition, and shape every heart to their own.

My friend Amr is known as the son of al-Asi, but in truth he could have been the son of any number of the reverend fathers of Mecca. His mother called him Ibn al-Asi and flattered that old man that the boy really did look like him. But the reason she did this, doctoring her marriage contracts for the illiterate if need be, was because al-Asi was the richest of her lovers, and all his other sons had died as children. Old al-Asi's lavish gifts kept Umm Amr in date wine and silks. Had the fruit of her labor been a girl, she would have blamed it on the pauper in town with twelve daughters already. In that case, she would have consecrated the child, as she herself had been, to the Goddess of love. Is that what those women did to my girl while I sat with my friend? The old Gods had their own ways of evening things out in this unfair world.

Actually, Amr did not look anything like al-Asi, and everyone knew it. I will withhold my opinion of whom he most resembled. There are people in high places who would not mind claiming the conqueror of Egypt as their kinsman. But they might well resent the insinuation that one of their reverend ancestors had indulged in such paganism. They flatter themselves as being among the first to reject all Gods but the One.

And Amr did look as much like his very feminine mother as any man could and still be superbly masculine. His beard was sparse, though always well oiled, his chin round and dimpled. But these features had hidden many an unsuspecting man's death on desert raids. Since Amr was (or was not) whose son he was, he could spill blood with practical impunity. Grieving kin had no one to take it out on but himself—and few would dare that. By the Gods' beneficence, by the red kerchief of the temporary wives flying above him since birth, he had not completely turned that bloody way. Not yet.

One other man in Mecca some said was my friend's companion in charm. This was my own father's son by another wife, Ummarah ibn al-Walid. He had all my father's assets of strength and beauty unmarred by the pox, which I'd suffered, and many others besides. God knows his mother thought him a true wonder and taught him to think so before he could toddle.

Taking up my responsibilities as head of our clan in my father's illness, I had been the one to bring my brother to Umm Amr's to introduce him to the ancient mysteries of the Goddess. In the same way, years before, my milk brothers and I had tried to do for the herdsman al-Harith, but I had more success in Ummarah's case. Perhaps I'd had too much success, in fact. Even though I'd fulfilled that other responsibility of a clan head—I had presented him with a wife and she with a son—my brother still came to pay his respects to the Goddess.

And so he stepped into Umm Amr's garden that afternoon, sending the priestesses scurrying into fewer clothes and abandoning my little painted girl so she came and sat on my knee.

"Say another poem, Uncle Amr," she begged.

I stroked her flower-crowned head but had to worry too much about my brother to encourage her request. What else could a clan head do to steady a young man so full of himself?

Rather than to see Ummarah shifting anxiously from foot to foot while he waited to worship, Amr called my brother over to join us on our cushions. He poured wine.

26

What is this religion wherein you have become separate from
your people, though you have not entered my religion nor that
of any other of the folk that surround us?
      —Words of the Negus of Abyssinia to Jafar
      ibn Abu Talib when he heard the words of
      the generous Quran as reported in a hadith

I fostered serious misgivings about my friend Amr's wisdom when he first invited Ummarah to join our circle in his mother's gardens. I did not want my little daughter, painted by whores, to get the wrong impression of the men of my family from his vain airs.

Does Amr have no sense at all to invite him so? I asked myself.

"Endure him for my sake, Khalid," Amr spoke in an undertone as Ummarah approached. "For my own instruction. His presence reminds me of the folly into which I could fall if I let knowledge of my own beauty get the better of me."

The conqueror of Egypt is that sort of man.

My little daughter reached over and tugged on my friend's sleeve. "Please, Uncle Amr, a poem."

While we witnessed yet again the signing of the marriage documents to get Ummarah a temporary bride, we began to discuss, once again, Muhammad the son of Abd Allah. Without poetry. Mecca held little other conversation in those days. The various merits of Umm Amr's girls seemed but a desperate diversion.

"What a lot of difficulties would be lifted if Muhammad could be made to meet with some fatal accident some dark night."

Amr studied the lamp flame used to heat the lumps of black bitumen for sealing contracts with more than necessary interest. This time, the terms for my brother's match were "until the white thread is distinguished from the black before sunrise." The fool Muslims would be at prayer.

"I do love it so when you recite a poem." Again we ignored the little girl.

"What a shame my cousin Omar didn't kill him one of those two times he set out to try," I said.

"Then we should have been rid of two madmen with one blow."

"What a shame that Muhammad's clan persists in supporting him."

"Yes," Amr agreed. "Anyone who attempted such an accident would bring so bloody a feud upon his head and the heads of all his kin—it would hardly make it worthwhile."

"What if we made a trade with Muhammad's kinsmen the Banu Hashim?" My brother surprised us both by speaking up; I had thought his mind too much on the rites of love he would shortly perform. "One of our young men for their Muhammad. A life for a life. Then they wouldn't care what we did to punish him, if he were our own."

I cringed at the stupidity of the suggestion. "And who is going to be willing to desert his own honored and ancient clan to become a son of Hashim?" I asked. "Just in time for them to kill him, too?"

"If a young man's clan asked him to, he would be honor-bound to go," Ummarah insisted. "Like you licked the hot sword, brother."

"Oh, you're suggesting I should give myself over to Muhammad's clan?"

"It would be like fighting in a war for the glory of the clan on the battlefield," Ummarah pursued. "You always say you long again for the Day of Dhu Qar."

Did I so? I smoothed the petals in my daughter's hair again and ignored another request for poetry. Rather than sweet longing—seeing once again the white camel and its sacred burden lurch forward, hearing the scream—memories of Dhu Qar continued to be as bitter as colocynth on my tongue.

"You make yourself out to be such a hero," Ummarah went on. "Licking hot sword blades, all of that. Well, here's another chance to prove it to the rest of us."

"What clan would be willing to give up a strong son, a man-at-arms?" I began, but Amr waved me silent.

Amr leaned forward over the writing table and let his great eyes loll under their heavy lashes. "I say, Ummarah. Why don't you go trade yourself for this Muhammad?"

"But I'm too young . . . There are so many more deserving of the honor . . ."

Amr and I turned all my brother's sudden and stupid excuses into a joking matter then. The time had come to see him off to the scented cushions with his chosen girl, with music and broad, bawdy jests like any groom to his bride. My little daughter—one hand in mine, the other in that of one of the other girls—joined the procession.

"Khadijah's husband, he recites poetry," my daughter said, more sulkily than any member of a wedding party should be. "He would recite if I asked him 'please,

O my uncle.' And I could recite to him."

Children do get the oddest notions, and then it is best just to ignore their fantasies. Recite to Muhammad, indeed! She should have been adding her little trill to those of the women who had spent the afternoon teaching her to do it.

❧

When our conversation from the brothel rose to the circles of our elders, however, where discussions were turned into action, the joke was ignored. My father, al-Walid, rose from his sick bed and led the delegation to Abu Talib of the Banu Hashim himself. He offered them his fourth son Ummarah in exchange for the person of Muhammad, blessed be he, to be controlled, finally, in any way our clan saw fit.

Blessed be the Merciful One Who, though He never willed that he should become a Muslim, nonetheless created Abu Talib, a man of honor. "This is not a fair exchange at all," he said. "You would give me your clansman to feed and clothe with the dainties and vanities he has become addicted to, while you only want my clansman in order to kill him. Take your treacherous bargains elsewhere."

This event wounded Ummarah's pride enough to keep him from infesting our circle for a while. By the time he did, the son of Abd Allah had given us something more important to worry about.

As is well known, at this time, under Muhammad's inspiration, some Muslims went across the Red Sea to seek asylum in the Empire of Abyssinia from what they termed our "persecution." This news unnerved Amr, usually the calmest of men. My friend's profession, when he cared to claim one, consisted of buying up fine leather goods from the tribes around Mecca or from the tanners' pits in at-Ta'if. These he shipped over to Africa where he traded them for skins with the life still in them—namely, slaves. We feared, not without reason, that with a colony stationed in Aksum, the Muslims could very easily take control of this commerce. They might also take it into their heads to aid the present Abyssinian emperor—or the Negus as he was called—to carry out his ambitions to extend his empire into Arabia. Amr, whose charms had long ago won him a solid friend in this Negus, determined to go at once in person. He meant to secure his claims and demand that the vagrant Muslims be returned to justice.

While we were discussing these matters, my younger brother Ummarah made his reappearance at the outer edge of our circle. To my surprise, he advanced humbly and quietly as becomes a younger man among his elders, where he may listen and learn but not presume to speak. This approach did not escape Amr's attention. He stopped mid-sentence to say, "And you, Ummarah ibn al-Walid, although the Hashim did not want you, you will come with me to Africa."

After the first twinge of jealousy, I accepted this arrangement with good humor. Amr had not asked me to accompany him because he wanted a second, someone to take his orders, not an equal as I was. Perhaps he hoped to show my brother what good use flashiness tempered with a little style could be put to. At any rate, it meant that I did not have to take Ummarah with me on the northeasterly route this year, tending him like a nursemaid when two of my father's other sons already competed with me.

My scribe asks: "Even so early, you thought of dividing the world between you, Amr ibn al-Asi and yourself? In trade then as you did it for Islam later?"

"The thought crossed my mind. If, with a little help from Ummarah, Amr could take all lands south and west, I could handle all the trade in the other two directions. I was not to be too far wrong, you see, though never in my wildest dreams had this conquering included more than just a controlling hand on the markets. It took the voice of the Prophet, blessed be he, to open the vision to include people's hearts and minds as well.

"But now we must add the complication of womenfolk. Pick up your pen again, fellow, and write."

Amr had been married to a girl of proper Qurayshi family according to old al-Asi's best desires. But Amr's concubine and favorite was one of his mother's own girls, a black Abyssinian slave named Bakarah he had given Umm Amr as a gift. His doting mother, Umm Amr, had returned the girl to her son later, well trained in all her best Goddess skills.

"A pox on all such demons," says my scribe as he writes. He who can never know the gifts of such girls.

Amr's first wife spent so much time visiting her mother and caring for their children that he would hardly miss her. But he was loath to travel without the second, the slave Bakarah. Especially on this trip to her homeland. He intended to let her visit her long-lost kin, to assure them they need not grieve or curse the year of famine that had forced them to sell her. Perhaps he wished to show the Negus by her presence, by her culture and her education, that the slave trade with Arabia was well worth continuing. Even the slaves benefitted.

So the envoy made their farewells to the Ka'ba and disappeared into the westward desert. They had hardly reached Jeddah on the coast before my brother forgot his hard-learned humility. He found himself in love with Amr's concubine. The infatuation was natural—Bakarah being the only woman in the group. Ummarah, however, was not content to moan and sigh like a poet when a woman was beyond his reach.

Ummarah decided to kill his master and my friend.

He plotted to push Amr into the sea during their crossing. But the girl Ba-

karah—to whom all passion was mere idle entertainment—kept Amr abreast of every development. My friend avoided the fateful shove until he was certain he could swim to shore. Then over he went.

When Amr appeared onshore, a little damp but having safely avoided the sharks, Ummarah pretended to rejoice at his master's miraculous salvation. "I felt so terrible, as if it were my fault."

And Amr pretended he suspected even less, saying, "It was a lurch of the boat. An accident that couldn't be avoided," until he could teach the young fool a proper lesson.

For this purpose, Amr enlisted the help of the Negus's queen, whom he had charmed on previous visits. This noble lady pretended to fall in love with my brother's beautiful face. Ummarah, flattered, instantly forgot all about the lowly slave Bakarah. He encouraged the queen's falsified fancies. When they were together in a compromising situation, Amr revealed the plot (as well as the queen's innocence) to the Negus. Then my friend stepped back to let the emperor extract punishment.

People today say the Muslim refugees worked a miracle and so ingratiated themselves to the throne of Abyssinia. I prefer the less faith-inspiring tale that I heard from Amr's own lips.

The Negus called up his sorcerers. They came in clouds of smoke and fire, black skin glistening. These sorcerers can stop a spear thrown at them a hand's breadth from their naked chests and watch it fall harmlessly at their feet. They drummed and danced and chanted. They gave my unwitting brother a potion to drink. They cast a demon of madness upon his already insubstantial mind. For years after, Ummarah wandered wild like a beast in the jungles deep inland, in the Land of Mist and roaring water, where the natives say the great Nile River takes its source.

Only some two or three years ago a young cousin of mine heard the tale and got fanciful notions about this beautiful clansman of his whom he had never seen. He decided to make the trip across the sea to Abyssinia himself to see if the madman could not be returned, by the power of the Name of the One God, to the community of the Faithful. He found my brother, the decades-old adulterer, a legend among the natives of the neighborhood. But when our cousin laid his hands on him to bring him home, Ummarah—or the demon within him—struggled and thrashed so much that he broke his own neck and so died. May rain fall gently upon his hard-earned nonbeliever's grave.

We sons of al-Mughira have never made any claim of blood against Amr for the fate of our brother. We know he deserved punishment. And my friend Amr ibn al-Asi endured disappointment enough on this journey without threat from us. This business with Ummarah distracted from the true purpose of his mission. It gave the Muslims time to prepare their defense.

And they were prepared, by the mercy of God. They recited to the Negus a new Surah from the Quran. They recited the nineteenth, which relates the stories of Yahya, whom Syrians call John the Baptist, and of Isa's birth by the virgin Maryam. The Negus, who was a monotheist, a devout Christian, wept to hear how Maryam shook the palm tree as the birth pangs came upon her.

Amr had to admit defeat and to return empty-handed to Mecca. And I see now that events were moving according to the will of Almighty God.

But I also see that perhaps it would have been better had I left my daughter in the desert, never brought her to Mecca at all.

27

Have you considered Allat, and al-Uzza
and Manat the third, the other?
What, have you males and He only females?
Behold, that would be a most unjust division.
They are naught but names you yourselves
have named, you and your fathers.
>—The Holy Quran 53:19–24, what has
>replaced the original "Satanic Verses" in the
>Surah of the Star

The hour between the last two prayers of the evening, "the time of herd dust" as it was called, settled over the oasis of Tadmor. Dust dulled the clappers on the bells of herds returning wearily from the day's grazing, milk heavy in their udders. The sun—exhausted, lying low in the west—thudded into every particle hanging suspended, and the scent of camel-dung fires and tired suppers weighted the air.

Sitt Sameh picked up more wool, stuffed it in the bosom of her dress to control it towards the spindle and began her story once more. "I had known there would be something remarkable about the day from the moment I woke up. Woke up in that strange town to which I'd been brought called Mecca. Dawn came with those curious streaks of light called shaytan's horns."

Rayah formed her fingers into a ward against evil. "As happens only once or twice a summer?" she asked, beginning then to recite "In the Name of God—"

"In those days—"

"In the Days of Ignorance."

"Very well, call them that. But in those days, 'shaytan' had not yet gained the meaning it now has."

"Of something totally and irredeemably evil and contrary to God's will." Rayah gave it as a statement of fact, but she felt herself relenting. She had always secretly found the spray of glory in the sky beautiful. She would like to be able to love it instead of fear it.

Sitt Sameh, however, would not be absolute. "I took this sign to mean that the spirit world was very active. We all did, in those days. It could be active for good as well as bad, so everyone took care that the first holy beggar she saw got an extra little something. Many a woman even went out of her way to make a special offering at the Ka'ba, to her personal shaytan or to Manat, She of fortune. A man would nod to his associates upon meeting and comment that yes, he could see it, active spirit, thickening the air like what happens just before a sandstorm."

"Were the Conqueror alive, God reward him," Abd Allah commented from his sick bed, "he would shiver at the mere thought of 'sandstorm.' He always did. His back, he said, would seem to burn again."

"But he did not suspend his business any more than the next man," Sitt Sameh countered. "Who knew but what those self-same spirits might make it a day of wonderful gain? There was as much chance of that happening as catastrophe, so we took our chances.

"Khalid ibn al-Walid went early, as was his custom, to pay his devotions at the Ka'ba."

"Rather, he went to be seen to pay his devotions," Abd Allah suggested, "for since Omar his cousin had converted to Muhammad and his brother Ummarah gone mad in the Abyssinian desert, Khalid Abu Sulayman, too, was suspect. I got the impression that he made a point to show the gossips daily that their suspicion was wasted on him, particularly on a day of awe-full omen."

Sitt Sameh nodded in agreement; no doubt that was true. She, as a child, had not been aware of all the reasons adults might do things. She continued the story in her own way. "Then he sat, as was likewise his custom, among the men to hear what news had blown out of the desert during the night.

"He brought me with him that morning. Or, as he would have taken care to say then, he brought his herdsman with him and his herdsman just happened to bring his little daughter. Abd ar-Rahman—that son of the Conqueror who has come all the way from Homs and now sits downstairs—he and I are very close in age. Khalid brought him along, too, not so much to teach him the ways of men, but as an incentive to al-Harith to feel free to bring his daughter. The herdsman always made such a fuss about it, certain that I, his girl, should stay at home. A poor man's daughter is often exposed and out of the harem, collecting dung for the fire or tending goats because there are no slaves. He frets more about her safety when he can afford that luxury to make up for the times when he cannot.

"I know my father—I mean al-Harith—was not comfortable with me finding a playmate in Khalid's son. He remembered old scars of his own and could not keep a grimace from his face when he heard Abd ar-Rahman call me a 'herdsman's child' in scorn. Khalid did nothing, at first, to correct the abuse, finding support in such proverbs as 'The boy is a boy even though he rules a country.'"

Abd Allah nodded. "He said that same proverb to me on occasion—about himself, I think. As he sat Conqueror in Homs."

"So I took the matter into my own hands," Sitt Sameh continued her tale. "A word here, a verse of poetry there got the boy whipped, his father making a man of him. As if whipping ever gentled either child or beast. I lectured Abd ar-Rahman myself at length, in a childish way, about how 'a truly great man is known by the charity and compassion he holds towards his dependents.'

"But I never ran away crying, as my father had done in the old story. I stood my ground. I was made of sterner stuff than al-Harith—my reputed father. What a silly boy such as Abd ar-Rahman might think had no effect on what I thought of myself. And what Khadijah's daughter Zaynab told me of her namesake, the blue-eyed warrior queen, gave me even less reason to listen to him."

Rayah understood that her mother was telling her not to worry about the Abd ar-Rahman grown to manhood and governorship downstairs any more than she herself had done as a girl. But this was a man who could have a scribe tortured for what he had taken in dictation—

"I suspect it was not his son's education that worried the Conqueror that summer," Abd Allah suggested. "It was his daughter's, that awesome charge he had been given by the voice of a shooting star. He was very jealous of what al-Harith could do for you that he could not. Amidst all you have to blame Khalid ibn al-Walid for, Lady, keep his devotion to you in mind. When al-Harith would pick up his little girl, fallen asleep on Khalid's carpet because of the lateness of the hour, the great Conqueror would fight tears of jealousy. Al-Harith was allowed to pat those little honey-colored cheeks as he settled her between the covers and the rugs. Khalid, rich as he was, was not. Al-Harith, lying propped up on an elbow, drifting off to sleep each night, was allowed to have her little face as his very last waking sight. This seemed to be the greatest of the world's injustices. Is it any wonder, then, that whenever he could, the Conqueror took your education in both of his hands?"

"Was the marketplace and Ka'ba what a man usually thought of in the education of a young lady?" Sitt Sameh countered. "He brought his son Abd ar-Rahman with us, not one of his acknowledged daughters about my age, of which there were plenty."

"Ah, but this was no ordinary young lady. 'She must learn the ways of the world and the ways in which spirit works upon the mortals here,' the Conqueror told me."

"But he didn't have you write such words upon your parchments."

"He still struggled with the same constraints, the constraints of his honor and his greatness. He was bound to teach you in the best way he knew how. You were, in any case, a gratifying student."

"Was I?" Sitt Sameh gave a fierce twist of her yarn.

"I'm sure you got more out of visits to the Ka'ba at four years of age than Abd ar-Rahman ever would."

Sitt Sameh considered the eunuch's words, delivered from his sick bed. She set her wool aside to get up and fetch him some more poppy juice.

"Just water," he asked her instead. "You will not keep me from speaking the truth with more sedative. You were more on the Conqueror's mind that summer long ago than was Abd ar-Rahman, his son. Heaven favored you, too."

"More than Abd ar-Rahman who now holds all the power?" she demanded. "He who is now governor of a great city, from whom I must continue to hide though our father is dead and who will soon pull me out into the light of day?"

"Do not fear, Lady." Abd Allah attempted to turn her gaze from the door-flap of the little third-floor room, her attention from the unseen space below. In that space, Abd ar-Rahman had installed himself as a guest whose high station overwhelmed the turpentine sellers. Abd Allah and Sitt Sameh had fallen to whispering, as if the man could overhear them two stories below. "I think you have some power over this half-brother of yours."

"No power to keep him from killing me and my daughter and so ridding himself of the embarrassment of our existence all together."

Sitt Sameh picked up the sword that still lay unsheathed on the rug before her. She turned the blade to catch the light.

She wouldn't, would she? Rayah's heart stopped. Resort to using it against a guest? She breathed again when her mother quickly set the blade down and picked up her spinning once more.

"You are not without friends," Abd Allah said with quiet urging. "God—or the Goddess, if you will—has not abandoned you yet."

Sitt Sameh looked at her daughter. The blue eyes were hard, as ever. But was their hardness a craving for protection? Had it always been? The same sharp fear that made a man reach for his blade and sometimes—God forbid—to swing it even before he knew what flesh might meet blade as he did? The dangers that had always forged steel in Sitt

Sameh's eyes were suddenly coalescing into actual persons, names from the past slowly gathering, with the fall of evening, into material threats.

Rayah decided it was best to say nothing. That same Abd ar-Rahman, the bullying boy of the tale she was hearing, held a place of honor in the majlis like a trap set against the harem door.

After a few twirls of the spindle, Sitt Sameh found the thread of her tale again. "I did love to perform a child's version of the devotions. I made great friends with several of the priestesses. And not just those in Amr ibn al-Asi's mother's garden, as the Conqueror's dictation would have you believe, although they had much to teach me of the powers of love. The women who knew Allat, Manat and al-Uzza, other aspects of womanhood, would sit and talk to me, with *me*, for hours on end.

"Abd ar-Rahman could not be bothered with such things. He always went at once to join the other boys around the well Zamzam, tormenting the old well-keeper until he was forced to throw the only thing he had at them—the sacred water. On hot summer days, that was great refreshment."

To Rayah's shocked gasp that the holy water could be treated so, Sitt Sameh replied, "Remember, child, it was the Time of Ignorance.

"And then—I was no longer talking to the priestesses. How did I find him they called the Prophet? How long had I sat thus? I cannot say. Two camels can find each other out over days of trackless desert. But there I was, perched upon Muhammad's knee."

"Precious blessings on him," Rayah added.

"But he was not the Prophet then, at least, not to me. And not to Khalid, either, nor to most of the town. He was a troublemaker, a hater of the old ways and, to Khalid, a destroyer of the Gods."

Rayah didn't want to hear these complaints as much. "But, Lady, what did he say to you, precious blessings on him?"

"He blessed me."

"*Al-hamdullillah*," Rayah exclaimed with wonder and joy. Her mother had been blessed by the Messenger of God himself.

"I think his words were, 'God bless you, my daughter. You will love the truth.' Something like that. I remember more clearly what I said to him."

"Which was?"

"I asked him why he sent his one daughter away to darkest Africa and made the other one to weep day and night."

"God forgive you, Lady, you didn't? Not to the Messenger of God. But what did he say in return?"

"If he said anything, I don't remember," Sitt Sameh said. "Khalid ran to us then. He snatched me away from the old man as he might snatch me from a fire. Even as he spat into the tangled henna-dyed beard and carried me swiftly away, we continued to stare at one another, visionary blue eye riveted to blue eye.

"'Never,' Khalid said with sharpness that made me start to cry in his arms. 'Never speak to that man again.'

"'But why, O Uncle?' I asked.

"'He is a very wicked man.' He'd succeeded in breaking our stare at last, making me spill it instead into childish tears.

"'No, Uncle, no,' I protested."

"There was wisdom in her discernment beyond all her years," Abd Allah commented, "more wisdom than emotion, for all her weeping."

"'He is not wicked,' I said. 'He knows goodness when he hears it. He only has to hear it, that's all.'"

"Then what happened?" Rayah asked as her mother threatened to stop the story again. Surely she didn't mean to say that she, at four years old, had been the one to speak that goodness to *him*?

"Khalid rejected my words, being too angry, too afraid, perhaps, to give the matter further thought. Seeing that I had either his or al-Harith's undivided attention for the rest of the time he had to remain in the Ka'ba precinct kept him distracted.

"But then whispers accompanied by chuckles rumored about the square: 'By Hubal of my fathers, old Muhammad is hearing his voices. Ibn Abd Allah is going to prophesy again!'

"All of Mecca knew the scene well. He they called the Messenger of God—"

"Blessed be he," interjected Rayah.

"He grew tense and rigid. His legs no longer folded gracefully beneath him but stuck straight out in front of him like the poles of a camel litter. The globes of his blue eyes started from his head so that the red veins in them were exaggerated and seemed to give him pain. I heard a buzzing in the air as if the spirit we had sensed since dawn suddenly amassed about the Prophet's head as bees swarm to their queen.

"Seeing his state, the Muslims rushed to their master's side, but they all knew better than to try and lend him a hand or some sort of support at a time like this. Such a move would be an interference from the tangible world, which was the last thing the Prophet—"

"Blessed be he," said Rayah.

"—Wanted in the midst of his divine communication. Besides this, his companions knew that the weight of heaven was pressing down upon their master. They could see that this weight turned the stones beneath him to dust. They knew from past experience that that weight could crush a man's leg or cause camels to buckle beneath him.

"With snickers and jibes, a crowd of unbelievers began to form a second ring, to take entertainment from what this new prophecy might be. Khalid did not wait to hear. He bundled me up in his cloak. He did not care what his son Abd ar-Rahman happened to hear, but he muffled my ears as he carried me from the sacred square. I protested—I found everything about Muhammad intensely interesting—but Khalid refused to listen to me as well.

"And then the square was filled with the Word of God. Even Khalid ibn al-Walid stopped in his tracks, me in his arms.

"Muhammad spoke slowly and clearly, as was his wont when what he spoke was revelation. He mouthed each sound carefully as if he, an illiterate man, were actually reading. He chanted letter by letter, like the strange sort of music that comes from a schoolroom full of young boys learning to read at their master's knees.

"These were the words he spoke as I remember them:

> "'By the star when it sets . . .
> Have you not considered Allat and al-Uzza
> And Manat, the third, the other?
> These are exalted females,
> Sublime swans ascending nearer and nearer to God
> And truly their intercession may be hoped for,
> Their likes should not be neglected.'"

"The Conqueror said those words would be remembered in the harem," Abd Allah spoke in a strangled sigh, quieter than a whisper, "try to forget them as men might."

Rayah froze. Sitt Umm Ali had never taught her words like these as part of the Holy Quran. Rayah knew they must be wicked, and yet she knew their source and couldn't hate it.

Sitt Sameh went on, oblivious to the crush of terror in her daughter's heart. "A great sigh of divine relief exuded from one end of the square to the other when these words had penetrated every ear. That sigh bounced off the smooth walls of the Ka'ba and returned to inflate every heart with joy. Muhammad had, in so many words, allowed the worship of our three great and ancient Goddesses along with his single jealous God. The sons of Mecca, tense and having been at each others' throats for so long, wanted to shout for joy. They wanted to clap one another on the back in congratulation. They wanted to toss their camel goads into the air and shout triumphant war cries.

"Instead, we all watched Muhammad's silent and pious action: he fell to his knees and prostrated himself forward upon his palms. Then every single man gave vent to the reverence and relief he felt. The entire square, like one great blooming flower as the peace of nighttime falls, folded itself up after Muhammad's example.

"At the edge of the holy precinct, which was as far as Khalid's flight had brought us, I wriggled out of his arms. I, too, turned, and bowed to the ground. As did Khalid behind me. Khalid's actions were in such haste and bewildering wonderment that he did not manage to face exactly towards the House. The careful observer would have seen that he was still turned in the direction of his last action before his knees rooted him to the ground. It was more directly to me that his idolatrous palms stretched out.

"Ignoring him, I prayed the same words Muhammad recited."

"Blessed be he." A creeping horror strangled Rayah's pious wish.

Without hesitation now, Sitt Sameh pushed ahead. "Only I did not echo the words as one with a sharp memory might after first hearing.

> "These are exalted females,
> Sublime swans ascending nearer and nearer to God.

"I spoke the words as a poet recites her own composition, as tenderly as a mother may say the name of her own firstborn, there beneath the shaytan's horns in the sky over Mecca. I know, and stayed bowed longer than any for that knowledge, that this was my own inspiration and that Muhammad had taken it secondhand."

And Rayah wanted to die, to rid the world of the burden of her blasphemous life.

28

بسم الله الرحمن الرحيم

**Believers, when you meet the unbelievers preparing for battle
do not turn your backs to them. Anyone who does shall
incur the wrath of God and hell shall be his home, an evil
dwelling indeed.**
—The Holy Quran 8:15–16

*How glorious were those few weeks in Mecca when the Verses of the Swans, as
they were called, reigned over us in peace. If Muhammad allowed four Gods,
surely he could be brought around to tolerate the rest. Clansmen, Muslim
and non-Muslim, embraced one another in the streets, a thing their differences had
forbidden them to do for so long. The refugees—all but my mad brother Ummarah—came back from Abyssinia upon hearing the good news, and there was more
rejoicing, more blessed homecoming. The rich feasted the poor, the widow and the
orphan found strong and righteous protection. We thought ourselves rather foolish
not to have seen the divinity of Muhammad's dream of paradise on earth before.
And the Muslims went about amazed that reconciliation could have been found in
so few words.*

*But God, the Merciful and Compassionate, willed that things should be other-
wise. Al-Harith hated the town; he insisted upon taking his family and returning
to the hereditary pastures of the Banu Tamim. And because anything I gave him
to do was obvious make-work, I ran out of excuses. The common herdsman finally
got his way.*

*I'm certain I'm the only one who felt the loss and saw the link: The moment my
daughter's influence was gone from the town, the bastion of peace built by harmony
between monotheist and pagan crumbled away as if it had never been.*

"I blame my cousin Omar's influence on the Prophet," I tell my scribe.

"Blessed be he. Blame, Master? You want me to write 'blame'?"

"Current fashion calls those same verses not Verses of the Swans but those of the evil shaytan. The moment my daughter was gone from Mecca, the angel told Muham-mad that those verses were to be replaced."

"The Satanic Verses," says the eunuch in a tone that would freeze the water of the fountain. "You remember what was commanded to be forgotten."

"Current fashion will praise my cousin and call his influence sublime instead of blameworthy."

"Current fashion aims for purity."

"And so is sterile. Current fashion prefers the dragging prose Muhammad—or God through Muhammad—substituted for the Verses of the Swans. But I heard them. And I remember the forge-heat of the original. 'By the star when it sets . . . Have you not considered Allat and al-Uzza and Manat. . .? These are exalted females . . . '"

"Master, I will not write them. Such evil words, such dangerous words."

"Leaving a page blank also sends a message."

"I won't write it."

"But women also heard," I say. "The harem will remember if you will not."

"Here, Master, have back today's coin and tomorrow I will send another scribe. But I myself will not write those words of Satan."

"Very well." I bow my red turban in a gesture of surrender. "No, keep your coin. What is it to me?"

My scribe's exaggerated breath calms somewhat. He thinks he has won, but I know I have, in this particular parry of pen against sword. They may try to hush it, but once it is written, the world will know. One set of words stood substitute for another. It is enough to know that, and blessed shadows have come to the desert again.

"Here," I tell him. "Here are the words you may write without compunction. Words that take the place of the Verses of the Swan in the Holy Quran."

"Has God adopted daughters from among those whom He has created, and chosen sons for you?"

"Or say some of the verses that were revealed afterwards:"

> *"What! Do they make a being to be the offspring of God*
> *who is brought up among silly woman's trinkets and*
> *is ever contentious without reason?"*

I hear Omar's voice in these replacements. Omar wanted a fight. He has always wanted a fight since first I threw him from the back of our mare. He was aching for the chance to prove that we had been wrong all along, that he had been right to follow an uncompromising Muhammad from the beginning. He wanted to toss our teasing back in our faces with dust and dung. He wanted the lofty position that such inspired forethought would give him when they won. Omar wanted a fight and, by God, that is what he got.

I went north with al-Harith and his family to return them to the pastures of the Banu Tamim. This time I stayed away from Mecca longer than I ever had before, seeing to lands my father had purchased in Syria, leaving him to see to things nearer home. Lands in settled places require so much more attention than desert holdings. I learned the lay of Syria—that would help me in years to come. During this time I married again—the first time I'd managed since that unearthly night at Nakhlah—the woman who sits behind me even now. More importantly, I made many trips across the Syrian desert, to trade horses—and to visit my milk family. I spent more time with the Tamimi than I had at any time since I was in my milk mother's arms, and I watched Bint Zura's little daughter grow, more than any child I claim as my own.

Would she remember me today, she a grown woman? I don't know. This little mite whose spirit had swayed the Prophet of the age: Sometimes I would hear her clear, high voice singing, improvising new words to old tunes. I would peek through the tent curtains like women peer at the men's world—and know more about it than the men who live there themselves. Then I'd see her trailing after her herds through the haze they raised just before the sun burst over the horizon. I would discover her asleep on rugs in the heat of the day, curled fists thrown with innocent abandon to either side of her head where the sweat dampened her hairline. I would hunker down where I was and watch. When she laughed and skipped with the other children among the guy ropes, I could never pay attention to the men's talk of pastures and horse flesh.

I did not come back to Mecca for two years. Finally I knew I must tear myself away, but then only when I had arranged to have al-Harith come with me once again, bringing the daughter I could not claim with him. I even saw to it that she had a grown woman's tassled litter to ride in on her camel. We set our mounts' noses south once more, with the profits of two year's trading in Syria in camel packs and a herd of twenty-five horses to improve my stock at home.

I was blissfully unaware of the fact, but I had had precious little news of what was happening in Mecca all the time I was gone. Only a rumor blew through the desert: The Quraysh have driven Muhammad from their midst at last. If that be the case, I thought, only peaceful profits lay ahead. Besides, Pleiades, "the many little ones," had risen; winter had begun. The weather turned cool, pleasant for travel during the day. More, the holy month of Rajab, "the respected one," would soon be upon us, meaning that no Arab would dare raid for fear of the curse of the Gods. I might quickly go and then return to the tents of the Sons of Tamim again.

Following the Wadi 'l-Qura, my men and I with our herd had already passed
the bleak lava ridge of Ash-Sharayf. We were just about through the lands of the
Banu Muzaina. The tribe, I knew, were fierce raiders if they ever dared to curse
themselves by ignoring the holy month and the presence in their tents of a son of
mine in fosterage. Another day's travel would bring us into Yathrib, a fair-sized
town, where we could resupply and rest within the protection of clay brick walls. I
could take care of certain finances with the Jews of Yathrib, too. The town was but
a week's travel away from Mecca. All the tribes between Yathrib and home were
securely allied with the Quraysh and presented no threat.

So I could not believe my eyes when al-Harith pointed to a plume of dust on
the horizon and said first "Riders" and then "Raiders." I rubbed my eyes to rid them
of the crusted sand and a certain sun blindness long hours in the saddle can bring.

Having ridden for a closer look and then returned, my herdsman assured me:
"They are armed for war and have no women or pack animals with them. Raiders."

"They come in broad daylight like this?" I asked, astounded at such brazenness.
Usually raiders waited until dark, the moonless time of the month, and until they
had watched an encampment from a hiding place beforehand.

What manner of flesh—or fire and smoke—could such raiders be, to break the
truce moon? By Hubal—and the God would surely stretch his blood-red hand out
to help me. I would keep an oath I had sworn before al-Harith and the Gods when
I'd been young. I would not submit to defeat in battle again, as long as I lived,
and surely not to such a blasphemous force. Now was the time to mount one of my
horses for speed in battle.

And then, in the corner of my eye, I caught a glimpse of the swaying litter, Bint
Zura's child urging her camel closer to her father—not me—for protection. The
vision of her mother's litter collapsing to the ground at Dhu Qar blinded me for
a minute. All that had come after— My stomach roiled as if the wells where we'd
filled our waterskins were tainted.

The best way to keep my oath—and to protect the girl—was never to get in a
fight. Stay at her speed, stay on the cursed camel. As a precautionary first move, I
turned the caravan off the track westward.

The approaching dust cloud moved faster than we did. Figures separated themselves out of the general blur. Fifteen at least, to my ten men. No wonder they dared
to strike in broad daylight. This wasn't a raid. It was a full-scale attack. I might
still win and keep my vow. But I'd lose horses, either dead or driven off.

I whistled my herd to a faster pace. We might outrun them. At least choose the
site of the unrolling. This open ground would not serve my road-weary company well.

Then al-Harith, struggling to stay even with his daughter's camel at the same
time, pointed westward. Another plume. As near as the first one, nearer perhaps,

but it had come on us invisibly because the wind blew their signs away from us.

"Good God," I couldn't help exclaiming. "Thirty men there. Forty at least. On their swift horses. And the two bands work in concert—see how a movement of that one shifts the other."

I swung my she-camel around to help control the gallop the horses had reached. The barren ground flew beneath us now, the camels' tails flying straight out from their solidly pumping thighs. Just tallying those dark shadows within the dust clouds would have made any other caravan driver slow, reel his company, and hope to bargain the lightest surrender possible. I, Khalid ibn al-Walīd, had made a vow. I would not surrender.

I reached down and caught the reins of my daughter's mount, pulling the beast to keep up. The litter rocked dangerously, and the girl inside squealed, "Eeeee," whether from excitement or fear, I couldn't tell.

"They signal us to stop," al-Harith said, struggling to keep up.

"By Hubal, I will not."

If I refused to halt and they caught up with us, however, this wouldn't be just an attack. It would be a slaughter.

My first maneuver westward had set a long, hardened lava flow between us and the eastern band of pursuers. That hardly mattered if the western band trapped us against the ridge of porous rock.

Within the litter, the girl had begun to recite something. I couldn't hear the words—a poem, a song? But the flow of the sound matched the lava's flow and captivated my whirling mind. The eerie red-black slipping past my camel's racing pads seemed a river turned to stone. Ripples had frozen on its surface like some enchanted world held under an evil spell. Its rounded edges bulged as if pottage had poured out on the sand—and stopped there for eternity.

I'd hesitated to drive the herd over the flow from the start. Lava is rough on horses' feet. What was the point? We were going to be trapped on one side of the flow or the other.

Then I noticed that, as my daughter's song rose, the stone flow was also rising: as high my camel's hocks, now her knees. Before us, gritty rock loomed over our heads. There, the lava formation was not a flow at all, but one of those strange conical shapes of the same strange matter, as if the stuff had once cloaked a mountain. The mountain within was now all worn away, leaving only this hollow, crumbling hull—and sometimes a naked lava pillar in their centers.

As God is my witness, my daughter had sung that formation into being, although none of my men seemed to think it miraculous.

"Quick," I shouted to my men, and signaled to make my meaning plain over the thundering hooves. "Drive the animals in there."

The strange formation was as close to a fortress as might be made without the hands of men, with only the whistling, invisible hands of the jinn. In fact, we call such places jinn forts, and some say they are haunted. But I couldn't care for that. Not now.

Just as I'd hoped, around the western side of the red-black flat-topped cone where the winds had scoured it, the lava wall had crumbled almost to the ground. Here we drove the herd through. They tripped and stumbled over the crumbled rock in their terror and sent up whinnies that echoed off the cone's far walls like jinn horses, increasing the animals' terror. Our beasts circled the space wildly for some time, but when they discovered there was no way out but through the same entrance that I still held with my men, they began to calm. Calm enough that I could think of shooing my daughter's mount in after them with the yelled warning to her to keep out of the way. Then I could think of something else, what was behind us instead of ahead.

Al-Harith had ridden around the cone to keep an eye on the eastern band. "They seem to have given it up," he told me. "The plume rises straighter and is not drawing closer."

"Very well. They are rival bands, not one mighty band split in two. The lesser band backs down from booty before the greater. But we still have the greater to wor-ry about." I pointed desperately westward. "Fifty men at least. And closing fast."

I set up the pack camels as a kneeling, solid barrier across the mouth of our compound. I set three of my best bowmen behind these backs. The other men and I quickly unpacked our sheaves of lances, our stiffened leather shields, every other weapon from the camels' burdens. I strapped on my heavenly sword, the baldrick crossing from shoulder to hip. Then we clambered up on either side of the fort's entrance, trying to conceal our positions among the rocks.

Once these preparations were made, we hadn't long to wait. The plume of dust grew thick among the remnants of our wake. The thud of their animals roared in upon our own. It was no use imagining they might not know where we had gone. Our prints set a path as wide and plain as some Roman road across the wind-purified sand.

I had no time for fear. I had one moment to get my bearings, to steady myself. One panting moment to recall my childhood exploit—how I'd stood in just such a position as Omar had ridden around Mount Arafat toward me at the head of a race.

Then once again I sprang, landing on the lead rider. No personal fury or youth made me clumsy this time. His was a wirey frame, tough as camel thorn. His head-cloth muffled his face against the dust, bound around a conical helmet. This left only his eyes, desert bloodshot, slit like the pits on a viper's head. His left arm bore a leather-bordered wickerwork shield; his right held the reins.

My grasping hand slipped. Rather than closing on yielding fabric, it met a layer of chainmail beneath. I did not get the firm grasp I wanted. By the grace of God, however, the wind-filled outer robe did not give. All the while enduring the heavy blows of its rider, I jabbed the horse with my knee.

We didn't ride together long. The beast whinnied and jerked as my knee hit its belly. It took my part then, and I wrestled my man, his back to my front, to the ground.

He landed uppermost, sharp bone elbowing my ribs. The rings of chainmail, barely padded, knocked the wind from my lungs. Blackness swirled in my eyes for an instant. Sand sprayed in my mouth and nose.

When my mind cleared, all around me, vaguely, I was aware of each of my men engaged with another rider. The rain of arrows and lances had stopped the enemy short before the fort's opening. Otherwise we might have been trampled to death. Screaming horses and screaming men backed up behind the narrow passage. They clogged one another's movements but kept our front to a manageable space.

My man, the leader, was still on top of me, his back to my front. In this difficult position, however, I'd succeeded in keeping a firm grasp on each of his arms. I yanked both arms down, extracting a grunt of pain from above. He kicked, connecting with a knee. Pain flashed all the way to my crotch, balling there.

He was trying to flip himself to face me. With his next kick, I surprised him by not resisting. Spitting sand, grunting, I kept the roll going until I heaved my opponent over, under me. He lurched like an untamed horse. I thrust my left arm across his windpipe.

Don't spend so long on one man, fool, I told myself. I would have to dispatch five, more, to make up for my less competent men, before our odds evened up.

Finally I could spare a hand to draw my heavenly blade. We were too close for it to be of any use, however. I settled for my short dagger instead.

It took forever to get the blade near anything vital, even once I had the upper hand. I hit hard armor beneath his robes. I hit his sword, his shield. He threw my arm off his throat and bucked up.

I've fought with women for their honor much like this. The notion crossed my mind. So thinking, I went for his groin and got repulsed there too, having to move quickly to avoid a strike to my own—and I hadn't had time to put on armor.

This fellow didn't want to die. He fought like a bull camel in rut. The studded leather rim of his shield caught me on the brow, sending blood to blind my eyes. The tails of my own red headdress tightened in a garrote around my neck. I gurgled for breath. Strength coursed like an inner armor through his every sinew.

And all the while he screamed something that I took to be his battlecry. Sometimes, though, between deafening clangs, it sounded like my own name.

Finally, I elbowed his sword arm to the ground and pinned it there. My right elbow got under his shield. My left hand groped for the headcloth muffling the lower part of his face—as raiders do so their prey won't see who they are, making vengeance more difficult. I didn't care who he was. I just wanted to avoid any neck armor.

The headcloth came free—and I began to join my voice to his, calling my men to halt.

The man I was straddling with my blade inches above his neck was my friend Amr ibn al-Asi.

29

Was God's earth not wide enough for you to emigrate somewhere else in it?
> —The Holy Quran 4:99, describing what
> the angels will say to those unbelievers who
> blame their disbelief on oppression in the
> countries where they lived

"*W*hy on earth did you ride on us so?" I demanded of Amr.

*Once the scuffles and arrows had halted. Once men began in won-
der to find old acquaintances and kinsmen among the warriors they'd
been intent upon killing not a moment before. Once I made certain al-Harith had
helped his daughter, shaken but unharmed, from her litter.*

"You saw those other riders in the east?"

*I looked for the old familiar grin from Amr as he said this, but he gave none.
So I just nodded.*

*"Raiders from Yathrib. They would have taken everything you have, horses,
everything, if we hadn't come when we did."*

*"Yathrib?" I repeated. "The Yathribis are a mild enough folk. More intent upon
fighting among themselves than against others."*

*My question went unanswered for a while as we had to sort out the wounded
from both sides and among the beasts. Fortunately, no human wound looked
serious, and they were about equal on both sides, so amicably we decided no
blood-money was owing. One of Amr's horses had caught an arrow through the
neck and would have to be put down. I gave its rider one from my own herd and
that was settled.*

*I suggested we light a fire. The sun had set. "It will help us to tend the wounds.
Some of them might want branding with the edge of a hot blade. And we might as
well cook the dead horse for ourselves as leave it for the hyenas. Then let me tell you*

about all the doings in the wide world: how the Roman Emperor Heraclius has had great success reconquering all the bits of his Syrian province the Persians recently conquered away from him.

"Here, men, is there some brush for kindling?"

But Amr stopped the search for dry brush. "Too close to Yathrib," he said. "Too dangerous. We cannot light a fire."

"Yathrib again. What is the matter with Yathrib?" I demanded. "Have its men all turned to jinn overnight?"

To my surprise, even this little joke of mine did not draw a chuckle from my friend. His sobriety made me wonder if indeed he thought it true.

"You haven't been here for many months, I think," he said.

Over by the couching camels, I heard a familiar little voice pipe up. "But my father, I am hungry."

Then I talked Amr into a fire. "Just a little one, here within the jinn's fort. The flame will not rise over its walls, and the horse flesh will not go to waste." And my daughter will not go hungry.

Finally my friend shrugged. "It's your profits you'll lose if the men of Yathrib find us, not mine."

Amr had aged since I sat with him last around a mound of qat. His beard was no longer oiled and carefully tended. It wore a month's worth of desert grime and unruly growth. Something serious indeed had happened.

What was afoot in Yathrib would shake the world in such a way that what passed between Rome and Persia would appear as no more than the squabblings of children. From that era, all time henceforth would be counted.

"I left Mecca in midsummer, a year and a half or so ago," I told him.

"That was right around the time these things began," Amr said.

The conjunction of events was just coincidence to him. But as he continued with his tale, I had to remember what I knew was no coincidence at all: When I'd left Mecca, al-Harith had ridden with me, bearing his little daughter before him on the camel.

"Not long after you left," Amr said, "Abu Talib died."

"The Gods send the rain gentle on his grave," I said. "But it was to be expected. He was an old man and hadn't been well."

"But, you see, he was Muhammad's uncle, the head of his clan. And just about the only one in that clan inclined to extend his protection to his nephew, with all his disruptive preaching."

I nodded. "But Muhammad's preaching had ceased to be so disruptive. At least, before I left."

"Well, that was only the respite of a brief, cooling rain. He started up again, the moment you were gone, worse than ever."

The moment we—she was gone from Mecca, I thought again, but let my friend continue.

"Abu Talib's heirs never had patience with their mad kinsman, and once the old man was gone, they let it be known that they removed their protection from the son of Abd Allah. Any man in Mecca could kill him then, without fear of blood feud."

"I'll wager you had men lined up for the privilege," I commented, poking the fire with my camel goad. Sparks showered heavenward, making the scars on my back burn once more. "By Hubal, I'm sorry I wasn't around to join them."

I suddenly longed to be back with the Banu Tamim, in the desert's peace. But I didn't say that aloud.

"You are right about that." Staring into the fire, Amr wouldn't meet my eyes.

"So Muhammad is dead. What can give you such a long face now?"

"I suppose we tripped over one another in our haste to be rid of him, and that is where we failed."

It dawned on me. "So he is not dead. That's the disruption."

Another shiver crept up my back as the dark, moonless night drew in. "Magic?" I wondered aloud.

Circling my right forefinger to my thumb, I made the sign of the evil eye, invisible to Amr but, I hoped, not invisible to the threatening spirits. Just in case, I spat besides. That might ward them off.

I wondered if we shouldn't have moved the herds out of the jinn fort before we settled in for the night. I had been used to seeing the power of magic among the Tamim, how their herds flourished every time a little girl in tousled braids hugged their necks. I had forgotten there were other, darker kinds of magic.

"So Muhammad still plagues the Ka'ba?" I asked. "No. Didn't I hear—? Yes, some rumor to the effect that he was banished?"

Amr had picked a stone up off the desert floor and began to pass it nervously from hand to hand. The old Amr I'd known could sit with complete calm among his red cushions for hours on end.

"He knew well enough the danger we wished for him," he said. "Not long after you left, he fled Mecca by night with some few of his closest friends and followers. The moment we learned they were gone, some of us went after them, on our swiftest horses."

"An excellent plan." I nodded. "A desert murder, with no witnesses. An even better way to escape the blood feud."

"Except we escaped nothing. Muhammad did. Got all the way, first to at-Ta'if and, when they wouldn't have him, safely to Yathrib." Amr tossed the stone with fury into the black desert night. It hit the sides of our fortress with a decided chink.

"We lost his trail. We never saw him."

"Can't you get the Yathribis to give him up to you? They're a compliant folk, in my memory. Too busy with their own feuds, I think, to interfere in others'."

"They offered him asylum, ya Khalid, my friend."

"The Yathribis?"

"He ate their dates and drank their milk. They'll never give up a guest with that in his belly. And now every follower of Muhammad has trooped after him there, and a good number of the Yathribis have converted as well. They've even changed the name of their town."

"What was wrong with Yathrib?"

"They call it al-Madinat an-Nabi now, the City of the Prophet, pure and simple."

"I won't call it that, by my life," I swore. "What on earth made Yathrib so placid?"

"It was their constant squabbles, what you've already spoken of. You know they had parties of Jews, of the followers of many Gods and tribes, all vying with one another for the outside trade. They were always pleasant to strangers while vicious to one another. Now it's just the reverse."

"They didn't put Muhammad in charge of their factions?"

"They did."

"By Hubal." I was beginning to understand Amr's haggard looks. "And this new, united Yathrib lies, like a tight-drawn noose, directly across our main caravan route to the north."

"Exactly. My men and I have been scouring this part of the desert for weeks now, and there are other bands of young Meccans as well. We must see as many caravans as possible safe around Yathrib so our supplies are not cut off. What if the Muslims got hold of these horses of yours, for example?"

He gave an almost invisible nod towards my herd—no more than clomping hooves and quiet nickering in the dark—before adding: "A disaster."

"They are not waylaying our caravans?" I demanded, full of disbelief.

"That is exactly what they're doing. Like some peevish desert tribe. Only much more numerous, much better organized."

"Surely they can be bought off with the usual safe passage fee?"

"Surely they cannot."

"What about giving our sons as hostages? My Sulayman should be of an age . . ."

"And would you give him, not to learn the pure ways of the desert, but Muhammad's godless ways?"

I had to confess I would not. "Hubal forbid. I'd almost see my heir become a Syrian eunuch first."

As the water in my garden fountain splashes over its black stone heart, I realize what I have just said—in the presence of a Syrian eunuch. The emerald in his ear doesn't shift as he scratches away at the words. The only thing that seems to notice is my own sprouting, cursed sensitivity. That I squelch and push on.

And what of my daughter? I wondered. Looking up, I was relieved to see that al-Harith, after having claimed some of the first braised horse flesh for his daughter, had come close to join our council. The girl, getting too big now to fit comfortably within the cross of his legs, lay on the sand with her head on his right knee, picking at a rib bone. Al-Harith laid the corner of his mantle gently over her shoulders.

"They speak of Muhammad, O my father, don't they?" I heard her dear voice ask.

"Yes," al-Harith replied.

"I remember him."

Wondering pride at the mind of this child—so young!—made me lose the train of my conversation, but it was al-Harith's place to answer her.

"Do you, my heart?"

"Yes. He spoke of swans. The Blessed Ladies like swans."

"He did. But hush now, child. The men have important things to discuss."

Amr didn't seem to remember either the swans or the child who had inspired them. "You must have been ignorant of the state of affairs here indeed to have thought to bring a child on this stretch of the trade route," was all the notice he gave to her before he announced, "So. My men and I will escort you home—protecting you against any other such Muslim parties as you saw on the eastern horizon."

I saw a shadow of the old Amr returned, flickering like the firelight across his face. He rubbed a shoulder where my attack had bruised him and grinned. "That is, if you promise not to attack us again."

I joined his smile with a laugh of my own. "By Hubal, I swear I will not harm you, old friend. And thanks for the offer. Certainly, I will take you up on it."

"I like this place, my father," the girl said.

I looked across the fire at the face of my daughter, her eyes, sapphire dark, wide with fighting off sleep. The flames danced there, like a spirit inside, longing to escape.

"The People of the Place shelter us here," she continued. "My song asked them to, and see, they did."

"Hush, child," al-Harith whispered.

"But I should tell you, my friend," I went on speaking to Amr lest he think I paid attention to children, in particular children not my own. "I meant to take the way past the shrine of Nahklah before turning west to Mecca." I wouldn't mention it to my friend, of course, but I had planned to bring my daughter to the spot where she was conceived, to share with her the magic of the place and to make offerings there.

"Can you come with us on that loop?" I continued. "If not, we could part ways earlier."

"I won't hear of either option," Amr replied. "We might even catch up with a caravan we met just yesterday that also thought they'd go that way to avoid the Muslims. And this will be of interest to you: One of your younger brothers—your father's namesake, al-Walid—is among those traders."

"And as for Yathrib—"

"Khalid, you'd never go to the City of the Prophet? After all I've told you? With Muhammad become warlike, and he and all his followers there?"

"No, Amr, I won't." I looked across the low-burning fire again to find the girl sleeping gently on her father's knee. "But you will not stop me, I hope, if I send my—" I stopped myself just before I said "my daughter." "—my herdsman and his daughter into that town to join the next caravan back to their pastures among the Tamimi. They are not Quraysh, not from Mecca, not traders except as I have hired him. They should not be dragged into this fight of ours."

"But Master—," Al-Harith began to protest.

"Al-Harith, I insist."

"Alone, Master?"

"I can't go with you to Yathrib. I'm sure to be recognized by some Muslim or other—maybe even by Omar, my own cousin."

How this strange religion of Muhammad's tears up families! My heart ached, thinking more of the little girl asleep across the fire from me than of my annoying cousin.

"With Amr here, I have plenty of herdsmen now," I went on. "Besides, think of your daughter."

Al-Harith acquiesced, never realizing how close I had come to saying "my daughter" again. Or at least "ours."

30

In the opinion of God, the greatest betrayal on the Day of
Judgment is for the man to reveal something to the woman in
confidence and vice versa, then to betray her secret.
—A hadith of the Prophet

The jinni came to Rayah in her sleep. Toying first with her hair, the beautiful boy from another realm twisted a loose tendril as he twisted dust in the desert. He had more substance in her dream than when she, awake, had seen him and seen the ruins of the Camp of Diocletian behind him, through him. His dark eyes shone bright in the midst of fire and lovelocks curled like smoke on his shoulders.

Now she felt the pressure of his hand as he took hers and played with her fingers.

His whisper in her ear sent a skitter of sand down her spine. "Do not marry that old sharif, my love. You belong to me."

Rayah tried to move her mouth to say—oh, so much. "Indeed, I do not want to marry him. But what else can I do? A girl with no family to speak of? What else will appease the old man's wrath against me? I wounded his pride so deeply when I brought Ghusoon and her husband together."

She was not certain how much of this she actually spoke, and how much not to the jinni but to Auntie Adilah. Auntie Adilah whose plump, good-natured face looked down at her as she came awake to gentle shaking.

"Come, slugabed."

Rayah groaned when she saw it was still dark out in the courtyard behind her aunt.

Her protests were instantly countered. "You can't oversleep today. Today when your groom comes to close the marriage agreement. Too much to do."

There was too much to do, too much to give Rayah even a moment to think. She helped to sweep and scrub the courtyard, lay the dust, constant in this heat, and carry out the best cushions for the guests. She had to chop the nuts, boil and pour the honey and rosewater syrup over the rich pastries they would offer to display her skills in the kitchen. She had to dress in her best, including Cousin Falak's new embroidered slippers that pinched her feet. Even then Rayah had to suffer every woman in the house to give her opinion and adjustments and press jewelry on her until her head ached with the weight.

And just when the shadows grew long and she was about to drop with exhaustion, it was time to put on a smile and descend the stairs to greet Sharif Diya'l-Din's female relatives.

Rayah ran up to her mother's door to beg once more that she come down and support her. Rayah might be brave enough to say "no" if just one other voice spoke with hers. The wishes—or orders—of the handsome jinni wouldn't suffice.

"You need not stay on my account," Abd Allah said from his sick bed. "I'll be fine."

Sitt Sameh gave no reply but to begin to recite a poem with an intensity that made Rayah back away and then run for the stairs. The first line of the poem described the sons of Malik, Nabit and Aws, early converts to Islam, and used an Arabic word Rayah did not know. She didn't know its meaning, but just the way her mother said it assured her it wasn't a good word at all. What faced Rayah below seemed less threatening.

Rayah lit the incense brazier. Her family had filled it with frankincense and rare rosewood, not pine liberally dowsed with turpentine, the fragrance that usually filled their home. As each visiting woman passed under the blue eye and silver hand over the harem door, Rayah knelt before her and offered the smoldering tray. One by one, the sharif's sister-in-law, cousin and a daughter nearly twice Rayah's age threw their hems over it and stood until smoke curled out between their seams and permeated every thread of their garments.

After that, Auntie Adilah and the other host women led their guests to the seats of honor with polite conversation. When they were seated, Rayah went from one to the other, taking up each hand and pressing it to her forehead obediently. She passed the food, careful to offer to the sharif's most senior female relative first, and the best portions.

When she sat, Rayah looked modestly down into her lap without saying a word, letting Auntie Adilah answer for her even when the visitors spoke to her directly. Rayah studied the floor, the mosaic newly whitewashed for the guests so that no tendril of vine or singing bird showed—images of the old times.

The fountain in the center of the courtyard around which they gathered sat silent, too. The trickle of the past few weeks had stopped completely for want of water; the family of the turpentine sellers had to stand in line at the well like everyone else these long, unseasonably warm days.

The women talked of that. They talked of many other things. On and on they talked around her until even the intricacies of many generations of all families ran out. They talked of everything and every family except the one comprised of Rayah herself and of her blue-eyed mother. But how could it be called a family when her cold, inexplicable mother refused to stand with her own daughter at this pass?

Because there was no trickle of water to cover words whispered behind hands, Rayah overheard the sharif's sister-in-law say to his daughter, "Whatever can be keeping that fool father of yours?"

"Just give her the gifts," the other woman replied. "He can't be much longer now. The old man will have fallen asleep. But they will nudge him awake—as the girl will have to on their wedding night."

So Rayah was called forward and had gifts presented to her: bracelets slipped on her wrists and ankles, a massive gold chain for her neck.

"It's been in the family twenty generations," said the sharif's sister-in-law.

The weight of the thing pressed harder.

The women of the turpentine sellers exclaimed their awe. In none of the previous twenty generations had they seen such objects given to a bride.

Rayah felt all the gold made her move slowly. As if his fire were buried under the metal, she heard the weakened voice of her jinni: "Do not accept these gifts from another man." She would never run through the desert with dust demons, weighted down like this.

"Bushra, go on."

Out of her slow gold stupor, Rayah caught this order from Auntie Adilah to her youngest cousin.

"I don't care what the boring men are doing." Bushra shook her little braids defiantly and helped herself to another almond-stuffed date. How long before they would weight that sauciness with gold?

"Bushra, you must," insisted Cousin Demiella, jumping down from the clay bench beneath the high air vent passing to the men's room. In her restlessness, she had climbed there to see if she could gather any more news, but the women were too numerous and talked too much, even though she begged them to hush. Demiella was able to report only that "there are a couple of strange men in there."

A couple of strange men? Rayah nearly threw off the gold and jumped to her feet. Two strange men could only be the governor of Homs and his Persian servant, the men who had beaten Abd Allah and broken his leg. What did they have to do with this unwanted marriage bargain? Were they the reason the old man was taking so long?

"All men are strange," commented one woman so that the company tittered with pleasure and shared knowledge—which they took delight in withholding from the perspective bride.

The laughter frustrated Rayah more; she shifted on her cushions under the gold. Fortunately, Demiella's curiosity frustrated her, and she begged, "Oh, please do hush." No one paid any attention.

"They are strange to you, dear, only because they are the sharif's relatives, and you are not used to such fine people," said Auntie Adilah.

"I don't think so," Demiella insisted. "I don't think the sharif knows them very well. They have taken the places of most honor, too. Everyone is deferring to them."

They could only be Abd ar-Rahman ibn Khalid and his vicious servant. Rayah wrapped her hands in gold until the metal cut into her skin to keep from crying aloud.

"But I can't hear what they're saying," Demiella pleaded. "If you would just stop laughing for one minute—"

Trying not to laugh made everyone laugh all the more.

"Bushra," Auntie Adilah threatened. "Go."

The little girl had been babied since a head injury had almost killed her a few months before. The touch of Rayah's hands—power she hadn't known she possessed until then—had melded the bones together again. But Bushra was the only female young enough still to wander unrestrained into the men's guest room, yet old enough to listen and remember. Enough babying.

After elaborate promises to restore her to the royal status she had enjoyed because of her accident, Bushra was finally induced to go. And, "I'll give you one of my new bracelets," Rayah whispered in the little ear.

"The sharif's not going to marry Rayah," Bushra announced when she flounced back. Rayah knew noticeable relief at the announcement.

"Of course he is," the sharif's sister-in-law said. "This little one must have heard wrong."

"I did not," Bushra insisted.

"Bushra, that's not the way to talk to the honored auntie."

"But he's not going to marry her. Someone else—what was the name? Abd ar— Abd something. And now I want my bracelet, Cousin Rayah."

Before speculation as to what this speech might mean could rise to a pitch, another figure appeared in the doorway under the lapis lazuli hand that guarded the harem. The women fell silent, although the figure seemed more embarrassed to find himself where he was than any of the women were. It was Lutfi, the youngest of the turpentine sellers' males.

"Rayah's supposed to come to the majlis." His voice cracked, and he disappeared.

Every gaze fell on Rayah. A dozen hands pulled her to her feet, swaddled her in a veil, then tore it off and threw on a borrowed one, nicer, although it dragged on the ground. Then they pushed her through the door.

Rayah felt the blue hand of protection leave her back. She took one hesitating step toward the heavy blur of men, down the passageway and around the bend.

"Go on," all her kinswomen said, remaining safe beneath Fatimah's hand themselves.

Then, from the rear, the crowd standing in the harem doorway parted. Rayah, too, stepped back as the new figure appeared in their midst. The figure did not wear the usual veil of Tadmor town. The black shell- and coin-dangling covering of the desert draped her head to foot, exotic, mysterious. And—and then the wind of the figure's rapid movement caught up the hem in a swirl, like the too-close passing of a dust devil. Rayah was quite certain she saw the blue lapis hand set high over the doorway pull back as if from flame. Beneath that veil swirled something unnamed, something demonic.

Sitt Sameh had not left the turpentine sellers' harem as long as Rayah had known life. Rayah had been convinced her mother never would, certainly not for her sake. Now, Sitt Sameh blew past her directly into the men's room and stood. Caught up in the wind, Rayah swirled after. She stood and stared.

The blue-black hem weighted with cowrie shells continued to gyre with a life of its own around the ankles of the desert-swathed figure. The body within, however, stood deathly still. And from deep in the stillness rose the voice. Rayah recognized the voice; she'd recently begun answering "Mother" to it. And yet—she didn't recognize it. Some dark power sustained it like the deep waters of a well may hold up a chip of wood.

Her mother stood in the midst of the men. Such was the confidence of her stance that no one would guess this wasn't something she did every day. With the desert covering her, she looked straight into the face of the man sitting facing the door, in the place of honor, with one knee raised and his arm draped lazily over it.

"Abd ar-Rahman ibn Khalid ibn al-Walid." She spoke his name. With no honorific.

Abd ar-Rahman ibn Khalid drew the knee back under himself protectively. He must have seen the blue eyes above the coin-sewn fold of veil. All the men had and, from the way they shrank back like mud drying against the wall, had clearly never seen anything like those eyes.

Abd ar-Rahman ibn Khalid collected himself more rapidly than the rest. He sat in the place of honor, after all. He forced a smile. "Bint al-Harith, I presume. Or should I say, 'Daughter of Khalid'? My own half-sister."

Sitt Sameh—Bint al-Harith, as he called her—ignored him. Instead, that shadow-sustained voice began to recite. Start to finish, she recited the verse Rayah had heard her rehearsing in the little room upstairs. Even so had Rayah often seen her mother splash a little oil into a pestle of healing herbs to loosen the ingredients to a salve. Or a powerful purgative.

Sitt Sameh spoke the verse start to finish like one long, thundering word. Not every man in the room understood it. But Abd ar-Rahman ibn Khalid did, for the desert Arabic was likewise his father's tongue. If the men did not understand the words, they could hardly miss the meaning; at very least, the power behind it.

And the word with which the whole began, the word Rayah hadn't understood upstairs— now she did, and her ears burned.

> "Bugger you, you sons of Malik and of Nabit
> And of Aws, bugger you, men of Khazraj.
> You obey a stranger who does not belong among you,
> Who is not of Murad nor of Madh'hij.
>
> Do you, when your own chiefs have been murdered,
> Put your hope in him
> Like men greedy for meal soup when it is cooking?
>
> Is there no man of honor
> Who will take advantage of an unguarded moment—"

The entire majlis waited for the final rhyming syllable. Sitt Sameh delivered it with one murderous arm piercing white out of the black veil.

"So to bolt away the hopeful arrows of the old man?"

No one in the room imagined "the old man" referred to the erstwhile groom Sharif Diya'l-Din, whose suit had suddenly become a minor issue. Everyone knew the original curse had been meant for Muhammad the Prophet. And since God had decreed Muhammad's death, the curse transferred to those who would use his name for present ambition.

31

Then occurred the sariyyah [raid] of Umayr ibn Adi ibn
Kharashah al-Khatmi against Asma daughter of Marwan....
She composed verses ...
The Apostle of God said to him: "Have you slain the daughter
of Marwan?"
He said: "Yes. Is there something more for me to do?"
Muhammad said: "No. Two goats will not butt together about
her ..."
The Apostle of God called Umayr, "Basir" (the Seeing One).
   —Ibn Sa'd, *Kitab al-Tabaqat al-Kabir*

"**I** heard that verse first from the very woman who composed it. May the rain fall gently on her grave."

Sitt Sameh, freed of her cloak and veil, sat small, thin and quiet, taking up even less space than before in the corner of her room on the third floor. At least it was the third floor, behind the protection of the blue-and-silver hand once more, away from the furor her recitation had caused down among the men in the majlis.

"Asma daughter of Marwan?"

Abd Allah spoke from his sick bed. Rayah found it difficult to read what was in the eunuch's voice as he said this name of a woman she didn't recognize. Something of the sense that this poem—and the name of the poetess who first recited it—were not suitable for her young ears.

Also, she had to wonder, "Mother, perhaps our patient's poppy juice is wearing off. Shall I decant more?"

His voice sounded as if his wounds pained him again. He certainly spoke the name "Asma bint Marwan" as if he thought doing so would bring renewed torture to his limbs.

"No, child," said Sitt Sameh, still as stone waiting for the hammer and chisel. "He'll take no more."

To Abd Allah, she said, "I mean Asma bint Maysa, not Marwan. She traced her lineage through her mother, as did many in the oasis. Before Muhammad." But the blue eyes looked sharply at Rayah.

"You met the poetess?" Abd Allah asked, more troubled, even, than before, although he wasn't asking for poppy juice, either.

Sitt Sameh nodded, and began the tale. "So we went to Yathrib, my father—No. I mean him they called my father, the herdsman al-Harith,—and I." Then the scene from the majlis seemed to creep up the stairs for a moment and weigh on her tongue.

Abd Allah encouraged her. "Yathrib which is now called the City of the Prophet, al-Medinah."

"Yes, we went there when Khalid ibn al-Walid heard of the raids the migrated Muslims were carrying out against his people of Mecca on their trade routes. We were not of the Qurayshi tribe and so should have been able to seek asylum in Yathrib without trouble.

"'We shall have to beg for some great man's protection,' I remember my father saying. 'Or we could pay for it with the great pouch of coins the son of al-Walid has given us.' I could tell by his voice that neither option gave a man much honor, but he would swallow it. After all, he was a man willing to claim another's child as his own.

"And then appeared Asma bint Maysa. Father—al-Harith—and I had just crossed out of the brutal, black-and-red lava fields east of the city, where the Banu Qurayza ran their camels. We had been the guests for two or three nights of this Jewish tribe. In the distance flowed the achingly green swathe of the date orchards, gardens and, in good years, tiny barley fields of Yathrib. Gardens divided from one another by something I, a child of the desert, had never seen before: fences made of palm ribs. Here and there among the green, the rooftops of the various tribal fortresses shimmered in mirage.

"'The Gods willing, we will make it before the dreadful heat of the day,' my father said, and urged our animals on.

"But then, right before us in the shade of a lone acacia—broken adrift, as it were, from the rest of the oasis—sat a woman with blue eyes.

"She had five young children, one at the breast, one on her knee. The others tumbled together like kid goats and kicked up the dust into twirling devils that rose as high as the tree around her.

"'Peace on you, O Mother,' my father wished her, making her kin so he could talk to her. 'Do you wait here for your husband, for your children's father?'"

Rayah saw the creases in her mother's face smooth as the long-ago day came back to her. "'No,' the poetess answered, slinging the baby to her back as she got to her feet. 'I am waiting here to welcome you.'

"It wasn't my father her eyes rested on. It was me. In shyness—didn't everyone always stare at my eyes?—I buried my face in my hands.

"'So this is Se—?'

To Rayah's confusion, Sitt Sameh again stopped herself from saying her own name. Abd Allah nodded on his pillows, recognizing the wisdom of this choice.

"What?" Rayah demanded.

Ignoring her, Sitt Sameh went on. "'Welcome, daughter of al-Harith.'

"I tried to hide behind my father's robe.

"'My shaytan said you would be coming,' the woman explained as she began to lead us back to her house in the city.

"'Your shaytan?' I peeped out from the robes and could not wait for my father to ask this question. A woman with a shaytan—? A poetess? I had to know more. Did words drum in her head under the heat of the sun as they did in mine to the swing of every camel I'd ever ridden? I had to know more.

"'Yes,' she answered, smiling down. 'My shaytan pays homage to yours, Little One. You are welcome to stay with me in Yathrib for as long as you care to.'"

The space between the tattoo lines on Sitt Sameh's chin and forehead narrowed again as the memory sharpened for her.

"In Yathrib, where Asma brought us, the festival celebrating the fertilizing of the palms had come. We were invited to join in as every young man carried a branch of male flowers up to a tree and tied them among the white sprays of female blossom. To encourage them, Asma showed me, we women danced and sang at the foot of the tree.

"'Go up, up the palm tree,' said the old, old song. 'Take hold of its boughs.' When the young man slid down, he would take hold of one of the women. They would come together under the tree to show the plant's flowers what to do while the rest of the group moved, laughing and singing, onto the next tree, the next young man."

Abd Allah looked unhappily up from his bed. "And this was the world into which the Prophet of God had brought his people?"

"The Muslims weren't too pleased about it, no. They—among them Omar and his twitching whip—mixed with the festivities, interrupting the songs with Quranic verses. But they were from Mecca, all merchants who glide over the surface of the land and do not understand what has to happen in order for the land to bear.

"Asma had just been chosen by a very handsome fellow. I had seen their eyes meet before he went up to the crown of the palm, and I know she let herself be caught.

"A man not her husband?" Abd Allah asked, pain increasing.

"Not one of her husbands, because, like women of her clan, she could take more than one."

"God forbid," Abd Allah moaned.

"Asma herself, being a famous and powerful poetess, had three, and which of her children belonged to which, no one knew. A man had more care for his sister's children than for his own—in those days. In those days the Muslims came to dispel with quirts and loud chanting. Asma had just lifted up her skirts for her partner when we had to flee.

"Afterwards, behind the safety of her walls, we ate the food that was meant for the festival—including a young dog roasted in a covered pit—in glum silence. Once she had seen us settled under her roof, our bellies fed and our feet washed, she, her husbands, and my father sat and talked long into the night about the evils they had seen that day. Then, around midnight, her shaytan came to her. My head on my father's knee, I roused when she began to recite.

"'And yours, child?' she asked once her verses were pronounced. 'What has your shaytan whispered into your ear?'

"For the first time, I understood what those words I heard in my head meant. I recited."

When her mother hesitated, Rayah tried to urge her on. "What did you recite?"

"Something about the old man. And then—"

"Then?"

"O Mother
You will not leave me an inheritance of necklaces for my wedding
Only a neck
To face the Sword of God
Not an embroidered veil for my face
but the eyes of a jinni
That glitter like the daggers
in the belts of men.

"Asma bint Maysa sat silent when I fell silent. I grew afraid I had spoken wrong.

"Then she said, 'Yes. My shaytan admitted he paid homage to yours. That you would be my heir.'

"When the talked turned to local politics, I wasn't so interested and probably slept a lot. 'Since the coming of Muhammad—' 'That's all gone, since Muhammad came—' 'A woman doesn't dare, not since Muhammad came to Yathrib—' These seemed to be all their talk.

"And then, I sat up straight as Asma recited what her shaytan had given her concerning Muhammad of Mecca."

Sitt Sameh sat up straight in her room on the third floor of the turpentine sellers' house. As far as Rayah could tell, however, her mother was no longer anywhere near conquered Syria. Somewhere in Yathrib before the coming of the Prophet changed its name—

"'So to bolt away the hopeful arrows of the old man.'"

"The old man." She meant Muhammad an-Nebi, him they call the Prophet, of course. With all the dark power of her shaytan's words, Asma bint Maysa had been asking the tribes who had given their allegiance to the Prophet in Yathrib to remember their honor, to consider their heroes he had murdered. And to exact their due revenge on the old man.

"Blessings on him," Rayah wished for the "old man." Then she knew that was hardly enough to counter the blasphemy she was hearing. She tried to speak the verses against evil from the Quran. Somehow, they jumbled. Instead, her mind went blank with horror.

Abd Allah spoke into the silence. "'Who will rid me of this daughter of Marwan?' Didn't Muhammad say that to a gathering of his followers when those verses of hers were reported to him in his new refuge of al-Medinah?"

"He did." Sitt Sameh seemed to be trying to shrink her words to their tiniest space. "And one night, after my father and I had shared Asma's hospitality for some time, zealous Umayr ibn Adi took the Prophet at his word. He was a kinsman of my hostess, one meant to guard her and her children in the place of a husband. But Muhammad had made him forget this most basic of duties."

Abd Allah ran his finger along the edge of his parchments. "Umayr was a friend of Khalid ibn al-Walīd."

Sitt Sameh only growled at this news. "Umayr crept through Yathrib's streets to Asma's house—"

The eyes, unblinkingly blue as the desert sky, stared straight in front of them. Sitt Sameh still sat with Rayah and the scribe, but truthfully, she was in the nighttime room in Yathrib where a single lamp flame flickered—

"I was there, sleeping next to Asma, among her five children. My father slept across her doorway, to show his gratitude for the hospitality she had shown us. The man— My father, al-Harith, tried to stop him. My father felt the blade in his heart first, and died without a sound. The man stepped over my father's corpse to Asma's bed, although few remember to mention the fate of a poor herdsman when they tell the tale.

"The man tossed us children aside; I still feel the bruise on my upper arm and the wrench of my hair," Sitt Sameh rubbed her arm as she spoke. "He stabbed her through the breast, slicing off her nursing infant's arm as he did so. Her wailing orphans stuck to me with their mother's blood. I became an orphan myself twice over in one night. An orphan and Asma bint Maysa's heir: vulnerable neck, blue eyes, and words of power."

32

بسـم اللـه الرحمـن الرحيـم

And the poets, it is those straying in evil who follow them.
See you not that they wander, jinn-led, in every valley?
And that they say what they do not practice?
—The Holy Quran Surah XXIV:224–226

Silence reigned on the third floor of the turpentine sellers' house. Somewhere in the dry streets, a vendor cried out his watermelons. A hoopoe sang a hollow "poo-poo-poo."

Abd Allah broke the silence. "They say news of Asma's death was brought to the Prophet, blessings on him. They asked him how vengeance was to be taken on the assassin Umayr, seeing that he was the kin who should have guarded the woman and extracted vengeance from any who dared to harm her. 'Two goats should not come to blows for her,' is what they say Muhammad said."

"And now my daughter—"

Sitt Sameh was back in the turpentine sellers' house. She was again the woman who had stood in the midst of the men and dared to toss Asma bint Maysa's poem into the discussion of her daughter's marriage. Tears—the first Rayah had ever seen her shed—glistened across the tattoos on her cheeks.

"My daughter has agreed to go with this man, this son of Khalid who says he is her uncle."

"Mother, I didn't say that," Rayah protested, although stronger here than she feared she had in the face of all the men. "Not exactly. I did say I was honored and would—would consider."

"My own daughter said she would go with him to Yathrib to marry his son, her cousin."

"Please, Mother," Rayah said, trembling with fear. "It's better than the old sharif. Even unseen, he must be better than an old man. And the grandson of the Conqueror, son of the governor of Homs— Mother, we are poor, destitute in fact. How can I hope to do better?"

"And have you no shaytan to tell you otherwise?" Sitt Sameh pulled her bent knee up to her belly as if against a cramp. "My daughter, looking at me with those blue eyes, dares to tell me she has never heard a shaytan's voice telling her anything."

Rayah looked down at the hands in her lap, clutching each other for fear. Her mother knew. Sitt Sameh had heard the jinni's voice, too.

"He just said I shouldn't marry the sharif," Rayah whispered.

"Ah. So. You admit it then?"

"Yes."

"But nothing else?"

"He did say—"

"Yes?"

"He did propose."

"Speak up, child. I didn't hear you."

The image of Asma bint Maysa, stabbed through with the baby at her breast, swam before Rayah's eyes. This is what happened to women who spoke what shayatan had said to them against the holy word of God's Messenger.

"He said we should marry, the shaytan and I."

Rayah said this, admitting to something she had meant to keep to herself. Who would not call her mad, *majnunah*, jinn possessed, for confessing she saw jinn? That she spoke with them like she spoke to women around her, and more comfortably than she spoke to human men?

She had thought her mother alone might not call her crazy, and that was even more reason never to mention it to such a one.

Rayah spoke her nine words even doubting such a thing was possible. She had never heard of it happening before, a match between the two worlds.

Rayah said it, hoping her mother would dismiss the notion as strongly as she dismissed marriage with Abd ar-Rahman's son and much more strongly than she had dismissed the match with the sharif. Rayah hoped her mother might reply with something like, "What nonsense. The sun on your head made you see and hear things. The world of clay and the world of smokeless fire can never mingle."

And then tell her how to avoid it. Such a union was certainly haram, not something a good Muslimah should consider. The Prophet, precious blessings upon him, in all his marrying to form alliances, never took a jinniyyah. And Rayah knew better than to even mention the subject to Sitt Umm Ali, whose hair might turn grey even through all the henna.

Instead of reassuring her, her mother remained silent, staring at her, as if Sitt

Sameh could not believe that even she could have given birth to one to whom such honor might come.

"And you would ignore a jinni?" her mother finally said.

"I did not know marriage—" Rayah could hardly pronounce the word. "—was possible."

"There are tales. In the eastern desert is a clan who claims jinniyyah as their foremothers. If the jinni is a ghul and not merely a shaytan, an adversary, who will make life difficult but make you stronger in the end— Ghuls, Allat shield us, have been known to trap unsuspecting men in the form of pretty women and then suck the life from them."

Abd Allah murmured a prayer of protection from his sick bed as if he needed more poppy juice.

Sitt Sameh stopped what Rayah had found an irresistible train of thought, fascinating and horrible as the sight of death, and concluded, "But mine only ever gave me poetry."

"'Only' poetry is dangerous enough. Too dangerous. I don't want this, Mother. I don't want to die like Asma bint Maysa."

"Allat and Manat shield you, of course not."

"And I don't want to be like you, friendless and hiding my whole life. Praise God, I do not receive poetry. As the Holy Quran says,

> "'And the poets, it is those straying in evil who follow them.
> See you not that they wander, jinn-led, in every valley?
> And that they say what they do not practice?'

"The Holy Quran must be generous enough for me." Rayah finally managed to pull in the reins on her tongue.

Sitt Sameh sat silent again, taking in the condemnation of one thing to which she had given her whole life by the other thing—her daughter. She swallowed the criticism—and then probably rejected it with her usual blinkered hardheadedness. Why should she listen to a younger person, after all? Younger and more confused.

"Far be it from me, your own mother, to curse you," Sitt Sameh said. "But it may be that your daughter may have blue eyes, too. And her gift might be poetry. Think on that."

Rayah thought. She thought of quoting the Quran to such a child, and the terror of hearing words of undeniable power coming back at her from lips her own womb had formed. Would it be better to bury such a child at birth? But the Prophet, blessed be he, had condemned that practice of ignorance as well.

"But do not deny that you can heal," Sitt Sameh said at last. "The good of the world—of every sick child or barren womb coming after Muhammad—needs you to embrace that gift."

"I use the words of the Holy Quran."

"But also don't deny that the jinn are part of your healing. And that one of them has asked for your hand in marriage in admiration for your gift. In support of it."

Rayah felt strong. She felt hope where there had been none before. Still, her heart raced with fear.

"We can expect the jinn to prepare the marriage according to their customs," her mother said, "and in their own time."

"I don't want any of this," Rayah insisted.

"Those who can see the jinn, as you and I, are few and far between. Abd Allah here," Sitt Sameh gestured to the eunuch, "cannot."

"I have no desire to," Abd Allah agreed, and Rayah had to envy him, even on his sickbed.

"But because others cannot see, we need only divulge to them what we want. It is like women in the harem, who can observe what goes on in the men's quarter but need not reveal what goes on in ours. That is part of our power. You need not, for example, bear the jinni's children, although surely you must pass your powers and your relationship to the Smoke World on to the next generation. As did Asma bint Maysa, may the rain fall gentle upon her grave."

Sitt Sameh leaned back, triumphant at her daughter's helpless confusion. Sitt Sameh touched the hilt of the blade that still lay on the rug before her. "Now, what I want to know is, what are we going to do with that stepbrother of mine, Abd ar-Rahman ibn Khalid, governor of Homs, waiting downstairs in the majlis, who wants this sword as your dowry?"

33

بسم الله الرحمن الرحيم

O God, rescue al-Walīd ibn al-Walīd!
O God, rescue all oppressed believers.
And God, be hard on Mudar.
O God, give them years of drought like the
drought years of Yusuf.
>—A prayer of the Prophet related by Abu
>Hurayra

The sky over the Valley of Nakhlah, a blue-white tent pulled taut, looked no different from any other sky I'd ridden under since parting from my daughter. Stones could fall from such a white-hot sky? Bits of molted metal from heaven? Jinn? It seemed impossible.

And yet, the scars on my back tingled as I drew closer. A wind came up out of nowhere, raising a twisting demon that ran before me. It disquieted the surface of the well water. It rustled through the fronds of the three sacred trees, a mournful sound. A restless spirit, thirsty, missing her child. Our child.

Abandoned in the sand, I saw the wreckage of a campsite. Had I left it there? Had the sandstorm of so long ago left so much—and for so long? The broken shafts of spears embedded in sand, arrows— Mine, in what had been a peaceful halt? I found it hard to believe. And yet, I reminded myself, this was a place of wonders.

"Bring the camel," I told my slave as I drew my divine sword. "No, not that lame one. The best." I'd yet to see the shrine's caretaker, but I was no Christian. I needed no priest to make my sacrifice.

"She lives, thanks to you." I whispered then, as I drew my blade across the long neck. "She grows. Thanks to the Goddess, she is beautiful."

I stepped away as the dangerous hooves flashed in the death throes, remembering the fall of the white camel at Dhu Qar. "If you and the Goddess are willing, I will continue to see her safe."

Blood pulsed onto the sacred stone, black with previous offerings. Tears pulsed down the desert-blasted skin of my cheeks. "I have sent her with al-Harith to Yathrib, to safe—"

Only now did the caretaker make his presence known, now that he saw proof that I came in peace and piety. He stepped out from his hovel of stone, its ragged tenting roof popping in the wind overhead. He stood and watched, wringing his hands, still wary, until I finished my devotions and cut his share off the dead animal.

"I see you are Qurayshi," he said.

"I am."

"Come to give drink to the souls of your dead?"

He didn't seem to recognize me from that night so long ago. Of course, he must see many, over the years. And he didn't need to know the whole. "By al-Uzza's will, yes."

The man shook his grizzled old beard and looked towards the ruin of a camp I'd seen as I approached. "I've never seen anything like it. I almost fear the Goddess may have abandoned the place after such sacrilege."

Flies had come instantly to the camel's spilled gore, walked in it, then walked on my face. The Lord of the Flies, I understood, Jews called some ancient and very thirsty God of their land.

"What?" I demanded. "What has happened here?"

"You do not know? But you are Quraysh—"

"What?" I raised my heavenly blade languidly. "I have been in Syria all this while. What happened here?"

"A raid. The Muslims made a raid on some of your people encamped here."

"They broke the sanctity of this shrine."

"The Goddess is a demon, so the Muslims said, and worth no sanctity."

I called a curse down from that blue-white sky, I who'd been none too pious myself, the last time I'd been here.

"Oh, it is worse than that, sir."

"Worse?" What could be worse?

"It happened just since the turn of the moon."

"This month? But this month is Rajab."

"Exactly."

"The sacred month, when all warfare must cease."

The caretaker shrugged. "And your people had already shaved their heads to indicate their readiness to enter the peace of Mecca's holy place."

Those lances had not simply fallen into the sand and broken. They had been thrown.

"What damage?" I asked.

"*Your people surrendered. The Muslims took them hostage to be held for ransom in Yathrib. And all the booty of a returning caravan.*"

Another curse. "*Is nothing sacred to this blasted son of Hashim?*"

"*What can I say?*" pleaded my host the caretaker. "*I remember, the leader of the Muslim raid kept yelling, 'Who wants to die a martyr with me? Who wants to die a martyr?'*"

"*This Muhammad has a shaytan!*" I cried. *The sky didn't blink.*

"*I would not say 'a shaytan,'*" the caretaker said with the cautious theology of a man in such a position, who lives off those who come to him, faithful to so many things they've lumped under one single tent. "*A shaytan visits a poet to give him another way of seeing things, a shadow to his light, an image that makes the distant mirage take form. This Muhammad wants to scuff over all shadow: one God, one prophet, one way of thinking.*"

I'd meant to camp at least overnight in the sanctuary. Instead, I pushed my caravan, even the fragile horses, on through the heat of the day to Mecca, to safety and council with my kinsmen.

But even as the old man and I had been commiserating thus helplessly in Nakhlah, Muhammad's new inspiration gave him and his followers all the justification they needed. "*They ask you concerning fighting in the sacred months,*" reports the Holy Quran. "*Say: 'Fighting therein is a grave offense, but graver still in the sight of God is to prevent access to the path of God.'*"

❧

I didn't want to leave Mecca the next season. I needed to be there, to add to the defense. But the stranglehold the Muslims in Yathrib had set across our trade routes required that every capable man go and bring a caravan back from the north.

Desire to check on the sons of Tamim also acted as a lure. Most of all, what had happened to my little girl? Stupidly, stupidly I had sent her and the stupid herdsman who passed as her father into the very lion's den.

In the lands of my milk family, what I learned did not help. The girl was not there.

"*And al-Harith the herdsman, her father?*" My stomach churned in a sick panic.

"*We heard nothing but that he died in Yathrib,*" replied my milk brother Mutammim.

"*Dead? Murdered?*"

"*So it seems.*"

"*By Muslims.*" I didn't have to ask. I knew. "*Revenge!*" I cried. I wouldn't lick hot iron for this one. I would shed blood.

"*Indeed, a sharif can gain no greater honor than to revenge the blood of his people, even the least of his herdsmen," said Mutammim, annoyingly slow to join me on his feet. "Al-Harith's blood weighs heavily on me."*

I could not keep my eyes from the sword I had hung from the tent pole upon my entry. No doubt this was the blood heaven and earth had been forged together to draw. "You will let the honor be mine, brother, I hope. The Gods willing, I shall leave at dawn."

"Not so fast, O brother. You may have the honor if you wish. However, I cannot learn the name of the one man whose blood we must take. A monster with a thousand heads, a new one rising every time one is cut off, that is what these Muslims in Yathrib are like."

"Must it be relatives of the man who actually did the deed?" my blind milk brother Malik asked. "Or would any Muslim do? They are treating one another as family against all real blood or milk bonds."

"Any Muslim will do," I assured him. But how we were to break one off from all the rest in their stronghold of Yathrib, none of us could figure.

"And the child?" I had to ask. "Is she alive or dead?"

Neither brother cared much for the blood of the child. She was only a girl, after all, although to my mind, only the Prophet himself would do for revenge if she were dead. Come the light of day, I didn't dare go into Yathrib alone to follow the traces.

I concentrated on bringing back my caravan. Denying the Muslims its riches would be a start towards weakening them. Failure to do so meant not quite as much to me as the little girl with the bouncing braids and her mother's eyes, but it would mean more than just ruin for Mecca. Our families were very likely to starve.

Close to the same spot as the previous year, my friend Amr ibn al-As and his companions helped me fend off yet another Muslim raiding party.

"That was close," I said as our camels slowed and fell in side by side, sway by sway. I wiped the blood off my heavenly sword carefully before returning it to its sheath.

"Let me tell you—" Amr was not breathing easily yet. His grim gaze darted horizon to horizon, not just toward Yathrib where our thwarted enemy still raised dust. "—What happened when Abu Sufyan tried to bring his caravan down from Syria last fall."

"They didn't capture Abu Sufyan's caravan, did they?" Abu Sufyan always carried the richest merchandise of the year. Very well guarded, his was the life support of more than half of Mecca. If they'd taken Abu Sufyan's goods, what hope was there for mine?

"Not for want of trying," Amr replied, and I gave a sigh of relief.

"We managed to get word around Yathrib to him, how things stood, and he took his caravan away by night and by another route." The memory, however, did

not seem to give my friend much pleasure.

"That must have caused him some loss, anyway. Taking a different route is always risky."

"That was not the greatest loss. An army of us was at the place they planned the ambush. You know it? The place called Badr?"

"The village of Badr? There among all those difficult valleys?" I knew it. The perfect place for an ambush. "You had a skirmish there?"

"A skirmish? I wish it had been so. And I am heartily sick of skirmishes. Badr was—Badr was a full-scale battle. That Day of Dhu Qar you always brag about?"

"You accuse me of bragging? I tell the truth." Except about the white camel and its sacred burden.

"Well, it was a day like that."

Something about his words made me feel the cold again, so that I pulled the cloak about me for warmth, although early morning sun was already over the eastern hills. "You won," I insisted. "You sent the bastards scurrying back to Yathrib with their tails between their legs."

Amr was silent. His silence lasted so long, I looked over to see if he had dropped off his camel from exhaustion.

"You lost?" I demanded, thinking I merely asked the chill air.

"We lost," came Amr's disembodied voice.

"Surely you outnumbered them."

"We did. Three or four to one. Besides a hundred cavalry. On your horses."

"And you lost?"

"Khalid, you can't imagine, until you've faced it, what this Muslim zeal is like."

"Are you telling me you think Muhammad's God actually helps them? More than Hubal? More than any other God? More than a strong right arm?"

An uncomfortable shifting came from Amr's direction. His saddle creaked with a helpless shrug. Such a gesture was so unlike my old friend that I wondered if another man sat in his place. I felt another shiver, the passing of jinn into their hollows before the heat of the day.

"How many dead?" I demanded.

He told me. "Of the great and powerful ones who called upon the name of Hubal of Mecca, seventy were killed on that day. Among the slain was your cousin and good friend—"

"Not Abu 'l-Hakam?"

"Yes. I'm sorry."

"The Gods quench his spirit's thirst," I said quickly. "I'll slaughter a camel at his tomb."

"It would be better if you slaughtered his murderer."

And I knew my hasty, pious statements had done little good against the haunting of Abu 'l-Hakam's restless spirit. I felt him there among the jinn.

"Any captured?" I asked.

"Seventy Qurayshi. Including—" Amr's voice stopped cold.

"Who? Who of my kin?"

"Al-Walīd."

"My father? Surely my old father didn't don armor and fight?"

"Oh, Khalid, you don't know that, either."

The voice coming from the darkness before me sounded heartbroken. This fatherless man knew the want of a father better than any.

"Your father died, in his bed. Three months before Badr, I should think."

"Oh, God," I said.

"May the rain fall gently—"

"I promise the swiftest of my mares as sacrifice, Father, to carry you through the next world's deserts." For the moment, I was too shocked to grieve.

"At this rate, Khalid, you will sacrifice every beast you've brought back from Syria. And we need them. Hubal knows we need them."

"But this was my father. Oh, God."

"Muhammad has cursed him to hellfire."

"A curse upon Muhammad, then. May he discover there's no hellfire in the next world at all. And this al-Walīd you say was captured—?"

"Your younger brother, your father's namesake."

"But al-Walīd is just a boy. We planned to circumcise him when I got back. His teeth aren't sharpened yet."

"Nevertheless, he went with us to fight at Badr. And was taken."

"Muhammad's demanding ransom for him?"

"A huge ransom. He knows your family."

"How much?"

"Four thousand dirhems."

That stung. "And it hasn't been paid?"

"Other ransoms needed to be paid. So many. And there is no one, you see, since your father's death, no one to speak up for the interests of your clan."

The weight of the charge fell on me like stones. It made my grief heavier. But it stiffened me like sandstone inside, too.

"Well, I am home now," I said.

"No, Khalid, you're not," Amr said. "Yathrib stands between us. We're here to help you get these horses home, however. They mustn't fall into Muslim hands. That band we saw earlier—they'll wait to waylay us at every turn. Our numbers should help to keep them at bay, and we will lead you around a way they avoid. Perhaps.

The Gods willing. But right now, we ought to set watchers before and behind."

"I did that already, Amr. You think I'm a fool?"

"A double watch, Khalid. You haven't been dealing with these Muslims all these long months. Not as I have." The weariness in his voice rose up to the dumb, dull sky.

"Khalid ibn al-Walīd is home now," I insisted. And touched the quirt to my camel's side, to ride on ahead to watch myself, to see it was done right.

❧

I could not leave my own brother in the disgrace of captivity; my first concern when I returned from Syria was to see to his ransom. I sent messengers to Yathrib at once, to Omar; I learned he had emigrated with the rest of the Muslims. The fact that we were cousins had no effect on him. It seemed that he remembered his broken leg and nothing else. Or that Islam was stronger than any other bond.

In the end, however, negotiations brought the sum down to thirty-five hundred dirhems. By that time, my pride wouldn't let me pay less than the full amount.

"Take it," I said, "and may it curse every Muslim who claims a share."

The ransom took the greater part of all the gold I'd brought back from Syria, what I needed to support a large and growing family of dependents. I didn't start making plans for next year's caravan, however. Every waking moment I spent hearing plaints of family and the rest of the town of the effects of the Muslims at Yathrib. Then I spent time seeing to horses, my own and others', ensuring they were battle ready and training young men to ride them.

And then my messengers brought agreement from Omar, and I had to go halfway back to Yathrib to pick up young al-Walīd.

I sighed deeply and bit my tongue from all the furious things I wanted to say as the boy passed from Omar's hands to mine at the edge of town under an acacia tree. A slender youth, with hardly any beard, al-Walīd nevertheless had so much of my father in his long, attractive face that I fought back tears. He had grown since I'd seen him last, but he was still very, very young. Young to see a bloody battle such as Badr, young to lose a father.

I must father him now, I thought, and put my arm companionably about his shoulders as I walked him away from the Muslims and to our fire.

The boy stiffened beneath my touch.

I remembered when, hardly older than he, I'd waited with the Banu Bakr for my own ransom that never came. Yes, I'd felt this same resentment against my father and milk brothers, that they hadn't moved to release me any faster.

I should have remembered another aspect of that youthful scrape: how the months with Hanzala ibn Thalaba had created bonds between me and my captor. So much so that I had fought on his side at the Day of Dhu Qar.

If I had remembered— But there is no use mourning what might have been.

What was, what God willed, was this: come morning, my men announced, "The boy is gone."

"He's just gone to relieve himself," I told them.

But when we were all packed and ready to return to Mecca, al-Walīd still hadn't returned. For one moment, my mind flashed back on the fate of al-Harith, all those years ago, the boy who would never been a man. The jinn. That put a bit of panic in my search. We tracked the long, thin footprints to a campfire, still warm to the touch.

"Omar and his Muslims camped here last night," my men told me.

"The Muslims have used spells and enchantments on my brother!" I cried.

What was the use of such raillery? I had to accept the witness of my eyes. My brother had submitted to Muhammad during his stay with the man in his city. It had been worth his youthful faith to walk alone through the desert night to where Omar had promised to meet him and return him to the community of the faithful. Omar and my four thousand dirhems.

I couldn't suppress my feelings: "By Hubal, I'd rather it had been the jinn. Does family mean nothing anymore? Does this Islam cut across all that's important? How shall blood feuds be settled in future?" Of course al-Harith weighed heavily on my mind. And his daughter. "What will keep hotheads from murdering one another when they no longer fear the stain to family honor? What, the Gods help us, will keep women faithful?"

So it seemed. And that my family was crumbling before my eyes, just as I had come to take it over from my father. This injustice I couldn't help but feel as a personal failure. But such divisions were no more than every other family in Mecca had been suffering since Muhammad first began to preach.

I told myself I should go, as quickly as possible, back to the Tamimi lands. I should do whatever was necessary to track down al-Harith's daughter. I would even claim her as my own, if possible. If necessary. If this world was going to take a brother, why couldn't I claim a daughter otherwise denied me? If prophecy were to take precedence over any tradition, why could I not choose the prophecy that seemed best to me?

But I didn't go. And I never got al-Walīd—or his ransom money—back. The Muslims used both of them to arm themselves.

34

بسم الله الرحمن الرحيم

**Solomon disbelieved not; but the devils disbelieved,
teaching mankind magic and that which was revealed to the
two angels in Babel, Harut and Marut.**
—The Holy Quran 2:102

T hat night, Rayah had very strange and vivid dreams. She flew in them. She floated above the desert like a mirage. Something dark she couldn't make out pursued her, and she couldn't fly fast enough. At the end, when her wings caught fire and her flapping arms failed her, she plummeted toward the ground. As the mirage slipped by her, giving way to fast-approaching solid ground, the jinni suddenly appeared beside her, the wind playing with his dark curls. He put out the fire in her wings with his smoky breath. He set her down gently in her own bed and, before he left her, his lips brushed her cheek.

Rayah woke, scratching violently at the cheek.

"It looks like a bug bite of some kind," Abd Allah suggested.

The eunuch met her outside Sitt Sameh's door, holding his splintered leg tenderly before him as he sat on a low stool. He had had to give up his sick bed to a woman from the town whose monthly course had failed for two full moons.

"She must be expecting a baby, God be praised," Rayah said.

"Hush, no."

Sitt Sameh appeared in the doorway and seemed ready to snap her daughter's head off at the suggestion she had overheard. Sitt Sameh made signs against evil and checked the potency of the mixture she was pounding together in her mortar to administer to the patient. In spite of her obvious anger at what Rayah had just said, the older woman still seemed anxious that her daughter should see what was turning to paste beneath her pestle. Rayah smelled anise among the dates and wild carrot seed; the small, woolly flowers of germander, parsley, sage, and everywhere-present black seed, which the Prophet himself, blessings on him, had pronounced was the cure for every disease but death.

"A woman's courses are a natural thing," Sitt Sameh went on. "You have yet to learn this."

She worked the pestle in such a way that Rayah was certain something more than mere utility was behind it. Something magical and emblematic. Something her mother might have learned from the priestesses of the demon-Goddess in the courtyard of Amr ibn al-Asi's mother.

"For her health and strength, her courses must come regularly." Sitt Sameh pounded with a flourish that made the stone mortar ring.

"For her health, if she already has seven children and a poor husband," Abd Allah, leaning on his cane and exiled to the shadowy corner of the rooftop, added to Rayah in similar exile later. They spoke out of earshot of Sitt Sameh and the woman, whose audible grunts and groans were bringing her to regularity once more.

And Rayah realized that naming the disease was sometimes as important as knowing which herbs to pound together.

When the woman slept from her exertions, Sitt Sameh finally left her to come out and join them in the lengthening shade. She took her first good look at the cheek Rayah had tried to tend herself with a salve of olive oil from the kitchen. Meanwhile, and in spite of the salve, Rayah had scratched the cheek raw. In light of the new importance Rayah had just learned to set upon the naming of disease, Sitt Sameh's pronouncement had more meaning.

"No bug makes a bite like that. That is the kiss of a jinni."

As if she could enter Rayah's dreams at will.

Abd Allah sucked in his breath and recited a verse against evil. "The Conqueror's son will never have such a one for a daughter-in-law. It looks like some sort of disease. Leprosy, God forbid, or something."

"Yes." Sitt Sameh didn't seem at all upset by this dire prospect, but looked at her daughter keenly. "The Smoky Ones of Any Place know how to stop those who'd thwart them."

Rayah felt a breath of desert wind that scuttled sand across the rooftop and made her shiver.

"If, God forbid, a simple salve is not the cure—" Abd Allah began.

"No. Such salves will not cure them." Not "it," but "them."

"What, then?"

Sitt Sameh smoothed a finger over her own tattooed cheek. "In the desert, every girl is tattooed to protect her beauty from the envious Smoke Ones. These settled people, they have no fear of the place where they've laid their bricks, of the very soil they've stamped into those bricks."

She shook her head at her daughter. Or was it disappointment with herself, that she had cowered too fearfully up in her room throughout Rayah's childhood, that she had failed to do things that ought to have been done?

"In this case—" Sitt Sameh spat on a corner of her underdress and used it to dab at her daughter's cheek. "Yes, see? The wounds are already in the shape the Ones of this Place prefer. Like mine—a triangle."

"But the Conqueror's son—" Abd Allah protested again.

"Yes. I think Muhammad and his most careful followers forbid making such offerings to place. Rayah, you know the truth of this. It is your cheek—which may never heal, or may leave a deep scar. It is up to you."

Under the steel-blue gaze, Rayah said, "It was the jinni. I must have the tattoo."

Later, when the woman's courses were renewed and she went home to her seven—not eight, thank God—children, Rayah took her place on the patient's bed. Sitt Sameh made a paste by shaving off pieces from her precious block of indigo and mixing it with camel urine; it had to be from a male camel. As she dipped a needle in the paste, she distracted her patient with a new event from her childhood.

❧

His poetess wife and his youngest dead at the hands of a zealous Muslim, one of the husbands of Asma bint Maysa took charge, just as Muhammad said every husband should. The widower needed a woman to care for him and his four remaining offspring. To get a woman, he needed the bride-price. He found the stray among his litter—me—and took me straight off to Yathrib's slave market to see what such a girl might raise.

If a master cares for his stock, he provides the shade of thin tenting. My new master, shaking his head over the deal he'd just struck with a poor widowed man, herded me under his shade with three or four other girls of about my same age. They were all Africans, whose glossy black skin attracted my stare like shards of shiny black obsidian. Their crying for their families made me cry for mine, although we shared a mere handful of words.

"Do you think a kind buyer wants anything but a cheerful girl?" the master demanded. He laid in with his lash to bring the point home.

The market stood in the open air at the foot of Mount Sal. Here, it easily captured the attention of caravan drivers, whose favorite campsite was at Zaghabah in Wadi 'l-Aqiq, waylaying them on the path to the wells and supplies of Yathrib.

And the caravan drivers did come by. Then the master was a different man. He would caress us with his crop to make us walk, to see that there was no limp. The potential buyers pried open our mouths to study our teeth as if we were horses. Another prod was meant to get us to strip, and if I or one of the other girls failed to understand the Arabic order quickly enough, they'd do it for us. Great hands tore at the worn fabric of our smocks and left us, after close inspection, to pull the frayed edges back together as best we could. Then buyer and seller haggled, repeated this inspection or that to make a point.

Every buyer exclaimed at my blue eyes and tended to let me be, not wanting that evil in his home. A black girl, branded by her skin from any too-familiar melding with free women, was preferred.

The man saw me before I saw him, since I was the one on display. Besides, I was trying to keep my eyes averted from wherever the next indignity might be coming.

"That one's an Arab," were the first words I heard him say. "What's her tribe?"

The seller shrugged. "She has no tribe, no kin to come looking for her. She will be whatever you are."

The man curbed his interest then, a ploy, perhaps, to bring the price down. He turned to platitudes with my master instead. "We are from Yamamah, the Banu Hanifa," the stranger said.

And then he said something that made me take in breath as Asma's blood by lamplight flickered once more before my eyes. "My companions have gone into Yathrib—or al-Medinah? Is that what they call it now?—to make a pact of peace with him they call Muhammad the Prophet. So I am left to guard the baggage."

My master grew cool in the midst of driving his other stock out of the tent. The man left to guard the caravan would not be the one selecting new slaves to take back to Yamamah after the embassy was over. But something in the way the stranger chuckled about his station made me realize there could be other reasons he wouldn't join his clansmen in submitting to Islam—which was the same as submitting to the Prophet. This made me look over the matted tangle of hair belonging to my companions to study him more closely.

He looked incredibly old to me. Although he was perhaps no more than thirty-five, grey already streaked his beard and sun wrinkles creased the corners of his eyes into permanent smiles. Those eyes staggered me the most.

Like Muhammad's, like mine, like Asma's, they were blue.

The man from Yamamah cast that kind, blue gaze in my direction one more time as he rose from my master's grudging hospitality to return to the caravan he was supposed to be guarding. I stood, too. One of the little Africans with me caught at my skirt; if I tried to escape, they would all feel the lash. She only opened my torn smock to the waist. Instead of indignity, I felt something I had never seen, only dreamed of. I felt the power of my mother as a virgin rising in the litter on the white camel, riding into battle. I didn't bother snatching the fabric shut, but stood like that and entered my own battle. I began to recite what had suddenly slammed into my heart like a saddle bag slung ready-packed over the beast of burden's back:

"And the joint stock which they have begotten
Among the race of Mutammim and Malik.
Some are great beams,
But the fire needs small kindling, too."

Ignoring my master, the man from Yamamah strode quickly back to me, where he squatted to come down to my level.

"And so you are not without a tribe and kinsmen after all, Little One? You have protectors in Mutammim and Malik, the sons of Nuwayra? The great tribe of the Banu Tamim?"

"I am Bint al-Harith, may the rains fall gently upon his grave," I told him, tears starting to my eyes even as I remembered my father and the way he had died across Asma bint Marwan's threshold.

"I'm sorry I don't know that brave Arab." The kind face smiled as if he guessed the man who passed for my father had, in fact, been no more than a herdsman.

"I am all the offspring left to him. And I alone must see to avenging his blood."

"May the Gods will that you do so, then." He made no comment that, as a slave, I might want to temper my ambitions. "And I am called Musaylimah ibn Habib. But I see and hear that you have a connection to another tribe as well. Through your mother, perhaps? To the Fire-Born Ones. Or am I—and my own shaytan—wrong in this?"

I took up a corner of my torn smock and sucked on the dirty, salty fibers to comfort me from the vision of what had happened to the last person I'd met who claimed to have a shaytan. I did not want this kind man to suffer the same fate—and was it my fault?

"Won't say, will you? Your shaytan gives you no more words today?"

I shook my head.

"Then I will let mine speak instead. The rumor in the desert is that a little girl with blue eyes gave inspiration to this Muhammad. She inspired him with the Verses of the Swans, which he later denied. Was that you, Little One?"

Again, I said nothing.

"Something from the world of shadows tells me it was, and that doing so has brought you to the slavers' tent. I will take all of this as true unless you deny it."

I denied nothing.

"Then let me tell you something. The Gods willed that my good wife died just this last season of rains—may the heaven water fall more gently on her now than it did in her last days. I had not thought to seek another companion, for her memory. But now my shaytan tells me an alliance with the Tamim would be a good thing—as well as closer ties with his own people of smoke."

The man from Yamamah gently parted the edges of my smock that had fallen together again. He laid his hand upon my flat chest.

It tickled. I giggled in spite of myself.

"I see you are not ready for such a thing," he said, "and I am not a man, unlike this Muhammad my kinsmen have come to submit to, who will take a nine-year-old child to his bed. It wouldn't matter if I were, I suppose, since I haven't the money to make it so. Nor can I buy you from under this slaver's scrap of tent and carry you back to your people to wait until you do come of age. I am the one they leave behind with the baggage, you see."

He sighed. "Ah well, by Allat and Manat, I still do have a shaytan." He winked at me. "See if the old man and I can't work some magic this night to make things go more in our favor."

True to his word, that evening, relieved of his guard duties by his companions, Musaylimah of Yamamah did come back to the slave market after the time of the Muslim's final prayer.

"I'd like to buy a lock of that girl's hair," he told the slaver. "I cannot yet afford to buy the whole, but one lock—"

The slaver shrugged at the odd offer, but finally agreed to the price of two coppers. He came at me with his dagger drawn. When I whimpered and shrank away, Musaylimah laid his hand on the slaver's arm and said, "Let me."

"But she is still my property."

"The cutting is part of my price."

The slaver looked from me to Musaylimah with a leer. Musaylimah ignored him. He gentled me with a singsong of poetry, something about young camels frolicking in winter grass. He undid a braid already several days worked from its weave with an "ah" of triumph, then held it up to admire by firelight.

Musaylimah carried my hair, still triumphant, to a clear spot away from the tent. Soon he had conjured, if not spirits, then at least a crowd, with more poetry. I dared to creep closer, too, and Musaylimah made certain I had a place right in front.

First, with his desert staff, Musaylimah drew a circle around himself. When he struck the ground, the circle burst into ankle-high flame. We all shuffled back with gasps of surprise.

From under his cloak, Musaylimah produced a dove, one of the Goddess's birds. I flinched as he plucked a storm of feathers from her. I tried to back away, glad I had not become the possession of such a cruel man. The circle of men behind me gave me no escape. Then suddenly, with a wave of his hand, the bird refeathered as good as new. He released her into the air to join her divine Mistress.

"I send a prayer heavenward to help my hopeless cause with this slaver," Musaylimah said with a wink that drew me forward again.

The rest of the viewers murmured with appreciation—all save one who cursed the Goddess in the name of Muhammad's one Allah and got shoved out of the ring.

Next, Musaylimah produced a narrow-necked bottle "fit to keep a jinni in" and an egg. He peeled the egg, made the shell vanish, then set the smooth oval on top of the narrow earthenware neck where it balanced precariously. He drew flame from his still-leaping cordon, set fire to the little twist of the lock of my hair and, quickly lifting up the egg, dropped the flaming wick inside. He replaced the egg and spoke in familiar tones to his jinni: "Take this egg, this gift to you. In return, help me to my heart's desire."

Another wink at me.

The egg lurched and trembled on its narrow neck, then slowly, slowly got sucked inside the opening. The viewers exclaimed more loudly this time, and some tossed coins into the flaming circle. Not nearly enough to cover the price of a slave, but some.

Musaylimah let the money lie as he spoke to his jinni again. "I command you now to return the egg whole as a sign if this desire of my heart is to be granted."

He blew over the mouth of the bottle where smoke still rose like the fire spirit himself. Slowly, the bottle rebirthed the egg whole, oval and white.

More coins flew, but not enough.

Finally, Musaylimah took up the edges of his cloak. Holding them like wings, he whirled himself around, extinguishing the flames of his circle as he did so. As hardly more than the whistling wind of his passing, I heard him say my name. That was all I needed, that and the urging of my own jinni. When the cloak settled down again, Musaylimah pointed to where I had been. To the viewers' astonishment, I had vanished.

He whom I was now calling my deliverer drew his watchers' attention to the spot where I had been and drew many more coins and a few small sacks of valuable incense as well.

The slaver pushed through to the edge of the blackened circle. "Thief," he cried, and tried to rush at the man from Yamamah.

All this while, I clung to Musaylimah's hairy legs, safe, hidden beneath his cloak.

"There, take your price," Musaylimah told the slaver, pointing to the wealth scattered in the dust all around us. "And there's more." Again he gestured to the spot where I had been. A fine folded cloak and a newly smelted bar of silver from Yathrib's Cradle of Silver Mine now sat in my place.

"I had those gifts of Muhammad the Prophet," he told me later, "as well as yonder young camel and its gear. When he met my companions, seeing with prophetic vision, the Meccan asked, 'And have you not a third man with you?'

"'Yes,' they replied, marveling at his divination. 'He keeps our mounts and the baggage.'

"'He is not the least among you that he should stay behind to guard the property of his comrades,' this Muhammad said as he handed out gifts to them for their submission—and yet these finer gifts for me, who never said I'd submit for one moment.

"And you see?" Musaylimah spoke as he tweaked my redone braids, the one still missing its little piece. "These gifts of that man who calls himself a prophet when he sees only light and never answered a dark shaytan's call—I have exchanged them for something better."

So it was, riding behind Musaylimah ibn Habib on his camel, that I returned to the tents of the Tamim where I had been born and raised.

"I will come for you again when you are a grown woman," he promised as he rode on towards the rising sun and his home of Yamamah. "Then, if the Gods and my shaytan allow it, I will make you my wife."

And so I waited and watched for the signs that I would be a woman, although they seemed so long in coming.

Something else happened that I should perhaps mention, when Musaylimah had just rescued me from the slavers. That very night, as he was leading me back to where his camels were couched, we were overtaken by great numbers of men heading out of al-Medinah of the Prophet. Beneath their banners green and black, the Muslims were amassing at the foot of the mountain known as Uhud. There, when the sun rose, a great and decisive battle was to be fought, believers against nonbelievers, Muhammad against his own native tribe of the Quraysh. Musaylimah tried to lead me out of the way so I should not be in any danger. But that sleight of hand he did not accomplish.

35

بسم الله الرحمن الرحيم

War is what you've known or tasted, not
a tale told in vague conjecture: if you
stir it up, you set on a hateful thing;
it is ravenous, once you whet its appetite
it bursts aflame; then it grinds you as
a millstone grinds to a dross . . .
War yields you but a harvest
of blood, not bushels and silver as the
fields in Iraq yield for the villagers.
                    —The qasidah of Zuhayr ibn Abi Sulma

When we Quraysh went out to take revenge on the Muslims for the Day of
Badr, somebody had to lead the cavalry. Somebody who knew what he
was doing.

I took up the charge, of course.

*We set out from Mecca at the end of the month of Ramadhan, under the rule of
the star ash-Shira, which many of us worshipped for the rains it brings. During Ramadhan, we knew, the Muslims fasted; we hoped that would weaken them. Having
called in help from every local tribe the Yathribis had wounded as well, we were
three thousand strong. Abu Sufyan led our army, all the profit of his last caravan
gone towards the outfitting of this force and to buying the devotion of mercenaries
from the desert. Never had that part of the world seen an army better armed and
mounted. Young men today would think nothing of it, for we now reach to the ends
of the earth with a hundred times that number. But it seemed great to us then.*

*We would be no mere stone-slinging mob to quiet Muhammad this time, ei-
ther. Seven hundred were fully equipped with armor of Jewish or prized Yemeni
make. I was able to mount nearly half that many. For the journey, my cavalry rode
the sturdier camels and led their horses. The rest of our army had only camels, but*

only a few had to pair up, and every man had at least a dagger.

We brought the Gods from the Ka'ba with us. They moved in the center of our horde: Hubal riding his own camel under an awning of red leather, marching to clapping camel skulls; the icons of Isa and Maryam. The only thing missing, to assure victory, was a virgin in a sacred litter on a white camel.

I tried not to think too much of my daughter. Much of what I did was for her, to save her if I could, wherever she might be.

No qubbah *litters led us, but at least a hundred women swelled our ranks in regular howdahs. My own sister Fakhta was among them. We'd married her to Sufwan before I last left for Syria, and in the normal course of things, she would have stayed behind with the rest of the suckling mothers. Indeed, I tried to get her to do so. But things had not gone in the ordinary way with Fakhta. She had yet to birth a child or even to conceive. I had a brief memory of my own barren third wife, her maddening amulets and charms, and so I let Fakhta come.*

Head of all the women was Abu Sufyan's wife Hind. Fifty and fat, she was a fearsome creature who had lost both her father and her brother at Badr, killed by Muhammad's giant of an uncle Hamza. Hind came, shaming the first sign of cowardice in anyone and screaming for revenge. She would take it with her own hands if necessary, but she had also hired an Abyssinian named Wahshi. A spearman of deadly accuracy, Wahshi was to have no other purpose on the battlefield than to find Hamza's liver. Hind had sworn before the Gods she would eat that vital organ.

Women's shrill trills, drums, timbrels and songs accompanied us every step of the way.

Taking the sea road, we covered the distance in ten days, and came within sight of the smoke of Yathrib's dung fires in the late afternoon of a Thursday.

"Friday is the Muslims' day of prayer," Amr told me. "So much the better. We will come at them while they are at their prayers."

Further reconnaissance decided against a direct attack on the town. Yathrib was not walled, but those of us who had been there before knew that sturdy brick house-fortresses of two or three stories flanked every entry.

"They could kill us all from their prayer rugs laid out on the roofs," Amr said. "They'll toss their wives' soup kettles over on us. And they are ready for us, every roof loaded with stones. There's even a mangonel, after the Roman fashion. We'd never be able to storm even one of those houses, never mind the hundred or so there are."

In spite of his words, I noticed some of his old cheeriness about him, a flush of excitement at the prospect of revenge. That lightened my heart, too.

"Well, we'll simply have to draw them out of their walls then, into the open to fight," I said. And Hubal willing, I added to myself, keep the women and children safe within.

What place would there be for my horses if we decided to take the place by storm, anyway? The rest agreed.

So, having made certain the Yathribis got a good look at our numbers and our armor, we circled north around the city. Here a bleak and rocky plain sloped slightly toward an empty, sandy wash.

"Perfect for my cavalry," I said.

A great mountain called Uhud rose its stern face between the plain, the famous slave market and the gardens and orchards of Yathrib. This barrier would shield our movements from the Muslims. They would have to send spies out; we might capture them, Hubal willing. So we let the women pitch their tents—the red leather tents of the Quraysh rather than the black hair tents of the desert—by a well or two near the wash on the plain of Uhud.

Come morning, the Muslims had yet to appear.

"I told you," Amr said. "They pray. They fast."

And so it seemed. We would have to do more to draw them. That day, therefore, we drove every camel around the mountain and set every man and many of the women on to Yathrib's gardens. Swords hacked at fodder, and that fodder loaded camels' backs. Men shucked their armor and shimmied up date palms. It was just the season when, as they say, you can gather dates in the dark because they have all come ripe. We Meccans cut down the rich, golden clusters. We stripped the ripening pods from every tamarind, the growing melons and cucumbers from every vine, trampling those we couldn't eat. We set our beasts to feed in the knee-high wheat.

My daughter may still be here, Hubal forbid, I thought. But we will win this victory and I will get her out before the starvation of these deeds affects her.

One of our number named Abu Amir collected a quantity of palm fronds.

"To what purpose?" I asked him.

"I've dug some pits on the path the Muslims will take towards Uhud," he replied. "I'll cover the pits with these fronds."

"Hubal has inspired you," I told him. "May you, with His guidance, trap a Muslim or two like wild animals."

No Muslim, however, left his fortress and his prayers to stop our pillage or to fall into any trap. In fact, those who lived in the small huts among the fields and gardens took their most valuable possessions, their farming tools that might have made useful weapons, and fled. They went to relatives within the town itself.

One old, blind man had been left behind, and he shouted at us: "A curse on Muhammad. A curse on him who riled up strife and left us open to such destruction."

His blindness reminded me of my milk brother. And I hoped there were plenty of others within Yathrib of the same persuasion. I had the men leave him a storage pit full of food and his old donkey.

"There," Amr said with deep satisfaction. In lengthening shadows, we followed the last of the laden camels back around Uhud to our tents grown blood-red in the lowering sun. "Let Muhammad and his followers fast for the rest of year as well as Ramadhan."

We set the watch, then, and waited to see what the morrow would bring.

Just at dawn, I came wide awake from a dream of racing my good mare Sadha twenty bow shots in a blinking of Muhammad's steel blue eyes. I would reap everything within my path into a great smooth swath with my heaven-sent sword—

The unnerving sound that had awakened me came again. My sister wasn't churning butter in the tent; a city woman, she always let the slaves do such things.

The sound was the Muslim call to prayer, those rich tones rising from the deep, black chest of Bilal, the slave and Muhammad's muezzin. Like the spate of a cloud-burst suddenly filling an empty wash with tumbling boulders and muddy water as heavy as bricks, the call rolled in a rush no man could oppose: "God is great, God is great . . . There is no God but God."

I confess it. For one dazed instant, I was terrified. I had never been so terrified, even at Dhu Qar. In an instant, I had my divine sword down from the tent's center pole and out of its sheath. Wildly, I roared for Fakhta to help me with my mail.

I hadn't even found the armor yet when a shout and a pound of hooves drew me to the leather-fringed mouth of the tent. Amr had just ridden up on his dashing black mare.

"Are the Muslims upon us?" I demanded. "By Hubal, did they sneak up on us in the night?"

Being the early part of the month, a mere slip of a moon had lit that night and set early. That would have lent perfect cover to such a maneuver, for men who knew the area well. Abu Amir's pits would have been lucky to catch a stray camel of our own.

"That's exactly what the Muslims did," Amr said. "Although I wouldn't say they're on us quite yet. They will take time to pray. But look, just look. Muhammad has his best archers—must be fifty of them—perched on the side of Mount Uhud."

"Damn," I said, shielding my eyes to see the bare planes of Uhud lit with the first orange sunlight. The tiny figures of men specked this light. Their bows were already strung to the taut serpentine curve and at the ready. "I should have thought to secure that face."

"And I wish to Hubal you had," Amr said. "From there, they can command not only the road to Yathrib and their gardens, but also much of the plain. Unless we can draw their foot soldiers out of range—"

"Out of range of those arrows will mean almost to our tents," I said with a sudden shudder of fear for the sake of the woman behind me.

The woman at this moment was Fakhta. I never should have allowed her to come. She stood behind me now, listening to all Amr said. She held the weight of my mail in her hands, trying to find the neck hole and sleeves. Because she hadn't yet become a mother, a certain maiden slenderness clung to her, a prettiness and innocence that didn't belong on a field where slaughter would soon begin.

I had to turn back to Amr. "Is Muhammad on the field?"

"There." He pointed.

Shielding my eyes, I could just barely see. On a low shoulder of rocky Uhud stood a cluster of men and a single horse. One of the men must be the Prophet. A pair of banners curled lazily over them: the white one declaring the Muslim's purity and a larger black one, the veil of Muhammad's child-bride Ayesha stuck on a lance. The sight of that ensign made me reach up and give the red silk I wore a caress. Muhammad and I shared common—

I stopped the thought and tore the turban from me, gesturing for Fakhta to bring the mail shirt.

"How many Muslims?" I demanded of my friend as the weight slipped over me from shoulders to thighs.

"About a thousand, I should guess. Only not all Muslims. Yathrib's Jews have joined him. We must have torn up their gardens, too."

"We still outnumber them three to one. I am content with that."

"Those were about the odds at Badr," Amr reminded me. "We lost at Badr."

I set a conical helmet of Yemeni work upon my head and let Fakhta help me tie the red silk about it.

"How many horse has he? All I see is that one on the ridge."

"Muhammad's horse. It won't enter battle. I think Yathrib only has one other steed, and it's here, too, though I don't know who's riding it."

"I don't care if the Great King himself sits in the saddle. My seven hundred, then, will be key."

I had a pair of laminate greaves and knee guards, very important for a mounted man going against men on foot. Fakhta helped me to lash those on my legs, and then she tried to give me a length of her veil to tie to my spear.

"Save that for your husband," I told her, adjusting once again the red silk about my turban. "Then perhaps he'll give you a son."

Turning from my sister, I murmured, "Bint Zura, for you. And for our daughter."

Then I went out to join Amr in the dawn.

36

Tastier than old wine,
sweeter than the passing of wine cups
is the play of sword and lance,
the clash of armies at my command.
To face death in battle is my life,
for life is what fulfills the soul.
> —Abu't-Tayyib Ahmad ibn al-Husayn al-
> Mutanabbi, tenth-century Arabic poet

Quickly, *before the Muslims should finish their prayers, I divided my horsemen into two wings. I gave one into the command of Ikrama ibn Abu Hakam, a steady, trustworthy man, and ordered him to take the left flank. He had lost his father at Badr; I knew he would fight like a demon for his revenge.*

"And, by Hubal, stay away from those bowmen." I hardly needed to tell him that.

I led my own group to the right. At no great distance, the plain abutted on a lava field. I would have to keep the horses off of that and avoid getting trapped against such a barrier by a Muslim offensive. That was why I took that flank for myself. Then I curled my legs up onto the saddle under me and leaned forward on the horn to rest until the way of the battle revealed itself.

With a thrill in my heart, I knew we made a brave sight. Even strung out only one man deep, the Muslims made a front that ours easily engulfed on either side.

Then, no sooner had we lined up and taken the measure of the enemy in this manner than a great band of Yathribis lowered their weapons and turned. Slowly and deliberately, they picked their course away from the front, back around the mountain. Our men jeered them, the Muslims pleaded, but these men—almost three hundred of them, I should guess, and the best armored of the lot—had already had enough.

"Yathrib's Jews," Amr told me, leaning on his saddle horn. "They've suddenly discovered that Muhammad's battle is not their own."

The Muslims were thus left with a force but a quarter of ours. The gap in the line looked like a mountainside after a rock slide. But those who stood and stayed showed no sign of following the Jews.

"Even better than Badr," I told my friend.

He replied with a "wait and see" twist to his face.

At this point, Talhah ibn Abu Talhah, under the white with black swallow-tail banner of the Quraysh, approached the other side. "Companions of Muhammad," he called. "You say your dead go to paradise and that our dead go to hell. By Allat, you lie. If you are so confident, let some of you come to face me. Are there any duelers?"

Ali, son-in-law to the Prophet, took up this challenge to single combat. I couldn't keep a gasp strangled in my throat as the Muslim champion's double-bladed sword took only a single swipe to bring the Qurayshi banner fluttering lifeless to the ground. Its ripples fell over Talhah's prone body.

Shrieks and howls rose from the women behind us. Over the rest I heard Abu Sufyan's wife Hind ululate in resonant, almost masculine tones.

Instantly, Abu Sa'ad, another son of Abu Talhah, snatched the banner out of his brother's blood. Almost as quickly, he too fell.

Amr gave me a look that said "I told you so."

I sat stunned and beyond feeling as, in under an hour, ten of Mecca's best warriors fell—most of them seething with revenge for losses at Badr, and most of them to Ali. I might almost have recited with the Prophet who said of his son-in-law on that day: "There is no youth full of manhood like Ali, and no sword comparable to Zulfiqar."

My own Sword of God had yet to swing a single time.

No Muslim blood yet stained the soil beneath Mount Uhud.

Hind's great African prowled here and there like a panther along the lines, in lion pelt, his spear ready on his shoulder. Hamza never came to answer his challenge. Muhammad's uncle must have been warned.

"You see?" Amr told me grimly. "It doesn't matter our numbers. If that one Ali can kill ten, we'd need many, many more on our side than are here now."

He was right. I could feel it in my men. Those ten quick deaths had taken from them all the morale the flight of the Jews had brought. I took a swig of my waterskin, spat, and longed for the dueling fire to burn itself out.

Finally, it did. Many who had sworn on our way to Yathrib how they would be the first to challenge the whole Muslim army to a duel had changed their minds. The silent fear hung heavily on our side that no brave Meccans remained.

Thank heaven, our Gods flowed then into the space between the armies. Whirl-

ing priests chanted; the sacred camel skull snapped threateningly. They affirmed that honor did indeed enfold all who fell in the name of the three hundred and sixty of the Ka'ba.

A howl of rage rolled from the Muslims as from one throat at this. They surged forward, swallowing the idols in their midst, and battle was engaged.

I swung my legs to my mare's sides, gripping her belly, and signaled my men to ride. In a mass we tried to push forward, to hook round the Muslims' rear and encircle them. I even had my first victim picked out. I'd send my lance through his back straining armorless beneath the simple white izar. Maybe I'd take off his head with my sword, if I didn't save that swing for his neighbor in the long lovelocks.

But the arrows from Muhammad's carefully planted bowmen met us like a solid, whistling wall. The rocks themselves seemed to be raining down on us.

Horses screamed. The sound made me sick, the sight was even worse. By Hubal, we might have left the horses home, for all the wounds they were taking, my beauties. The man next to me tumbled from his saddle with a shaft in his eye.

I waved my unspent spear in a desperate signal for my men to pull back before those of us in front should be shoved to certain death. Again I was obliged to watch and wait. Slowly but steadily, the smaller Muslim force pushed the Meccans back. By Hubal and by al-Uzza, I was choking on my own helplessness, as I had done at Dhu Qar. For all that I was fully mounted and in fine armor, I might have been a woman. I might have been bound in leathern thongs again and sitting in a prisoner in Hanzala ibn Thalaba's tent.

Twice more I tried to hook behind the enemy and engage; twice more I was pushed back.

I had dreamed the night before of racing my mare and the dead falling like sheaves around me. Now I was forced to admit to reality, and that reality was that I was completely inactivated by no more than a handful of archers that Muhammad had carefully placed among those rocks.

Those archers, on one knee, their arrows stuck in a handy row, point first into the ground before them, did not fire so very rapidly. Each bolt, however, was deadly accurate and had such power behind it that I saw arrows pierce full armor. Ikrama, my second, had tried the same maneuvers on the left and pulled up short before the same barrier.

By noon, still unable to charge, I had turned my mare's flank to Uhud in order to watch as the battle line pushed behind me. I rolled my eyes heavenward for aid and found none. Only sky was there, strained nearly to white by the weight of sun and dust. Through it spiraled a throng of vultures, awaiting their turn.

I held my position more from frozen frustration than from any courage or sense of duty. I had not yet had a chance to strike a single blow for Hubal and the Ka'ba's *three hundred and sixty various Gods. I watched the Muslims swarming past my left side; I was a spectator at the procession of a religion that was not yet my own and of which I had no understanding. I might have been drugged and asleep on my couch, watching the antics of a dream in which I had no part.*

By God and by my life, I had sworn never to lose a battle again. Let me die first, I prayed. But I could not even find a likely Muslim sword held in my direction that I could fall upon and end the shame of that immobility and helplessness. My horse beneath me tripped about in the little half-circle that well-trained animals make when they smell battle and are yet reined in. She and I had very much in common.

It was difficult to see through the haze, but a long, high-pitched scream told me when the Muslims reached our tents and our women.

"Shouldn't we go to their rescue?" Amr demanded. He had been raised among women.

I fingered the red silk and swallowed hard through a painfully dry throat. Some of my men didn't wait for a signal from me. They were already riding hard for the tents. One of the screams seemed to be Fakhta's, and it made me wince. But to set horses among guy ropes and women would be to squander their advantage. The only advantage, slim though it might be, left to us.

"No," I told Amr firmly. "Hold," I shouted back to the men. "Hold."

I had sworn I wouldn't lose, not this, not any battle. I couldn't lose. Gods, how was it possible? Maybe I should just ride. Ride out into the arrows the bound or two it would take before some bolt found me. That was the only alternative to failure.

By Bint Zura, by our daughter. Almost wildly I worked the red silk through my fingers—

And then, it happened.

37

**Adopt positions opposite those of women. There is great merit
in such opposition.**
—A quote from Omar ibn al-Khattab

Abd Allah felt well enough to sit up and read his bits of his parchments again.
Even as he pushed them aside now, pleading exhaustion, Sitt Sameh rocked
forward, eager to begin this part of her tale.

"You know what happened next?" the eunuch asked.

"Of course," she snapped. "Wasn't I the answer to Khalid ibn al-Walid's prayers to
all the 'demon' gods?"

And she began.

❦

"Come away, child," kind Musaylimah told me.

We stood together on an outcrop of rock, watching the battle rage between the
Muslims and their kinsmen from Mecca beneath the mountain of Uhud. "So Muhammad has done away with the old proverb one used to be able to depend on, 'My
brothers and I against our cousins . . .'"

Rising dust made it more and more difficult to see exactly what was happening
as the day pushed towards noon. Within the sunlit dust, figures moved like jinn. Still
I could tell—because of his seat in the saddle in the midst of his horses—which was
that strange foster brother to our sharif, Khalid ibn al-Walid. He refused to let himself
be enchanted by the dust. Why, I couldn't understand, except that Muslims held the
mountainside between him and the pitched tents closest to me, where the Meccan
women watched and encouraged their men. And now and again the Muslims on the
height clouded the sky with arrows. These burning jinn, too, Khalid ibn al-Walid
refused to engage.

"The Muslims have carried the day." Beside me, Musaylimah shook his head with wonder and a little sadness. But he didn't really feel the loss personally; he was native to far Yamamah, after all. He could carry me to safety there, out of the way of this mad fight between brothers.

"Come away then, Little One." He took my hand and smiled as if nothing was wrong, although he'd begun to look uneasily at the Meccan women's tents. "Having so recently won your freedom, I would not like to see you fall into slavery again."

Allat bless him, he probably wanted to shield me from the sight of the more brutal acts of pillaging which, even among Muslims, were already beginning upon their fallen foe.

I would not budge, however. "How can the Muslims be winning?" I demanded. "There are so many more of the Meccans."

Musaylimah shrugged. "It is the will of heaven," he started to say.

"No, it is not the will of Lady Manat," I insisted.

"Well, perhaps She has been forced to succumb with a blade to her throat." Musaylimah must have already seen scenes like this beginning among the tents surrounding Hubal's red leather.

"No." I refused to believe it.

"They say he is a great magician, this Muhammad the son of Abd Allah." So spoke the magician I'd seen pull an egg into the narrow neck of a bottle.

"Then it will take more than arms to defeat him. Where is your magic?"

"Ah, to have the trust of a child. Alas, Little One, I may be able to refledge a bird by sleight of hand. This sort of magic, however, is beyond my skill."

Then I heard a voice.

My mother's voice.

"By Allat and Manat," I said. "Such magic is not beyond my skill." I could hear my own young throat shrill with anger as I said it, my utterance carrying only because it had my mother's underneath it with the solid sound of the soil of a grave.

"Indeed, Little Blue Eyes?" And the smile playing about Musaylimah's lips was only half a fond adult's indulgence.

"Of course. When women deal with men, they must always resort to magic."

With strength rising from the grave's soil, I broke free of Musaylimah's grasp and ran down the outcrop. My guardian was right behind me, faster on his grown man's legs although he was no longer young. Before he could quite stop me, however, he saw that I ran not for the center of the dusty battle, but towards the tents of the women of Mecca. He knew the Muslims had already begun their pillage at the far side of the encampment, and the confidence with which I ran in between the first guy ropes gave him pause.

"Women of Mecca! Women of Mecca!" I cried. "Do not lose heart. Have you no *qubbah*? Direct me to your white camel and your *qubbah*."

At first the terrified women could only stare at me over the heads of the screaming children they were trying to pack up for flight. They did not have a camel to spare, most animals being on the field with their men. And, not being desert people, they didn't have all the mysteries of the *qubbah*. They had the Ka'ba instead, and the Ka'ba was a week away.

Two or three fleeing beasts might have run me down as their mistresses whipped them in panic. Only my upbringing as a herdsman's daughter kept me from harm. Behind me, Musaylimah leaped back and aside again and again for cover. His call of my name came again and again, but more and more distant, as if expecting at any moment to pick my lifeless body up out of the dust. I could not wait for him.

At last, one breathless woman took a second look at my blue eyes as she scurried for the safety of the open desert. She pointed me in the direction I was going anyway, towards the center of camp.

Hubal and his bull camel—a rust-colored one, not white—rested under his red tent. One lone toothless, whispy-haired old priestess with breasts sagging to her waist was making the God's safety her first priority. She knew, as I did, that were the statue to fall into Muslim hands, they would hack it to carnelian powder in a moment. She wasn't strong enough for the task, however.

I ran to the God at once. First, I made quick obeisance, holding my palms upturned before me to receive a blessing, then approaching to bend and kiss the silk-draped platform on which the God stood. His form was that of a crowned and very virile man carved in carnelian. Like his male member, his right hand rose aloft in blessing. Having broken off at some point in the past, the carnelian hand had been replaced by a hand of gold.

That metal caught the sun's rays and threw them towards the struggling Meccan soldiers to no effect. Nevertheless, I rubbed a hand over each of his, the one of gold, the one still of carnelian and the third, that part only given the name "hand" to avoid hazarding fertility. All three were smooth and shiny from countless other similar devotions. I massaged the blessing from my palms into my head, face, and neck.

Once I'd made this proper, if hasty, greeting to the God, I caught up the two poles on my side of the platform He stood on.

"Come, Grandmother," I said to the sagging-breasted old woman. "Help me get Him to the camel litter."

To my surprise and hurt, she didn't take the other two handles. She came at me instead, hissing through her toothless gums.

"Fie, Hubal curse you, you wicked slave child, child of the desert. Only those of pure blood of the Quraysh should dare to touch fiery Hubal—or die of his wrath."

I wasn't afraid of Hubal. I knew my devotion had not offended him. The violence of the old priestess, however, did send me staggering back a step or two. Doing so,

I knocked over the silver vase stuck with seven arrows that always stood at Hubal's carnelian feet for use in divination.

The priestess will really beat me now, I thought, giving a little cry of foretelling.

She did not. Instead, staring at the arrows spilled on the carpet beneath Hubal, she herself winced and took a step or two backwards.

"But you are," she said, amazed. "The God has spilled His arrows, and He never lies. You are the true-born child of a true-born son of the Quraysh."

The old woman is surely mad, I told myself. My father was the herdsman of the Tamim, al-Harith, may the rains fall softly upon his grave, dead at the hands of a follower of Muhammad. Her eyes have grown old in the service of Hubal, and she has read the arrows wrong.

I knew that the arrow test was sometimes used for newborns to see if they were bastards or not, and whether their mothers should die for adultery. Nonetheless, I told myself, perhaps I am so small and insignificant that the arrows pointed beyond me to some of the true-born Qurayshi woman. On all sides, these women were screaming and running from the Muslim pillagers who had begun to slash guy ropes, bringing down the Mecca tents, trapping booty and new slaves beneath.

But there wasn't time to discuss all this with the priestess. "Help me put him in his litter, Grandmother," I cried.

In a moment, we had slid the platform into its place on the camel's back. Just enough room remained behind the platform. I shrugged my dress off my shoulders, draping it over the belt at my waist. My breasts were revealed as no more than soft mosquito bites of promise. I instructed the priestess that she should do the same.

She hesitated, but I did not. The screams and smells of burning creeping closer told me I could not hesitate. I climbed into the red leather litter, settling Hubal between my knees.

The toothless mouth worked, trying to find words to tell me that, no matter what the arrows said, this act would be my death. It hadn't been so far. She could see that. Musaylimah, who had just trotted up to the space around the God's makeshift shrine, saw the same thing. He called my name, then fell silent.

A twist of battle dust, roiling jinn, started the camel to his feet, back legs first, then front. Words from the Land of Fire, from those sleeping in the dust, formed themselves in my mind.

"O you sons of the Servant of the Holy House! Defenders of our homes!"

The priestess gaped without a tooth to show. The loose neckline done long ago with fading red and blue embroidery slid away from her boney shoulders. She had to lift the grey, wrinkled sacks free over her waistband, but those breasts that had spent themselves giving life were the perfect match to mine at their first budding. To my mind, we formed an icon of fertility as powerful as ever Hubal was with his golden hand.

"Get the others, your kinswomen, to do the same, Grandmother," I told her. "The accursed Muslims will do that for them soon enough," she protested. More verses came to me. I said, "Teach them to chant:

> We are the daughters of the stars.
> We move to you among the silk cushions,
> Light as the feet of doves.

"Tell them to stop worrying about these Muslims now attacking them.

> "Musk perfumes our camels,
> Pearls burn around our necks."

"How can they escape thinking of this fate?" she asked.

I told her that as much as they could, they must center their attention towards the Muslims high on that mountainside. And sing this spell:

> "Come, come to us when you have vanquished.
> For you, we extend rich cushions."

"And draw more pillagers and rapists down upon us?" the old woman shrieked. "Ah, Hubal, that I lived to see this day of Your great betrayal."

"Hubal has not betrayed you," I insisted, "nor has His gracious Mother, the Mother of all Gods and all life, Allat. The archers will be enticed into thinking the battle is over. They will fear that they are missing out on their share of the spoils, that their Muslim brothers will not share with them. You will draw them away so that the son of al-Walīd's horse may engage and entrap the Muslims, if the Gods are willing."

The old eyes finally held understanding and away she went, old grey breasts jiggling.

Beneath me, Hubal's camel was moving, causing Musaylimah to step out of the way and simply stand and stare. The words continued to come, swaying now to the camel's gait. I sang them aloud, and Mecca's women, one after the next baring her breasts, joined me in them as the magic caught like fire in dry grass.

> "If you advance, we will embrace you.
> But if you should retreat, 'Away from us! Away!
> If you do not win, you are not ours.'"

❧

As Sitt Sameh leaned back against her cushion, weary with memory, Abd Allah pulled the lamp towards himself and turned to his next parchment page.

38

بسم الله الرحمن الرحيم

We went forth from the barren desert against them,
Forming as it were a streaked girdle to Radwa in the morning.
When I see war's flames leaping over the fire stones,
Reaching the squadrons, flaying men with their heat,
I am sure that death is truth and life a delusion.

    —From a poem by Amr ibn al-Asi, the con-
    queror of Egypt

My prayers were answered. The spur of rock before me suddenly came to life as the archers who had kept me so at bay began to leave their posts and clamber down. The fleeing women, raising the skirts to reveal their bangles—and wonder of wonders, their breasts as well—had been too enticing. The archers had to take their share of the spoils.

I watched as one views a miracle, unable to do anything but struggle to believe the possibility. Could the Muslims have forgotten that I still stood here with a hundred mounted men? But the smell of spoil makes men blind and stupid, much like sharks who kill their own when the smell of blood enters their brains. Perhaps our ferocity alone is not the reason our tribe the Quraysh is known for such creatures of the sea.

Muhammad's archers, forgetting their oaths, sprang down from their aerie. They started across the plain, strewn with the tempting dead and wounded, and most of the companions who had stood with the Prophet went with them.

"My love! Our dear daughter!" I exclaimed as something between a magic spell and a battlecry. Then I gave the battlecry my men would answer—"On for Allat! On for al-Uzza!"—and charged.

I whirled my spear over my head. Pushing as close as I dared to the edge of the lava field, I waved my men to ride like the wind into the now-free space.

Amr galloping beside me sang a song for joy at the top of his lungs that echoed the fearlessness in every heart:

> *"We went forth from the barren desert against them,*
> *Forming as it were a streaked girdle to Radwa in the morning."*

By Bint Zura, no, I would not lose, even against God's own Prophet.

The same wondrous chance had just then opened up to Ikrama on the other side of the field. In no time at all our charges had met. We had not only succeeded in encircling the Muslim army at the very moment when they lost discipline in the looting. We had also opened up the field to our swift and superior horsemanship.

I was moving now. I was fighting, and the battle madness overcame me. As the first man felt my divine sword, I yelled, "Take that, you wretched dog's son! Tell your God when you see Him that it was I, the father of Sulayman, who ended your miserable life!"

And Ikrama, gloating like the sun upon a summer's day, reeled his horse to dance parallel to mine and called out another gain. "Up the defile!" he shouted over the roar of battle like wind in our ears. "We've cut Muhammad off from the body of his men."

It was true. The Prophet of God stood in the defile with but a handful of companions. Some of these were only his women and his water carriers.

Muhammad and his companions had wedged themselves between two rocky spurs with the mountain mass behind them. The way to them was so rocky and steep that we would have done better to be mounted on goats than on horses to attempt to fight on that terrain. Ikrama had already thrown his horse's reins into a nearby bush and dismounted. Swords in hand, a dozen of his men were at his heels.

I would have loved to claim the death of the son of Abd Allah to my own hand. But, "He's yours," I said to Ikrama. He'd dismounted first. I contented myself with acting as his cover and with slowly pressing the mass of Muslims out into the open plain, into the arms of Abu Sufyan and our main force.

Out of the battle dust, a bare-breasted woman, beautiful Amra bint Alkama, danced in front of Hubal's camel with a tambourine. Beneath the red leather awning of his litter, the God rode—and something I could not see clearly because of the shadow. Amra's breasts swung as she bent to pick up the fallen Meccan standard. She yelled for our army to take heart and return. She had been the object of pillage by the Muslims, but now she sang out the words many have since credited to Abu Sufyan's Hind. To me, they always had a deeper origin than that:

> *"We are the daughters of the stars.*
> *We move to you among the silk cushions,*

Light as the feet of doves.
Musk perfumes our camels,
Pearls burn around our necks.
Come, come to us when you have vanquished."

Hind herself was too occupied to join in the song. Her Abyssinian had found his mark. The giant form of Muhammad's uncle Hamza lay prone in Uhud's dust with an African spear in his guts. Hind, that fearsome lady, broke the spear aside so she could attack the form with her own dagger.

"Revenge! Rest in peace, your thirst slaked with this blood," she cried to Badr's dead.

Then she pulled the dark, quivering liver from the cavity as matter-of-factly as she might have done from a chicken in her kitchen. And she bit into it, warm, while the blood coursed down her ample bosom.

The shout went up behind me, "Muhammad is dead! Despair, O Muslims, for your foolish imposter is dead!"

Now indeed did Muslim despair deflate their zeal. Spur my horse as I might, I could not kill them as fast as they threw down their arms and fled.

In very little time we had gained the field and stood milling about as men do at such times. Laughing and congratulating one another, some wariness lingered, as if to ask, "Is that all, then? Is that all there is to it?" Or again, "You who come to me with extended hand, does not someone rise behind you whose blow I must shield myself from as there has been all day?"

Our women went about among the corpses as women do, wailing for their loved ones when they found them and taking trophies of the enemy. So I found my sister Fakhta, and went to her to embrace her, hoping to learn that she'd come to no serious harm when the Muslims had overrun the tents. Six paces from her, I stopped in horror. She was covered in blood. My first thought was that she'd been cut open from the breast bone down. I had seen men in such a state, their bowels bulging out. I had caused it in not a few.

"O my poor sister—" I cried.

She came to me, laughing. She hugged me. Then I saw, felt, her neck and wrists well hung with bleeding Muslim noses, ears, and—most important for her—male members.

"Praises are your due, O son of my father." Fakhta unashamedly dangled a piece that did not belong to her husband for my inspection. "Brother, you've caused revenge to cool my heart so that a seed fertilized by this blood might have a chance to grow."

She wore these trophies all the way back to Mecca till, dried and hard, the parts swarmed with maggots and stank. And, in fact, no more than nine months after Uhud, she brought forth a fine, healthy son. But now the rumor ran around that uhammad was not killed at all.

"By Hubal, I saw him fall," Ikrama swore, riding up to me on is reclaimed horse. "Not by my hand, though. Another."

"You'd better go up the defile and see," Abu Sufyan ordered me.

I took a few men along. In case there was any doubt, we would end it forever. We passed Hubal's camel on our way. The God had paused to catch His breath. We saluted Him, and He watched us hurry on our way.

"Glory to Hubal! Glory to al-Uzza!" I shouted up the barren hillside.

"Glory to God, Most High and Mighty," a solitary voice replied.

I could not see where it came from. The late afternoon sun burned in my eyes, though I flung up an arm to shade them. The sound echoed unnaturally against the walls of the defile.

"We have al-Uzza and Hubal," I shouted again, to give myself courage. "You have no al-Uzza and no Hubal."

"We have God as our Lord," the voice answered. "You have no Lord."

"Is Muhammad among you?" I asked.

To this there was no reply. I smiled in triumph to Amr at my side. I shouted the same thing twice more and again received no reply. Then I asked in the same fashion after Abu Bakr, Muhammad's second in command, after Omar my cousin, and after al-Walīd my brother. Likewise I was given no reply.

"They must all be dead," I said triumphantly to my companions. "Come, we will find their bodies on the field."

But then I heard a voice I knew as Omar's. "You lie, O enemy of God," he shouted. "Those whom you have counted are alive, and there are enough of us left to punish you severely for your disbelief."

I laughed scornfully at these boastful words, for none had yet even dared to show his face above the rocks of Uhud. But I called again, "God protect you, son of my cousin. Is Muhammad really alive?"

"By God, yes. And even now he hears what you say."

I felt a curious shiver at my cousin's words as if a shadow had fallen over my position. Such a shiver a man gets when he feels that indeed some God is listening to every word he says. I rejected the feeling quickly as only my battle sweat drying off. I heated my blood with fire again as one by one those leaders of the Muslims I had asked after showed themselves upon a ledge of rock.

The Prophet, blessed be he, was indeed sorely wounded. Ikrama and his charge had left him cut with a sword both on his head and on his shoulder. Other attacks with stones had broken out his two front teeth and mashed links of his chain mail *helmet into his cheek. And then, trying to escape, he had fallen into one of Abu Amir's frond-covered pits.*

But he'd been helped out. And though these wounds might appear fatal in the confusion and exaggerated heat of battle, they were wounds any determined man could recover from. And this determined man had his God behind him.

Amr and I and the rest of our companions scoured the hillside for the man, seeking to finish the job. Night fell too quickly, however, and the companions managed to spirit him away.

"Thanks be to God," my scribe exclaims as he puts the final flourish to the Battle of Uhud.

"And the Muslims would not face the problems we had later," I add, not letting him set down his pen quite yet.

"What is the matter with you?" I asked more than one of the Meccans as we took our triumphant route homeward. "You took no hurt and go home laden with spoil."

"Muhammad spat on me," a pale, thin voice replied from cloaks huddled in the warmest sun.

And in every case, the man rolled from his saddle, dead, before we ever reached Mecca victorious.

We buried them on the way, and the looks in the eyes of the men around the shallow graves told me we were not finished with Muhammad ibn Abd Allah yet.

My younger brother's taunts still rang in my ears from their echo off the mountainside. And they were words that make any loss a conquest for those who believe: "By God, our dead are even now finding a joyful welcome in Paradise while your dead burn in hellfire."

39

His truth is clear as daylight. How can compulsion advance religion?
—The Holy Quran, Surah II

That was the beginning of my differences with Abu Sufyan, commander of those opposing the Muslims, then when I rode back to all the Meccans and dampened their triumph by announcing that Muhammad yet lived. For some reason, probably intense frustration, our commander blamed me for this oversight.

"If anyone but high heaven is to be blamed for the fortunes of war, let it be Ikrama who reported the imposter dead when he had only fallen wounded," I complained.

And perhaps, as others say, Abu Sufyan did not carry a personal grudge against me. He held it rather against anything and everything that had seen him for that brief moment turn his back on a force of Muslims half the size of his own and run.

I said, "We should quickly turn and take the town of Yathrib while her defenses are scattered and weak in the desert. Such raiding would in some part recompense us for the expense of this campaign."

But all the old man could think of was home.

It was inevitable. To every man comes a time when he grows weary and loses the daring of youth. Perhaps our differences that seemed so insurmountable were really only one difference, and that was the difference some twenty or so years make between men. Any man not touched by God, as was Muhammad.

For the next two years, not only I, but every man in Mecca pressed for a return campaign. Abu Sufyan put us off with lame excuses. All the time, our lack of trade made us weaker and weaker while Muhammad, who claimed to be interested only in the world to come, daily gained.

Some five years after Muhammad left Mecca for al-Madinah, two years after our victory at Uhud, came the event I would hardly glorify by the name of battle, even though we did set out with an army of ten thousand. Such vast numbers, one would think, could surely sweep away all in their path. But at al-Madinah we found ourselves confronted by a very non-Arab stratagem. Muhammad had a Persian advisor who had taught him to surround his town with a deep ditch. We were forced into the tedium of laying siege, which few Arabs can endure for long.

I am grateful now that I was present there, for I learned how not to set siege by Abu Sufyan's bad example. Such knowledge served me well in Persia and Syria later. But we Meccans had taken no thought for the supplies needed for a month's camping. Mecca was ten days' ride away, and we were forced to forage about the neighborhood for food and kindling. Such women's work unmans an army quickly. The single time sheer frustration drove me to jump the ditch with my cavalry behind me, Abu Sufyan failed to give us proper support, and so I was forced to withdraw. In twenty-three days, we fought no more than to let eight men get killed, an equal number from each side.

The men, even the commanders, began to complain out loud that they had better things to do with their time back home. Then, one night, when the wind came up and brought a late winter storm, Abu Sufyan, the man we called our general, packed up his gear and left.

My friend Amr and I were the very last to follow his example. In the end we did; we left for home, too. I do not call giving up a siege a defeat. But what does that do to the morale of an army when its leader heads for home the moment a strong gust of rainy wind blows out his fire?

The Muslims, we heard later, had been in worse straits than ourselves. The entire town had been without food for two days when we lifted the siege. Another day, two at the most, would have seen them capitulate, finally and for good, Prophet or no.

And we had packed up and gone home.

Upon our return to Mecca, Abu Sufyan received word that one of his own daughters was in al-Medinah and that, over his head, she had become one of Muhammad's wives. The old man truly lost all will to do battle against God's Apostle.

Once he did authorize me to make a raid, after I had pestered the both of us sick. But then not only did he give me false instructions and poor intelligence (I got better watching the horizon for myself), but he gave me so few men that I could attempt nothing.

The Muslims had come to try to make the pilgrimage during the holy month, you see, and Abu Sufyan was afraid that on such a mission, his daughter might be with them. How can one follow a man who concerns himself with such trivial things? A true man would see to it that his own self-willed and shameful daughter was the first to feel his sword, if she had done what Abu Sufyan's had done in defiance of him.

Wasps settle heavily upon the overripe pomegranates fallen in my garden, the splattered, obscene fertility of their seeds. I think of Abu Sufyan and his daughter. I have just condemned the man to this scribbling boy who will never have son nor daughter, who can never know. I condemned the man for hardly less than I was guilty of at the same time.

All this while, my own daughter was growing to womanhood among the Tamim, as far as I knew, without a glimpse of her refreshing my eyes for one moment. I let other men's foolishness with their children rule me—

But my scribe taps his quill in his ink. I must push on with my tale.

The thought gnawed at me fiercely: I am living here in Mecca with a pack of useless cowards. All the brave men have migrated to al-Medinah and fight for Islam.

I had vowed before heaven and by my own life never to accept defeat. Though I had hopes heaven might help me from tight spots when I found them in fulfillment of that vow, I knew well enough that no God favors a fool lest He be proven likewise foolish. Besides, what was the use of such a vow if one never got a chance to prove it, but was kept in town with vague excuses? There we sat like women waiting for something to happen, while the Muslims in al-Medinah were led by Muhammad to prove themselves on foray after foray.

Again, the smears of pomegranate like blackening blood make me fall silent for a while. My daughter, the fruit of my only true love—

My scribe discovers he must prod me. "Will you say nothing here, Master, about how the Prophet's message of the Compassionate God pricked your heart to conversion?"

"That would be proper, would it not? It isn't popular to attribute conversion to any religion—especially not this religion—to crass motives of politics and personal ambition. But this is my story, and I will for once tell the truth. I will not mouth after all the others the rote declarations that speak of the changing of a heart of stone to one fresh and flowing with new life. I was stifled there in Mecca under Abu Sufyan."

I was stifled. And I had not seen my daughter.

"Write that down, fellow, and say then that I had the sense to see which way the wind was blowing."

He doesn't like it, but the fellow begins to write.

And though I don't expect him to write this, I murmur as his pen scratches. I speak so softly, how can he even hear me? Just between me and the fountain's water, I make confession: "Only one power I have known in all my life has had the strength to command my heart; one power I could not control. That is that power passed from mother to daughter to granddaughter and which now resided in a girl named the daughter of a herdsman, al-Harith. I will confess that this power had something to do with my conversion to Muhammad."

For six years, the Prophet's blockade of the trade route had kept me from visit-
ing my milk brothers, from hearing any news of them or of their dependents. By
God, she would be grown by now, practically a woman. Perhaps they would have
married her already. To whom? I wondered. By God, I hoped he was not such a
clumsy fool that I should be forced to kill him for her sake.

Then I remembered how Muhammad had allowed himself to be touched by
that same power I worshiped. The power had touched him a single time, that is
true, and he soon recanted his reaction to it. One single inspiration was still better
than the dead souls I saw about me in Mecca. They carried out their rituals before
dumb figures of stone and wood not because anything had touched them, but be-
cause they were afraid to open up their hearts and feel at all. They were afraid to lift
one single foot from the plod of their fathers and to risk a dance step in love of life.

Such thoughts touched my heart, such thoughts moved me and directed my ac-
tions, not any verse of Quran. I admit this with some reluctance and with some fear
of future judgment, but with no hesitation as to its truthfulness.

The night came when I could not bear these feelings trapped within me any
longer. I thought if I did not get out past al-Medinah and make contact with the
source of my spirit, I should shrivel down to nothingness.

Abu Sufyan cursed me: "What? You can't stay and fight like a man?"

But I knew that ability was the only thing he would miss me for. This one
thing he had denied me for years. His words only goaded me on quicker and more
resolutely to action.

That night, I traveled with a string of horses behind me towards the Drinking
Gourd and its North Star. Alone, the doubts that had kept me indecisive all those
years rode beside me as clearly as if I had companions. My pride sat a hard-driven
camel stallion with a nasty temper.

The ancient gods? I knew they had come to our rescue at Uhud, but that had to
do with the women. Now the old idols seemed to mince beside me on three hundred
and sixty prissy mounts, slowing progress down. My harem, my children? Those I
left behind in Mecca did not adorn qubbahs; if matters went well, I would send
for them, and Abu Sufyan would be glad to see the last of the extra mouths to feed.
I carried all I needed for a new harem in my balls rocking against the saddle.

Aside from the girl in the Tamimi encampments beyond al-Medinah.

In the desert night, I had no doubt in the existence of shayatan. An army of
them marched at my side, whispering, screeching sometimes with the sounds of
hunting owls. This ride, however, did not mean I had to leave them behind. Not
at all.

Didn't Muhammad preach of Satan?

Amid this unseen throng, I saw a campfire burning in the distance. I made my mount kneel and, drawing my dagger, crept up to it on foot, the throng left behind.

In the firelight sat both Amr and Uthman ibn Talhah, a man who had lost two brothers to Ali during the duels beneath Uhud. I knew what they were doing there. And I knew I had made the right decision.

I stepped into the firelight, dagger at the ready. "Traitors," I called them.

Amr and Uthman scrambled for their weapons, but I slammed a foot down on Amr's sword and caught Uthman by the neck so the next move he made would be onto my blade. Then I tossed them both casually aside and stepped to warm myself by the fire.

"Traitors," I said again. "To run off to convert and leave me behind."

We laughed together heartily at that. Omar and Abu Bakr were men who could challenge me as opponents, but old friends like Amr and Uthman I would much rather fight beside than against. We traveled on together after that, and in daylight.

On the outskirts of al-Medinah, I sent a message in to my younger brother al-Walīd, to intercede for me and my friends before the Prophet. In that topsy-turvy world, the younger brother had to take care of the elder. With al-Walīd, I went into Muhammad's humble house first while Amr and Uthman waited outside.

Muhammad sat with others in majlis. He didn't look up at our entrance, nor even when al-Walīd gave my name.

Into the edgy silence, I made the profession of allegiance and (secondly to me, at least) of faith. Then I presented my sword—my sword from Bint Zura and Rudainah—to the Prophet, laying it at his feet and backing slowly away. My heart thrumming in my throat, I knew I was giving him the chance to snatch the weapon up and drive its heavenly blade straight through me. In that moment, I didn't care, one way or the other.

The Prophet, blessed be he, a man who appreciated fine weaponry as well as things divine, picked up my sword and studied it. His appreciation was so keen that for a moment I thought he might claim it for himself. Thanks be to God, he did not, but soon gave me mine again.

"O son of al-Walīd," Muhammad said, "use this sword of heaven now to fight for God and not against Him." My hand and my pledge were all the vengeance he asked for.

40

بسم الله الرحمن الرحيم

Of her who will give us a full sieve,
Oh may her little son grow up a rider.
Of her who will give us a full bolt,
Oh may we lead her son to a bride.
Of her who will give us a large handful,
Oh may the grave open for her enemy.
Of her who will give us a small handful,
Oh may her eyelashes grow thicker.
                    —A prayer for rain of the Rwala Arabs

everal of the students from Sitt Umm Ali's Quran class had left off their memorization to come to the turpentine sellers' house. Several, but not all. Sitt Umm Ali and the parents of the rest had warned that a good Muslimah would not do as these were going to do. Rayah had always been a good student, striving for understanding and obedience. Had the meeting been at any other house, she would have stayed at home. But the girls had come to her.

They sat about the fountain in the courtyard, its emptiness echoing and emphasizing why they had come. With them were a number of girls Rayah didn't know except that their dress was from the desert. These had blown with their families into the Tadmor oasis where the fountains had run dry, but at least one spring still had water for herds that were so thirsty they had to be carried. Such people did not believe in drinking themselves except after sunset lest they make the jinn jealous.

"Such desert people," Sitt Umm Ali had warned, "will follow the jinn if they appear to them in the guise of their dead parents. It is a hadith; the Prophet, precious blessings upon him, condemned these people so, for he knew well their blackened hearts."

Rayah thought of the jinn conjuring dead ancestors to life. What else had Abd Allah's parchment done? And yet—and yet, her heart knew their hearts now, and couldn't so easily condemn.

"We heard you were to be married, Rayah," one of her friends interrupted her thoughts and the rite, unable to hide a note of envy. "Is that why you haven't been coming to class?"

"I'm not going to be married, inshallah," she replied.

"If my parents, God forbid, matched me with the old sharif Diya'l-Din and his smelly teeth, I would deny it, too," said another girl.

"I will not marry the sharif," Rayah insisted, forgetting in her fervor to mention God at all.

"No, she won't. Not the sharif."

Rayah felt grateful for this sober girl's belief in her. Then the girl went on. "Do you not know that the governor of Homs is here in Tadmor? The son of the Conqueror himself, living under this very roof among the turpentine sellers. That is the man who has spoken for our Rayah and overpowered the sharif."

Rayah wanted to deny that accusation even more fervently than the rumor about the sharif. Fortunately, the girls from the desert had more pressing issues on their minds and changed the subject.

"But this is not why we have come," they protested. "Not because of whom she will marry but because of who she herself is."

"She has blue eyes, yes," piped up one very little girl, not more than five or six, her uncovered hair a dusty mat of tangles. "That's what we were told, even in the middle of the desert. Blue like a pool of water. Blue like the sky that will not rain. We must make her cry."

At the mere sound of such concern, Rayah felt the tears come to her eyes. She forced them back, however. For sake of the rite, which must make its demands on the whole community.

"You must come with us and beg for help from the Mother of the Rain," two or three other voices said together.

Then more voices, including a number from the Quranic class, chimed in to chant verses much older than those that usually occupied their tongues:

> "O Mother of Rain! Rain upon us.
> Wet the mantle of our herdsman.
> O Mother of Rain! Rain upon us.
> With pouring rain allay our thirst."

As the men discussed the lack of rain in the majlis of the turpentine sellers, Rayah had overheard Abd ar-Rahman—the son of the Conqueror Khalid himself—say: "God, all praises to Him, has dried up His heavens because although we have brought truth to them, the people in these lands we now control are not good enough Muslims."

But the man who was her great-great grandfather had prophesied, "The coming salvation of the Arabs." Of course, he had been mad, jinn-touched, opposed to her mother's mother. He hadn't spoken truth, because salvation had not come through his daughter. Nor through hers. And hers had actually recited Satanic Verses in opposition to true revelation.

But what if salvation were not only in one revelation, burning like the single sun, nor in one woman, now dead. What if it came every day? In one well. In one patch of shade. In one drop of rain. In one tear.

Her uncle Abd ar-Rahman had said these good people were not good enough? Wishing to counter the man she feared was enough to make Rayah consider a different path. "Don't we need the Mother Herself to make the circuit with us for such a rite to work?"

Even as she asked the question, Rayah felt the shiver across her shoulder blades, knowing that such a thing would be anathema to Sitt Umm Ali. Probably to Abd ar-Rahman, too. The girls from the Quranic class with whom she usually sat before that dominating woman didn't blink. They had been praying for rain in the new Islamic way for a full turn of the moon, along with their fathers and brothers. What Sitt Umm Ali might say of obedience to one's menfolk no longer mattered. No drought had punished the land like this since the coming of Islam. For rain, the prayers of women, old prayers, alone were known to be efficacious.

"We need a woman's gown." Rayah heard her own protests growing feebler.

Even as she said it, Auntie Adilah came down the stairs among them, looking back at where she had just been on the roof spreading dates to dry. Water was too precious right now to waste on laundry. Yet, folded in her hands she held a length of desert cloth.

"Sitt Sameh asked me to give this to you," she told Rayah as she passed the bundle to her.

The girls stirred with excitement and awe on the coping of the empty fountain. So there was indeed a woman named Sitt Sameh. Some even spoke another name, a name so wicked, Rayah refused to believe it could be her mother's.

When she unfolded the bolt, Rayah started to ask, "How—?"

Auntie Adilah shrugged before moving on with her work. The fact that only one well in the oasis still held water made her chores more strenuous these days. She had stopped insisting that Rayah help her, however, once the group of girls had arrived, begging. "Most of what is said in this courtyard floats up to Sitt Sameh's room, if she has a desire to listen," was the explanation the auntie gave.

Once she had unfolded the garment with all the girls watching wide-eyed, Rayah saw that it was, in fact, a woman's dress, one she had never seen her mother wear. Women of the desert wore such things, coins and shells adorning the bodice. Heavy woolen tassels in reds, yellows and greens like camel ornaments dangled among the stitches. Rayah had only ever seen her mother, hiding she realized now, in the most somber of black or indigo clothing of the settled lands.

"It is a desert dress. Yes, that is best," exclaimed one of the desert girls.

"A dress for a kahinah," agreed the eldest of them.

With that hint, Rayah had to agree that the decorations did give that impression. Many of the embroidered symbols were clearly protective and magical.

Two girls quickly lashed together a pair of sticks into the form of a cross. The others took the dress reverently from Rayah's hands and fitted it onto the framework thus created. The full sleeves drooped lifelike from the two stick arms. The stick of a neck rose ghostlike from the tasseled collar.

By this point, Rayah had had time to discover the three extra pockets her mother had laced within the aging fabric. The contents of these pockets lent extra weight to the stick figure it would not otherwise have had, two at the breasts and one as a pubic bone. Rayah's fingers told her, even through the heavy black fabric, what the pockets contained. They were the three wooden goddesses, Allat, al-Manat, and al-Uzza, which her mother kept hidden under rugs upstairs. Once these figures had ridden in honor within the curtains of a *qubbah* at the head of the Taghlib tribe. In those days, the rains never failed to green the dunes in the proper season. One of those images bore the toothmarks of Rayah's own great grandmother, the kahinah Umm Taghlib, as she sought aid in her labor to bring forth her daughter, Rayah's grandmother, on the outskirts of Mecca itself.

"O Mother of Rain!" The girls hoisted their effigy high with a shout.

"Now you must lead us, Blue Eyes," they told her.

"I should not—"

But she did, clapping and chanting with that emblem of three generations of desert women flapping above the other girls' heads behind her.

Through the day, they made a parched, weary circuit of the town and the oasis. At every door, at every tent, they stopped and sang:

> "O Mother of Rain! Rain upon us.
> The evil is still tormenting us.
> O Mother of Rain! Rain upon us.
> Clouds of dust are still blinding us.
> O Mother of Rain! Rain upon us.
> The specter of want speeds towards us.
> O Mother of Rain! O Hungry One,
> A real flood let our share be."

At every dwelling, the inhabitants—usually the women for, Rayah noticed, the men knew enough to stay clear of such magic—gave a little something. Often it was only a handful of cooked barley scraped from the bottom of a pan, a few salted chickpeas, or a dipper of water. Still, by the time they finished the circuit, with the sun riding low over the towers of the dead, the girls had two cloaks full of food to end their fast.

They posted their Mother of Rain outside an open-sided tent in the ruins at the outskirts of town. She watched, stick-faced, over the division of the spoils, gently twisting and flapping in the breathless air.

Rayah avoided eating her fair share, although the other girls pressed it on her for her part in the leading.

"There is no cloud in the sky," she protested, thinking perhaps that the governor of Homs was right after all. The people of Tadmor and of the desert around had not submitted with hearts contrite enough. "It is as God wills."

I am not submissive enough, she thought. Her mind ran on, and she was too exhausted to call it back.

She saw how thin and hungry the other girls were, especially those from the desert. In lean times, the best food would go to their brothers, who must be strong to run their desperate raids. Some of the girls had even resorted to the old trick of tying a stone into their girdles over their bellies to help still the pangs with a mock feeling of heaviness.

When Rayah saw that, and when they still pressed her to eat, the tears started to her sun-dried eyes once more. This is not Islam, she told herself. But the more she told herself that, the more the rent in her heart hurt, the more the tears came.

Then she could not stop them.

God could not be pleased with her actions that day. A Goddess made of nothing more than twigs and an old dress? A Goddess human hands could dismantle in an instant and make vanish into the coals under their cooking skins or fold away among their cushions and blankets? What sort of divinity was this her group of friends still put their faith in, for all their recitation of "There is no God but God"? God, the new, jealous, single God, must rise up and curse the heavens even more for such folly. He would turn the very inert stones against them to gnaw at their hungry bellies beneath the ragged girdles.

Such a God never gave birth, was proud that he never had. For this reason, He must disavow the efforts of all women back to Eve, even of one woman struggling alone in a *qubbah*, with a block of ancestress-shaped wood between her teeth. What must He think, then, of what Rayah and her friends had attempted that day?

The jinni was there. She knew he was, the beautiful boy who said only kind things to her but against whom her outer self wrestled. Such a hard struggle, against this adversary. She couldn't win. It broke her heart. And it would never be over. She must wrestle her shaytan every day, and only ever to a tie.

Rayah caught at a sob. Even as she did, a wind stirred through the Mother of Rain's dress, sending her swinging on her wooden prop. The coins and shells jingled. One of the secreted idols knocked against the pole. Rayah wept some more.

"Look," exclaimed the oldest of the desert girls. "Tears in the blue sky."

Rayah tried to dry up her emotion like the desert in a drying wind, but the girl stopped her. Rather than calling attention to Rayah's emotion, however, she pointed out across the desert where, over the burning sunset, purple clouds were gathering.

"Cry more, O Blue Eyes," she urged.

To help her, many in the group worked up their own tears. To do this, they exchanged tales of woe, including stories of younger siblings who had died during the recent hunger, often because they were female.

❧

Rayah scurried home through fat, hot rain drops. The bundle of gown and idols she had perched where no one would think to look for it: on her head, beneath a jug that rang in deeper and deeper tones as the rain it caught rose higher and higher.

Rayah knew her cheeks were drought dirty, streaked with the raindrops she'd lifted her face to catch on her tongue as well as with her own tears. Just in time, just before she bolted into the narrow close, Rayah pulled up her veil to cover her face. The jinni at her shoulder, she was certain, had whispered, warning, "Cover." Although perhaps she merely reacted to the smells of chamber pots and rotting kitchen scraps. The moisture resurrected months of old smells in this confined space.

For Abd ar-Rahman the son of Khalid, governor of Homs, stood in the alleyway, watching the rain fall. Watching for her.

So she managed to avoid her own doorway. She slipped instead into the courtyard of the two kind, elderly sisters who shared a house wall but whose door, in the twist of streets, opened around the corner.

"I thought you might appreciate my jug of fresh rain water," she said, reaching up to remove what stood on her head.

They thanked and blessed her, pouring her offering into their heavy jar. However, they were watching their own cistern, an ancient cross etched in its side.

"And we know to what the miracle is due," said the one, who had lived more years before the name of Muhammad was known in Syria than after, with a quavering voice.

She closed one wrinkled hand over Rayah's where she held it folded protectively over desert dress and Goddesses. The woman's sister, even older, traced the cross, as she had done with her own spittle throughout the dry days.

After dutifully watching with them for a while, Rayah returned home over the connecting rooftops.

Later, from the safety of her mother's room, she did hear the governor railing at his hosts, "Rain or no rain, I will have that girl for my son to wife. I will have my father's sword if I have to tear this ancient house and its harem down stone by stone."

Vain were the turpentine sellers' quaking attempts at appeasement. "Can you not say, O lord governor, that all will be as God wills? You, good sir, a companion of the Prophet, blessings on him, must know that what will be is in His hands and not our own."

Tiptoeing past the noise, Rayah rejoiced that the Mother of Rains was a divinity that could be dismantled and packed away under her own mother's carpets and cushions once more.

THE END

SUGGESTIONS FOR
FURTHER READING

I can't begin to list all the sources I have consulted for this work during the thirty years it was my passion. I content myself with listing those the reader may find the most useful—and only those in English.

Let's begin with the Quran. I consulted three different English translations: the Arberry, which many consider to give best the flavor of the original; the Everyman-Rodwell; and the Abdullah Yusuf Ali. In some cases, when quoting, I made choices of my own.

For biographies of the Prophet, you may consider:

Karen Armstrong, *Muhammad: A Biography of the Prophet*

Martin Lings, *Muhammad: His Life Based on the Earliest Sources*

Maxine Rodinson, *Muhammad*

F. E. Peters, *Muhammad and the Origins of Islam*

Betty Kelen, *Muhammad: The Messenger of God*

W. Montgomery Watt, *Muhammad at Mecca, Muhammad at Median* and *Muhammad, Prophet and Statesman*

Then there are biographies of Khalid ibn al-Walīd himself. The best of these, *The Sword of God: Khalid bin Waleed*, by the Pakistani general Syed Ameer Ahmed, is now available online, complete with sketches of the battles. Two others are *Khalid bin Walid: The General of Islam* by Major S. K. Malik and *Khalid bin Walid: The Sword of Allah* by Fazl Ahmad.

Of the great number of Arabic historians who've dealt with this matter, one of the ninth Christian century, al-Tabari, is available in a multivolume set in readable English translation from the State University of New York.

More than anything else, my love for pre-Islamic poetry spurred this work. There simply isn't enough of it to satisfy me, but there are translations and discussions by Christopher Nouryeh and Charles James Lyall. AJ Arberry, as with his interpretation of the Quran, provided his wonderful *The Seven Odes*. A slim but very interesting work is *Religious Trends in Pre-Islamic Arabic Poetry* by Hafiz Ghulam Mustafa. Please note that I have given the proper poets' names with the verses that begin each chapter, but when I have used them in the body of the story, the credit went where the plot demanded.

Besides the time I spent living on the edge of the Arabian Desert, which I consider the most formative of my life, modern anthropological studies and earlier travelers to these places helped me to create the world. They make wonderful reading, too, including:

The Manners and Customs of the Rwala Bedouin, where I found the Mother of Rains ritual, and *Arabia Deserta* by Alois Musil.

Drinkers of the Wind by Carl R. Raswan

Personal Narrative of a Pilgrimage to al-Madinah and Meccah by Sir Richard F. Burton

A Pilgrimage to Nejd by Lady Anne Blunt

The Arab of the Desert by H. R. P. Dickson

For my account of the Bisha trial, I am indebted to Larry W. Roeder's article in *Anthropos*, "Trial Law and Tribal Solidarity in Sinai Bedouin Culture."

I constantly consulted the articles in the *Encyclopedia of Islam* including those on Khalid b. al-Walid, Sadjah bint al-Harith, Tamim, Taghlib, Banu Bakr, Malik and Mutammim b. Nuwayra, Dhu Kar, Kuraish, Lakhmids. . . Well, the list goes on and on.

J. Spencer Trimingham's *Christianity among the Arabs in Pre-Islamic Times* might also be of interest.